WHERE ALL ROADS LEAD

Devon Richards

All Roads Adventures Publishing

contents

ALSO BY DEVON RICHARDS

SHORT FICTION:

Minotaur

Two Shots: The Damon Black Mysteries

Billy...

NOVELLA:

Ripples

SHORT SCRIPTS (Produced):

Infiltrator

Wolves at the door

NON-FICTION:

Get your s**t together – Fast! (Forth-Coming)

NOVELS:

Ever Lurking in Darkness: A Damon Black Mystery (Forth-coming)

COPYright

W HERE ALL ROADS LEAD

Dedication

No writer gets to this point in their life – their first publication - without a great deal of support, both emotional and financial, during their journey.
In my case, the road was much longer, and only made possible and even remotely tolerable by the following people –
Annie, Mike, Chris, Cilanne, Heather, Kerry, Carrie, Miko, Margaret, Ren, Tara, Jessica, Eirinn, Sabrina, Melyssa, Sandi, Andrea and Rebecca
Also need to mention my tabby, Minion, who had been with me for 18 years –
My constant companion and constant interrupter of writing supreme
And, of course, Dave
Thank you all for taking the journey with me
DR – J

Prelude – The Mage's Dark Fate

Arnath, Trellith and Shrakar stared into the depths of the crackling campfire and wondered how things had gone so terribly wrong. They could hear the boy, Garthe, as he bawled unconsolably nearby in the darkness just outside the firelight.

The elderly mage Morgosh, Gathe's master, was their companion since the trenches of the Orkan civil war, nearing twenty years ago. A mere hour ago he had been killed, horribly. Such a death none of them had ever seen, and as veterans, that was saying something. In the last days of the war, the battle that raged within the Orc borders was a slaughter unmatched in the histories of all four kingdoms. What had just happened to Morgosh was far more disturbing.

Arnath, a powerfully built man, trained by the King's Guard for war, looked sheepishly up from the fire at his companions. From across the fire, they too – Trellith, a five-foot tall dwarf and Shrakar, a green-skinned, seven-foot tall half-Orc – looked up and met his eyes. Boon companions who'd adventured together since wartime, they could easily see the same question behind all of their tear-reddened eyes.

What in the bowels of darkness had happened?

Days before they were in a town just to the south, Umdra, one of the northern-most towns in the country of Farsuum. Umdra sat so far to the country's north it was above the border of the Orc country, Kolgatha, which dipped down like an unwelcoming smile all the way into the neighbouring country of

Vallasen, from which Arnath and Trellith hailed. While still Farsuum by rights, people did not dare venture into the far north of the country. Not only did the Orcs freely wander there, it was where the ancient ruins of the once-great kingdom of Arkonia stood, and the none of the lore surrounding Arkonia's demise sounded inviting. The word "accursed" was used frequently when referring to the fallen empire and the land its overgrown remains occupied. Arkonia, however, was once an incredibly wealthy nation, and the legends and rumours surrounding that fact drew both brave and foolish adventurers like Arnath and his friends in droves to the lands others so feared.

Around the common room of the dingy outpost they had stayed in, word travelled quickly of just what they were going to attempt – Raid the Arkonian ruins, seeking whatever treasures they held. That made peddlers of maps and spells from all over Umdra, purveyors of blessed ancient artifacts and all manner of lore-coloured trinkets appear like fireflies in the night.

"If this doesn't work, we will come back here and kill you, you know." Morgosh said to the latest of the oily sellers of must-have wares designed to help them penetrate the golden chambers beneath Arkonia's ruined temples. The man, a rat-faced, flinty-eyed peddler dressed in all black, looked at everyone around the table in the darkened corner of the tap room. All of them – The big warrior man, the dwarf with a bow over his shoulder, the half-Orc in the leather armour, even the boy, the older mage's apprentice – were giving him a stern look that confirmed they would do exactly what the elderly magician had said. The peddler calculated for a second, swiftly snatched the rusty key from Morgosh's palm and raced through the crowd for the door.

The companions immediately burst out laughing.

The boy aside, they were all former soldiers, and though they'd chosen the carefree, sometimes lawless life of the adventuring road, they were all honourable men and the killing of strangers was beneath them. Still, it was fun to portray those types of rogues when Morgosh's latest grift required it. The impish old mage had a gift for fooling others out of the essentials they needed as a party to survive, and it often was the only thing that kept them fed. Rather than resenting the times when necessity bade Morgosh usurp his leadership, Arnath played along and they all reaped the rewards.

"Well, there goes another one." Morgosh said, turning back to the table, his bushy, white eyebrows raised.

"Has been quite a stream since we got here." Arnath said, his lips near his ale stein.

The boy turned to Morgosh and asked, "Are they all selling useless baubles, master?"

Taking a swallow, Arnath lifted his chin over the rim of the stein and was about to speak, but a stern look from Morgosh across the table silenced him. Trellith and Shrakar caught the minute exchange, anticipating the coming argument. Since the boy, now 10 years-old, had joined their party almost a year ago, it had been very hard for Arnath, Trellith and even Shrakar to fight their fatherly instincts and join in the teaching of the boy. These many years seeking fortune on the adventuring road had denied all of them the chance at any kind of family, and the temptation was great for all three of them to treat young Garthe as a kind of surrogate son.

Looking away from Arnath, Morgosh leaned over toward the boy, so his elder's whispy voice could be heard over the talk and shuffle of people in the large ale room, and said, "Oh no, lad. Some have genuine articles to sell. We just have to tolerate many charlatans before genuine articles present themselves. It's the way of these things."

"Those not brave enough to risk as we do, try to eke out a living off of what little profit we might gain for our efforts." Arnath said, looking at Trellith and Shrakar, but saying it loud enough for the young lad to hear.

Morgosh, miffed at Arnath for deliberately stepping on his toes, flicked a glance his way, but he did not disagree with Arnath's statement, so he nodded at Garthe saying, "Yes, that's quite right."

Drinking again, Arnath looked over the rim of his stein, and saw the angry mage's eyes boring into him.

Before any argument could ensue, and Arnath and Morgosh had argued quite passionately since the boy joined their ragged company, the attractive dwarf serving girl arrived with a tray full of frothy drinks.

"You must have read my mind." Arnath said, plucking a stein off her tray by the rim.

"From a gentleman at the bar. He wishes to speak to you about your destination. Says he has something you need." She said, her voice heavily accented in the musical sound of dwarf country in the southernmost points of Vallasen.

"Well, send our patron over." Arnath said, peering across at Morgosh, who was going to have to take the lead on the interviewing of another likely fool. He did buy them a drink though.

As she turned away from the table, she set down a drink in front of Trellith, saying, "Cousin."

A salutation Trellith returned, joining once again in the running joke between them that started a couple of days ago. She'd told him she was from one of the many dragon-burnt villages to the far south. She didn't know who her family was, they having died when she was so young. Trellith tried to put some humour into that sad fact by stating they'd best not get involved, lest she be a relation and they make fools of themselves to their remaining family. They referred to each other as "cousin" since.

As she walked away, waving the man at the bar over, all at the table saw the man emerge from the darkness, limping as he moved toward them. He was a tall, swarthy man, brown-skinned, like the noble families of Vallasen. But with his pronounced limp, which presented more as an unhealed war-wound rather the effect of disease, and his near-shabby clothes, there was an unseemly air about him. Though the least unruly-looking of the bunch that had presented themselves of late, he still fit well into their company.

When the dark stranger finally reached the table at his hobbling pace, Morgosh bade him to sit in the only free seat – The one next to the looming presence of Shrakar. The wars were long ago, but the presence of a half-Orc in these northern towns often rankled quite a few nerves. Sensing the test in it, the stranger looked at Shrakar, not at his cheerful face, not in the eye, but at the Allied Sergeants crest bolted to the left breast of his shoulder armour. Once the stranger saw Shrakar was one of the thousands of young Orcs who joined the side of the three kingdoms to stop the fighting, he sat down without hesitation. A pained expression crossed his face as he settled in the chair; clearly even bending that knee just to sit was an ordeal.

"Welcome, friend. Many thanks for the drink. We hear you have something that may be of help to us in the ruins of Arkonia." Morgosh, raising his stein toward the man.

"I do. Something that could be of great value to you." The swarthy stranger said in an almost high-born accent. Placing his goblet down after returning their toasts around the table, his face became serious. "There is however a delicate question I must ask..."

"You wish to know if we can pay for whatever you are peddling. And handsomely, if the item you have is of worth." Arnath said across the table, somewhat glibly. They had been having this same conversation for days now.

"Yes. Again, I had no wish to be indelicate."

"Think not on it, friend." Morgosh said with a throwaway gesture. When he turned to Arnath, the big warrior dropped a coin purse on the table with a *thunk* so loud it drew jealous and scheming glances from the nearby tables.

The stranger's expression went from momentarily impressed to narrow-eyed. He realized quickly that this cunning adventuring party had marked him for the benefit of the less savoury characters around the tavern. Whatever they gave him, not matter how big or how little, those willing to do him harm would now know he had it. A clever way to divide the numbers that would be tempted to follow they themselves into the night. Ignoring the invisible target they'd placed on his back, the stranger reached into his coat and withdrew a slim leather tube, saying, "I acquired this on the way home in the final days of the war. I thought it a unique souvenir, but as my fortunes have taken a downward turn..."

He extended the slim leather document protector toward Morgosh, who took it, quickly unlacing the leather thongs that held the cap on. Immediately upon placing his thumb inside the tube, to begin the action of sliding the document out, Morgosh's expression brightened. "Oh, powerful!"

When he got the parchment out, Morgosh spread it flat on the table with both hands and closed his eyes. "Yes, yes indeed. Garthe, come feel this." Morgosh said, pronouncing the boy's name like "Garth – Ah", the traditional way of his home region in between the mountains that divided Farsuum and Vallasen to the south.

The boy mage slid off his chair, stood close to his master and placed one of his small hands between Morgosh's large, gnarled ones. Like Morgosh, Garthe too closed his eyes.

"You feel that, boy?"

"Yes, master." Garthe said, his eyes still closed as he turned his head from side to side, as though searching the corners of his mind. "It is alive with energy. It's very strong."

From across the table, Arnath looked at the swarthy stranger, asking, "What is it?"

"From what I was told, it is spell to bring down magical wards. A tool for getting through doors, thresholds, walls even, if they are warded to keep people out. I can't be sure. I can't read it." The stranger said, matter-of-factly.

"Strong, indeed." Morgosh said, opening his eyes and finally looking over the parchment. After a long scan from the top of the page to its bottom, Morgosh nodded and looked from the stranger to Arnath as he spoke. "You might not read the ancient Arkonian, but I do. It is as you say, it is a spell for disabling impenetrable wards. A breaching spell. We'll need this."

"Finally, some progress." Trellith said, to which Shrakar grunted his approval.

Arnath nodded, and patted the fullness of the coin purse that still sat on the table. "Then we should talk price."

No one had noticed that Garthe had stepped away from the table, rounded behind Morgosh and now stood beside the stranger. Just as the stranger was about to speak, to name a preliminary figure, his jaw froze open, nearly slack and his eyes took on a distant quality.

From under the table, a green glow emanated. Familiar to all in the party, Morgosh rolled his eyes and looked under the table to see that, indeed, Garthe held his green healing stone between his fingers close to the swarthy stranger's bad knee.

Entirely cross with his charge, Morgosh pounded the table with the side of his fist. "Garthe! I've told you not to do that."

"But he needs it." Garthe said, not looking away from his ministrations.

"Yes. But you must get permission to do spell work upon someone's person – Always!" Morgosh said in a stern tone. Angered though he was at his apprentice's lack of etiquette, he did not try to stop him physically from completing what he was doing. Interrupting a spell whilst it was still being cast was incredibly dangerous.

Garthe's ability to heal was how the party had discovered him. Mage births were so rare, since mage's themselves could not seed or bear children, that when a child was born with potential abilities, they attained a kind of celebrity quite quickly. Garthe, however, was from an isolated village tucked within the mountain chain between Farsuum and Vallasen – a place where word neither travelled in or out of. The party only strayed into the village in desperate need of food after yet another failed adventure. Morgosh could sense his presence immediately and began the lengthy process of convincing Garthe's parents of the need for he to apprentice under another mage as soon as possible. Untrained mages often turned their powers recklessly toward darkness, having had no discipline in their use. His reluctant parents eventually conceded to release their son to Morgosh's care, knowing full well the law of the land, and the lore around dark mages. Though the goodbyes were tear-filled, Garthe's parents took heart that their lives would be enriched by the kingdom, once Morgosh reported that he had taken on a new mage as apprentice to the great mage Orpha at the palace. Parents were handsomely rewarded for loss of their magical children by the crowned heads of all three kingdoms, as those children would grow to serve the kingdoms for the duration of their lifetimes.

Even Morgosh, who worked alongside the great healing mages during the war, was immediately astonished at the boy's healing ability. For a completely undisciplined mage, Garthe demonstrated incredible power. Even now, all those around the table could see the rictus of pain on the swarthy stranger's face relax into a tranquil visage of relief. He continued to sit entirely still, his head lolling slightly back even after the green light from the healing stone faded away and Garthe rounded the table to return to his seat. Settling his chair, the boy avoided his master's angry glare.

Morgosh's judging eyes were not locked on Garthe for long, as the stranger in black stood up from his chair and made the most pleasure-filled of sighs. He sat back down again, without any of the pained hesitation that punctuated his descent into the chair when he first joined them. Fully seated, the stranger raised and lowered his leg, slowly and quickly, the widest of smiles on his face.

He looked across the table at Garthe, and said, "Thank you."

Arnath, Trellith and Shrakar also gave the boy approving nods, all of them wishing a healing mage of Garthe's power had been with them in the trenches of the war and beyond. Were that so, the table would be surrounded by a dozen or more friends who they'd lost in combat and misadventure over the years.

Morgosh turned to the man whose brow had previously been knit in a permanent pained expression, and was now relaxed in utterly contented relief, saying, "You're quite welcome. As you can see the boy is not only talented, but also quite generous with that talent. I do not wish to interrupt your reverie, but we still need to discuss the price of this spell."

"No, we do not." The stranger said, a wry expression on his face. "Your young companion has restored me to the man I once was. You have, all of you, changed my life forever. Take the spell, you owe me nothing. I hope it brings you the luck you need to succeed in your treasure hunt. Good journeys, gentlemen."

And with that, the stranger effortlessly stood from the table and strode toward the door, with only the slightest wobble of years of muscle imbalance in his now confident gait.

*

They left Umdra the next day and were well into the forested hills to the north a day later. As they crested another of the many rolling hills, Arnath and Morgosh had allowed themselves to fall behind the others.

Up ahead, Trellith and Shrakar hiked up the hill, side by side, as Garthe rode high up, seated on one of the shoulders of Shrakar's armour. Several paces behind, out of earshot, Arnath and Morgosh continued an argument they had been having for going on a year now.

"The boy is not yours to teach, Captain." Morgosh said, repressing his fervor. "I wish I did not have to repeat myself, but our previous conversations on the matter seem to not have taken root."

"They've taken root enough. You said the same thing the last time. I remember." Arnath said, taking long strides up the hillside, thus fOrcing the mage to nearly trot to keep up with him. Arnath was a good-hearted man with a keen mind, but he often found the subtle use of his brawn spoke volumes over any words.

"And yet you still feel the need to interject your snippets of martial wisdom any time the boy asks me a pointed question. It is as though you can't help yourself."

"I can hold my tongue when needed, when I feel it makes sense." Arnath said continuing to look ahead at his friends who were nearing the crest of the hill. "He is a child from a very isolated region. Why travel the world, if not but to become more worldly? In travelling with us, one would hope the lad would get further education than spell craft and the art of the grift."

Morgosh was visibly rankled by this, taking extreme umbrage with Arnath's not-so-subtle slight of his character. "We do not *have* to travel with you in order for my education of the boy to continue." He said, making the threat and almost meaning it.

Arnath turned to Morgosh, reached out and gripped the old mage by the front of his long, white robe. At first, Morgosh was shocked. Arnath had never once used violence to try to win an argument with him. But when the warrior put a finger to his lips, beckoning for silence, Morgosh immediately understood.

They were in danger.

And from the squinting, side-long expressions of Trellith and Shrakar, who had slowly made their way back down the hill towards Arnath and Morgosh, weapons drawn, they knew it too. Arnath let go of Morgosh and drew his sword. Shrakar had kneeled down to allow a clearly frightened Garthe to jump from his shoulder and race into the arms of his master.

In short turn they all heard it – the crunch of leaves and bracken on the forest floor. To Arnath's ears it was the sound of people with no serious training trying to be stealthy, and failing miserably. They didn't have to wait long to see who pursued them.

They emerged from all sides, a band of filthy curs, ten in number, and Arnath recognized them immediately. They had occupied the tabled one spot closer to the door of the ale room where Garthe had healed the peddler. Their whole company emitted a gasp when Arnath dropped the soft purse on the table in order to impress the swarthy spell seller. After that gasp, their table had grown eerily silent, as though quietly plotting.

"Greetings, travellers." Said their apparent leader as the group reached equidistant positions surrounding Arnath and his companions. His smirk and defiant rasp let on the group's intent toward Arnath and the others.

Trellith, who stood closest to the leader, his nocked arrow pointed at bald cur's face, said, "And what would you travellers be after? That was a long trot to catch up with us from Umdra."

At which the bald cur only grinned, and said, "Yes, it winded us some. But the prize is worth it, we thinks."

"And what prize do you think we have for you?" Trellith said, not taking his aim from the man's eye for a second.

"When those coins hit the table, sure convinced that down-on-his-luck noble gent you had money to pay for that parchment 'o magic. But it sure convinced us the weight of it was worth killin' ya for, as well." The bald cur had said in a voice that sounded like he had practiced to perfection a charming menace over a great many years. He himself must have believed his own snake-like charm, for he looked utterly baffled when Arnath and the others started to snicker at him. He scowled and barked, "What you all laughing at?"

Arnath pulled the hefty purse from his belt, untied the thong, loosened the opening and readied to throw it at the cur's feet. "I think we need to shed some light on the subject." Arnath said, turning pointedly toward Morgosh, and then tossed the purse.

It sailed the brief distance toward the bald cur, and when it landed at his feet his entire party's eyes were on it. And all of their jaws dropped as the coins spilled out... The mere half-dozen coins mixed in with a plethora of squashed construction nails and rocks that gave the deceptively bulky purse weight. Before the ten thieves could retaliate for the effort this deception had cost them, they were suddenly blinded by a piercing white light.

*

Later, as the sun began to set, and they were within sight of one of the many ruined ancient Arkonian temples, Arnath and Morgosh were concluding their discussion, this time on friendlier terms.

"Yes, I suppose we should abandon the ruse with the coins. It's just worked so well." Morgosh said, a veritable pang of loss in his voice.

"Worked very well at attracting cut-throats and thieves. This must be the fifth or sixth melee we've had over that infernal trick." Arnath stated, still aggravated they'd had to fight at all.

"Seventh." Trellith said gruffly from behind them, which neither Morgosh or Arnath questioned, knowing well the dwarf's gift for numbers.

And a melee it indeed was. When the shocked bandits all looked down at the near-worthless contents of the purse, Morgosh pulled out and shook his illumination ampule – a glass container filled with a potion of liquids that got very bright when shaken – prompted to do so by Arnath's phrase, "Shed some light on the subject." Entirely blinded, the thieves were easy prey for Arnath and his companions, who had trained with the King's guard of Vallasen during the war. Even with their greater numbers, Arnath, Trellith and Shrakar had easily felled them all in a short turn, trying their best to not inflict fatal wounds on their out-matched opponents. Even Garthe joined in the battle, he too having been readied for it when he heard one of many of Arnath's secret tactical phrases. Under the blinding light his master held above his head, the boy pulled out his slingshot and struck no less than three of the thieves in the head with its heavy pellets.

Afterwards, to discourage further pursuit over the rough terrain by the group of vanquished bandits, Shrakar and Trellith stripped off their many boots. They carried the footwear all the way to the next river they came across and dumped all the would-be robber's boots into the chilly, rushing waters.

Morgosh sighed and slowed his pace, allowing Trellith to pass them by. "I've been thinking about what you said earlier, before we were so rudely accosted."

Arnath stopped and looked at the mage full-on, asking, "What part?"

"Oh, the notion that the boy needs to be worldly, especially since he will travel far and wide, healing many kinds of folk as he goes." Morgosh paused a moment, and then completed his thought. "I think in this you're right. You and the others should be teaching him the skills he'll need to survive no matter where he goes. My own master taught me much about subtly bending people to your needs. Those skills now benefit us as a party on a daily basis."

Arnath smiled and patted the old mage on the shoulder, gesturing for them to catch up with the others. "And to think, it only took you almost a full year to come around."

"A full year, many an argument and seven violent attempts to rob us of coin we didn't have."

*

Twilight was upon them as they reached the base of a hill, one shaped quite differently than all the other rolling mounds they had crested over the past two days. Though as overgrown with grass and trees as those all around, this one had a noticeably conical shape. As soon as they saw it, they knew they'd come to the place marked on the map they'd bought several weeks ago.

Arnath, Trellith and Shrakar inspected the overgrown, ancient Arkonian temple's base with torches – Arnath and Trellith walking in opposite directions around its circumference, and Shrakar climbing up the structure and navigating around it from some twenty feet up.

Morgosh and Garthe stood close to the ancient temple that was hidden under near a thousand years of overgrowth, with their hands held up, palms out, and felt for any magics within the structure. Morgosh searched for the magical energies, his eyes closed and spoke softly to Garthe the entire time, instructing him on what to "feel" for as he reached across, into the magical plain. Garthe's brow cinched for a moment and he opened his eyes. He tugged on Morgosh's robe and pointed to a spot higher up where the conical structure rounded away.

"Up there, master." Garthe said with total certainty.

Morgosh was just shifting his palm in that direction, when Shrakar appeared in that exact spot, waving his torch down at the others, and called out in his croaking Kolgothan accent, "Up here! Found shaft up here!"

"Good lad." Morgosh said, patting his ward on the shoulder. "Now let's gather up the climbing equipment."

*

Once they had all made the short climb and were inside the corridor Shrakar had found, they relied on the illumination ampule for light, instead of using torches. Ancient places had very little circulation, and burning what little air there was within them was just not smart. Morgosh led the way, occasionally stopping to read the ancient text carved and painted along the walls. Much of the painted text of the Arkonian glyphs was faded or chipped away, and Morgosh often bade Shrakar, who held the illumination ampule up high as they progressed down the dust-choked corridors, to bring the light closer, so the old mage could get a sense of what the fragmented script conveyed. After reading the words in the ancient, dead tongue, Morgosh would think on them and then point down a darkened corridor, saying, "This way."

Shrakar, his war axe in one hand and the bright ampule held high in the other, led the way. Any threats that sprung out at him would likely never reach the rest of party. Shrakar was a gentle soul who took much joy in the many creatures in the animal world and enjoyed making children laugh, but in battle he was an unbeatable hellion – Many were the individuals whose last inkling before they fell was utter shock at how fast he could move his giant Half-Orcs bulk. Morgosh crept along behind Shrakar, peering around the half-Orcs broad back as the light was introduced into every new corridor they came upon. Garthe stayed close behind his master, and Trellith stayed close to Garthe. Depending on what they were doing on any given time during their journeys or raids, each man took responsibility for Garthe's safety as was needed. Shrakar was up ahead with the light, Morgosh was guiding them by reading the ancient tongue around them and the magics infused in the temple, and Arnath brought up the rear, listening with his keen ears to the encroaching darkness that crept after them with every turn. That left Trellith, who didn't mind the boy at all, but for his never-ending questions. Even now, as the rest of them steeled themselves for an attack out of the shadows, the boy prattled on.

"How can you be sure she isn't really your cousin?" Garthe asked, speaking of the barmaid in Umdra at near full volume.

"That's just the thing, lad. I can't." Trellith replied in a truly hushed tone, a way of hinting at the boy to keep his voice down. Voices echoing off the ancient stone of these winding corridors at full volume might well wake up something better left in slumber.

"But how do you know she isn't?" Garthe said, emulating the rasp of a whisper, without lowering his voice all that much.

At this, Morgosh tapped Shrakar on the elbow, bidding him to stop. The old mage turned around, glared angrily down at his apprentice until the boy hunkered away from his gaze. Morgosh then looked up, wide-eyed, at Arnath and indicated the boy with his open-palmed hand, as though to say, "*You wanted to teach him, so teach him.*"

As Morgosh turned from them, concentrating on the cuneiforms on the walls, Arnath knelt down to be face to face with Garthe.

"Do you know why your master is cross with you?"

"I was only asking questions..." The boy said, visibly upset.

"I know. And those are good questions. You travel with folks of differing species, and knowing their ways is indeed good. But, when immersed in darkness, with potential dangers around every corner, there is only one question that really, truly matters." Arnath said, being sure his whispered tone gave no hint of scolding.

"Only one? What is it?" Garthe asked, amazed at the mere idea.

Arnath leant in closer and whispered, "When all around is dark, not even a star to be seen, the most important question is *"What can hear me?"*." He then put a finger to the boy's lips, and then one up to his own ear, illustrating that it was time to be quiet and listen as best he could.

Arnath picked up his sword from the cobbled floor and rose to meet Morgosh's still-judging gaze. Rather than comment on Arnath's ability to school his charge, the mage merely tapped the symbols on the wall and pointed down the corridor, quietly saying, "This way."

As they continued on into the darkness, it took a great deal of effort for Arnath not to explode with laughter when he saw young Garthe turn to Trellith, as the boy put a silencing finger across his lips, shushing the visibly irate dwarf.

*

The chamber they descended into was tiny. It matched the incredibly narrow, winding stairs that led down into it. Shrakar had to tuck into one corner to allow the others in through the slim doorway.

Morgosh took his ampule from Shrakar and approached the far wall, which was barely ten feet from the open doorway. "Odd place for a vault." The mage said as he began to read the symbols covering the entire wall spanning the chamber.

"That had to be a prison of some kind up there." Trellith said, a perplexed looked on his face. Though he knew little of the ancient Arkonian culture, he knew design and building well enough to know you did not put a sealed treasure vault in the sub-basement under a multitude of prison cells. He and Arnath exchanged a concerned look, having noted that not only was the location odd, but that there were bones, or mostly fragments of them, scattering the floor at the base of the far wall. They looked up from the grisly sight to watch the mage stop in his approach to the wall, his hand held fully out.

"Powerful magics, indeed. Almost like something masking over..." Morgosh said as he reached toward the wall with his eyes closed. "Garthe, you stay back. Feel the energy from afar. There is something here, I'm not quite..." His voice trailed off a moment, and then he turned toward them, holding up the leather tube they acquired in Umdra.

"What say we try it?"

"Wait!" Arnath said stepping forward as much as the small space allowed. "You say there are magics at work here, but why not see if we can breach it... our way?"

Though he was a mage trained in the ancient tradition, Morgosh often saw the simple wisdom of the old soldiering lunks he travelled with – Why expend a valuable spell when the wall might give with a good bashing?

"Very well. Have at it." Morgosh back towards the narrow doorway, ushering Garthe back up the landing of the slim staircase.

When everyone was tucked up the narrow, winding stone stairs, Shrakar hefted his great war axe up, aimed the butt-spike at the base of the weapon's long handle at the wall, and let out a snorting breath. He bolted forward, two short but powerful strides, driving the spike towards the wall.

An echoing *CLANG* rang out as the spike stabbed into the wall, and was, along with Shrakar, repelled away with great force. The half-Orc and his great axe flew across the tiny room, to land roughly on either side of the door. It was fortunate the axe wasn't driven down the center, into the staircase, for it sure would have mortally harmed Arnath and Morgosh, who were closest to the threshold.

Arnath leapt out of the doorway and to Shrakar's side. The half-Orc was sitting up, dizzily rubbing his head. "Wall no break. Only skull." Shrakar said after sitting up fully, his one eye shut as he winced from the pain in his head. Arnath helped him up, and guided him to the stairs, where the big half-Orc sat down to the immediate ministrations of Garthe and his green healing stone.

Certain his injured friend was in good hands, Arnath turned to Morgosh, who had emerged from the stairway to make room for Shrakar, and asked, "Did you see it?"

Arnath referred to a light, the faintest limn of blue, that appeared over the surface of the wall when Shrakar's spike struck it. The blue sheen was strongest where the spike made contact and faded as it radiated away from that point. And as soon the Orc and his weapon were repelled the colourful layer that protected the wall once again became invisible.

"Oh, yes. I saw it. Powerful spell indeed. Shrakar could bash at it all day, for weeks even, and have no effect." Morgosh handed Arnath the light ampule, then removed the slim leather spellcase from his robe and rolled up his sleeves. "No, this kind of warding requires an equally powerful magic."

"The writings, on the wall, do they say what kind of spell it is?" Arnath asked cocking his chin toward the wall covered in writings from floor to ceiling.

"Oh, just the usual – "Doom be to those who would breach these precincts", etc. No different than we've seen before, I assure you, captain." Morgosh answered casually as he undid the leather binds enclosing the leather tube.

Arnath nodded and moved back to the doorway, allowing the mage room to cast the acquired spell.

Morgosh slipped the spell parchment free, allowing the leather container to plop to the floor. He cleared his throat loudly as he unfurled the parchment. Needing one hand free to cast, Morgosh affixed the parchment between his thumb and pinkie fingers, to keep it from rolling up again. He then held his other hand out, palm towards the warded wall and began to speak the words on the parchment aloud. In the tiny space Morgosh's incantation of the ancient Arkonian tongue boomed.

Arnath, who stood behind Morgosh, and Shrakar, Garthe and Trellith, who were crammed tightly into the little stairway, all waiting with patient fascination as Morgosh read from the parchment. The mages voice rose and fell in deep, rolling bass tones as he read the entirety of the parchment.

When he was done, and the last echo of his voice faded away, Morgosh looked at the wall curiously, allowing his outstretched hand to slowly fall to his side.

Arnath remained still as he looked curiously from Morgosh's back to the wall. "Did it work?"

"I don't know…" Morgosh said over his shoulder, not taking his eyes from the wall. He could not see or even feel anything different since casting the spell. Most times there was something, some sign, a shift in the feel of the magical plain, even sometimes a noise, that indicated that a spell had taken effect. Here, there was no such thing.

Feeling a sense of defeat, Morgosh's shoulders slumped. Though he brought much more to the party than his magical abilities, his talent for breaching impenetrable wards was the one thing most needed when hunting for treasure in ancient tombs. And it looked as though this time he had utterly failed.

"I don't know what to say. The spell must be faulty. Inappropriate for this kind of warding. I really don't understand. Much of the wording within the spell matches what is written there on the wall." Morgosh said with quiet humility.

Arnath wasn't willing to give up so easily. He unsheathed his sword and hefted it up, readying to see if the spell had indeed broken the wards, the same way as Shrakar had before Morgosh had read it.

Before Arnath could take a single step toward the wall, some invisible force seized Morgosh's body, freezing him in place with his arms flung out to his sides. Though his knees were bent like he might crumple in a heap, the forces held him rigidly in place above the stone floor.

"Morgosh!" Arnath exclaimed, as he stepped forward, reaching out to help pull the stricken mage away from the wall.

"No, don't, Arnath! Don't touch me! Stay back!" Morgosh shouted urgently, only able to turn his head a few meager degrees.

"What is it? What has you?" Arnath asked, resisting the urge to defy the mage's command and intervene.

"I don't know! A defense within the wards? Something beyond them...?" Morgosh answered with questions of his own.

"What can we do?" Arnath said, stepping as close to Morgosh's side as he could without risking contact.

"I don't know. I don't think there is anything you can do."

"Let me help, master!" Garthe said, trying to leave the stairway. Shrakar held him back, worried the boy might break Morgosh's edict and get caught up in the captivating spell.

"No! Keep the boy back! All of you stay back." Morgosh shouted. With visible effort the mage managed to turn his head toward Arnath, enough for the two of them to look each other in the eye. Arnath was stricken by the pain and anguish he saw within his friend's eyes. "You can't help. I can't even help myself. In all my experience, I've never encountered a power such as this. I know no spell to repel it. I can feel it reaching into me... down into my very soul."

"Listen to me carefully, Arnath. The books, the spell books amongst my things, are for the boy. He should have them all." Morgosh continued, speaking of the gear they had hidden in the nearby woods so as to explore the ruin unencumbered. "I'm sorry, Arnath. I don't know what went wrong. I hate to leave you like this. I know you'll do right by the boy."

"Leave us? We'll find a way, friend." Arnath said, and as the last was spoken he was close enough to see a red mist spanning from the wall to various points on Morgosh's body. At first, Arnath thought it was the magical field that held the mage captive. Then he realized, it was Morgosh's blood.

Whether the spell was indeed faulty, or the warnings on the wards were real, the forces that held Morgosh were literally sucking the life from him.

Arnath followed the tiny streams of blood emanating from his friend, to where they were disappearing within the wall. Once again, he looked at the base of the wall, and saw the piles of fragmented bones there. Arnath realized he was completely powerless to save his friend.

Morgosh's body tensed, the cursed spell holding him so tightly his feet were no longer touching the floor. Through his clear agony, Morgosh was able to shout out, "Get the boy out! All of you - GO!"

Slowly, Morgosh began to float towards the wall. Though levitating, the mage struggled against his bonds, his jerking movements appearing as though he fought an invisible demon.

Arnath stepped to the doorway, and flicked the back of his hand at Shrakar and Trellith. Dumbstruck by the sight of their friend floating towards the wall, his blood now pouring out of him in gouts, they still obeyed Arnath's silent command. Shrakar gathered up Garthe, who struggled still to get free of the half-Orcs grasp, and the trio disappeared up the stairs.

"Master – no!" Garthe's cry could be heard echoing from the corridor above.

Arnath turned to see Morgosh's wriggling body had just nearly reached the wall.

Making contact, the mage tried to push away with his hands. Then the flesh was ripped from his hands, consumed by the wall itself. Then the bones within started to sink into the wall. Morgosh let out a scream of agonized terror as his body made contact with the wall and began to sink into it. Pulling his head back away from the wall as long as he could, Morgosh continued to scream, blood streaming from his mouth, forehead and eyes, as he inched ever closer.

Finally, his face made contact with the accursed stone, and the mage's screams gave way to gurgles like those of a drowning man. Those gurgles stopped as the last of his body was consumed within the stone. His robe, which had many of his bones still within, crumpled in a bloodied heap on the chamber floor.

Arnath stared aghast at the weeping oval of blood on the wall where his friend had once been, then turned and ran from the chamber.

*

"Into the very stone, you say?" Trellith asked again, after they had had enough time numbly staring into the fire.

"Into the pores of the rock itself." Arnath said, not wanting to picture it further.

"By the dark, what cruel curse." Trellith said grimly, as he passed his pipe to Shrakar, who wiped away a tear and put the pipe to his mouth. After a couple of puffs, the brows above Shrakar's sad eyes raised up.

"What we do now?" Shrakar said, his already croaky voice rendered even more brittle from all the tears. Maybe it was too soon to ask, but Shrakar was not one to mince words in his second language, the common tongue of the three kingdoms.

Arnath took the pipe from Shrakar and passed his wineskin to the half-Orc, saying, "I'll say this much right now – I'm not going back in there."

"No treasure is worth that chance!" Trellith scoffed, smacking his palms on his knees. "If there was even the remotest, the tiniest possibility that Morgosh accidentally activated some defensive curse within that tomb, we'd be fools to walk back into it."

Shrakar nodded at Trellith's words, and passed the wineskin to Arnath, who said, "Then we are all in agreement. There is something else though…"

Arnath turned over his right shoulder, and looked pointedly at the silhouette of the boy who sat just outside the firelight. When Arnath turned back he saw Trellith and Shrakar knew exactly what he was speaking of. "He made no request, I swore no oath, but still, they were his final words to me."

"It just isn't… feasible. These last, what, fifteen years, we've been up to our necks in all kinds of trouble. Barely survived some of the scrapes we've gotten into. To do that with a…" Trellith looked over to where Garthe sat in the dark, letting that complete his thought. He turned back, and said in a lower voice, "I just don't think it can be done."

Shrakar shrugged, saying, "I could protect."

"Yes, you could, but not all the time." Arnath said in a low tone. "Compound how we feel right now at Morgosh's loss. That's how bad it will feel when some terrible fate befalls him and he ends up like Lanea and Dalgar did. And now Morgosh."

"Our numbers have dwindled drastically in recent years." Said Trellith, acknowledging the many friends who had all met terrible ends as they adventured across the three kingdoms over the years. Now, with Morgosh gone, there was only the three of them left of the original adventuring party that had struck out together at the wars end.

"There is that, and the plain truth of it. He is a mage in a kingdom that has been starved for mages since the war." Arnath said as he punctuated his words with the pipe that had been handed to him. "It is callous to think he can learn better under us than under, say, Mage Orpha at the palace. We take him back to his parents and inform the kingdom he is there, awaiting a new teacher. Traipsing around after us will only get him killed."

"Or you might be killed without me."

Startled, the three warriors turned to find Garthe now within the firelight, standing in the space between Trellith and Arnath. How long he had been there? What all had he heard?

"You can't take me back. You can't. I've learned so much on the road with you. And you need me too. How many times have I healed you of mortal wounds? Each of you? How many times? Well, if you take me back home, I won't be there the next time. Will you let your party dwindle down to nothing because you didn't wish to care of a boy?" Garthe's entreaty spilled out of him, between sniffles and tears.

"You've heard our stories, been through many a harrowing turn with us, you know the dangers you'd be facing." Arnath said, not questioning, but as a warning.

Garthe wiped away tears, and said, "I know."

"If you commit to this, to keeping the three of us alive should we be felled by misadventure, which seems to be the only kind we have, you have my – our - solemn promise that we will endeavour to seek out mages and the written teachings of mages, so that you may continue to develop your skills. But understand, your survival is not entirely in our hands. We are drunken fools seeking treasure. What little skill we have surviving in this world was earned on the battlefield. We can offer you no home, no hearth. You'd be your own number one guardian, as we ourselves are. Do you understand?"

"I do." Garthe said, his tears now fully dried.

Arnath nodded solemnly, looked to the others and saw no disagreement in their eyes. He then gestured for Garthe to sit at the fourth log around their fire, which had laid empty until now.

Garthe crossed around the fire and sat. He looked at the others, then to Arnath.

Again, it was Shrakar who broke the silence. "Where we go now?"

"In the morning, we'll chisel markings into the opening in that ruin, warning people it is an accursed place. Then I think we should go back to Umdra, and try to find the peddler who sold us that spell." Arnath said without having to think about it.

"Why?" Trellith said eyeing Arnath sidelong. He thought he knew the answer, but wanted to hear his captain say it aloud.

"I want to know where he got it from, from whom." Arnath said. "Was it the spell that killed our long-time travelling companion, our friend, one of the last master mages to survive the war, or was it something within the tomb itself? Wouldn't you like to know? I see a fog of vexation upon my mind for a long time to come if I don't find out."

"And if we find him, and he won't tell us anything?" Trellith asked.

Arnath was unable to shake the image of the dying mage, even as he looked at Garthe for a moment, considering. He hoped not to be a disappointment to the boy, their new charge, but knew also that a hard price had to be paid for sending Morgosh into the jaws of death. He looked deeply into the fire and shrugged; his mind made up.

"Then we kill him."

PART ONE: WHERE THE ROAD ENDS

CHAPTER ONE

T**here it was again!** Arnath was sure he'd heard something this time. A kind of skittering echo from the cavern below them. Startled by the initial echoes, mere moments ago, Arnath immediately had the party douse their torches, leaving only the pinpoint of bright daylight from the opening up the cavern slope to guide them. He held his broad warrior's frame stone still as he listened, waiting for those elusive sounds to resound again, if only to ascertain if their source was nearby. A lifetime of adventuring had taught him that this kind ominous, hanging silence never bode well – It was the whisper of some incredible terror about to explode forth upon them. Instinctually, his hand tightly gripped the hilt of his sword.

Listening for the distant sounds was made all the harder by the rattle and scrape of his nearby companions as they stuffed their newly acquired chest of gold into a large hide and metal-rivetted backpack. Arnath turned toward them, his boon companions for decades, hoping they'd be prepared to leave this place in a hurry. One thing was certain, whatever he'd heard could surely hear them as well, with all the noise they were making.

Sensing Arnath's concerned gaze Trellith and Shrakar looked up from their labours, fingers still speedily working on the straps and belts of the pack.

"Quickly." Arnath seethed through gritted teeth. Trellith and Shrakar peered past Arnath into the threatening darkness. Beyond their leader, further down the throat of the cave another member of their party, their mage, a boy in long robes, stood with his back to them. Without further words, Trellith and Shrakar gathered Arnath's meaning and re-doubled their efforts. Things were about to get hairy.

The mage who stood down the rocky slope was Garthe, now a tall teenager of 17-years, still the most recent to have joined their company. One of his skinny arms held up a glass ampule; a tiny jar filled with liquids that grew extremely bright when shaken. After telling everyone to douse their torches in the many puddles at their feet, Arnath had instructed Garthe to have his magic ampule ready, but to not light it. Not yet. Like Arnath, Garthe looked down into the descending maw of darkness and listened, turning his large ears this way and that. In the roughly eight years since Garthe joined their company, the boy had proven himself time and again by standing point between the party and some incredible threat, all the while swallowing fear that would unman many a warrior. It earned him the lasting respect of the grizzled veterans he travelled with.

Seeing that Shrakar and Trellith were finishing up with the pack, Trellith buckling the last straps across Shrakar's broad green chest, Arnath stepped quietly down the tunnel to stand at Garthe's side. Still listening, Garthe flicked a quick glance toward Arnath, who shrugged a silent query the boy's way.

"I don't know." Garthe whispered, immediately cringing at the tiny echo his voice had created.

"But there is something?" whispered Arnath, his voice near silent.

Days before, they had been in the town of Moorgate, a few leagues away. At the trading post, the proprietor had offered them a map that supposedly led to the once-great kingdom of Ulg. The legends surrounding Ulg spoke of an arrogant king that had angered their god and the very earth then swallowed the city whole, cursing the errant populace to eternal damnation. Fanciful as such tales were, Arnath knew from experience that they often contained some kernels of truth. A city was buried under the Ulgrew mountains – a chain that was prone to earthquakes - and cities contained gold. The rest was nonsense meant to explain the tremors and cave-ins to the superstitious. Besides, the map was cheap and they had already planned on heading in this direction.

Now, deep within the largest mountain in the chain, with only a distant pinpoint of sunlight guiding their way toward escape, Arnath began to question whether they had indeed awoken some unearthly force. He didn't heed the spiritual all too much, but in his travels, he had seen things – Things that bolstered his lifelong distrust of the supernatural. He believed enough to fear and hate the curses that at times befell them, and that was spirituality enough to sustain him.

Hearing the creak of straining leather, the chime of gold coins settling, Arnath and Garthe turned from the darkness to see Shrakar slowly getting to his feet. Their half-Orc friend was very strong, but this gold was an incredibly heavy prize. It took all four of them the early part of the day to get it this far from out of the bowels of the mountain. Seeing Shrakar had straightened his back, was steady on his feet, Arnath gestured at him, and Trellith also, with a flick of the back of his hand, ushering them to get a move on. Both old soldiers, Shrakar and Trellith gave no questioning look, they just turned and began the trudge toward the light at the upper end of the cavern.

Arnath leaned in close to Garthe, and whispered. "We'll walk slowly behind. Bring up the rear. Keep listening for..." Letting the last hang. Surely there was something. They could all feel it – a change in the air - as soon as they wrenched the chest of gold from its resting place. But what...?

Patting Garthe on the shoulder, Arnath gesturing for him to follow. Gulping down fear, the young mage began to slowly proceed up the slope, his upper body turned slightly, wanting to continue monitoring the cave behind them. They'd only taken a few steps up the cavern slope when they heard it.

Arnath and Garthe froze instantly. Peering into the darkness, Arnath thought hard on the sound. The echo aside, the only thing it bore similarity to in his recollection was the rattle of bone dice on a stone tavern floor. Yet it sounded like it came from the roof of the cave. They waited for several moments for the sound to report again. When it did not, they continued to move up the cavern slope.

Again, the noise resounded, and this time it did not stop. The cascade of echoing dice grew louder as it clattered towards them.

Arnath nodded at the fear-filled Garthe, "Shake it. Cover of dark does us no good anymore."

Garthe vigorously shook his hand, the liquid within the teardrop shaped vial immediately unleashing a glow so bright he and Arnath had to squint against it.

Their eyes adjusted after a moment and then they saw them.

What first appeared as an army of man-sized crawling insects, lining the walls, roof and floor of the cavern, turned out, on second glance, to be skeletons. Hundreds of them. No – thousands of them! They crawled in speedy pursuit of the party - on the floor, walls, roof of the cavern, bones tapping against stone, jaws on the lolling skulls gnashing. Those that had skulls. Some were mere portions of the dead. Whatever had a remaining elbow or knee or socket to crawl with. For a collection of rattling dead things, they were threateningly fast.

"Run!" shouted Arnath, rousing Garthe from the shock of the sight. Both of them turned and ran with all they had.

Arnath could hear the urgent clattering gaining on them. He calculated their speed against Garthe's ability to run. His speed would not hold. Another escape tactic was needed in order for them all to survive. He cupped one hand beside his mouth, and shouted a command ahead. "Shrakar, Trellith – stop!"

They did, and turning back saw the undulating nightmare coming up after them for the first time.

"Unbuckle the pack. Trellith, you and I will carry it. Shrakar, take the boy." Arnath commanded them as he and Garthe caught up. Shrakar immediately dropped to one knee, and hastily began to unbuckle the pack with Trellith's help. To save precious time, Trellith pulled the centre buckling straps away from Sharkar's chest and hacked through them with his knife. The pack fell to the cavern floor with a jangling thud.

Without hesitating, Arnath and Trellith each grabbed one of the straps and took off, the surprisingly fleet dwarf matching Arnath's pace. Arnath looked over his shoulder as Shrakar snatched Garthe up by the waist, tucked him up under his powerful arm, like he had a hundred times before, and then started to race up the tunnel after them.

The rattling bone army practically nipped at their heels. They were gaining fast!!

"Garthe – The inferno spell! The one you got in Kilanthy!" Arnath shouted over his shoulder, racing toward the light under the weight of the heavy gold chest. Turning forward, his breath heaved, lungs and legs burning from the exertion. The rising slope was not so severe that they would tumble back downwards again if they fell, but it was just enough to tax the body harder and harder with each stride. A quick glance confirmed that Trellith did not have much more left to give either. Arnath focussed on the growing light of the cavern opening and hoped for his life that the boy understood him over the noise of the chattering bones.

Garthe was being jostled like a ragdoll, his legs flailing in front of the running Orc, as he faced the on-coming horde of gnashing skeletons. How did they get so close?!

Carefully easing his body sideways, so as to not wriggle out of Shrakar's grip, Garthe reached into his cloak and slid a leather-bound note case out of his waistcoat pocket. He carefully unlaced the thong enclosing it, gripping it against each jostling buck of the Orc's pumping legs. Despite the buffeting his body was taking, Garthe easily found the ancient spell inside the valise, removed the paper and restored the folio back to his waistcoat. Steadying the ancient parchment in his hand, Garthe began to read.

As he read the words aloud, reciting the elongated bass sounds of the ancient Ufranduu tongue, the paper began to spark at the top. Then it began to burn, eaten by a bright flame from the top of the page downwards, the words consumed as Garthe spoke them.

In the distant darkness of the cavern, far behind the roiling bone army, a golden glow appeared. It grew larger with each new phrase Garthe read, building from its initial tiny glimmer to a white-hot intensity that encompassed the entire circumference of the tunnel. The wild cascade of raging bones took no notice of the giant ball of fire that began to match pace behind them, then quickly overtake them. The magically-produced flame enveloped the skeletal remains, burning through the bones instantly, reducing them to mere dust inside its all-consuming fire.

Garthe tucked away his no-longer-needed light ampule, his eyes following the last smoldering remnant of the burning page as he let it go, the incantation complete. Fear struck hold once he saw that the skeleton army was right on Shrakar's heals, and now the ever-growing results of the inferno spell was racing up to meet them as well.

It took all the breath Garthe could muster to yell, "Shrakar – RUN!!" over the sound of the rattling bones and the roaring wall of encroaching flame.

Already feeling the heat on his back, Shrakar gritted his teeth and strained to unleash a last burst of speed. Even with his dangling passenger, Shrakar, his sandaled feet swiftly pounding on the cavern floor, easily closed the ground between himself and their treasure-laden companions up ahead.

Nearing the mouth of the cavern, Shrakar felt the heat on his back grow from scalding to blistering. He didn't turn back. He could hear the skeletons searing, the piercing soul-screams of once-alive things, as the magical flame ate ever closer to him. Shrakar could also hear the young mage Garthe let out whimpers of fear and pain as the flames licked ever closer to his head.

Up ahead, Shrakar's companions were at the lip of the cavern, uncertain if they could make the jump before them.

Shrakar let the flames at his back decide for their whole party.

As he barrelled toward the lip of the cavern, Shrakar gripped hold of Garthe's robe, spread his powerful arms and heaved forward with all the power his legs could muster.

Tackling his companions over the side of the mountain, Shrakar just barely spared them from the enormous column of fire that blasted like a volcanic eruption out of the mouth of the cavern. The roaring column of blazing fire shot into the sky, hurling charred bones and ash all over the mountain.

The party fell, tumbling away from the now-collapsing maw of the cavern, haphazardly bounding like skipping stones down the mountainside.

Whether it was the inferno spell, or the magics activated when the companions stole the chest of gold, the upper portion of the mountain began to rumble. With hundreds of deafening cracks as ancient stone broke apart and the shrill, elongated scrapes of rock grinding against rock, the peak of the mountain began to collapse into itself, returning into the earth.

Arnath tried to keep an eye on his companions as he plummeted down the mountain, now accompanied by pinwheeling armadas of stones and boulders, all of which seemed to want to hit him as hard as the rocky ground did on his uncontrollable descent. The last thing he thought before blackness took him was that he had lost his grip on the hefty pack with the treasure chest inside. If one of his companions did not have it, it would surely be buried under the mountain, and all they had fought for, this whole foolish adventure was for naught.

*

Arnath sat up abruptly with a roar in his head and his body in excruciating pain. He took a bleary, one-eyed look at his surroundings. Reaching up to his face, he found his head tightly bandaged, the wrapping covering over one of his eyes. He'd survived, that much was certain. Dead men didn't need their wounds dressed.

By the light of the large fire near his feet, Arnath found Shrakar as the Orc limply pulled his bloody arm from the crux of two thick tree branches, allowing Garthe to take over the ministering of it with his glowing green healing stone. Shrakar must have anchored it between the branches, and forced the bones back into place. That was the roaring – Shrakar's yelp of pain.

Arnath sat up fully and instantly regretted it. Some parts only ached mildly; the rest was in utter agony. That he lived through the plummet down the side of the collapsing mountain struck him as defying impossibility. His every ache and pain disagreed. Yes, it was entirely possible to hurt this much. The price for his survival was a near-death pummeling.

He looked around again. Shrakar and Garthe were close by the nearest tree, but where was…?

"Did we live? Did we all live?" Arnath said, looking around with great concern. Not another boon companion…

"We live." Shrakar nodded at him, speaking in his deep croaking basso, the highly-accented voice of a native of Kolgotha, the Orc country just a few leagues to the north. Garthe looked up from his ministrations, cocking his chin toward where the mountain once was. Even in the dark of night, by only the light of their fire, Arnath could see that the once mighty mountain was now merely an impossibly far-reaching pile of jagged rubble and an immense cloud of hanging dust that went all the way up into the sky.

"Trellith went back some time ago. Searching for the remains of the treasure."

Arnath's heart sunk. "Remains?"

A heavy scraping along the rocky ground nearby drew their attention and Shrakar growled into the darkness. Arnath reached for his nearby sword, which was not there. Realizing his sword was likely buried under the mountain, Arnath whipped his hand up to his left breast, and found his weathered Captain's clasp, his rank insignia from the war, his only prized possession, was still fastened to his ragged cloak.

"It's only me." Trellith emerged into the firelight, as battered and bandaged as the rest of them. He held one of the straps of Shrakar's pack over his shoulder, dragging it across the ground like a yoked animal. Exhausted and covered in rock dust, Trellith dragged the mangled pack within arms reach of their places around the fire and then collapsed next to Arnath, a cloud of rock-dust puffing off of him.

Arnath looked at each of his companions around the fire, felt a swell of relief they had all survived, and then stifled a laugh. He knew it would hurt too much to let a full belly-laugh overtake him. What amused him about the sight of them all, even what little he could see of himself, was the utterly bedraggled state they found themselves in and imagining how frightening they might look to a passing stranger. Their motley appearance drew undisguised side-long looks as it was, even when they looked their best.

As he began to search the remains of the pack, Shrakar's heavy, jutting brows tilted up and down, creating comic expressions over his small white-rimmed black eyes. Along with his brow line, his jaw worked from side to side, which like all Orcs was set in an underbite to accommodate the two large, protruding tusk-like teeth that jutted up towards their cheeks. Between the brows and jaw, it produced periodic comic expressions which human children found very funny, and thus made them unafraid of the once great enemy of the recent wars, even though their parents still were. Topping that off with the fact his arm was wrapped in a bloodied tourniquet, he was covered in rock dust and parts of his green skin where bruised near black, Shrakar looked a horrific and hilarious sight indeed.

Right next to Arnath, Trellith looked no better. Though most of his skin was covered, the signs of a recent battering were still evident. His five-foot tall body was covered in twice as much rock dust as the others, as he'd just come back from standing in the dense cloud that hung over the rubble.

Garthe had settled on his left in front of the fire, and Arnath could see his normally studious looking clothes were torn to shreds and powdered in rock dust too. Again, Arnath stifled a burst of laughter at their atrocious appearances. They were by no means a fancy lot, but, outside of the wars, he could not a recall a time wherein they'd looked worse for wear.

"Half." Trellith said, righting himself, clearing the dust from his throat.

"Half?" Arnath inquired, breaking free of his reverie over their tattered appearance.

Trellith pulled a wine skin from his belt, downed several gulps and passed the skin to Arnath. "Half or perhaps less. All that's left of our treasure."

"Ah. Half." Arnath said dourly, and took a long drink from the skin. How they had marvelled, withholding shouts of glee when first felt the weight of the chest. Arnath estimated half of it to still be of a respectable, even incredible, fortune. It was certainly more gold than they had ever seen in one place. They were rich men, for a short time anyway. Wiping his mouth, he smiled wryly. "At least that is better than what is left of us."

"Not by much." Trellith said bitterly as he stood, retrieved the skin and took another long draught.

"Thank you." Arnath said, hoping his gratitude would appease his disgruntled friend. "Thank you for going back."

"One of us had to. Searched by lamplight for hours. Tomorrow the remains of the mountain will be covered with the curious from all around the countryside who saw the fire and dust cloud. Had to get some of what was ours." Trellith said his voice trailing away. As he sipped from the skin, his eyes became distant. "Held on for as long as I could."

"What's that?"

Garthe had removed a green stone from a pouch hung around his neck, and held the stone close to Arnath as he muttered an incantation under his breath. The stone began to glow, casting a bright green glow in Arnath's direction. Arnath sharply inhaled, and upon a long exhalation, felt much of his pain disappear. This was the boy's innate skill, what he brought to the party. For an untrained mage, his gift as a healer was extraordinary.

Arnath inhaled another deep breath and said, "Thank you, Garthe." He pronounced the boy's name like "Garth-Ah" as fit the region the young mage hailed from.

Shrakar still searched through the tattered remains of his large pack. Much of the smashed boards and hinges of the treasure chest were still within, but they would never enclose anything ever again. The treasure that remained was clinking heavily around the bottom of the bag. When Shrakar emerged from his search within the tattered leather and canvas sack, he turned toward the others in the firelight, he held a long pipe, a poke of smoking leaf and a wineskin three times the size of Trellith's. "It not break." Shrakar smiled happily.

"Well, that's something." Arnath returning his smile.

Still watching the crackling fire as though elsewhere, Trellith took another swig and said, "As we fell down the mountain. I held onto to that pack for as long as I could. When Shrakar tackled us..."

"I no meant to..." Said a guilty Shrakar, mid-sip from his huge skin.

"We know." Arnath said, assurance in his voice. "You saved our lives. Better to fall down an angry mountain than to be consumed by the infernal fire."

His momentary guilt assuaged, Shrakar took another sip.

Trellith nodded his agreement. "You saved our hides, indeed. Only to have them battered by every rock on the way down the mountain. After Shrakar hit us, I saw you lose your grip. I held on, letting that blasted chest drag me down the mountain and vice versa. Somehow, I don't think it was as injured as I was, by me slamming into it."

"Still, you live to fight another day." Said Arnath, receiving the skin from Trellith once again.

"May that day not come any time soon."

Trellith's words caught Arnath mid-sip, causing him to sputter somewhat. Wiping his mouth, Arnath passed the skin to Garthe, eyes taking in Trellith fully. Trellith only ever pointed out the negatives when he spoke with a degree of sarcasm, his humourous way of offering his captain alternatives. As doom fraught as those alternatives might have been, it was quite unlike him to present them without some modicum of bravado. Arnath was always the one whose strategies were built around worst-case scenarios. It wasn't like Trellith to come right out and say he didn't have any fight left in him anymore. "What's that, friend?"

For a moment Trellith stared into the fire, saying nothing. He worried a twig in his hands, tossing the pieces into the fire one at a time, finally saying, "For these good many years, I have travelled with you, Shrakar and the others, long gone. Our party have lived, fought, warred and died together. After all that, to be killed in the midst of a task that leaves us no richer than any other we've survived...? As the years go by, one would think, one would hope, the prizes would grow, and ourselves with them, richer."

Arnath heard the words and felt their bitter sting. Not just because his friend had suggested their time as an adventuring party was likely soon to end, but because those exact thoughts had been haunting his private moments for some time now. Once, in the wars, he had been run through with a sword. It did not hurt as much as his body did right now. How many more of these fortune-seeking, near-death adventures were left? The fact they were not killed this time smacked almost of a divinity that Arnath held no faith in. By the infernal dark, they were drunk when they bought the map. They'd bought the map knowing it was a fool's errand, thinking it would lead to nothing, and it had nearly killed them all. What if the next quest did? Become like those skeletons, the accursed, unburied dead, no loved ones left to speak kind words? *Only a fool dies for nothing.* Strong words spoken by his first drill sergeant before marching off to the frontlines of the Orc civil war. Never truer than right now, twenty years later, battered body seated around the fire with his only surviving friends. Those friends would number a great many more had they not gone adventuring after the war. Who could honour the friends we lost in moments such as these if we three were killed chasing some foolish prize? he pondered.

Arnath nodded at Trellith's words, eyes now locked on the fire as well. "What could we do, companions such as ourselves, should our adventures end?"

The four sat silently for a time, Garthe sipping quietly from the skin, knowing they were not speaking of him. He still understood the importance of what was being discussed. The warriors who took him into their party, despite his young age, veritably raising him like a son, were discussing hanging up their swords forever. Garthe knew better than to disturb them with his tears, so he held them back.

Strangely, it was Shrakar who spoke, "When I think of old age, I think of place. We go, long ago. Wooded but rocky hills. Big rocky mound. Town built around. A ledge I could look over the lake. People swam, played, laugh. Not many bothered by sight of Orc."

Garthe didn't know what Shrakar was talking about. It must have been before his time with them. But he could see by Arnath and Trellith's faces they knew the exact place.

"The rocky ledges above the lake at Kroman's Town?" Arnath asked, more to confirm for himself.

"We stocked up before going after the jewelled horn of Cromanii. The King's guard were chasing us." Trellith said, nodding, remembering the time well.

"But never found us. Never came." Shrakar said.

"That double-back we pulled on the trail must have worked." Arnath smiled. "Of course, they just had to show up as we entered the chamber of the horn."

"Leagues away." Snorted Trellith. "I remember that place too. Good wood. Good stone. Many metals to work with. When I think of a place to go, to open a smithy, I account for those things."

"A smithy." Arnath said nodding, having only heard of his friend's old profession spoken of a few times in the years since the war. "I liked the outpost there. No nonsense, always good advice. What was the owner's name again...?"

"Roberge. Gave good advice, indeed. Sold proper maps too." Said Trellith, casting an embittered glance at the mountain. "No maps to suicide missions like this."

"What about training?"

The three warriors looked incredulously Garthe's way.

"What?" asked Trellith, baffled by the boy's question.

"Did they offer any kind of training at those outposts? For warriors, mages and the like." Said Garthe, genuinely curious. "How could they sell climbing hooks and ropes, and not tell parties how to make the proper knots, pass on what they learned of their use?"

"Oh, those traders weren't warriors." Said Arnath, stifling laughter. Sometimes the boy's notions were as fanciful as his old master's.

"But you are."

This observation held Arnath, Trellith and Shrakar momentarily dumbstruck. Then, gradual smiles grew on their faces. Arnath leaned over to look at mound of Shrakar's ruined backpack, and asked, "Half, you said?"

"Not enough to keep us rich for the rest of our lives. But, certainly enough to set up shop for the rest of our lives. Buy the land. Fix up the old outpost. Put a proper smithy out back." Said Trellith, already ruminating.

"We train warriors. They come get supply, find maps. While they stay, we train." Shrakar said

"That's right. And by training with the young warriors who come through, we stay in fighting shape ourselves. Old, but not old and fat." Said Arnath, seeing the appeal of the idea.

"That's the spirit." Said Trellith, standing up, reaching over and snatching his skin back from Garthe.

"I could stay with you." Said Garthe

"Oh. You wouldn't want to find an elder mage to apprentice under, to train you formally?" Arnath asked.

"They will come to us." Off their quizzical looks, Garthe elaborated, "Each party will have an experienced mage..."

"Hopefully." Said Trellith, deliberately ribbing the boy.

"Yes, hopefully." Garthe replied, not falling for Trellith's goad. "And each of those who come through can teach me a bit of something in exchange for their lodging."

"That's well and good, but how will you pay your way?" said Trellith annoyed at the suggestion of free lodgings for one type of customer, and not dwarves at that.

"How else? With healing, of course." Said Garthe, pointing at the many dressed wounds around the fire. "It is a town after all, towns have townsfolk who fall ill."

For the first time since the dreary discussion of aging out of one's chosen life had started, the four of them looked at each other knowing tomorrow offered promise.

Arnath wrapped the remains of his cloak about him, touched his captain's clasp and settled his back against the log. "Let us sleep. Trellith is right – this mountain will be crawling with people in the morning. Besides, we have to get to the exchange two leagues away, turn in all this gold for jots. We can't carry all that jangling weight around and be quarry for thieves. We're businessmen now."

CHAPTER TWO

The morning after they'd been caught in the collapse of the mountain, they arose with new purpose and soon found that optimism, however burgeoning, was not balm enough for their wounds. The hike to the livery in the nearby township where Arnath and his companions had boarded their horses was excruciating. A deep river half way to the stables provided some relief. They crossed it on foot, allowing themselves to periodically submerge fully as they went across, and thus got entirely clean of the clinging rock dust that had rendered their appearance so ghostly the night before.

On the opposite bank, as he allowed himself to drip dry, Arnath looked into the waters and smoothed his long, light-brown hair back with his fingers. With all the rock dust gone, the grey that grew from his temples was now the only frosting in his hair. He took the covering bandage off his eye and assessed the damaged. Thanks to Garthe, who had treated them all with his healing stone once more before they set out, the bloody wound was healed. The swelling and deep bruising would take days more to go away. He'd been injured many times during his years on the adventuring road, and he hoped this deep, stinging one would be the last. Even in the rippling water, he could see how the multi-coloured swelling distorted the features on the one side of his face. The youthful crinkles, the smile lines that made him look surprisingly younger were swelled away.

That was something that he'd retained, despite his middle age, the visage of a care-free young man. Looking at himself in the waters, he worried the mountain had permanently beaten that air out of him. As he stood up, flexing his knotted shoulders, other more immediate pains replaced his thoughts of the cost of his life of wandering.

They felt only a hair's breadth better upon reaching Moorgate, the large city to the north-east, a necessary stop to relieve themselves of their ill-gotten gold. Before exchanging the treasure for banker's jots, they divvied up a tiny portion so that each of them would have pocket money, giving a slightly larger portion to Garthe so he could replenish their food and medicinal supplies for the journey onwards. Heading into town they made a quick agreement to not separate. Moorgate had been partially razed during the Orkan civil war, and Shrakar received some hard looks during their first visit. Despite Shrakar wearing his Allied-Sergeant's crest on the left breast of his leather armour, a signal to all that he'd had fought for Vallasen and the other allied kingdoms during the war, many people this far north reacted to the sight of any Orc with great offense.

The upraised eyebrows of their bankers, however, were the only noteworthy ripple in their trip into town. Despite the four of them knowing they'd lost more than half of the Ulgrew gold, the remainder still looked like a more-than impressive mound to the accountants they chose. The bankers weighed and divvied the gold, calculating how many jots their treasure was worth. Banker's jots were hard slabs of darkly lacquered wood, lengthier than a fully open hand and inlaid with gold symbols delineating specific amounts. Their value was recognized throughout the three kingdoms. Arnath and the others agreed to get many, many jots instead of one great one. Many jots could be split amongst them for safety, and distributed to potential suppliers of their imagined new business.

After banking, they ate – steering clear of the inn where they had purchased the map - resupplied and left, electing to sleep on the road, rather than in town. Though banker's jots weighed less and were less impressive than a mound of gold, they still represented a great temptation for thieves who might overhear their bankers talking in the taverns about the adventurers who rode into town with a treasure mound of strangely stamped gold coins.

For that reason, they stopped by the smith's quarter and fully re-armed themselves. Arnath got a new broadsword and dirk, Shrakar got a new war axe – Luckily the kind that would boomerang back to him when thrown, just like he had in the war, Trellith got a good bow and a quiver worth of arrows and Garthe got a new sling shot and a pouch full of rough metal pellets. It took some searching, but Trellith also found a replacement for the retractable seafarer's glass he'd had in a leather case on his belt. His old one was so much shattered brass and glass under the debris of the mountain. They all took their time with re-arming, purchasing equipment they could trust. Losing their weapons to the folly of the road was nothing new to them, so they'd learned to scrutinize the replacements well.

It was the same for horses, though their current ones did not need replacing yet. Horses, like weapons, came and went quite frequently over their years of adventuring. So much so that Arnath and his companions did not bother to name the beasts anymore, beyond "my horse" or "our horses". The attachment to any one animal, like the fetishized feeling of luck a particular weapon brought, was a waste of time and energy better devoted to survival.

Another thing purposefully replaced along with their weaponry was much of their outer wardrobe. They couldn't go riding into Kroman's Town, expecting to set up shop there, looking like they'd had their already threadbare road clothes torn to pieces. Trellith kept his bycocket hat, boots and outer leather coat and replaced everything else. Arnath kept his boots as well, but threw away every-thing else, making sure to remove his clasp from the ragged cloak before dis-carding it. Garthe kept his leather waistcoat and boots, but replaced everything else, even finding a hooded mage-styled cloak in the same brown that actually fit him much better. Shrakar got lucky, for he found a lace-up, short-sleeved shirt in Orc-size, despite the town's overt prejudices. He didn't really need it, but Shrakar, already shy of the black beauty marks that amply dotted his green skin, found the large, multi-coloured bruises quite embarrassing. Orc culture took a great deal of pride in their skin – be it tattoos, scarification or simply not looking like you just had the stuffing beaten out of you.

Arnath joked, as they paid for the last of their garments, that if they kept this up, they'd be well on the road to respectability. Trellith rejoined with a quip that he thought that was the general idea.

Once Garthe had made purchases at the apothecaries and grocer's mar-ket, re-supplying them for the road, they saddled up and set off out of town. Moorgate had actually taken them a considerable distance out of their way. It was a two-day ride north-east of the King's Highway, or King's Road, as it was also commonly called, and their hoped-for destination, Kroman's Town, was directly east along the King's road from the Ulgrew mountains. So, they rode roughly overland south east, until they returned to the safety of the wide main traveller's road that cut across the northern part of the entire kingdom, stopping only to sleep, eat, tend their horses and wash and relieve themselves. The forest that lined the south side of the King's road had periodic cut-outs for just those things, a hospitable traveller's road being a point of pride for this dynasty of kings, not only here but in the neighbouring countries, Kruendaal and Farsuum, as well.

Taking advantage of the feeling of unity after their great allied victory over the Orcs, the kings of Kruendaal, Vallasen and Farsuum agreed to build a road system that spanned across the north of their countries, linking them together as one great traveller's road. This was part unity and part strategy, as having a direct road across the north of their three countries provided a way to quickly move masses of troops should the Orcs ever become a problem again. And from a budgetary standpoint, the northern tips of their countries were the narrowest part, where the breadth of the three countries were the slimmest, and therefore the least expensive to build across. Descending southwards, all three of the side-by-side kingdoms fanned out like wedges, or widening skirts, and the farthest southern point across them was so wide that the notion of any building project that spanned them all was laughably impossible. So, the fertile farmlands to the north of each country got a well-maintained trade road and within those individual countries many far-reaching roads branched off southward. While the royal seat of Kruendaal was to the extreme south, more than a hundred leagues to the southwest of the now-collapsed Ulgrew mountains, the royal houses of Vallasen and Farsuum were a relatively short distance from the King's Road, a mere week's ride from where Arnath and his companions were now.

They rode in pained silence, the warmth of sunset on their backs. Another long day was ending, and none too soon. Every league brought continuous, painful reminders of their recent ordeal.

With the thick forest blanketing the view to the south as far as the eye could see, the only place to look for a variety of views was northward. Arnath watched that northern view, now bathed in the golden sunset, noting features he'd already seen or never had on their many journeys heading this way over the years. Every passing league had a couple of farms, their fields of fully grown crops stretching towards the forests to the north. Occasionally, they'd pass an overgrown ruin, jutting up from the ground in the middle of a farm field. Farmers left them be out of respect for the ancient kingdoms the three current ruling ones were built upon. From his years of adventuring, Arnath knew these occasional ruins in plain sight were never accompanied by treasure. No - gold was always hidden away in dark, foreboding places.

There was a lulling peace to these sunbathed northern views, enough so to help push thoughts of his pained body and uncertain future a tiny bit aside. Mostly his mind wandered.

Arnath had met Trellith and Shrakar during the Orkan civil war, which started nearly thirty years ago. Though most humans thought it an internal matter, saying *let the damned Orcs kill each other*, the war began to spill over into the human kingdoms and not by a little. The north, the breadbasket of three kingdoms, was being razed. By royal decree in all three separate kingdoms – Vallasen, Kruendaal and Farsuum - conscripted armies were recruited to augment their already standing ones, and Arnath, a young man at the time, got swept up into the fight. From a youth drilling with the King's guard of Vallasen, to barely surviving his first bloody battle, eventually rising via attrition and skill through the ranks, witnessing heroism and atrocities along the way, he'd survived until the war's end. Trellith was one of many Dwarven archers from the dragon burned mountains of the far south assigned to his platoon, and the only one who survived to the end of the war with him, his trusted lieutenant for the final brutal battles. Shrakar was one of thousands of unarmed Orcs who approached the human encampments wishing to join the human efforts to stop the bloodshed. The Orkan races were already beyond decimated at that point, and many of the young Orc-kind saw the conflict as pointless, the inner squabbles of religious leaders seeking power, nothing more.

That tide turning moment saw a quick end to the war after several decisive victories, the last of which, at Isthmar within the Orc country of Kolgatha, saw Arnath and company fighting side by side with the King of Vallasen and his brother Prince Domar to vanquish the last of the zealot armies of the Orc clerics. Soon thereafter, Arnath and his fellows were decorated and released from the ranks with back pay. At first, their party consisted of twelve war-weary soldiers, all accepting of Arnath's leadership, all wanting to strike out for fortune. Over time, by misadventure, their numbers were whittled down. Dalgar, an archer and Arnath's closest friend, got swept away by a raging river during a daring but ill-thought-out treasure hunt. Morgosh, the skilled mage who served with them on the front lines, and who eventually brought his boy apprentice Garthe into the party, was completely consumed by either a faulty spell or a curse upon the treasure trove they were raiding – The truth of which they had all long accepted they would never know. Lanea, whom Arnath loved deeply, was killed by a giant spider in a cave system connected to the ruins of a castle that bore no treasure in the end. Of the dozen original adventurers, only he and Shrakar and Trellith had survived the adventuring road.

Such was his life, the only one he had known. Filled with the pain of loss and other sorrows though it was, he felt himself already mourning for it. Arnath could see it on the faces of his companions as well, as they rode in near-meditative silence, each of them straining to find peace with the decision they'd made.

*

As the sun disappeared, Arnath's horse began to shake its head with displeasure, and, taking the cue, Arnath pointed to a large, semi-circular cut-out in the forest edge up ahead on their right. They languidly veered off the road, losing the place they'd held between a guarded diplomatic party from Kruendaal ahead of them and a migrating family stuffed along with everything they owned in a covered wagon to their rear. The soldiers guarding the travelling diplomats had given up their suspicious backward glances when they spied Arnath's dented cloak pin. Emerging from the wilds, taking their place on the road, the family behind them did their best to keep their children from shouting at Shrakar's back. In time the children quieted down on their own, realizing that the giant half-Orc would not so much as turn around and make one angry face for their amusement.

They led their horses to a long post that spanned above a wooden trough. Shrakar grabbed the wide bucket that hung from the side of the post and trudged into the woods. Trellith took out his spade and began to dig a fresh fire pit. Garthe unstrapped his pack from his horse and began to withdraw his pots and the makings of their supper. Arnath rearranged the thick resting logs provided by the site to better suit their number. He stopped briefly to politely wave at the travelling family as they passed by on the road, then finished placing the logs around Trellith's pit so that each man would have his traditional place around the fire.

Shortly, Shrakar emerged from the forest, a bushel of wood and bracken rolled up in his arms, the water bucket sloshing in his fist. He dumped the wood by Trellith's pit, immediately stepped over to fill the water trough. As their horses leaned in to drink, Shrakar disappeared back into the forest. He returned again in short turn with more wood, which he left outside of their log circle, and the water bucket refilled. He placed the bucket down next to Garthe, who was chopping vegetables and dried meat on a cutting board from his pack. Garthe picked up the bucket without comment, poured some water into his small iron cauldron, sprinkled a portion of spices into the cauldron before placing it next to Trellith's fire pit. For his part, Trellith arranged the wood, bracken at the bottom, in the fire pit and struck a long pipe match, which he eased in amongst the bracken. Before long, the fire had fully grown and the water for their dinner began to boil.

Shrakar had placed feedbags on the horses and took their saddles off, before sitting down near the fire. After arranging the logs, Arnath had gone back to the stream and bathed. Each man in turn would, as the makings of Garthe's hearty stew simmered at the edge of the fire. Dressed in fresh travelling clothes, Arnath emerged from the forest and picked up his new sword. Leaving it sheathed, he placed his hands wide on it, from hilt to tip, and began to stretch his upper body. The loud pops of his joints and his grunts as the knots in his muscles, generously provided by days on the road, began to loosen up drew no comment from the others. Over the years, Arnath had maintained much of the physical training regimen he'd learned in the King's Guard, and it had kept him in fighting shape, despite his age.

Each man saw to their comforts as they settled around the fire – Trellith with his pipe, Shrakar with his wine skin, Arnath with his exercises. Such was their routine for perhaps a decade on. Garthe, who stirred the stew whist reading an unfurled scroll of anatomical drawings in his lap, fell right in with it when he had joined them.

When Garthe said, "It's ready.", it was the first time any of them had spoken to each other all day.

*

After their supper, Garthe had washed up its makings in the river, Shrakar had taken the horses' feedbags off, placing a blanket over each horses' back, each of the men settled in around the fire, content in body, if not in mind. As they passed wine skins and pipes back and forth, as was traditional around any fire, Arnath thought perhaps it was time to break the silence about his feelings of dread.

"These past few days, I've been thinking…"

"As have I." Trellith interrupted. "Can you recall what the best of the outposts we've stayed in had? What made them good, I mean?"

Arnath was glad for the abrupt stymying of his melancholia, and truly grateful to his right hand for putting his thoughts back where they should have been – on the task at hand.

"Food for all kinds." Said Shrakar. "From all places."

"Yes. And differing ales. Wines from afar too." Said Arnath, joining in.

"A proper library. At least a corner in the pub with scrolls to loan." Said Garthe, pipe held thoughtfully in his hand.

"Beds of all sizes. Orc size beds." Shrakar nodded, his eyes on the fire.

"A good selection of supplies – rope, carry-alls, climbing steel." Arnath added.

Trellith nodding, looking at each of them. "Yes. And where do you suppose we will get all of those things?" Spying Garthe's impish expression, Trellith held up a silencing hand, "No, boy, don't say it. Not from another outpost. No, we as purveyors of such goods have to find and have those things readily on hand for our patrons."

His captain's instincts kicking in, Arnath realized where Threllith was going with his notion, and blurted, "Supply lines."

"Yes." Trellith again nodded. "We need to develop supply lines, much like those needed when we served in the war, to ensure that *our* establishment is a place of good repute."

Noting how Trellith had emphasized "our" in his statement, Arnath understood he was still talking in hypotheticals. "We've had little opportunity, travelling over-land as we did. We completely missed the last town."

"Quinhaven. True. But along the road as we travel, we should start to develop relations with persons who supply things. Any type of things, really." Trellith said firmly, outlining a plan of action for the days ahead.

For his part, Arnath was impressed. And rather glad to have his leadership usurped for the night. Their whole trip thus far, he needed to be thinking ahead, instead of wallowing on the loss of the past.

"Trellith, you shame me. I should have put my mind to these things…"

"Oh no, friend. I too spent a goodly portion of our ride thinking on days gone by." Said Trellith, refilling his pipe. "But a single keen thought helped me snap out of it."

"Which was?"

"Should we do this, lay down our bows and axes and swords, foregoing all adventures and dedicate ourselves to the care of those who are just beginning theirs, we had better be damned good at it."

*

The next morning Arnath awoke refreshed, and was immediately alarmed by a strange sight. Two men, both carrying spears, their backs to the encampment, stood on either side of their forest nook at the edge of the road.

Arnath sat up, shook off his bleary-eyed lack of focus and took a long, hard look at them. They weren't doing anything, merely standing, their backs to the camp site.

Just as Arnath began creeping his hand towards his sword, both men turned toward him. Arnath realized, upon seeing the colours of their knee-length, leather-trimmed cassocks in the morning sunlight, they were fresh-faced King's guardsmen. Noting that he had awakened, both of the young men clad in the blue and gold of the King's Guard saluted him, likely out of respect for the battered captain's clasp on his covering cloak, and walked onwards down the road.

Rising, Arnath stood and ambled over to the spot they once occupied. Further down the road, he could see other such guardsman minding the rest nooks in the forest. This was part of the service provided by the King's highway – protection for the travellers that slept along its length. He had heard long ago that since the war soldiering in the kingdom had turned mostly into domestic protection, with an emphasis on the highways.

Arnath could not imagine a life of soldiering that was so sedentary, so peaceful. Carrying out orders to protect sleeping travellers from bandits at night instead of being the fodder for a thousand Orc axes. As he turned away from the road, heading towards the river, picking up the water bucket as he went, he began to see the sense of it. Maintain a standing army during peace time, but keep them on their feet, always keep them moving. Keep them ready to race headlong into whatever the next great battle could be.

*

Later, on the road, they discussed what kind of suppliers should be paid for in advance, which should have accounts opened by leaving a deposit of jots, and who should be paid only upon filling an order. It helped pass the time as they cleared the great forest and began to emerge into the long stretch of farmlands on the road to Kroman's Town. Coming upon the first farm, they found themselves quite nervous, battle hardened warriors though they were, as they turned down the road to the main house. None of them knew what to say.

In the end it turned out alright. Initially, the farmer and his wife, Nestar and Gilea, were afraid to open their door for a group of ruffians, their faces and bodies still battered from their spill down the mountain, and accompanied by a large half-Orc at that. But, after hearing who they were and the intent of their visit, they were welcomed inside, offered tea and some food. Each man in turn tried haltingly to explain what they planned to do – They wanted to run a new type of outpost in Kroman's Town, as a combination inn and training center for passing adventurers. Excited by the idea of new customers themselves, Nestar and Gilea dictated a list of what they could supply in regards to food stuffs to Garthe and sent them all happily on their way.

The men collectively breathed sigh of relief. That was tougher than tackling a monster in any dungeon. But the next time should be easier.

They soon realized that none of them was a born salesman. That was the talent the long-absent Morgosh brought to their party. They would have to rely on their collective instincts in order to woo their new suppliers. But for Garthe, they were grizzled old soldiers who luckily carried no battle-weary bitterness in their manner. The pain of loss, certainly, but none of the moroseness that overtook so many veterans and prevented them from finding their next place in life. Maybe choosing to adventure and travel to differing places these many years had worn a much of that edge off. Either way, they were all grateful for it with each passing farm they visited.

*

Their heads swam as they wrapped up their discussion riding into the next town along the King's road. There was so much to do. And they were leagues from Kroman's as yet.

Solindar was a little more than a half-day's ride away from Kroman's Town, depending on your pace. It was the largest nearby township and almost entirely populated by Elves. Arnath and the others surmised they would need to leave a substantial deposit with the many elf craftsman in Solindar. Figuring they were far enough away from conspiring ears in Moorgate, and still under the protection of the King's road, they had decided to split up to best make use of the time. Separately, they would seek to attain things for the outpost that fell under their individual specialties.

Arnath would start their accounts at the main bank, as well as search out ancillary supplies for their outpost - maps, rope, various carryalls and such. One could never have enough carrying space on a quest. Trellith would find materials to build a good smithy, and the building blocks for swords – steel, coke, tools. Elves were famous for forging, and Trellith knew that this town was the only stop he would need to make to get a proper works going. As discussed before, Shrakar would concentrate on things that would make Orc-kind more welcome at their inn, as well as the many tools needed to train fledgling adventurers. They couldn't exactly train young swordsmen with real swords. Elfwood mock-ups would need to be made, and in all sizes – Broadswords, longswords, dirks, throwing knives and more.

For his part, Garthe sought out the healers of the township in the hopes of starting a medicinal trading relationship with each of them. He gathered he might have to wait to start training under other mages perhaps until after they had actual lodgings to trade. Garthe already knew that visits from senior mages would not be frequent. Many mages, young and old, were killed during the war, and mage-births were rare. Since mages were incapable of fathering or mothering children, their births were a random occasion, looked upon as auspicious throughout the three kingdoms. When Morgosh had come across Garthe, quite by luck during the party's adventuring travels, he remembered, despite being only nine years-old at the time, that Morgosh had told his parents that Garthe was the first mage-born he had heard of since the end of the war. The rarity of such births, and the powers that accompanied them, accounted for the awe-like reverence folk afforded mages in general and the willingness of all mages to abide by the ancient oath, "*Let No Talent Squander*", an edict that saw that all mages who needed teaching would get it.

Garthe hoped that the mages here, and also those that came to their outpost over time, abided by the code and would teach him all his deceased master no longer could.

After sunset, they met at the inn with the largest dining hall, one that would accommodate Shrakar for headspace. Here, sitting down at a large table, a new map unfurled in between them and their black bread trenchers and ales, they discussed the logistics of their inn. Garthe had arrived later, after they had ordered food and drink. He brought with him a tall stoic-looking elderly Elf. Without being asked, the old Elf took a look at each man – at Trellith's bound ribs, Shrakar's arm and Arnath's still swollen eye. After looming over each man, prodding each of them, asking a question or two, he stood upright, turned to Garthe and said, "Yes. Excellent work. See me tomorrow." And strode toward the door without further cordiality.

Garthe sat, relief on his face, and took a long draught from the ale they'd ordered him. "He was impressed. I think."

The three older men watched the old Elf leaving, suspicion in their eyes. If he was to take over the teaching of their boy, he had better be of sounder character than Morgosh was. Whilst Morgosh was a respected member of their party, a veteran of the wars like them, he was also more than a bit of a grifter. This served to the party's advantage when they found themselves without coin. Morgosh would bring them to the richer quarters of whatever town they were passing through and present them as the *"guardians of the chosen one"* – Garthe – a miracle child born of the impossible union of two mages, attaining for them free food and lodging, whilst spinning further non-sensical lore of the boy's prophesied greatness for their awed and honoured hosts. Though his impish lies and ability to con people out of just about anything came in handy when supplies were needed in the trenches during the war, or for getting them out of trouble when they ran afoul of the King's Guard, such qualities were useless if Garthe was to ever develop into a proper mage. Especially now that they'd decided to leave the road behind.

"Good lad. Eat. See what you can add." Arnath turned back as the old elf disappeared and patted the map that occupied the space between them. Earlier, while they had waited for their food, the three of them had marked off places they knew from their various adventures, farms and breweries that might supply them, other inns where they had stayed. Anything that came to mind that might help them in the business of aiding travellers. Before Garthe had arrived, they came upon the notion of maintaining a master map, one that would need updating and copying somewhat frequently. Garthe looked at the map, immediately understanding the meaning of their markings and picked up the quill.

After Garthe had made more than a dozen markings on the map, between mouthfuls of a stew trencher and sips of ale, their table was approached by a tall, dark-skinned elf with piercing brown eyes and short-shorn tight curly hair.

"You are Arnath?" He asked in a basso voice.

"I am." Arnath waved his hand at the others, then at a free chair. "And these are my fellows. Please sit, drink with us. You are...?"

"I am Lorta. The builder. Word had just reached me you wished to speak." After saying this, Lorta sat down, turned to a lithe, blond elf serving girl who approached the table and spoke to her in Elvish. Before she turned away, Arnath pointed to his drink and swizzled his finger around the table at the others, nodding to her. She nodded back, curtsied and flitted away.

"Not just any builder, I hear. *The* master-builder is my understanding." Arnath said to Lorta.

With a humble tilt of his head, Lorta said, "I have reached the age to have many apprentices."

"Your humility does you proud, but we have known of your skill since long before our turn in life had us seek you out." Declared Trellith from the other side of the table. "The town hall at Sa'ensbourg is a glorious work of art."

This brought enthusiastic replies of agreement from around the table, and another acknowledging tilt of the head from Lorta. "My first triumph after apprenticeship. I appreciate your compliments, gentlemen, truly. I see it as my purpose in life. The thing that I am meant do."

As the serving girl returned with a tray bearing their drinks, Lorta looked at Trellith quizzically, "You mentioned a turn in yours. The "thing you are meant do" has changed, I take it."

"It has." Said Arnath, moving an elbow to allow the serving girl to set down a new tankard of ale. "We have decided to hang up our swords and open a truly unique outpost. One that functions as a training center as well as lodging and supplier."

"Also, a medicinal stop, a clinic. For both travellers and the township." Beamed Garthe, a little too loudly for the lovely serving girl's benefit.

"Intriguing." Lorta said, rolling his drink flute between his work-gnarled fingers. "And what township would that be? Surely not this one. All the services you mentioned are covered many times over here. Aside from the training, that is."

"We mean to purchase and take over the old outpost down the road in Kroman's Town." Arnath said, raising his ale to his lips. The serving girl gave a sharp intake of breath and almost spilled Trellith's new ale as she set it down.

"Shimalena," Lorta addressed her as she regained her composure. "Leave us for a time. I will raise my glass when we need more."

Shimalena gave a guilty nod and whisked away from the table. All around the table the men could feel the change in mood, their eyes shifting from the elf girl's fleeing figure back to Lorta's most serious face.

"What is it?" enquired Trellith.

"What don't we know?" said Arnath, bolstering the query.

"Gentlemen," Lorta intoned matter-of-factly. "The outpost at Kroman's Town was completely destroyed some time ago."

CHAPTER THREE

The ride from Solindar to Kroman's Town the next day was soul-crushing. Though their intentions had not changed, they might now have to consider building an entirely new structure, and they were fairly certain their remaining jots might not cover such an endeavor. Not with the land, taxes and all the other expenses of building thrown in. It was so difficult to know for sure; None of them had ever done any kind of legitimate business using large sums of money before.

The entire ride to Solindar, for every stop they'd made, no one had warned them of the fate of Roberge's outpost. They realized they had put forth to their new suppliers their desire to open a new outpost, not refurbish the old one. Those foggy details changed nothing.

Before beginning to discuss what he and his apprentices could do for them, Lorta endured a lengthy barrage of questions about the destruction of the outpost in the heart of Kroman's Town. How had the fire started? How many died in the fire? Was there anything left of the building? How much of it? Many tankards and flutes of the fruit cider Lorta preferred were consumed before the conversation turned toward the potential for Lorta and company to build anything for them on another site and what it was they wanted built.

Though there was much conjecture on the matter, it was agreed the events of the disaster went something like this: An adventuring party were staying at the outpost after a successful raid on a long-forgotten treasure trove. They had celebrated long into the night, keeping Roberge and much of the central street awake. For all their alcohol-fueled good cheer, the party had a problem that had burbled forth during the celebrations. For some unknown reason, the party had set out with two mages. And not the usual Master-Apprentice combo, but two old, experienced mages, both as stubborn and stodgy as one would expect them to be. During the nights celebrations the two mages began to argue over who would get what of the magical items they had obtained. Though there were many to be had, a good haul no matter how the items were divvied, both mages had designs on possessing the same things and would not back down.

When mages fight it seldom comes to blows. Sizable as it was, the outpost was not large enough to sustain a battle of two drunken magicians for long. The wooden structure began to take damage immediately as the two mages hurled explosive spells at each other, yelling obscenities in ancient tongues the entire time. Their fellows in the party sought to interfere, but too late – the battle had already awoken one of the disputed magic items, and it cast the deciding blow. The resulting explosion utterly destroyed the third and fourth floors of the building, and set the rest immediately ablaze.

The first and second floors were for the most part saved, thanks to the efforts of the whole town and the nearby source of water, a spring pool in the back yard of the outpost. But in all, twelve lives were lost, including the stout old proprietor Roberge, who Arnath and his companions remembered fondly. Only two members of the raiding party partially responsible for the disaster survived. Much of their treasure was saved from the magic fueled flames, a prize now split just between the two of them. After being forced to explain what had happened under threat of violence, they left Kroman's Town very rich, but utterly reviled men.

Having seen the extent of the damage just once, and only in passing, Lorta was only able to give them a brief, however technical, description of what remained of the building. Arnath and his friends did not like what they heard.

They traded doom fraught "what if" scenarios the entire ride from Solindar to Kroman's Town. Could they build onto the remaining two stories? Would the damaged foundation beams take the weight? Would the water damaged boards on the remaining two floors have succumbed to rot? How long might it take to clear the back courtyard, which they sought to use as their training center, of the heaped debris from the top floors? Had any effort been made by the township to clear the debris, or sell the property? They could arrive and find an entirely different building in its place, owned by someone who had just set up shop and was unwilling to sell. The not knowing was maddening.

So consuming were their thoughts and discussions of the many potential worst-case scenarios that they neglected to stop at any of the farms they passed along the King's highway. Only once did Arnath allow his mind out from under the dark cloud of impending failure, and the reason shook him to his core just as deeply as all the darker meditations of the day.

As the sun began to set, the party was passing a small farm. Some details about it seeped into Arnath's troubled mind as he lolled in the saddle. Despite being estate-size in acreage, only a portion of it was planted, the rest lay fallow and untouched. The portion that did have the symmetrical growth of planted crops wrapped around either side of the sizeable farmhouse, extending all the way to the road. Corn on one side, a mix of various vegetable plants on the other. Lazily observing these details, Arnath missed the emergence of a woman who stepped out of the corn rows closest to the road and into the golden sunlight.

Once there, and Arnath had laid eyes upon her, she was all he could see.

The woman was tall, strongly muscled and had flaming red hair that curled over her shoulders. She wore a sleeveless, faded green field tunic that became leggings rather than a skirt. One of her bare forearms bore quite a scar, perhaps from a labouring accident and the elbow above it seemed to only straighten to a crooked angle. Her face, however, did not reflect the gnarled soul of endless toil. Instead, she had a look of enthusiastic curiosity as she peeled one of the ears of corn open, checking its ripeness. Her wide, bright eyes – the same blue as his own, Arnath noticed – played over the corn with a hint of satisfaction. A genuine pride in her work.

Such was the feeling Arnath himself would hope to attain in his new life. The undoubted setback they rode towards would not thwart he and his fellows' ambitions. One day, however far off, he too would feel the satisfaction of knowing he made something to be proud of. What could she, this passing beauty, tell him of this future life, he wondered?

Since his youth, having been called up to the king's army, a traditional life had eluded him. Arnath had come from a farm family, and knew one day he'd be expected to marry one of the girls from the nearby farms. He would raise children and crops, and one day his children would marry and do the same. After the Orkan wars however, he could not stomach the notion of returning home to live life off the land. A thirst for adventure had grown in him that would never be quenched by pushing a plow and tiller. He had known many women from his youth onwards, mostly via harmless dalliances or an exchange of coin, but none from traditional courtships. Lanea, the warrior woman he had known since she had served under him in the last year of the war, was the closest he had come to such a conventional bond. The two of them had often laughed at the notion of being married under the King's law, two treasure-raiding warriors constantly in mortal peril. And their mockery of the institution had been proven right when she had died in the caverns under the Black Hills. What good was marriage to people whose very lives were so fleeting? But now, here he was, in his middle age, and wanting to put adventure behind him. Should he not consider all the possibilities such a life now offered?

Lost in this revelry, Arnath had entirely missed the fact that lady farmer was now looking right back at him.

How could she not look at this scurrilous band of battered men as their horses loped past her farmstead? Especially when the human man, the one closest to her age, stared agape at her, with eyes lost in distant memory?

She might have thought him rude if not for the fact that she could likely tell he was not staring for the lurid pleasure of it, and that his mind was entirely elsewhere. Besides, she was quite enjoying a good long look at him too. Though battle-hardened, he was handsome and tall. Despite his age, still muscled like a warrior. His light brown hair leaned closer to blond in the sun and had grey spreading from the temples. All things measured, maybe he was the kind of man she would like to know.

The wool of lost thoughts pulled away from Arnath's eyes when he realized the woman, who was now joined by a boy of twelve and a girl of seven, her children perhaps, was waving at him. Arnath clapped his jaw shut, sat up straight in the saddle and awkwardly returned her wave.

"A true beauty." Said Trellith, noting the change in Arnath's posture. "Shall we not stop and find out if her farm could supply us?"

"No." said Arnath curtly. "See the un-tilled acres? She likely grows food only to feed her family."

"Right." Said Trellith in exaggerated agreement, chuckling at real reason for his friend's trepidation.

Reaching the edge of the property, the woman's children now waved to them as well. Shrakar waved back, making his funniest "Scary Orc" face, which drew explosive laughs from the children.

Trying not to be too obvious, Arnath snuck one last look over his shoulder at the woman who had stirred him so, before turning to the road ahead.

*

They reached Kroman's Town well into the night. Even in the moonlight from the King's Road, they could make out many of the features they'd fondly remembered.

Sitting on the northern side of the King's Road, Kroman's Town could easily have been missed by all passing by. It was situated against a gigantic rock formation known as Kroman's Mound or just "The Mound". This immense range of smooth rocky mounds created a landmark that could be seen from leagues away, but everything behind it, on the northern side, might as well have been invisible to the rest of the kingdom.

The rock ledges Shrakar had spoken of around the fire, days ago, were on the far side of a tall and severely angled formation that started just across the King's road. The locals called it "The Fin", and with good reason. The tall, slim hump of rock looked very much like the rounded fin of an aquatic creature – If that creature had fins that were thirty feet tall. The thin side that faced the King's road was mostly smooth, only occasionally dappled with hand hold-sized divots. One of the long sides of the slim oval shaped landmark ran parallel to the western road that led off the King's Road into the town.

Passing by the fin, their heads craned back to view its curving summit, Arnath and his fellows marvelled at the marbled textures in the long, flat surface of the rock. Where it began to curve around again, they could see the many tiers of ledges that Shrakar had so enjoyed. Underneath those many ledges, the base of the fin dipped into waters of a sizeable inland lake, big enough for perhaps fifty families to sit around and enjoy its sandy shores comfortably. Those brief beaches were surrounded by grassy fields dotted with trees, particularly on its north and eastern sides.

The western tip of the small oval lake disappeared from their view as they continued up the road, the view briefly blocked by a large, long boathouse that dominated the length of the southern side of the shore. Where this structure began also saw the beginning of a fence to their right, along the grassy rise on the opposite side of the road. This fence surrounded a vast riding yard at the back of the white-washed stable building, a fair-sized three-story barn that could likely hold twenty-five horses.

Past the length of the boathouse, their view of the lake once again opened up. The eastern tip of the lake met with grassy land and a large tree that sat slightly to the north side of the shore. Beyond that tree, across an acre-wide stretch of tall grass, stood a thick forest, spanning as far as the eye could see. To the east, further tall grasslands gave way to the base of the mound where the many of the businesses on the north side of an up-and-down arcing main street jutted out from the mound upon supporting columns. These single-story buildings were half supported on their southern facing sides, where their entrances let out onto the mound itself, which was paved and cobblestoned over to create the town's wide main street.

As their horses rounded the corner of the stable yard fence, Arnath and his companions swore they could hear music coming from one of those high-perched buildings.

Across the road from where the stable yard fence began to curve into the town proper, there stood a two-sided, head-high decorative gateway on the grass. This welcoming, symbolic gateway seemed to serve the purpose of stopping people from trampling all over the grass from the town to the lake, and it must have worked, as only the grass between the gates leading straight down to lakeside was worn away. Everywhere else the grass was thick and lush. That purpose aside, it looked nice – another pleasant accent in an already pastoral looking town.

Rounding the fence, Arnath and friends were met with the breath-taking view of Kroman's Town proper.

The many quaint buildings of Kroman's were built right up against the base and sides of the hulking rise of the mound, the summit of which created a dark halo over the town in the moonlight. With only one deep cul-de-sac and one long street, the tiny town consisted mostly of densely packed three and four-story buildings. The enclosed cul-de-sac started just off of the stable gates, where a tiny town square stood with a wide fountain at its center and a large announcements' board sitting on its west side. The blind alley that rose upwards beyond the fountain consisted of a ring of buildings, most of them having businesses on the ground floor. At the top of the rise stood a larger building, presumably the town hall. The businesses and homes wrapped all the way around until they ended with the one right next to the stables – the sheriff's office.

The old outpost was up the other, high-sloping street that fed straight away from the stable doors. From here, Arnath and company could not see the remains of the old outpost in the darkness and were dreading that sight enough to wait until the horses were fully tended to.

Luckily, the stable was open, lit by lanterns and staffed by a seemingly friendly man named Jaross. He remarked on the beauty and strength of their horses, and led them inside. Welcoming though he was, Jaross continually gave sidelong looks at Shrakar, muttering how the Orc had better not eat any of the many barn cats that occupied the stable. Arnath chose to ignore the man's bigotry this one time, hoping the stableman was the only citizen of the tiny town Shrakar would need to win over.

As Garthe paid Jaross in coin, explaining they would like a few days feed and board at least for their horses, Shrakar took off their saddles, rubbed his big hands over each horses' back and put their blankets on them. Outside, Arnath and Trellith passed a pipe back and forth, and remarked on new sights to be seen since they were last here. One thing that struck them was the number of businesses and multi-storied homes around the circular, dead end road that were shuttered, or had completely darkened windows, not a candle or lantern in sight. Arnath and Trellith exchanged a look as they thought the same thing – The outpost was not the only business that had abruptly left this little town.

The four of them walked up the rising main road, weapons and cloaks on, packs slung over their shoulders. Knowing what terrible sight might befall them over the crest of the hill, each man did their best to stride as though they walked toward their future, and not toward the crushing of a dream. As they walked up the rise, the celebratory music they'd heard grew louder.

Reaching the top of the hill, they could begin to see the ruin of the old outpost. Lit by the noisy ale hall across the street, the building looked blackened and unstable. Crestfallen expressions overtook them all as they descended the short distance over the hilltop and down the level of the outpost. Ignoring the celebrations across the way, they gave the wreck before them harsh appraisals with furrowed brows.

"Support beams for the remaining floors look... *okay*." Trellith said, elongating the last syllable.

"Must have broken the door off to fight the fire." Said Arnath, looking at the boarded-over space that once had an ornate, elf-carved door.

"We'll need the upper floors," said Garthe as he craned his neck up at the charred top of the second floor. "For the exact reasons there was a fire. I have to be on the top floor."

"Yes, yes, boy – to prevent the smell of potions and such from rising through our guest's rooms. As you said on the road. Firstly, we'd need to see if those foundation columns would support a structure that high." Trellith said, his head tilting back to look all the way up as well.

"For that we need a look inside." Arnath said, cocking his head at Shrakar.

Shrakar stepped forward, wrapped his fists around the boards, and tore them free from the door frame. The noise gave them a bit of a start, but they soon relaxed, realising the revels across the street were far too noisy for anyone to hear them. Shrakar pulled away all the boards, set them aside and then they all slunk their way into the burnt-out building.

*

The inside of the defunct outpost was black as night until, with the sound of swishing liquid, a bloom of white light illuminated the entire first floor. Garthe walked ahead of the party, holding high the tear drop-shaped ampule of luminescent liquid. He shone it this way and that as they crept down the main corridor. The front corridor, long main desk, common room off to the right and ascending stairs near the back door all appeared to be in salvageable shape.

Passing the stairs on their left, the long ale room disappearing on their right, Arnath gave the stair bannister a shake. It creaked angrily but did not give. He and Trellith exchanged a look: A good sign.

They reached the end of the front corridor that let out onto the back courtyard they so needed to open their training center. It was why they had their heart set on this place. The large semi-circular space they recalled would be large enough to train with swords and bows, to create a climbing wall up the rock face, to house Trellith's smithy in one corner and more. And there was the spring pool, a fresh source of water needed to run a business such as this. As Garthe stepped out, his light bathed over the back courtyard, and one of their worst fears was confirmed. The villagers had indeed piled up the debris from the fire back here in the courtyard as Lorta had said. Shrakar motioned to Garthe, who understand straight away and handed his light over to the tall half-Orc, giving them all a better look at the wreckage as he held it up high. There were three high mounds of charred wood, chaotic pyramids of blackened timber pointing up the rock wall and towards the starry night sky. So big around at the base were the debris piles they went all the way from the back door of the inn to the cliff face that created the natural wall at the back of the property.

Before any building could be done, all of this would have to be cleared away.

"Well, it's not impossible." Trellith said, eyeing the corner where his smithy would ideally go.

"No. Not impossible." Said Arnath, his voice hesitant. The work ahead of them was going to be harder than any tomb raid they'd ever been on. "We could clear a space and set up camp with a fire for tonight. First, we should head across the way and see about some food."

They turned back into the inn, and almost immediately upon setting foot inside were confronted by strangers blocking the exit to the street.

"They'll be no food for brigands such as you tonight." Said a fat, moustachioed man in a garish red cloak, practically encrusted with medals of honor and office. He held a thin rapier at the ready, and two other rough-looking men stood just behind him.

"Sir, we are not brigands. We've come here to…"

"Search for treasure and perhaps magical items hidden in the ruins of the outpost. You're not the first." Red Cloak interrupted Arnath with obvious contempt. "Come along, or we'll force you."

Arnath looked at the rapier and at the cudgels the other two rather shabby, uniform-less men had. They were clearly enlisted on the quick. It took Arnath some effort not to laugh as he estimated how quickly he and his men could kill these fools.

The two enlisted men's eyes flicked over Arnath's party, their weapons and Shrakar's sheer size and swallowed down fear. "Sheriff, don't you think we should call for…?" asked one of them in a shaky voice.

"Nonsense." The Red-cloaked town Sheriff quipped, and then to Arnath, with his rapier held pointedly up, "Come along, I mean my business."

Arnath turned to his fellows, shrugged with a smirk, and then turned back to follow the Sheriff out of the ruins of the outpost.

*

Shrakar had to wedge himself, crouched down quite uncomfortably into one corner, in order for the four of them to all fit into the jail cell.

From inside the cell, Arnath and the others could hear the Sheriff and his toadies rifling through their packs, the hired men occasionally exclaiming at their finds.

"Look at this! I know this clasp. One of those men is a captain in the King's guard."

"Nonsense. They probably stole it." Rebuffed the Sheriff in an unsure voice.

"Will you look at these jots!" exclaimed one of them. "Wait... Why would monied men want to raid the old outpost for treasure?"

"I don't know... Shut up! Fool!" said the Sheriff in increasing trepidation.

"These scrolls, these books – These are mage's books. It's ill-luck to accost a mage like this, me thinks..." One of the lackies said, to which the sheriff finally had no indignant response.

In that hanging silence, Arnath noted he could no longer hear any music echoing from up the street.

Then, the outer door banged open loudly and a party of hysterical persons were shouting at the Sheriff all at once. From the muddled exchanged, the only phrase they heard from within their cell quite clearly was, "The dowry is gone!"

After a brief whispered exchange, the door to the cells opened and a rather festively dressed, elderly man of tiny stature stepped in. He held his eyes low over a dour face. "Which of you is the captain?"

Arnath stepped forward to the bars, "I am Arnath. Formerly of his majesty's guard."

The man nodded, swallowed and said, "The Sheriff says you wish to refurbish the outpost and re-open it for travellers."

"That is true. We were only on the property to inspect it, to estimate our workload in the coming weeks. We meant no malfeasance." Arnath said.

"Very well. Please listen to what I have to tell you. We are a small community. Since the old outpost burned, we have had no need of a large constabulary. Rough adventuring types don't come through here anymore..."

"But..." Arnath said, knowing something further was going to be attached to those swatches of local colour.

The formally dressed man told them he was in fact the mayor of Kroman's Town, and tonight his son was wed. The festivities were held in the large hall across from the old outpost. Some men had attended, strangers who pretended to be guests of either nuptial party depending on who asked them. Right up until just moments ago, when the six of them made off, at threat of sword point, with the bride's dowry chest.

"We have no one to make pursuit. No one with a warrior's skills. Some old soldiers do live here, but are away on reserve muster. And our Sheriff is an... administrator." The Mayor turned to the Sheriff, who listened to the exchange indignantly.

"Go on." Arnath said, enjoying the pompous Sheriff's discomfiture.

"Good Captain, what would it take for you and your men to pursue the thieves, and retrieve my new daughter's dowry?"

Without a moment's thought, Arnath said, "We'll need our weapons and packs back. Our horses from the stable. And... the land title deed for the outpost, signed over by you outright."

Arnath's fellows beamed at this, as did the Mayor. The Sheriff visibly his ground teeth when the Mayor energetically motioned for him to open the jail cell.

Chapter Four

Arnath took Garthe along with him, and they rode a good piece down the road that connected eastward out of Kroman's town to the King's road. Shrakar and Trellith climbed high into the rocky hills, and would descend down from high on the mound, hopefully meeting their quarry in the middle.

At the last cut-out before the eastern town road merged with the King's road, the place where still-frightened wedding guests had told them they'd seen the thieves disappear, Arnath and Garthe came upon two alert Guardsmen. They were crouched down in one corner of the cut-out, peering into the thick forest. Arnath and Garthe lashed their unneeded horses to covering trees on the other side of the cut-out and quietly trotted over, keeping as low as they could. The soldiers saw them approach, and might have reacted defensively had one of them not recognized Arnath.

And Arnath recognized him too as they kept low and sidled up along side the guardsmen. The one next to Arnath was one of the soldiers who kept guard over them as they slept on the King's road many nights ago. He was tall, with very short dark hair and an innocent yet keenly intelligent face. He leaned in close to Arnath.

"Captain." The young man said in a low whisper that still conveyed respect.

"Aye, retired." Whispered Arnath back. "We've been sent by the elder's of Kroman's Town to find a pack of thieves. I am Arnath, the boy is Garthe, a mage and healer."

"Private Apaulon, sir. This is Private Terrio." Apaulon whispered. He continued as Arnath and Garthe exchanged nods with the terrified-looking Terrio, a ginger-haired boy who could not have been older than Garthe, and who notably did not fill out his uniform tunic. "We'd heard someone making loud revels up in the hills. You can just see the firelight reflecting off those trees there."

"Good eye." Said Arnath, squinting up at the trees over the crest of the hill that occasionally flickered red-gold upon their trunks. Were they just celebrating travellers, they could have had their revels on the roadside, in a camping cut-out, and fully under the protection of the King's guard. Such a thing was perfectly legal. Travelling or not, life must be lived. But to hide away in the King's forest, light a fire and carry on loudly, doing who knows what – that was entirely suspect. "Fools. They celebrate within sight of their crime."

"What did they do in Kroman's Town?" Apaulon asked, and Arnath explained about the wedding party and the dowry chest. After which Apaulon told them in hushed tones that the roads to the east were on alert after a family immigrating eastward via the road had been set upon by thieves who had murdered the lot of them. From what the guardsmen could discern of the aftermath, the family had no valuables worth taking. When Arnath questioned young Apaulon further, his deep feeling of dread had been confirmed. The family were none other than the ones who shared the road behind Arnath and his companions for so many leagues along the King's highway.

"Damn them. Much as we might like to, we can't kill them. Not all of them anyway." Said Arnath, strategizing the battle ahead.

"Why's that, Captain?" Apaulon wondered aloud.

"There will need to be a tribunal. Sworn testimony that these are indeed the killers of the travelling family. Otherwise the search for them will go on and on, a drain on the resources of the King's guard. No, a conclusive report, the men brought to justice. An end to it." Arnath said, feeling as official as his former rank granted him. He looked at Apaulon, who suddenly understood the official duties fell on him to report the incident to the kingdom.

"What do we do?" said Terrio in a quavering voice that sounded as though he hoped they would do nothing. Arnath looked Apaulon in the eye for a moment, and Apaulon gave an acknowledging nod.

"I defer to your wisdom in this, Captain." Apaulon said. "We are yours to command."

"Right." Said Arnath unceremoniously, and turned to Garthe. "Have anything?"

Garthe pulled a small bulb of sack cloth from his pack. It had twigs and wood peelings sticking out of the top, like the stems of an onion. "Once near them, I will light this and throw it amongst them. We'll have a few seconds to subdue them after they are disoriented by the explosion."

"Explosion?" said Terrio with total astonishment.

"I'll give a whistle as I lob it. That will give all of us time to cover our ears." Garthe said, ignoring Terrio's befuddlement. Garthe smirked, fully understanding there were those who approved of the strategic use of battle magics, and those who simply choose a kind of ignorance regarding their use, and they were about to go into battle with one of each.

"Right." Said Arnath, immediately understanding the plan. They had done it perhaps a dozen times before, mostly for purposes less noble than these. "The four of us will make our way up the mound. Spreading out as we go, until we fully surround them outside their firelight." As he spoke, Arnath made gestures with his fingers depicting the pattern they would follow. Keenly trained, Apaulon watched Arnath's hands intently, immediately understanding the geography of their attack.

"Once the explosion occurs a short melee will ensue. My companions – the dwarf and half-Orc you saw us with the other night – will likely attack from above, from the highest point on the mound. Steer clear of them."

"Understood, sir" Apaulon said.

"You travel with a half-Orc!" Said Terrio agog and at full-volume.

"Quiet, fool!" seethed Arnath, and gestured for them to proceed up the hillside.

*

In a sunken clearing on the other side of the hill, six ragged and dangerous men took turns standing, dancing and revelling over a small chest, its contents glittering gold in the fire light. Each in turn would run his fingers through the gold coins, letting them spill with luxuriously noisy clinks back into the chest. Or miming with the stacks of jots, as though the jots might be playing cards, or a lady's fan or throwing knives. All took a turn looking through the various gems at the firelight, wondering loudly at the geometric patterns created by the flickering of the flames.

All this took place under the watchful eye of their leader, a scurrilous cur with a mop of black hair, dressed in black and brown leathers. He celebrated with his men, passing the mead skin back and forth, the entire time watching every single jot, jewel and coin. His flinty eyes told a tale of the near future, when his companions, and thus the shares to be divvied, would number far fewer than five.

Up above, further up the slope of the hill, Shrakar and Trellith read the leader's intentions, even from their distant perch. Crouched down in the darkness, Shrakar leaned on his axe and Trellith on his bow, watching the revelling party, awaiting a signal.

"Should just wait till the leader starts killing his men. Let him reduce the numbers for us." Intoned Trellith quietly, drawing a grunt of approval from

Shrakar. Trellith took off his hat, spun it round and put it back on, so the pointy brim was now out of his eyeline. Squinting toward the clearing, Trellith pulled an arrow from his quiver and nocked it on his bow. "Any time now."

A moment later, Trellith spotted a flaming projectile arcing into the camp, and heard a loud, piping whistle. "Ears!" barked Trellith, and they both covered their ears over.

They felt the concussive force of the explosion from their position all the way up the hill.

Immediately they got to their feet, Trellith taking aim and Shrakar bounding down the hill in a wide arc to avoid getting arrows in the back.

Around the fire, which was only half as bright since Garthe's incendiary grenade had landed near the logs and had blown many of them asunder, the black clad cur and his men reeled in agony. Most had been blown over, and all of them had their hands clasped over their ears.

Within seconds, Arnath and the others were upon them. Only the black cur and one other realized what was happening and drew weapons. That other standing thief saw Arnath, Shrakar, Apaulon and Garthe emerge from the shadows and ran for the only open spot in the ring of trees around the clearing. Terrio had arrived too late to his spot and when he did, his arms were upraised instead of on guard. The other thief drove his sword clear though Terrio's mid-section and shouldered him out of the way. Terrio was likely dead before he slumped to the ground.

Apaulon raced to the spot where the other had disappeared into the night and sheathed his dirk. Two arrows whizzed passed him, and drilled into a tree next to his head. Apaulon steadied his footing and turned toward the slope into the forest. Peering into the dark, he saw the man bounding down the hill and, after a quick estimation, hiked his spear up to his shoulder and hurled it into the darkness. The man made it two more bounds and then fell hard.

Arnath and Shrakar made quick work of the others, bashing them unconscious, leaving them for Garthe to bind. Only the black clad cur was left standing. He nervously shifted from foot to foot in front of the chest, sword in hand, one ear pouring blood. Arnath approached him, sword ready and said, "It's pointless. Lay down your sword."

"Rather keep it, and this," the Cur said, pointing at the chest and its glittering contents. "Wouldn't you?"

"Wouldn't I what?"

"Keep a share in this chest. Soldiered enough, ain't ya? You and yours join up with me, this is just the first of it. Treasure and gold, the rest of your lives." The Cur said, absolutely believing he could talk his way out of this.

For his part Arnath did think on what the Black-clad Cur offered. But only in as much as he hoped he never once sounded like this oily scoundrel when he proposed a life of adventure to his war-time companions. Like the kind of man who would kill a travelling family for no reward, or rob a wedding party for its dowry. This quick ponderance had filled many of his happiest memories with a tinge of sadness.

"Your choice, mate." Said the Cur and, seeing Arnath's distraction, lunged at him, sword point first.

But this petty, murderous thief stood no chance against Arnath's disciplined military training. Arnath swiftly blocked the Cur's sword, stepped in to meet the Cur's attack and drilled his sword into the man's chest with full force. For a moment, the Cur still lived, his shocked face next to Arnath's.

"My companions and I have made our choice." Arnath seethed, then relaxed his sword arm, allowing the Cur to slide off his sword and fall to the ground, dead.

*

A couple of hours later, Arnath stood at the entrance to the large hall across the street from the burnt-out hulk of the old outpost. He nursed a tankard of ale and looked wearily at the wreck, thinking hard thoughts.

They had brought the bound men down from the mound and slung them over their horse's backs for the short ride back to the jail in Kroman's Town. As they did so, Apaulon lit a torch on the far side of the road, away from the forest, to alert other guardsmen that they were needed. In short order, a chorus of hooves could be heard beating their way down the road. Four horses soon arrived, a sergeant and three privates astride them. After they dismounted, Apaulon gave a quick report, including the involvement of Arnath and his men to the Sergeant, who shot a look of disapproval at the inexperienced privates that had saluted Arnath.

The sergeant heard all of it, and got Arnath's word he would sign off on the testimony when the time came. Apaulon lagged a bit behind as the guardsmen headed into the forest to take care of Terrio and the dead thieves. As his men started up the road towards Kroman's Town, Arnath remained behind with Apaulon.

"Was he the first?" Arnath asked, nodding his head up the hill.

"Yes." Apaulon said, a tad lost.

"How do you feel?"

Apaulon thought on it a moment, finally saying, "Numb really, Captain."

"Lad, it's just Arnath between us." Arnath said, trying to break through the young man's military discipline. "As to feeling numb, that's good. Harsher feelings, those that would crush you, shall come to you later. But numb is a good way to feel about it now."

Apaulon nodded blankly, then turned to join his fellow guardsmen at the scene of the carnage up the hill and complete his report. Arnath watched him go, and felt some pride for the youth. To be a soldier, kill instinctually, but feel remorse some time later was a good thing. The mark of someone with a good heart. He himself had shed bitter tears nights after he had first killed an attacking Orc during the war. As those travails continued, and he rose in rank, he would find himself surrounded by the dangerous few who took unseemly pleasure in killing and greatly anticipated the next opportunity to do so, like the cur he left dead at the fireside. Fortunately, those who took undue pleasure in death didn't last long in war. They were unreliable in the field of battle, seeking their own pleasure over any strategy and that always led to mistakes that spelled their doom. Few missed them when they were gone.

Arnath rode back into Kroman's Town, where Trellith and Shrakar had forced the four murderous thieves into the cell that they themselves had occupied earlier. Each of them gave the Sheriff a brief overview of the events of the night, and explained the King's Guard would be by later to take confessions from the thieves.

After settling their horses at the stables once more, the four of them walked back to the outpost laden with their packs and camping gear, the mayor trotted up behind them, waving a scroll above his head.

"I found it!" He declared his voice echoing off the high walls on the south side of the street. His breath huffed as he caught up beside them. "It took this whole time, but I knew it was there."

"Is that the land deed?" asked Arnath, reaching for it. But the mayor clutched it to his chest.

"No, no, no. Not like that, my good man."

"But you agreed!" barked Arnath, a little too harshly.

"And I still do." Said the Mayor, unfettered by Arnath's explosive change in mood. "Gentlemen, think on it – You want to open a business on this land. That makes you part of a community. This community. Allow me to introduce you, a bit of ceremony for your heroics. Then, all in town will know your names and will trust to do business with you, even our half-Orc friend. It is the least I can do for you after saving my son's nuptials."

Arnath thought on it, and it made sense. Like the farms all around that would supply them, the businesses closest to them would be their most frequent suppliers and neighbours as well. One formal introduction to all of the town's folk would take the burden of doing it a hundred times over off their shoulders.

"Allow us to stow our gear, and change into fresh clothes first." Said Arnath, heading towards the entrance to the old outpost.

"Of course, of course," the mayor said, rocking on his heels in the street as Arnath and company disappeared into the darkness of the old outpost.

When they emerged from the front door into the surprisingly bright torchlit street a short time later, having quickly bathed in the spring pool and freshly dressed, the entire wedding party greeted them with a thunderous cheer.

*

After being welcomed into the decorated hall, which was normally the town ale house, the mayor stood on the dais where the wedding party sat, and gave a rousing speech about how mere a hour before they had all been terrified to witness a horrible crime, a wedding spoiled, a future ruined. But no – Fate smiled upon Kroman's Town today, for today a party of retiring adventurers had come to lay claim to the old outpost and build it up again to its former glory. After a brief misunderstanding with the Sheriff, (who blanched at the mention of it, when all eyes turned his way.) they volunteered to retrieve the stolen dowry, and set the celebration aright.

"And retrieve it they did!" the Mayor shouted, throwing up his arms and receiving another thunderous cheer. With that he cleared his throat, asked Arnath and his men to come forward. He introduced each of them in turn, and then presented Arnath with the title deed to land the outpost stood on. Arnath thanked the mayor on behalf of them all, and announced in short turn they would need able bodied men and women to begin the project of rebuilding the outpost. Many of the guests beamed at this. These men not only sought to restore an eyesore on the main thoroughfare, they wanted to employ the townsfolk too. Fortune smiled upon them all.

Then, the wedding celebration resumed, with a renewed vigor. Arnath and his men stood aside, wishing not to outshine the nuptial couple. But even from the outskirts of the party, mingling folk made there way round to introduce themselves – the local baker, herbalist, scribe, tailor, chandler, washer women and many more. Trellith met the town's elderly blacksmith, who had been looking to retire. They discussed at length the logistics of disassembling his smithy and moving it to the outpost. Everyone was thrilled to hear Garthe was a healer, for all in town had had to travel to Solindar for their medical needs for quite some time. The bride even dragged Garthe onto the floor for a dance, and after gave him a kiss that made him blush in front the entire party.

Things were winding down as Arnath leaned on the threshold post, and looked ponderously at the wreck of a business they had won. In short turn, Trellith joined him at the doorway. Arnath could detect dark thoughts lingering within Trellith, something he first noticed on the way back from the melee on the slopes of the mound.

"What is it, friend?" Arnath asked sincerely.

After a reluctant silence, Trellith mumbled, "I missed."

"What's that?"

"Up in the hills, when that thief killed that poor young guardsmen, I sought to shoot him down before Apaulon had to intervene." Trellith said, staring into his ale. "And I missed."

Arnath was lost for words at first. This was a unique circumstance since the beginning of their days together. "Sorry, friend. Age has at times rendered my hand unsteady as well."

"My hands are steady as rocky pillars, mate." Trellith said in mock offense. "No, it's my eyes. A half lifetime of staring into the fire of the forge... I'm not seeing well in the darkness."

After a moment's thought, Arnath said, "One could almost say we owe the Ulgrew mountains a debt."

"A debt! That tumble nearly killed us!"

"Very true. But it also woke us up to the notion that we are not so spry anymore. That swords look better perhaps over mantels than laid upon the chests of dead men. Your eyes are just another indication of how right you were."

"How right I was?" Trellith scowled, losing his friend's point.

"To persuade us to take this course. And to do it right."

Humbled, Trellith looked into his ale, "Well, yes, of course."

"The boy met all the medical practitioners in Solindar. Perhaps he'll know someone who can help." Said Arnath, knowing Garthe surely would find a solution.

"One can hope."

"One always can. You know what else one can do?" asked Arnath with a smirk on his face.

"What's that?" said Trellith, clearly having had enough words of wisdom for one night.

"One can admit that after a night of incarceration, battle and revelry that one is tired and needs sleep."

At that, Trellith finished off his ale and nodded, "Yes, one can certainly do that."

*

They made camp around a small fire in the back courtyard. It took them a while to get a quite drunken Garthe to sleep as he loudly sang the songs he'd heard at the wedding party. When he finally did loll off, Arnath stayed awake for a brief time, eyeing the piles of charred debris like they were symbols of both his old and new life. Big, hulking reminders of the nothing he was leaving behind, and the labours, stacked upon stacked upon stacked, that lay ahead.

CHAPTER FIVE

The **following weeks** were a whirlwind of sweaty work, frustrating set-backs and, in some cases, surprising romances, for Arnath, Trellith, Shrakar and Garthe.

The very day after the wedding celebration, the mayor had posted an announcement on the large decorative message board by the fountain in the town square, one quite similar to the one he'd made during the reception. On fine parchment paper in filigreed lettering it stated that Arnath and party were new residents to the town, were men of good character who had served the crown, including their large half-Orc friend, and that they were undertaking to reconstruct the outpost. Able bodied persons with any useful skill may apply to Arnath or his companions when work was beginning every morning.

He might as well have opened a floodgate upon them.

They had intended in the first days to merely sketch out ideas for the alterations to be done to the two standing floors they had. Trellith went in the early morning to the local scribe, intending on buying reams of sketching paper, quills, ink and charcoals, as well as formal map-making rolls and several blank ledgers. When he was there, however, he noted the scribe, Vormand by name, wore spectacles over his eyes and they discussed at length who he should see in Solindar about his eyes. It turned out Trellith had met one of them at the main pub – The tall, elderly elf who gave each of their wounds a quick exam. Vormand said the elfin healer was named Shimar, and that his companion Garthe would be lucky indeed to apprentice under him.

By the time Trellith made his way back to the outpost, a que of men and women had lined up down the street outside. Hiding his surprise, Trellith bid them good morning and went inside to find even more people in the back court-yard. Arnath and Shrakar had put several men to work creating long bundles out of the three piles of charred beams that towered over the yard. The intention was to haul the smaller bundles through the front corridor, out the front door and into the street. The problem was what was to be done with such an enormous amount of useless bracken after they got it outside. They couldn't leave it in the street. So, the bundling continued, everyone getting filthy with ashen soot, until they could begin to move the bundles.

Not only had they recruited people to disassemble the woodpiles, they had also involved several women in the washing and feeding of the labourers. Fires had been built in the remains of the kitchen at the back of the building, the place where Trellith's smith would eventually go, and the women were cooking food stuffs they had brought by the basket-load in the morning. They had fresh damp towels hanging on an improvised line for the workers to clean their hands and wipe the soot from their eyes, and a hot water bucket for them to drop them in when done.

After hearing of the dilemma of the bundles, Trellith set down his parcel, walked back through the front corridor, and upon reaching the door found a young woman, a tall waifish girl with freckles wearing quite manly work pants, at the front of the worker's line. Trellith flicked a quick glance down at her sturdy shoes, and asked, "Can you run, girl?"

"Yes, sir. Yes, sir, I can." She chimed right away, in an accented lilt. A far-southerner, like Trellith himself, for sure.

"Good. Run off to the mayor's office and tell him we need to speak to him."

"Yes, sir" she barked a tad too loudly, and turned on heel, disappearing up the street.

Trellith nodded politely at the next person in line, and went back inside.

*

"You see the dilemma, your honour? No work begins until this mess is cleared away." explained Arnath, standing with Trellith and Mayor Bunlop.

"I see, I see." The Mayor said, looking more in wonderment at the work they had accomplished in one day than thinking on the problem. By now the charred wood piles were greatly reduced, one of them gone entirely. The bundles made a snaking train around the courtyard, ready to be hauled away.

While half the workforce continued the job, the other half ate soup and bread near the improvised kitchen, watching the work and awaiting a decision from the mayor. With them was Illona, the skinny girl who fetched the mayor, who ate soup and peered over Garthe's shoulder as he sketched out floor plans on Trellith's newly acquired paper.

"Where does the town get rid of its refuse?" Trellith asked the mayor.

"Oh, the far side of the mound, across the King's road." The mayor said. "We have men take it away, maintain a safe fire to destroy it. But this is already destroyed. And it would take weeks to haul of this around the mound."

As Arnath nodded in agreement, he heard Shrakar call out from the other side of the yard, "The lake!".

Not sure if he took his meaning, Arnath shook his head at Shrakar as he approached. The half-Orc was trying to wipe his massive hands clean with several towels, quite unsuccessfully. "We can't throw all this in the lake. It will destroy it. Look at the spring pool."

Most around the yard did. Though it was fine to bath in before, since they began moving all the debris near it and using it for washing water, it was a sickly, polluted black, utterly permeated with millions of particles of ash. It would likely take a week or more for the waters to clear again, back to their pristine crystal form.

"Not in lake. Around lake. Big fire pits. We chop charred wood; people use in fire pits for cooking outside." Shrakar, gesticulating the whole time, as though it made his Orkan accent easier to understand. But Arnath understood immediately, and turned to the mayor.

"Would anyone disapprove of that?"

"Of you constructing permanent firepits around the lake for visitors to use? No, of course not. Brilliant, Brilliant, Shrakar!" the mayor exclaimed, joyfully punching the half-Orc on the thigh and clearly hurting his hand in the process.

Arnath turned to the men still bundling the wreckage, calling out, "Stop! Stop that work! Get cleaned up. We've got something else to do."

*

In short turn a large group from the outpost, including all those who stood outside awaiting work, were marching toward the lake. The swift Illona and several others were sent from house to house, business to business, to borrow as many shovels as were available in town. Eventually they found enough for each person who now marched west out of town, down the hill toward the lake. One of the workers, a man perhaps a decade older than Arnath, struck up a song in deep bass voice, and the other townsfolk joined in. It was a ballad of Kroman, an ancient king most took to be myth, and the tale of his finding the Mound, the singular rocky mountain the town was built on and around. Arnath and his men didn't know it, but they listen keenly, and were able to join in with the repeating choruses.

Arnath reasoned, though they were new to town, the town was now their home, and learning the town song was only fitting.

*

The next day they woke up quite stiff, muscles knotted from a hard day of bundling charred logs and slats of wood, then shovelling a dozen huge fire pits, half as deep but near twice as long as a grave each, equally spaced around the nearby lake. Arnath got up, checked the spring pool, which was still thickly sullied by ashen particles, and got on with his exercises. Shrakar joined him for a short bit, and Trellith started his assessment of the space where the smithy would go. Garthe awoke later, as teenaged boys are wont to do.

Again, a line of workers had formed and Trellith let the ladies who'd fed them and kept them clean inside first. Once they had breakfasted, Arnath went outside and looked over the workers. He ushered swift-running Illona and the tall black-haired older man who struck up the song the night before inside. Arnath noted with a smile that all the borrowed shovels leaned on the wall outside, awaiting their owner's retrieval. Arnath asked patience of the workers awaiting assignment outside and went back in.

It turned out the older man was Illona's uncle Shamuth, brother of her long-deceased father and one of the few old soldiers who lived in Kroman's Town, those that were away on muster the night of the near-disastrous wedding. Arnath took him aside for a private conversation as they both enjoyed bites of the hot, stuffed vegetable buns the ladies had brought. "You've fought, Shamuth?" Arnuth asked in a low voice.

"Aye, Captain. The seventh regiment." Nodded Shamuth, immediately earning respect from Arnath, who knew of the feats of the brave, but ill-fated troop who held the lines to the south of Arnath's position in the final days of the Orkan war. To bolster his point, Shamuth pulled up his left sleeve, revealing a scarred brand of seven notches in his forearm.

"Good." Said Arnath, patted Shamuth on the arm and guiding him over to his pack, which lay on the ground with his other belongings. There he knelt and then stood to face Shamuth, his sheathed dirk and its belt in hand. "Take this. You'll need it to escort young Garthe to Solindar."

"I couldn't, sir." Said Shamuth. His trepidation was clearly not about the assignment, but in receiving and be entrusted with so fine a weapon.

"You can, and you will." Said Arnath, reaching out and stretching out the belt so Shamuth could turn into it and belt it up. "Good. Garthe is going to Solindar today to get some supplies for his trade, and, more importantly to the bank there to break one of our larger jots into coin. You'll escort him there and back, protecting our – your - payroll until you return."

"Understood, sir."

"Now to your niece." Arnath turned and waved Illona over. She dashed over, still holding a half-eaten hot bun. "Illona, we'll need to send posts to Solindar and the surrounding area daily. Unfortunately, we don't have a..."

"A postal pennon!" she enthusiastically interrupted, mouth still full of chewed bun.

"Right." Arnath said, trying not to join in with her uncle who snickered at her oblivious lack of manners. "Ask at the town hall or the mayor's office if they have the pennons. If not, you'll need to ride to the nearest depot."

Illona swallowed hard, eyes agog. "The nearest... That's Morley. That's leagues away. I have no horse."

"Worry not on that." Said Arnath turning away toward the burnt-out kitchens at the back of the outpost. He spied Trellith there, his back to them, making measurements with a knotted cord and called out. "Trellith! We need your horse today!"

"Feed her some apples first, or she'll throw whoever rides her." Trellith merely grunted across the courtyard, not bothering to turn from his task.

In an instant, everything around them changed. Arnath and Shamuth were about to laugh at Illona's expression of discomfiture at the notion of being the rider of an unfriendly horse for an entire day, when the courtyard was bathed in an intense crimson light.

Before the light enveloped them, Arnath recalled a high-pitched whine coming the spot where Shrakar was beginning to take apart another of the rubble piles. He shielded his eyes from the blinding light and looked that way.

Shrakar reached down toward the source of the searing, painfully bright spot of crimson light at the bottom of the woodpile.

"Stop! Don't move, Shrakar!"

All eyes turned away from the piercing light, to see Garthe had revived in his bedroll and was reaching out toward Shrakar. "Back up! Edge slowly away from the object!"

Shrakar did as Garthe said, resuming his full height and stepped away from the glowing woodpile. Arnath turned to see Garthe rifling through his pack. His hands emerged from the pack wearing a pair of black gloves and holding a blackened wooden box. Arnath had seen the gloves before, though Garthe had had no occasion as yet to use them. They were covered in ancient Elfen runes, especially at the wrists and cuffs.

Garthe bolted over to the spot, knelt before the glowing object and without hesitation plucked it off the ground. His arms trembled, as though fighting against invisible resistance as he slowly turned and deposited to the screaming red jewel into the black, elf-wood box. He closed the lid, which immediately restored normal daylight to the courtyard. As quickly as he could, Garthe wrapped a golden cord around the box, which glowed brightly for a second, and then faded to a normal appearance, sealing the box closed with its magic spell.

Arnath and Trellith raced over to Garthe, where Shrakar was already at his side. Having just awoken, the boy's hair was a wild mop. Added to that was the fact that he now glistened with sweat.

"Garthe! Are you alright?" Arnath exclaimed as he knelt beside him. Still trembling, Garthe nodded.

"I am alright." Garthe said peeling off his ornate gloves. "The rune-gloves protected me from the object's magics. I've never felt such power. It felt almost alive."

"What was it?" Trellith enquired, half-knowing the answer already.

"It was as I feared." Garthe said, eyes thoughtfully on the elf-wood box. "The object that destroyed this outpost was not itself destroyed. Those mages sought to possess it, awaking the artifact and everyone nearby paid the price."

Having found their courage, the others in the yard had come over to hear what manner of conjuring had just assailed them. Many had even raced in from outside once the terrible shrieking had ceased.

Garthe put one of the gloves back on, picked up the box and crooked out an elbow to allow Shrakar to help him to his feet. Everyone kept a good distance from Garthe as he was led over to his pack, where he knelt down and he stowed the terrible object away.

"I shall take it to Solindar, to Shimar the mage." Garthe said, loud enough for all to hear. "He'll know what to do with it."

Once everyone had breathed a collective sigh of relief, the cooking women began shooing the outsiders out of the yard, admonishing them to wait outside till called to work. Arnath turned to find Shamuth's face still blanched from the experience, and the fear of what lay ahead.

"Needn't worry. You shall have plenty more men with you on your trip. I want no uncertainty until that *thing* is out of our custody." Arnath said, not hiding his disdain for the dark magical object.

Arnath turned from Shamuth, who looked somewhat relieved, and clapped his hands loudly. "Alright. Let's form into gangs, and begin the work!"

*

Much was accomplished by nightfall. Shrakar and Trellith had divided the work gangs, which encompassed everyone who waited outside, into groups. Two thirds of them would haul the bundles through the front corridor of the outpost and into the street, a task the wracked unholy hell upon the front hallway and the men moving the bundles as well. As the bundles were shoved through, they scraped along the walls, sending blasts of black ash in all directions and scraping up the mostly undamaged wood of the back doorway, front hall, the long front desk, threshold to the tap room and the interior of the front door. All of it would need to be re-carved and refinished when the elf craftsmen arrived. The hands, faces, chests and thighs of every man involved got terribly splintered with every tremendous heave.

Those workers awaiting in the street would lay the blackened bundles on carts and haul them all the way down to the lake, some staying behind to chop up the debris with axes inside the firepits.

Those not picked for these arduous duties were personally selected by Arnath, with Shamuth's help, for their military experience to escort Garthe to Solindar and back. Along with Garthe and his four escorts, Arnath and Trellith sent along letters to Lorta and the other elf business owners they had established relations with during their last stay there. These letters mostly comprised of work progress reports, and requests for supplies already purchased to arrive by certain dates. With those, a very specifically worded letter to the bankers in Solindar authorized Garthe to act on their behalf during this and further visits. As Arnath handed over the letters, he reiterated his instructions at unnecessary length. Not because he had any mistrust for Garthe or any irresponsibility his youth brought to the task, but because many a time he had seen magical objects have a strange, enchanting effect on the minds of those who got too near them. It was only after he was fully assured Garthe's faculties were not affected by contact with the destructive red jewel did he send the party on their way to Solindar. Losing Garthe as they had lost Morgosh would be a heartbreak that he simpler could not recover from.

Within town, Arnath sent Illona to the mayor's office to request a postal pennon for the outpost. These triangular, sky blue flags hung on white poles diagonally over the street beside the front door of a home or businesses, letting the King's post service know that a letter, scroll or package awaited pick up. Riders on horseback and in carts rode through town, travelling either east or west, picking up and dropping off posts as they criss-crossed daily along the secure King's road.

It turned out there were no pennons in either the mayor's office or the town hall, everyone in town had simply grown used to coming to this very building to pick up and drop off parcels at the post office on the ground floor. Illona was fairly certain the captain wanted his deliveries made to his front door, so the mayor quickly scribbled a formal request for a new half-dozen pennons for Kroman's Town in general, one of which was for the outpost's immediate use. Illona would take this to Morley, bringing the pennons back with her.

Arnath took the time to walk Illona down to the stables, bringing apples for all of their horses. He had Illona feed and stroke Trellith's brown mare, until it was used to the girl's presence, and then readied her with a saddle to ride.

Before she rode off, Arnath bestowed on her a very short dagger that hung from a leather thong around his neck. It was meant to be hidden within one's shirt, and quickly ripped out of its upside-down scabbard as a weapon of last resort. Illona was confused by the gift, saying "What use would I have for such a thing?"

Arnath told her in a most solemn tone without humour or flirtation, for she was a child in his eyes, that she was a beautiful young woman, and there were those without honour who would sully a fine girl just for the sake of doing it. Also, though the road was full of allies, King's guardsmen whom she should wave at and draw attention to herself, so that they might note her presence along the highway, that there were also pockets of danger, places where the guardsmen were spread too far apart, and that was where she must be most careful.

Unsure if she had heard him fully, since Illona had dreamily blushed from the moment he called her beautiful, Arnath sent her on her way, up the rising road across town, past the outpost and out of town eastward toward Morley.

Striding up the hill himself, Arnath almost reached the outpost, when he found his way blocked by a man he knew, but whose name he'd forgotten.

Arnath felt no shame in his lack of recall as he'd met him on the night of the raucous wedding celebration. He did remember that this was the owner of the large town mead hall which had been tented over and festooned with garlands and flowered wreaths for the wedding party. All of that was removed now and the hall was merely a long low-slung building, with architecture similar to the rest of the town, its open doorway standing directly across the street from that of the outpost.

The man who stood there was in between short and tall, quite stout but not in a blubbery way. He had thick, dark hair that was cut in a squire's fringe over his forehead. That thick darkness also showed upon his face, where he had a dark shadow of beard that looked impossible to shave away, no matter how sharp the razor. He had a short-sleeved shirt with open laces in the front. An apron hid his pants, but below it one could see one booted leg and one well-worn wooden peg. He stood with his fists on his hips, eyes locked on Arnath as he strode toward him.

With that leg, Arnath thought, he had to be a man who stood his ground and fought. Running away was not an option. Arnath choose his next words carefully.

"Hail, good sir. I hope our work has not disturbed you."

"Not the work so much, Captain, but I have words for you anyway." He said in the town's common southerner's lilt, despite its northerly location.

"And what disturbs you, good sir." Arnath said upon reaching the man.

"Enough with the "good sirs", Captain Arnath. It's just plain Durnly now. Ain't set foot on a King's navy vessel in more 'en twenty years."

"Fair enough, good Durnly. What troubles you?"

"I don't mind if your workers be coming in all covered in soot. A man's labours makes him quite thirsty. But for your whole workforce to be in and out, using my commodes like garrison latrines, making a mess and no purchases… I'll not have it anymore. Hear me?" Durnly let forth all of this sternly, without babbling.

For his part, Arnath felt immediately ashamed of himself. With the million details they needed to cover whilst rebuilding the outpost, he'd forgotten about latrines for the workforce. Of all the things. He himself took a short walk every morning to the woods at the edge of town, and put no thought into how everyone else was taking care of their business. And the neighbouring business had suffered the brunt of it.

"You have my apologies, Durnly." Arnath said humbly, and thinking quickly, gestured toward the mead hall. "Perhaps we could sit down and discuss our future business relationship."

"I'll not be bought off in this, Captain." Durnly said, repulsed. "Where I'm from one does not repair injury with coin."

"I feel the same. However, there is the matter of my opening an ale house wherein the guests will also be briefly living, right across the street from yours."

Durnly looked over at the door, where a work gang led by Shrakar were hauling out another giant bundle of burnt debris. "Across the street…" Durnly said ponderously, imagining his future loss of revenue.

"I have no wish to harm your business." Arnath said. "So, let's go inside, and discuss how we will arrange things for ourselves as neighbours."

Durnly nodded, and followed Arnath down the short stairs into the mead hall, still gazing back at the door that could spell doom for his livelihood.

*

After a full tankard's worth of discussion, Arnath and Durnly shook hands on a long-term business proposition. Yes, the outpost construction workers, of which there would be ten times as many in the coming days, could use the mead hall's commodes in exchange for the hired cleaners maintaining them several times a week. The ladies would continue to make breakfast and lunch, but when the work day ended those workers not going home to a meal would be encouraged to go to the mead hall for dinner. The same would be the arrangement after the outpost opened. The outpost would have no kitchens, that space would be occupied by Trellith's forge, and all food ordered by Arnath's customers would be prepared by the kitchens of the Briny Sea – The name of Durnly's mead hall it turned out. Similarly, all the alcohol purchased for the outpost would be purchased by Durnly, including all the imported fare designed to entice foreign travellers, and sold to the outpost a little over cost to abate any losses Durnly might endure from the outpost's clientele not ever visiting the Briny Sea.

The matter settled, Arnath found himself still quite embarrassed by having glossed over so important a detail. Imagine a former military commander utterly forgetting one of his company's most basic needs. Damn my old age, he thought as he made to cross the street.

Looking across the way, Arnath saw Shrakar, his green skin near completely blackened by ashen dust, heaving yet another ungainly bundle of wreckage out the door. Arnath could tell by Shrakar's knitted brow that perhaps he had been away from labouring with the others too long, playing the business man whilst others worked. Arnath had seen that disgruntled scowl before and knew it was time as captain to step up.

As Shrakar helped the others get the bundle atop a rolling palette, Arnath said, "Alright brother, that's enough for now. Take that down to the lake and wash away that soot."

Exhausted, Shrakar nodded, gave a mock salute with an equally deflated grunt and turned away to join the others who guided the palette down the hill.

Already unlacing the front of his shirt, Arnath stepped into the outpost, and said, "The rest of this wreckage is mine."

*

On the King's Road, part way to Solindar, Garthe and his escort came across a familiar landscape, and a familiar face. Working in her fields close to the road, a red-haired woman Garthe recognized from their trip toward Kroman's Town turned at the sound of the many approaching hoofbeats, and smiled.

"Hail, good Merynda." Said Shamuth, motioning the others to stop their horses.

The woman, Merynda, clapped the dirt from her hands, and wrung them clean on her apron as she approached the road. "And to you, Shamuth. What brings such a pack of soldiering old dogs my way?"

"The young master has business in Solindar." Shamuth said, indicating Garthe. Leaning closer to her, Shamuth cupped one hand beside his mouth, and said in a mock whisper. "Business with a great deal of money involved."

"Ah, so you escort a young man of great means, do you?" Merynda asked playfully, knowing full well the company Garthe kept.

"Allow me to present young master Garthe, mage and healer." Shamuth said, his deep bass voice taking on the tone as one announcing guests at a ball. "Garthe, this is Merynda, the lady owner of this farm."

Garthe dismounted from his horse, and walked over to her. They shook hands, Merynda's eyes alight upon his. "A healing mage? At your age?"

"Apprentice mage, actually. But healing is my natural gift." Garthe said, not letting go of her hand. As the last words fell from his lips, he began to turn Merynda's hand upside-down and curiously traced his forefinger along the heavy scar on her forearm.

"Pay him no mind, Miss." Said one of the rougher of Garthe's escorts. "Proper wizard, he is. Why just this morning, we saw him..."

Shamuth raised a silencing finger at his companion, and he was immediately quiet, a guilty expression on his face. All the escorts exchanged a knowing look, all thinking the same thing. To reveal the boy had money that they guarded was no thing, they were all capable men. But to reveal the presence of a magic jewel that had killed a dozen of their neighbours and put a blackened scar of the face of their home for years was surely to court an early and terrible death.

Merynda, however didn't hear the exchange, entranced as she was by Garthe as he held his green healing stone at her elbow.

"Farming injury?" Garthe asked as he ran the glowing stone over her outer elbow in circles.

"Battle, actually."

"Merynda was one of the few "Maidens of steel" deployed towards the end of the war." Shamuth said, a hint of pride in his voice. Garthe met her eyes with respect. In hearing tales from Arnath, Trellith, Morgosh and even Shrakar of the tumultuous course of the Orkan war, he had been told of the closing days, when the three kingdoms were near out of young men to recruit, and thus the kingdoms had found as many able bodied farm girls as they could to train. Train them they did, putting them through their paces as hard as they would men. As Shamuth had said, by the closing days of the war only eight platoons of these maidens had been deployed to the front lines, and though less than half their numbers returned from the war, all had distinguished themselves in battle.

Garthe finished his circular motions, and put his stone away in the pouch he wore around his neck. "Try it now." He said to Merynda, and she let her arm fall to the side. She marvelled that it could extend all the way straight, something it had not done since she'd taken an Orc war hammer to her already weakened shield. Merynda flexed her arm up again, and there was a loud pop of muscle and cartilage, so loud it surprised Garthe's escort. Merynda gasped at the sudden relief of things popping back into their proper place.

She flung her arms around Garthe's neck, and exclaimed, "No one has ever been able to... Thank you!"

Garthe stiffened for an embarrassed moment, and then returned her embrace. Shamuth and his men again exchanged a look, one that conveyed their bolstered respect for their charge.

As she walked him back to his horse, her arm in the crook of his, Garthe gave her a pre-written list on parchment of food stuffs they would need regularly at the new outpost.

"Ahh, turnips, yes. I saw you travelled with a half-Orc." Merynda said, turning to face Garthe. "And what of the man you travelled with?"

"What of him?" Garthe asked back, not catching her meaning.

"She has her eye on the captain," joked one of the escorts, in a school boy tone.

Shamuth turned to him, and rather than chide the man, said. "Can you blame her?"

This drew a deep laugh from all the escorts. For his part Garthe, seemed to gather Merynda's intent. As he re-mounted his horse, he said. "Captain Arnath shall be quite busy over the next month or so. Keep an eye on the road. There will be many caravans of elf craftsmen travelling back and forth. But as they wane..."

"The work will be ending, and the Captain not so busy." Merynda said. She patted her arm, saying, "Thanks again, Master Garthe."

"A pleasure, lady Merynda. Hope to see you again soon." With that Garthe rode on, and each of the escorts bid her goodbye in turn.

Merynda returned to her labours, now with more vigor, having been relieved at last of so long and painful a burden.

*

In the late afternoon, Trellith had called upon the old smith, Kortell. They drank tea, ate and talked as Trellith took measurements of the smithy with his knotted rope, taking notes in one of his many fresh ledgers. Kortell mostly tried to pry nuggets out of Trellith regarding the blazing magical object that had appeared in the back courtyard, once again rearing its ugly head since destroying the old outpost. No doubt it was the talk of the town. Kroman's was really a village in size, but with its densely packed populace and businesses, it had everything a town had, only in a tinier space. And news travelled fast, literally from window to window at times.

Trellith did his best to describe the arcane event and concentrate on his measurements. Kortell paced, pointing at features of the smithy, particularly where things were fastened together and then prattled on with his endless questions.

"I wonder if this has something to do with the many intruders caught skulking around the rubble in the outpost yard?" Kortell pondered aloud, not expecting Trellith to know the answer.

Trellith made a quick numerical note, lest it get away from him, and turned pointedly to face Kortell. "Intruders? What intruders?"

"I thought you knew, being that the Sheriff arrested you, thinking you were the same rabble." Said Kortell, very pleased to have Trellith's full attention.

"He did seem a mite aggressive for a fellow shooing away trespassers."

"That's because you weren't the first." Kortell passing Trellith back his re-filled tea. "Over the months after the outpost was destroyed, my, before the smoke even settled, the sheriff began to catch interlopers rummaging about in the back. Some, perhaps most, were just scavengers, adventurers like you plan to serve, looking for a few quick gold coins. But the last few times, he had a fight on his hands. A black robed man offered challenge back and then disappeared into the night. The town was in quite a tizzy for a while. Imagining a cut-throat intruder beside every bed at night, and such."

Trellith rubbed his beard thoughtfully for a moment. Perhaps he should stop by the sheriff's office before heading back to compare his measurements at the outpost. Hearing Sheriff Daruun's descriptions of the brigands that sought out the jewel might decide what the next moves should be, if any at all. From a tactical standpoint, he found himself on the unsteady ground of not having enough information to even fathom a plan. The mysterious object was dangerous, yet someone seemed to want it. Garthe had taken it away to a senior mage, but would they who sought it out know that? If they did not, were the workers at the outpost in any danger? Were Garthe and his escorts?

The not knowing was enough for Trellith to pack up his gear and leave Kortell in a bit of a huff, worry causing him to almost let go his manners entirely.

*

Evening found Illona watching the stars above the road as though in a dream. The sky and scenery that stretched on and on as she and the mare loped down the King's road was a welcome balm to the busy and occasionally irritating day she had endured.

Upon arriving in Morley after an uneventful few hour's ride, she had no bearings with which to find the postal depot. It was only after exploring many a busy street, the mare's reigns in hand, did she see the building with a huge pennon hanging overhead. The postal flag was four times the size the ones she sought out and served as a sign for all, declaring "This is the postal office!".

Inside, Illona stood in the short line of people awaiting service. When it was her turn, she stepped to the counter and found herself opposite a fat, pallid-faced man with wispy blond hair and what seemed to be a permanent expression of disdain. Setting aside her instinctual dislike for the man, she smiled and placed the mayor's request parchment on the counter. "Good afternoon, I have request from the Mayor's office in Kroman's Town."

Upon hearing the name Kroman's Town, the man embedded behind the counter looked at the request parchment as though Illona had placed a portion of excrement before him. It was only when he leaned over to see if no one was behind her and that she was all his to play with, did he deign to pick up the parchment and look it over.

"I see," the porcine man said, feigning interest. "And do you work for the mayor's office in Kroman's Town?"

Illona struggled for a moment with her answer. "Not really. I'm in the employ of Captain Arnath, I suppose..."

"But you claim this is the signature of the town mayor?"

Realizing her first instincts about the man were correct, she bit back what she truly wished to say. She often did. She was normally quite a shy and nervous person, and not one to argue, but Illona could feel this arrogant clerk getting an angry rise out of her. Illona had had school masters like this since she was a little girl, people who took great pleasure in frustrating others and watching them squirm. Those old experiences informed her to let this worm have his fleeting pleasure and to remember why she was there in the first place. Above all she didn't want to let down Captain Arnath and, by proxy, his travelling companion, the handsome mage Garthe.

Without allowing her feelings of revulsion to change her face, she calmly said, "Claim? Oh no, it properly is. The pennons are for the whole town, not just the outpost."

"Ha!", the irritating man laughed. "Kroman's has no outpost! It was destroyed ages ago."

"I know that. I live there. The outpost is being rebuilt anew and it requires a pennon, as does the town post office for other businesses."

By now a number of persons had begun to line up, some with scrolls and packages, others with paper receipts to pick up a package. Illona could hear them making complaints under their breath. In her own frustration, Illona completely missed the quiet approach of another person, a woman, behind the counter.

"And yet your request has no town seal from the mayor's office. Where, pray tell, is the wax seal?"

Before Illona could explode angrily in the snivelling man's face, the women behind the counter snatched the parchment out of his hand with lightning speed, and gave it a cursory glance, her brows knit. Looking down at the man, whose shoulders were already hunched against the coming barrage, the woman barked, "Really, Barynth! Must you with every girl who comes through our door?!"

The tall woman had neatly piled up greying black hair and wore a crisp, black business dress that covered even her feet. She pointed towards a door next to the counter. "That way, miss."

As she passed through the doorway, Illona could hear as the woman seethed, "All of these people had better have been served by the time I return."

Illona had walked into a long corridor that ran the length of the building. A door at the far back of the hall stood open and the light of sunset shone through. The tall women stepped out of nearby door from the reception kiosk, and motioned for Illona to follow.

"Allow me to apologize for Barynth. He is unpopular with women, as you may have surmised by his appearance, and therefore uses our kiosk as a kind position of imagined authority over them when he thinks I am out of earshot. Pathetic, really." The woman said, gracefully traversing down the hallway, Illona's request parchment fluttering in her hand.

"I've known many like him. I'm grateful you intervened. Where my thoughts were leading might have ended me up in your jail." Illona said, her fleet feet doing their able best to keep up with the tall woman's incredibly brusk pace.

As they reached the back door, a thought occurred to Illona, "Do people hereabouts not like Kroman's Town?"

The woman paused on the long veranda that spanned the width of the postal building's rear, and looked Illona in the eye, "I wouldn't say dislike, my dear girl. Since your traveller's outpost burned, many people have taken on Kroman's Town as a symbol of ill luck. The outpost was destroyed, the town floundered, businesses shuttered, and many of the young left, seeking fortune elsewhere. You are the youngest person from there I have met, perhaps since I was your age. It became a town aging towards death, and no one wants to be reminded of that. People poke fun at Kroman's as they would ward off a terrible fate for themselves." Then she turned and continued down the veranda steps and into the large, enclosed yard that sprawled out before them.

Illona froze a moment, thinking on what the tall woman had said. It was true, she might have been one of the youngest persons in the whole of the town. Everyone else was like her uncle, or older. Their healer had died ages ago. No wonder she fancied Garthe. Mage or not, he was the only truly suitable boy her age she'd met since it occurred to her she liked boys.

Illona shook off the troubling thoughts, and looked across the postal depot yard, taking in the sight. Though the path was clear where the tall woman walked, the rest of the yard was packed tightly with people, equipment and storage spaces. On the far left, post workers of all genders, most fairly young, loaded up packs on horses or horse-drawn carts, with parcels, scrolls and sealed letters. Many of the post drivers dickered over who was going to get closer to any given destination faster, therefore who should take a disputed package. "But I'm going south-east. I'll get there faster, ya clod." "Ya only going south-east after you get rid of that whole wagon load. I'll get there two days before you. Don't be so thick."

These weren't so much arguments as they were prideful chides of people who were good at their jobs. A kind of goading comradery to see who was better at putting things on people's doorsteps faster than any other. To Illona it was wonderful. She could see herself doing all of this one day. She smiled, took an invigorating breath, and leapt from the porch to pursue the tall woman.

Catching up, she found the tall woman as she unlocked one of the many wooden sheds that lined the right side of the path and had disappeared inside. She popped back out holding a large white canvas sack and vigorously shook the dust from it. Holding it out for Illona to take, which she did, the women examined the mayor's request and said, "Six all told. I know for sure a new outpost means new businesses, so I'll give you seven. A good number for the town's renewed luck."

Later, Illona found a tavern that had a station to feed and water Trellith's mare, and to have a dinner sandwich herself. She sat on a stool that faced the town square and watched people coming and going in the twilight. She found herself surprised by what young people were wearing, having only seen old people in their work clothes most of her life. Some of the fashions she admired greatly, like the shirts the occasional passing elves wore. Others, that she surmised were from further south, where the royal court was, made people look foppish and ridiculous. She realized she must have looked a rube in her sturdy work pants and shoes, but then she wouldn't be here long, and that impression would be lasting for no one.

Into the night, on the King's Highway heading back to Kroman's town, Illona looked up at the stars over the northern farm fields and marvelled at their beauty. Such a day she'd had.

Occasionally Trellith's mare whickered in protest and Illona had to adjust the canvas sack of pennons that awkwardly hung from the saddle. Shifting the position meant the sack would only drum gently against her side as they loped down the highway, instead of painfully digging into her haunches.

With the mare's comfort being her only real task as she dreamily rode through the starry night, Illona was quite oblivious to the presence of the man who rode up next to her until he spoke.

"Lovely evening." He said, he himself admiring the stars as their horses came alongside each other.

Illona, though startled, gave no sign of it. Her eyes flicked from the sky to the man, and she gave a nervous nod. "Yes. Yes, it is."

Inwardly, she chided herself greatly. Here was one of the foul men the captain had warned her of, and then was caught unawares dreaming amongst the stars. But, maybe not...

Still keeping her head back as though looking skyward, she gave the man a thorough examination. He looked to be just past his mid-twenties. Though dressed in all black from head to toe, that black was comprised of leathers, suedes and silks, all of it embroidered in shining silver thread. The outfit struck her like a mix of the fashions she'd liked today and those she found garish. It looked perhaps like a monied person had themselves an outfit designed to make them look like a rebellious scoundrel. To attack her, try to drag her into the woods and violate her, would utterly ruin an outfit that likely cost more than her mother had ever made in her life.

As well, his face did not speak of anything dastardly. Even in the dark it was easy to see his skin was a light, even pale brown. His eyes were light brown too. His black hair was swept back from his forehead and behind his ears it fell to his shoulders. Around his mouth he had styled a ringed beard and moustache, which further accentuated his appearance as a kind-of theatrical cutthroat.

He was, however, quite well armed. A small bow hung from a quiver on his back. Around his body was a second bow, the longest she'd ever seen, one almost as tall as the man himself. A dirk in a finely tooled scabbard lay on his thigh. Illona imagined there could even be more. His gloves alone, which went all the way up to his elbows, could have concealed all manner of small arms.

Perhaps he rode to a costume party in a nearby township. Though she wished not to anger a stranger, she still wanted to test the waters of her costume theory. "I like your outfit. It's really quite... distinctive."

"Oh, thank you." He said, with a smile. "I'm pleased you like it."

"To what occasion do you travel in such finery?"

The man gazed on ahead down the road, saying, "Oh, no occasion. I travel to Kroman's Town. I hear there is much going on there of late. And you?"

Illona gulped back a lump of fear. What was she to say? If she admitted she was from Kroman's, she'd be stuck riding with this strange man all the way there. And it was hours away still.

The road ahead provided her with an escape. On the opposite side of the road, standing on either side of a cut-out where a camp of travellers slept, stood two King's guardsmen. Even in the darkness she recognized one of them as Apaulon, the brave guardsmen who helped retrieve the stolen wedding dowry alongside Captain Arnath and his men. He'd made Illona nervous when she saw him in the street, retrieving the thieves to take them back to court for trial, because he made her feel the same as Garthe did, all flush and flutter.

Illona quickly chose the lesser of the two embarrassments, and turned to the man in black, saying, "Do excuse me, good sir. I see a friend I wish to speak to. Good journey." And before the man could respond, she kicked her horse to a fast trot across the road.

She didn't dare look back. As she approached the campsite, Illona was relieved to see Apaulon smile at her in recognition, and reach for her reigns. "The Captain sent word you would be on the road."

Apaulon's cheer drained away as he saw the fear on her face as she dismounted and nearly leapt into his arms. "What is it? What's wrong?" He said, feeling her embrace around his neck almost tight enough to choke him. After a few moments, Illona relaxed, uncoiled herself from him and looked down the road.

"What is it?" Apaulon enquired again, both confused and concerned.

Illona looked down the road and saw the man in black had ridden quite a bit onwards, his head once again tilted up towards the stars. He hadn't stopped, wasn't lagging in wait for her.

"I don't know," she said, "Perhaps it was nothing."

*

When Trellith returned to the outpost after a long talk with the Sheriff, he heard quite a commotion going on out back.

He raced down the ash-blackened corridor and emerged into the back courtyard to find Arnath holding two of the workers at bay with a borrowed sword. One of the workers held out a dagger, and clutched something to his chest, the other had his fists balled up and stood ready to spring.

"Put down your knife, lad. I will not ask again." Arnath said just as Trellith moved within his eyeline. Seeing Trellith, Arnath cocked his chin at the unarmed man, indicating who he needed covered. Trellith edge closer to the seething man who held his fists ready to strike.

"I saw it first! It's not fair, him bringing a knife into it." Exclaimed the man Trellith stood near, mistaking Trellith's stance near him for an unspoken declaration of allyship. Standing closer, Trellith recognized the two arguing men as those recruited by the Sheriff to arrest them their very first night in town.

"And what did he take from you?" Trellith said, edging even closer to the man. As he looked across at the worker who bore his knife, Trellith could see around the courtyard as well. Workers stood frozen, afraid to get near the conflict, especially with the captain's broadsword out. The cooking and washer women huddled by the fires, eyes wide with fear.

"A gold coin, I saw it on the ground. When I pointed it out, he ran and scooped it up, the dirty thief."

"I grabbed it. It's mine!" The other man declared in a near-shriek.

"How is that fair, you bloody scavenger?!" The raging, two-fisted man said, taking another threatening step closer.

Trellith held up a halting hand in front of the man near him, and then turned to the other. "May I see it, please?"

"See it?" the man nervously queried.

"Yes. I'd like to see it and assess if it is valuable enough to merit all this. You do know you two could be quibbling over fool's gold."

"Fool's gold! No, it's..." but it was too late. As soon as the man open his hand and looked down at the coin, Arnath took one quick step, swatted the knife aside and smashed the man in the face with the fist wrapped around his sword grip. Trellith turned and by the sternness of his expression alone stopped the other man from rushing over for the coin.

Arnath reached down and picked up the coin on the ground near the unconscious man. He then strode over to the other man and handed him the coin. "This is yours. Now sit down next to him."

"Thank you, sir. But, why do I..."

"Sit down!" Arnath barked with a fury that startled everyone. The man nearly dropped his gold coin as he sped over to sit cross-legged next to the man sprawled on the ground. Arnath then turned to the cooking and washer women, saying "Summon the sheriff."

The closest of the washer women bolted from the yard.

"Hold on now! I didn't do nothing wrong." Protested the seated man.

"You didn't? This is a place of work, not some brawler's tavern." Trellith said in an admonishing tone.

Arnath turned and marched over to the edge of the courtyard, re-sheathed his sword, leaving it with his things. He turned and addressed the courtyard in a voice loud enough to be heard. "This will happen again. The old outpost housed a group of successful treasure hunters before it was destroyed. There will be gold aplenty buried in this debris. Should you find a coin or two, they are yours to keep. A bonus for your labours. But secret them away. Do not brag or stir up jealousy. As my friend said, this is a place of work and we are your work captains. Whilst under us, you must conduct yourselves honourably and fairly. Squabble all you wish about the matters and politics of the day. It helps pass the time as we work. But if you come to blows for any reason, you answer to us. If you make ready to do or do serious violence on another, the law becomes involved. That's what I have to say on it."

Many around the yard nodded at Arnath, some smiling at the notion that clearing the yard had just become a treasure hunt. Seeing the gleeful expressions, Trellith stepped forward, "One amendment to the captain's decree, treasure you keep, yes, but any documents or weaponry you find hand them over to us. Especially maps, even if it is a fragment of one, we will want it."

"There you have it. Gold is yours, weapons, maps, documents are ours. Now let's call it a day. We'll resume in the morning. Go get clean, if all this grime will even come off. Those not going home, sup at the Briny Sea, as is our arrangement. Go now, you've all earned your pay." Having said the last, Arnath noticed a man nearby about to ask a question, "Ah right. As you know, we are keeping record of who worked on what days, etcetera. Our payroll will arrive in a day or two, once master Garthe completes his business in Solindar. Have no concerns on that score. Again, you have our thanks for a hard day's labours."

Many gave half-hearted hails to Arnath's speech, all too tired for a proper cheer. The men and women lined up to grab hot, wet towels from the washer women and began to scrub the soot from themselves. Trellith marched over to join Arnath, who waited his turn at the back of the line.

"Was a good thought, about the maps." Arnath said, taking a towel from one plump women.

"Well, if we are truly going to maintain a master map, and supply copies to those who wish them, we shall need the ones maintained by the old outpost. Surely not all of them burned up in the fire." Trellith said as Arnath scrubbed his face and neck with the towel. When done, Arnath turned his head from side to side for Trellith's approval. Instead, Trellith scowled and shook his head.

"No?"

"Not even close." Trellith said.

"Perhaps I should join Shrakar at the lake." Said Arnath, who turned just in time to see the sheriff step through the back door, past the line of the exiting workers.

*

Garthe decided to call upon Shimar immediately upon reaching Solindar, even though it was well into the night. The burden he carried demanded the breaking of decorum.

He knocked on Shimar's door, having instructed Shamuth to send someone to secure them rooms at the inn. Shamuth and another man, the burly and flinty-eyed Fernlow, stood watch on the house, awaiting Garthe. The door to the slim three-story house of white stone and curving Elf-wood cracked open and revealed an unimpressed Shimar.

"Ahh, Master Garthe. Can this not wait until tomorrow?"

Garthe leaned in close, and quietly said, "I have the object that destroyed the old outpost."

Shimar's eyebrows raised as high as they could on his normally stoic face and he waved Garthe inside.

Upstairs in Shimar's laboratory, both Garthe and Shimar had donned their spell protected gloves and also darkened goggles that fit tightly over the eyes. They were both thankful for them as Garthe untied the magically bound golden string that held his protective box closed and a blinding blast of shrieking crimson light streamed out of the box.

Shimar only took a protracted moment to lean in closer to the box, not daring to reach inside, before slamming the box closed. He resealed the golden string, which glowed for a moment and then bound the box shut. Shimar removed his goggles and gloves, and Garthe followed suit. Garthe could tell the elder mage was quite concerned.

"What do you think it is?" Garthe asked, genuinely hoping he knew.

"I can't be certain. I've read of familiar things to this, but I had better check first." Shimar said worrying his chin with his fingertips. "You are leaving this with me?"

"I hoped I could…"

"Of course, of course. You were right to bring this to me. You say it was in the wreckage of the outpost?" Shimar strode towards the stairs, and Garthe followed him down.

Near the front door, Shimar said, "I shall know more tomorrow, once I have consulted my library."

"Thank you for taking it off my hands." Garthe said sincerely, then remembering the many purposes of his visit, pulled a small parchment scroll from within his cloak and handed it to Shimar. "For tomorrow as well. Like we discussed on my last visit."

Shimar opened the scroll, and after a glance said, "Yes, I already have these items ready for you. But no need to carry them to the inn and back here again tomorrow. They'll be ready when you head back to Kroman's Town. Call on me after midday. We shall get to the bottom of this."

They said their goodnights, and when Garthe got outside he found Shamuth and Fernlow looking at him with embarrassed faces. All up and down the street, whether on foot or from their windows, Elves of all ages stood looking in trepidatious awe at Shimar's house.

The blinding light of the magic stone must have blasted out of his windows, and any other cracks in his walls and ceiling, illuminating the entire neighbourhood.

"So much for our secret mission." Shamuth said meekly, as they mounted their horses.

*

Later, at the inn, after Fernlow had billeted their horses, the five of them sat around their table and cast dour eyes into their ales. Each of them – Garthe,

Shamuth, Fernlow, Tindall and Amorth – were trying their best to speak light of their situation. It was, at least, out of their hands now.

The only ray of light for them was the lovely Shimalena, who recognized Garthe from his last visit, and spent extra time at their table, particularly near him, when she brought them fresh pints.

"Ahh, to be a young man again," joked the grey-haired, hawk-faced Tindall as he wiped froth from his moustache.

"Aye, the lad's got the pick of the litter. From here to Morley." Ribbed the bald-headed Amorth. "Even Shamuth's niece is circling the boy."

This all rather embarrassed Garthe, who turned to Shamuth, saying, "They can't be right. That isn't right, is it?"

Shamuth merely shrugged, tugging the poor boy along. "I have to admit, she has been behaving quite a bit differently since ya came to town. Not badly, or poorly, just a bit bolder perhaps. All that nervous energy. I think that she just wants you to notice her. You're a mage after all, and a young one at that."

Garthe felt a heel, for he hadn't really notice her. Well, perhaps the subtle curves of her slim body, her wide smile. In a flash, he changed his mind, realizing he had noticed her after all. And he felt a letch for noticing nothing of her other than the parts he liked to look at.

To move the conversation away from himself and Shamuth's niece, Garthe asked a question about something said earlier, "Gentlemen – why is it that there are so few young persons in the vicinity of Kroman's town?"

This drew raised eyebrows and concealing shrugs at first from around the table, until, finally, Shamuth spoke up. "I imagine it's because of the end of the war."

"Not just that. The old outpost bein' destroyed. Has a lot to do with it." Tindall said, more adding onto than rebuking Shamuth's point. Each of the older men around the table in turn told of how after the war many who returned to Kroman's Town simply did not have children, the long-lasting conflict having sapped much of the joy out of their lives. And those families that did, found their children, most now grown, wanting to leave en masse after the explosion at the outpost.

"T'was like the destruction of the outpost marked an end to the end, if you will." Intoned Shamuth. "The mayor's son was only just married, and he and his bride are already gone. Bought property to the north, no intention of returning after the honeymoon."

Tindall's face was set in a ponderous expression, and he aired his thoughts. "You think, young mage, that the object buried in the yard was accursed? That it spread a kind of negative energy in the town?"

"Oh, most certainly. Shimar will tell more of it tomorrow, but I think the miasma that drained your town of its last remaining youth likely has something to do with the gem. I heard its call when I held it. It most definitely "wants" something." Garthe said, feeling a shiver up his spine as he sipped at his ale thoughtfully.

This drew collective shiver from the men around the table as well, a shared revulsion at the thought they had been manipulated by dark magics against their will for years.

Only the appearance of Shimalena, with a tray of fresh ale mugs, broke the prolonged silent meditations on things bleak and mysterious.

*

Down at the lake, Shrakar periodically nodded off, having bathed and built a fire in one of the many pits they had dug and filled with the outposts charred debris. He had a wineskin in one hand and smoking pipe in the other, yet still the drain of the day's labours forced his eyes shut. Shrakar perked up a little bit when he was joined by Trellith and Arnath, who looked a sight all covered in the black soot. Trellith carried a roll of fresh clothes for Arnath, who was just too dirty to carry them and not soil them.

Shrakar awoke enough to offer them the skin and pipe, as is mannerly by the fireside. Each enjoyed a few toots of Shrakar's strong pipe blend and swigs from his skin before handing them back. In his dreamy state, Shrakar heard them talking of moving the smith and Arkonian gold. That brought up memories! They had tried for the fabled gold of the lost Arkonian cities not once but twice. The first time yielded nothing. They might as well have been on a cave exploring expedition. The second time, attempting to open a sealed chamber, the mage Morgosh read from what they guessed later was a cursed spell scroll, the magics of which hideously consumed him and left them charged with the care of his talented apprentice, Garthe, then a boy of only 10-years old. With the death of a travelling companion and the seriousness of having to take care of a young boy foisted upon them, none of them felt the will to continue their search for the Arkonian treasure, and they returned to the west. Recalling this, Shrakar surrendered to dream.

*

Seeing Shrakar was drifting off again, Trellith gently grabbed both his pipe and wineskin from him. "We'll ask to see any of the gold they find. Politely, of course."

"What will you hope to gather seeing it?" said Arnath after taking a long draw from the pipe. He exhaled sharply and began to strip off his clothes.

Trellith took the pipe back and sat on the log next to the slumbering Shrakar. "Firstly, just to see where most of the gold had come from. If it is from all over, then we needn't think anything of it. Plunder upon plunder. The accumulation of many such raids. But if it is all from the same place... "

Arnath let the last implication hang for a moment and then said, "If it is all from the same place, Arkonia, then the party who died in the outpost were successful at what we ourselves failed to do."

"Twice. Which brings to mind a frightening question; Did our friend Morgosh perish because he read aloud a cursed spell, or was it because he tried to cast within the Arkonian tombs, which themselves were cursed?"

Arnath scowled. "Magical curses. Hate them. Always have."

"You need not tell me, friend."

"To think we dodged so many over the years, only to retire to business, and have one claw at us from within our very doors. From a treasure we ourselves did not plunder. One could think the curse was upon us." With that Arnath picked up his dirty clothes and strode, bare-assed, down the grassy slope and into the lake. Near the oval shore, around the whole lake, many bathers, the outpost's labour force, scrubbed off the dirt and ash from the day's work. Each bather's vigorous activity created ripples that radiated and intersected in the center of the lake.

Left alone, for the sleeping Shrakar was no company at all, Trellith alternated between swigs on the skin and pulls on the pipe. He could barely make out Arnath swishing around in the water with his poor night vision. Trellith didn't want to think like the captain. Huge-hearted man though he was, Arnath's mind would often travel first to the worst-case scenario, perhaps as a habit of battle preparedness. Trellith himself liked as much information as he could gather, so his guesses were closer to facts. Thus far, he didn't think the jewel, the gold or the other minor details had anything to do with them. The fact that this was where they as a party had decided to retire, and that this was also where the cursed jewel had surfaced was a matter of mere geography. Coincidence, nothing more. Or so he hoped. They never did find the swarthy man who sold them the spell that was supposed to get them passage into the Arkonian vaults, and their investigation into the matter went no further. Morgosh was gone, and there was really nothing more to be done about it.

Trellith heard two people approaching from the direction of town. Though they were close, he couldn't focus on them until they drew near the light of the firepit.

"Ah, Apaulon, Illona. What brings you out tonight?"

Apaulon and Illona stood side by side in the firelight, Apaulon looking amused and Illona entirely embarrassed. "I came upon Illona on the road. I'm afraid she had a bit of a fright."

"A fright?" Trellith asked, a worried tone in his voice. "You weren't accosted on the road, little lady? Say it isn't so."

"No," said Apaulon, "A fellow traveller, yes, a man, but…"

"What Man?!!"

Arnath's incredible barked query startled them all. He stood at the lakeside, seething, ready to tear Illona's assailant limb from limb.

With only one glance in Arnath's direction, Illona gasped and immediately leapt behind Apaulon.

And then they all realized. It was entirely possible Illona had never seen a man naked, let alone one built like a lifelong professional warrior. They suppressed gales of laughter as Trellith threw Arnath his fresh, clean shirt, one that thankfully hung well past his loins.

"I'm sorry for my rudeness, Illona. Please tell me no one hurt you on the road." Arnath said, putting his shirt on, both red-faced and utterly bemused.

"I'm fine. I got frightened by friendly stranger. That's all." her muffled voice said from between Apaulon's shoulder blades.

"A man riding alone. He likely just wanted a riding companion to pass the time." Apaulon said.

"I got the pennons." Illona's muffled voice claimed. One of her reedy arms shot out from behind Apaulon holding aloft a brand-new postal pennon.

The absurd image made the three men laugh. It was a hearty release of tension, considering moments earlier they thought the poor girl had befallen something terrible.

But their laughter was cut short, all of them realizing something was wrong.

The night around them had grown brighter. A red-golden glow reflected off the grass, illuminating all of their features. As they turned to see what was causing it, all of their jaws dropped in horror.

The roof of the stables was completely ablaze.

*

It was merciful fate that most of the outpost's workforce were in the lake at that exact moment. Had they not been able to race from the waters and sprint up the hill to the edge of town, the horses would not have been saved.

Trellith awoke Shrakar immediately by dashing the burning pipes contents on his shoulder. The giant half-Orc sprung up, enraged, but saw the fire and ran. By the time everyone reached the building, Shrakar was already inside, unlashing all horses. People outside, in their soaking wet work clothes, tried to stop the horses as the hysterical beasts ran from the building. Those horses that could be subdued were led away and lashed to the lake gates. Others had bolted fearfully into the night.

Arnath took command straight away. He barked orders in every direction until buckets and water were in organized lines. He turned to one man, realized he was the one brandishing his knife earlier, figured quickly Sheriff Daruun had let him go with a warning, and said, "The spring pool! Bring pots of water from the outpost spring pool!"

"Aye, captain!" the man said and bolted up the road.

Arnath looked around for Shrakar. He had left the barn since all the horses were freed. Where could he be? They needed his great height to reach the burning roof.

Just then, Shrakar gave a great growl from behind, and Arnath turned to see Shrakar striding up the hill, each hand dragging a canoe that had been dunked in the lake and was sloshing full with water. He dragged them up the cobblestones, settling one between Arnath and the beginning of the bucket line.

The second canoe Shrakar picked up, keeping it steady to avoid spilling. Once he got it balanced on one shoulder, he wrapped his fist around one pointed end and flung his arm wide. A wall of water blasted sidelong out of the canoe, and soaked the roof. Near half the flames sizzled out.

The townsfolk cheered, and Arnath turned to him. "Good man. Again!"

With that, Shrakar picked up the canoe and bounded back to the lake. Many from the bucket line that spanned to the town fountain raced with the buckets to the water-filled canoe on the street next to Arnath.

Illona filled her bucket, and turned to pass it to the next person in the line. To her surprise, that person was the fancy-dressed man from the road, his foppish outfit sullied by all the splashing water and the sweat of intense labour. He held a hand out, calling out, "Come on, girl!". She gulped down her fear of the stranger and passed him the bucket.

It only took one more canoe full of water for Shrakar to completely douse the roof. Brave members of the bucket line then ran inside the stables and soaked any smoking wood within.

Jaross sat on the cobblestones and cried at his misfortune. His entire stables now smoked like a busy smith's works. As Arnath approached him he got to his knees, saying, "Bless you, Captain. You saved my livelihood, you did."

As Shrakar emerged from the stables, holding many cats coiled in fear in his arms, Jaross stood to his feet and pointed at Shrakar, shouting, "Damned be the man who judges this brave soul in my presence! Despite your beliefs, despite the wars, he saved the horses and barn cats, he did. Prove himself, Master Shrakar did, in my eyes. Light be on you, Master Shrakar, friend to all animals, and a right neighbour he is, and the dark be upon you who would judge him otherwise."

Jaross declared this for all the town to hear, eyes and nose streaming, many around them bursting into tears at his words, until Shrakar embraced him and allowed the man to fall into his arms, weeping.

Arnath looked around, and saw that only a few horses had managed to be tied to the decorative fence that stood on either side of the lake path. His was there, Shrakar's, and another he did not recognize, the rest were nowhere to be seen. "Damn! The horses are scattered. We'll need to search in the forest around the lake."

"I can help with that." Arnath turned to see a swarthy stranger, dressed in fine, if somewhat water damaged clothes.

"How will you do that? On foot, those woods will take you all night."

"On foot? Oh no." The stranger made a sour face at the mere suggestion, turning his head, blew a loud whistle. From the darkness came a whinny, and shortly the man's regal black charger galloped up to him. Illona remembered the horse, but hadn't seen its face. It was all black, but for socks of white fur over each hoof, and from its eyes to its nose had a long white diamond of fur.

Illona set down the reigns and saddle she'd carried out of the stables, as were many of the others, removing everything of value that the smoke and water could damage. Then she stayed hunkered down, behind Arnath's back as he talked with the stranger.

The man in the fancy clothes strode up to his horse, and mounted onto its back in one swift move. Gathering up the reigns, he said to Arnath, "That fence won't do for the night. Too close to the smoke. The animals shan't like it. Where shall I bring them?"

After a moment's thought, Arnath said, "The first cut-out on the far side of the hill. Others will be round to help you shortly." He pointed along the rising curved main road, and the stranger looked, nodded he understood.

As he rode off, Arnath turned and found Illona right in front of him. "Goodness girl, what are you doing?"

"That was him." She said, wide-eyed.

"What? The fop with the beautiful horse?" Arnath said in disbelief, a thumb pointed over his shoulder the way the stranger had gone.

"Yes."

Nearby, Trellith was laying bridles and reigns flat on the ground. He gave a snort and said, "Him? He looks like a rich man on holiday. He wouldn't have hurt you."

"My mate and I have known brigands aplenty, and I assure you, Illona, he is not one of them." Arnath said, his hands on her shoulders. "Next time I send you out of town, I shall send an escort."

Illona beamed at this, "So, I get to go again?"

"Of course, you did a very good job, despite the foolishness with the stranger. I take part in the blame for that. I should have sent a couple of you, instead of you alone with a head full of warnings of rape and robbery." With that Arnath flicked his hand, ushering her on to continue helping the others. As she dashed off, he looked down at Trellith, who continued to straighten out the leathers on the ground.

"Can they be saved?"

"I'll need the oils from inside. Hope they didn't burn up." Trellith thought a moment and said, "Captain, we're getting deep into the night here. Perhaps we should..." letting the last hang just as he did in the field when he wanted to suggest the Captain give a particular order, without letting the others under his command hear the second-in-command making such decisions.

Arnath understood him immediately, "Too right." He said and cupped his hands next to his mouth and called out, "Hear me! All who work at the outpost, tomorrow is a rest day! There will be no work tomorrow. Spread the word!"

There were some hearty hails from all around. Just then Apaulon came up to Arnath, somewhat winded. "The signal torches are lit. On both sides of town. Guardsmen should be here soon."

"Good. We'll need some stationed at the first cut-out on the other side of the hill. Our horses will be returned there. Illona's "attacker" is off looking for them now." Arnath said.

"The man in the black finery? Here?" Apaulon asked, a little dumbfounded.

"Helped us fight the fire, and now he's off seeking our horses. One would think Illona might have been wrong about him." Trellith said from his place on the ground.

This drew laughs from Apaulon and Arnath. Apaulon then said, "I'll go to the top of the hill, the spot near the outpost door where I can see from either direction where the first guardsman come."

Before he turned away, Apaulon saluted Arnath, and they both laughed at the boy's inability to break command habits. As Apaulon ran up the cobblestone road, a woman approached. She carried two squat stools under her one arm, and a long wooden vessel in the other. Arnath recognized her as Feila, Illona's mother, one of the town seamstresses and washer women. She was tall and freckled like her daughter, but unlike her daughter dressed in the draping feminine whites of her profession, rather than the strangely manly clothes Illona wore.

"Careful now. The oil is still hot from the fire." Feila said as she set the tall wooden vessel down near Trellith, and set the stools on the ground.

"Bless you, woman. You save my poor knees." Trellith said as he sat down on his stool, and took a rag from her to dip into the oil. Together they began rub the oil into the damaged leathers.

Arnath was feeling somewhat out of use, and thought he'd best check inside the stable, perhaps root out the cause of the fire. He got not two steps toward the stable when he heard Apaulon urgently calling "Captain! Captain Arnath!" from the top of the hill.

*

As he raced up the hill, Arnath could see Apaulon standing at the doorway of the outpost. When he got closer, he could see the nervous expression on the boy's face, the tremble in his hand as he pointed into the outpost. "There, sir." Apaulon croaked, his voice quavering.

With his borrowed sword still beside the lake, Arnath stepped into the doorway and knelt to grab a long piece of broken wood. He hefted the burn-blacked cudgel and strode down the hall. In the moonlight, he could see a shadow on the ground in the back courtyard. Getting closer, he saw the shadow was a fallen man.

Stepping into the courtyard, Arnath knew who it was right away. In all the excitement of the fire, he forgot that he had sent this man to get the large pots from beside the spring pool. And on the ground near him was one of the many deep cauldrons the cooking and washing women used during the work day, the ground all around it freshly wet. He'd done as Arnath asked, but something stopped him from leaving here. Arnath stood over the man, and poked him with the burnt wood. No movement or response. Then Arnath knelt, taking the man by the shoulder and rolled him roughly onto his back.

Two things were immediately revealed. The man's knife was there on the ground. He had had time to pull his weapon on whatever assailed him back here in the darkness. The other was that he was without a doubt dead.

Both his face and hands were twisted in a rictus of painful death. Whatever killed him caused great agony before sending him into the blackness. Up his left side, spreading up from under his shirt, was an undulating black pattern that looked like chaotic lighting bolts on his skin. This ugly pattern mired his pale skin all the way up his neck and across his taut cheek.

Arnath stood again, looking down at the man whose name he didn't even know with pity. This day he had been accused of theft, shamed before his peers, taken to jail and then died in unimaginable agony. A horrible final day.

Arnath turned, stepped closer to the doorway, and called down the corridor to where the young guardsman waited. "Apaulon! Fetch the sheriff. And the mayor, if he is about."

Apaulon bolted out of sight. Again, Arnath turned to looked at the contorted man on the ground. His thoughts drifted back to what he'd said about curses by the lakeside. By retiring from adventuring, and opening this outpost, Arnath and his companions had sought to avoid this kind of fate – a hideous and unnecessary death at the hands of something cruel. One is not killed by giant spiders if one never goes into the spider's den. And yet, here it was – That very kind of death by harsh misadventure, in the quiet of his own backyard.

*

Mayor Bumpol and Sheriff Daruun stood over the body, looking at it with consternation in the lamplight. Trellith knelt beside the body, teeth gritted as he looked closely at the black lightning pattern under the poor man's skin. "Dark magic. Has to be."

"When does the boy return?" The mayor asked.

"Likely around sunset tomorrow. Perhaps later. We did give him much to do." Arnath said, estimating Garthe's return home. His knowledge was desperately needed at the moment.

"So, the fire was some kind of distraction?" the mayor asked.

Arnath and Daruun shared a look and a nod. "Had to be. The robed figure I've chased off before must have wanted time to thoroughly search the courtyard." Daruun said.

"But he didn't expect I'd send people to fetch pots from here. They must have been surprised, struck the man down before he could raise the alarm." Said Arnath, nodding grimly down at the corpse.

"Seems to be the way of it." Trellith said, standing up. "Whether the robed figure will return is the question. Did they have time to feel out that the object was no longer here?"

They all looked around the courtyard. Even with the piles of wreckage gone it looked a mess. Tons of sand and water had been used to put out the smoky wreckage of the old outpost. This sludge had since dried into a thick mix of dried mud and debris that paved over the entire back courtyard. With the conical wreckage piles on top of it, finding anything without the benefit of magic would have been impossible.

And he had dark magic, that was for certain. It weighed heavily on Arnath's mind. Garthe knew some combat magics, but was primarily a healer. If this dark mage came after him, seeking out the jewel, could Garthe even defend himself?

Just then, Apaulon emerged from the outpost corridor with another man – The judgemental sergeant with the greying red hair and beard who had been there on the night they rousted the camp of thieves. "Sergeant Graten has arrived with a contingent of guardsmen."

The Sergeant did a slow walk around the corpse, eyes agog. Finally, he joined the group, saying, "My captain, your little band seems to attract all kinds of trouble."

"On that score, I'd like a word." Arnath said, gesturing for the sergeant to follow him.

Arnath stepped into the street after he and Graten had walked through the front corridor of the outpost. There he laid out the details involving the finding of the mysterious jewel, and how the sheriff had already encountered a shadowy figure who hunted for it. After telling the sergeant how Garthe had taken the jewel to a senior mage in Solindar, Arnath requested that guardsmen be sent to escort the boy back, despite him having a capable escort already.

"The men I sent with him are good men, experienced. But if this dark mage has his mind set on the jewel, thinking that master Garthe has it..." Arnath said, bolstering his case.

But Graten held up an interrupting hand, and nodded. "I see your point, Master Arnath. I shall send riders to escort your party back."

"Thank you, sergeant." Appreciating not only the cooperation, but also that here, in private, Graten made a point of not calling Arnath by his former rank.

"Merely a precaution. The majority of us shall stay here and see to the unpenned horses, help with initial repairs at the stables and such." Graten said, more to himself, planning his duties over the next several days. His eyes flicked a moment, a thought occurring to him, "This dark mage, they do keep returning to this spot. One might imagine it would be from nearby. There haven't been any suspicious strangers in town of late, have there?"

*

Arnath, Graten and two torch-bearing Guardsman approached the cut-out quietly. Having gone down to the lake to retrieve his possessions, Arnath was now fully dressed, and fully armed. With his sword out, he stepped into the second cut-out away from town on the short eastern road that led to the King's road. They could hear the stirrings of the many restless horses, who had been rounded up over the course of the night and tied to a strong improvised line that spanned the first cut-out on the road closer to town.

As discussed earlier, Sergeant Graten bade Arnath take the lead, as he somewhat knew the man and there would be less likelihood of confrontation. Arnath stepped up to the legs sticking out from under the small, upright bivy by the dead fire and tapped on the side of one of the ornate boots with his sword.

Immediately, the flaps of the man-sized tentment flew aside, and revealed the swarthy stranger, a dagger in his hand. Arnath had raised his sword, which now hovered near the man's chin. "We would have words with you."

Having just awoken, the man in black took a moment to realize what was happening, and then said, "Of course." He shoved his dagger into the ground near Arnath's feet. "All my other weapons are over there." he said, indicating his pack and bows and quiver.

Sitting forward from his bivy, he said, "What can I do for you gentlemen?"

"You're aware a man was killed in the village tonight?" Graten asked.

"I am." The man in black nodded. "From what I know, I was helping to fight the fire at the time. Afterwards, I was helping gather up the horses."

"We know you can't be actually responsible for the death, but considering it took place on the night you got here, we would like to know what your business is." Graten said from his position behind Arnath.

"I understand." The stranger looked around Graten at the young soldiers with him. "Send the boys away."

"What's this?" Graten said dumbfounded.

"Yes, man - to what purpose?" Arnath said, a little annoyed at the man's tone.

"I can tell you who I am and why I am here, but only you. The lower ranks are full of rumours, and it can't become widespread that I am here." The man said, his voice now completely sincere.

Arnath thought on it a moment, then turned to nod at Graten. More curious than assured, the sergeant then turned to the young guardsmen, took one of their torches and bade them return to the village and help at the stables. Not needing to be told twice, the two young man trotted off towards town.

Arnath and Graten turned back, fully expecting an answer. The man rose slowly, his hands still up and went to his pack. He rummaged in it briefly, fully aware Arnath was near him with his sword at ready in case what came out of the pack held any threat. The man in black drew his hand out and showed them both what was in his palm.

It was an ornate metal badge of office, perhaps twice the size of a saddle conch. Like a saddle conch it was mounted on a slab of thick, tooled leather. The badge itself was cast of interlacing silver and gold with a sparse few highlighting jewels at points. The sculpting was that of the seal of the king. Anyone who bore such a badge had every right to speak on the king's behalf, in any situation, including outranking generals at war.

Red-faced, Arnath immediately slammed his borrowed sword into its scabbard. "If only you'd said..."

"I'm sorry, good sir. Had we known..." Graten blustered, attempted to perform the traditional upper-breast touching salute and nearly burning his beard with the torch in the process.

His sword away and his hand free, Arnath made his salute with more dignity, reaching up across his chest and covering over his captain's clasp, a gesture that traditionally meant "I am yours to command."

The man gestured for them to relax, and said, "I'm the crown's arcane investigator. I've been sent by the palace to investigate the disturbance caused by the magic object in your courtyard. I am Heflynn, of the court of King Kordollon."

Arnath's eyes grew wider, "Heflynn? As in Heflynn, son of Domar?"

"The same." Heflynn said, uncertain how Arnath could know him.

"The last time I saw you, you were this big," Arnath said, smiling and holding his hand at his waist. "You were in the front row at the ceremony wherein I received my last decoration, dangling your feet from your chair and bored to near tears. It is good to see you again, my prince."

"Prince?!" said Graten, near choked for breath.

"Heflynn is the third son of the king's brother, Prince Domar. I fought beside his father and uncle, so long ago."

"Yes. At the battle of Isthmar." The prince said, nodding, entirely familiar with the tale.

"That's right." Arnath turned, looked at the stars, recognized the ones he sought and pointed to the northlands under them. "About fifteen leagues that way."

When he turned back, Arnath saw Graten's face was nearly purple from lack of breath. Perhaps the poor man was not equipped to not only meet a prince this night but also to learn that Arnath, a man he had shown no small measure of disrespect, was one of the legendary heroes whose image was carved into the fresco that completely wrapped around the entire second floor of the royal palace.

*

The next day, as people cleared the burned wood away from the stables, taking it down to add to the lakeside fire pits, Garthe and his bolstered escort arrived back in Kroman's Town. Though the guardsmen had told them about the stables, upon arriving Garthe and his men halted and looked around the site, confused.

"Where shall take our horses then?" Tindall asked.

One of the guardsmen, a sharp looking girl with strawberry blonde hair, pointed a gloved hand up the hill. "Over the main street to the first cut-out."

The riders followed her lead as she led the guardsmen up the hill without pause or protest. She had practically taken over their lives from the moment she and the other three guardsmen arrived on horseback in Solindar. Her name was Listrelle – not the more feminine Listrella, she'd pointed out – and she meant business.

People stopped to watch the line of horses as it clopped up the main hill. Word had travelled swift as the wind that not only did Garthe return with their payroll, he might also be able to provide some answers in regard to the horrible death that had occurred in his absence.

One person who stepped forward to trot alongside Garthe's horse was Mayor Bumpol. He did his best to keep up with his short legs, saying between breaths, "Hail, Master Garthe. You've seen the results of the fire, no doubt. There were many injuries whilst fighting it, all fairly minor, but people will be wanting to see you."

After thinking on it a moment, Garthe said, "In a short time, I'll have a clinic at the front door of the outpost. Give it an hour or so, so I may get organized. Will you spread word?"

"I will, I will, good sir! Welcome back!" And with that the mayor was off like a tiny shot, no doubt to ready a proclamation for the town message board.

"Going to be keeping you busy." Said Shamuth as they crested the hill, nearing the front door of the outpost. Looking that way, Shamuth nodded his head toward the door, "Speaking of busy..."

Garthe turned as Illona stepped out of the outpost, a white canvas postal bag worn across her body like a sash. Upon seeing Garthe she immediately froze, but relaxed when he waved at her and smiled. "Illona, good to see you."

"And you master Garthe" Illona said, her cheeks flushing red.

"Can I send you on an errand? For the outpost, of course."

"Of course, master Garthe. Anything."

Garthe halted his horse, and said, "I need you to go to the town seamstresses, your mother or Leina. Ask for three sheets of the cleanest but lowest quality cloth. One sheet is to remain intact and the other two are to be cut into strips, say the size of a wrist. Shall I write it down?"

"No, no, I catch your meaning. One drop cloth and a plentiful number of bandages. Right?"

"Exactly. And when that is ready, if you didn't mind assisting me with our improvised clinic, I'd be grateful for the help." Garthe said, a smile in his eyes.

"Of course not. I mean I wouldn't mind. I mean, I'd love to!" Illona turned red faced in embarrassment at that last blurt, and ran off like a shot down the street.

"Good lad. You tried at least." Shamuth said, joining in the nods of approval with the other members of his escort.

"If you say so." Said Garthe as he dismounted his horse. "I hope in time we can just talk without her being so nervous. We can't be much in the way of friends if she is."

"That'll come, lad. Trust me." Said Shamuth, readying to detach his saddle bags.

Up ahead on the road, Listrelle had turned back, a look of consternation on her face. "Are we not going to put up the horses?"

"Outpost business first." Shamuth said, then patted the saddle bag he had over his shoulder, just like Fernlow, Tindall and Amorth, the saddle bag letting out a loud jingle with each pat.

"I see." Listrelle said, her brows knit, clearly disliking the disruption of the plan in her mind. She then ushered her own men onwards to billet their horses in the cut out at the bottom of the hill.

*

Emerging into the back courtyard, Garthe and the others found no one else there.

"I wonder where'd they be." Tindall said.

"What should we do with these?" Fernlow asked, patting his coin-stuffed saddle bag.

"Perhaps down at the lake. Dirty work, taking care of all this, and the stables as well." Said Shamuth pointing at the charred slats of wood just over their heads.

"Could go to the Briny Sea, get a table by the door, watch out for them." Said Amorth, shrugging.

Turning to Garthe for a suggestion, all the old men froze. Garthe was stepping lightly forward, one creeping step at a time, his left hand outstretched toward the ground. To Garthe's old escorts his movements seemed unnaturally slow, as if guided by magic.

Garthe reached a particular spot on the ground and he circled round it, keeping his palm over the spot. He then knelt, letting his hand dip down and hover over the area, back and forth, his eyes closed the entire time.

His escorts stood very still, partly in fear of what they were seeing and also out of respect for the young mage at his mysterious works. They kept still even when Arnath, Trellith, Shrakar and a swarthy stranger quietly stepped into the yard. Arnath moved beside Shamuth, who whispered, "The place where the body fell?"

"Yes." Whispered Arnath, nodding.

"Went straight to it, he did. Our guardsman escort made no mention of the position or anything."

Arnath again nodded, and moved silently toward the boy. Shrakar and Trellith did the same. Reaching him, they knelt around him and waited.

As he passed his hand over the spot again and again, Garthe began first to sweat, then to tremble. Then, as though bursting free, Garthe's eyes opened and he fell back into Shrakar's arms. At first, he was surprised, but then greatly comforted to find all three of his surrogate fathers kneeling over him.

"Tell us, Garthe - What it was?" Arnath asked gently.

"Yes, son, what do you know?" Trellith said.

Sitting up with Shrakar's help, Garthe nodded. "It is indeed black magic. The blackest."

Curious looks passed between Treillth, Shrakar and Arnath. All of them had dealt with dark magics wielded by evil men in their time. This time, it felt different...

"The creature who committed this murder," Said Garth, sitting up under his own power and adjusting his robes. "... was a Necromancer."

Unsettled looks passed among everyone in the yard.

A practitioner of the blackest, most reviled of the dark magical arts had walked among them just one night ago.

END OF PART ONE

PART TWO: THE OUTPOST

CHAPTER SIX

The night Garthe had identified the dark magic as necromancy, a forbidden part of magic that manipulated the veils between life and death, he busied himself by building a ritual fire over the spot where the dead man fell to cleanse the ground and begin the brewing of a salve for the townsfolk's many burns.

As he did this, Garthe also laid out his day in Solindar, with Shamuth, Amorth, Fernlow and Tindall filling in details, as well as assisting with his works. They had awoken early, ate at the inn and gone directly to the bank, where Garthe presented his jots and letters to the elves who recognized him from their last visit, but not his escort, who could have been kidnapping extortionists in their eyes. Once that was cleared up, Garthe deposited a great deal of money in the account of the Lorta the builder, and then received four saddle bags of counted coin, that would comprise the outpost payroll for approximately a month.

They then went to Lorta, to speak to him and his foreman, a muscular elf name Taishen. Garthe gave Lorta the account deposit receipt and then showed them the many drawings he and the others had done. Lorta and Taishen spread the drawings out on a huge table, calling over their specialists. There was no debate about where to begin – the smithy, obviously. But once that was established, it was as though an explosive Elfin war council had broken out, each specialist arguing over whose craft should be layered into the five-story structure next.

"Best you leave it to us, good lad." Said Lorta, realizing their human guests had been entirely cut out of the discussion. "We shall see you all in three days time."

They lunched at the inn, Garthe nervously fretting over whether the elves would even follow their instructions. He got to see the lovely Shimalena one more time before leaving town, a detail that seemed to be of more importance to Garthe's old guardsman to than to the thoroughly embarrassed Garthe himself.

They went to several other businesses after lunch – Tailors, leather workers, Elfen smiths who worked primarily on magically infused weapons, and more. The goal being to establish further contacts with service providers that the outpost itself could not provide. Clients heading west toward Solindar could pick up an order made from the outpost in a matter of days, those heading east could receive their order via post in relatively the same amount of time. In time, such relationships would be developed in Morley and other places to the east of Kroman's Town.

At noon, all four of them went to Shimar's. The escorts waited outside when Garthe was welcomed in and introduced to an ancient-looking elf from a town further to the south. The further south you got the more puritanical, traditionalist the elves got, and thus were more immersed in their elder lore. Though she was old, Shinthala was not crone-like. She leant on a long staff; head held with great dignity. She bade them all sit, and asked many questions of Garthe, her voice thickly accented as she spoke the common tongue. When her questions ended, she nodded and removed a scroll from the folds of her robe.

"Shimar has shown me the stone. And from your description of jewel I believe it to be one of the many live-stones." She unfurled the scroll in her lap, and read to them an account of how a live-stone, a tool of necromancy, was a man-made jewel that could hold within the lives of many, a kind of archive of the souls and wills of many persons and of how one had taken possession of a man, and made him kill the new husband of a recently widowed woman who had been married to a cantankerous mage.

The mage had reached out with his essence from the stone to interfere with the lives and happiness of living persons. Garthe thought on this, realizing the mages who had fought until the stone destroyed the old outpost may not have even wanted the stone at all. It simply bade them to kill each other so it could absorb their energies.

While it was easy to get lost in dark thoughts as they waited for the healing salve to boil, there was one thing Garthe received from Shimar that brought some happiness. He reached into his pack and produced two monocles of thick glass that hung from the same hide thong. To Trellith he said, "These are only temporary. When Shimar comes to fully stock my lab, he will examine you more thoroughly and fit you for a proper pair to wear across your nose."

Trellith looked at the two monocles that hung on the durable leather necklace. One was a bubble of clear glass, the other a bubble of darkened glass. Trellith fit the dark one into his eye socket and looked directly into the fire. His heart filled with elation right away. Within the fire he could see every nook and cranny of the burning logs, and even the tiniest flaky ashes, and without the brightness hurting his eyes. "That's it! I can see!" He said drawing a celebratory clap from his friends.

As they set up a table and lanterns on the street outside the outpost, Garthe continued his story as he ministered the wounds of the many who had helped fight the fire at the stables. Illona soaked bandages in the pot of hot healing salve and Garthe would bind bandages over their burns, and pass his healing stone over them. For each person he gave a different instruction: leave these on for two days, you should be alright after tomorrow, come see me in three days and I will redress this.

At one point, an old woman was saying her thank you's after receiving Garthe's care and placed a handful of coins on the edge of the table. "That's not necessary, ma'am." Garthe said, about to scoop up the coins and hand them back.

"Wait!" exclaimed Trellith and disappeared into the outpost. A moment later, he reappeared with a ledger and a quill, and took his time writing a note, his new clear monocle affixed in his eye. He then tore off page and laid it on the edge of the table, pushing the old woman's coins onto the bottom of the paper.

The top of the paper said: For Jaross

From then every patient laid some coin on the paper, those that didn't beg off until the outpost payroll was doled out.

And so, the line continued, and Garthe continued with his story.

*

Much to his surprise, when Garthe left Shimar's house, with a full sack of mage's supplies and a promise from Shimar to come and help him fully set up his practice once construction had begun, he found their numbers had doubled.

Along with his older, war-weary escorts, a party of young King's guard had joined them, led by a beautiful, if haughty, young woman named Listrelle. She informed them of the deliberate fire set at the stables, and that a man had been murdered in the courtyard of the outpost. And that he had been murdered by magic.

This prompted Garthe to return to the house and warn Shimar and Shinthala of what had happened before they left. The two elderly elves looked at each other with grave concern, but said they knew what to do.

From then on Listrelle took charge, dictating the pace of their ride back to Kroman's Town with persnickety detail. She even tried to stop Garthe's escorts from slowing down to receive a basket of turnips for Shrakar from Merynda on the road back, much to the embarrassment of those under Listrelle's command. But Shamuth wouldn't have it, the spurning of a gift because of a sense of urgency. It was just plain bad manners.

As Garthe finished his tale, the last of the line of patients were treated. And by then, Shrakar had finished all the turnips Merynda had gifted him.

*

The next day Trellith set up a table near where the washer and cooking ladies normally worked, and began to dole out the back-dated payroll. The entire workforce lined up outside, and one at a time gratefully signed for the pay owed them since they had begun to bundle the wreckage piles. Many left a coin in a box Trellith had set at the edge of the table to support the re-roofing of Jaross's stables.

One man in line was barely recognizable. He had freshly cut hair, new work boots and pants – which had a pair of new work gloves tucked in the waistband, a fine lace-up shirt and his formerly ruddy teeth looked as though they had been cleaned. It wasn't until he approached the table and gave his name as Kewin that Trellith and Arnath recognized him. He was the two-fisted man who had argued with the ill-fated man who died by magic just the other day. Arnath surmised watching the man at the table that, after the sheriff had released him, he had spent his Arkonion gold coin on making some needed improvements in his life, rather than on a month-long drinking binge. Arnath respected that, especially after he saw Kewin toss two valuable silver coins into the charity box for Jaross.

Rather than leave after he was fully paid, Kewin stepped over to Arnath, his head down in humility, and said, "Please, Captain, I know I caused a disruption the other day. And I never woulda done it if I knew poor Bowdry was near such a horrible end. But, please Captain, don't dismiss me from your work force. I had no real profession for some years until you've come. I promise I won't fight over the gold with anyone. The chance to find any would change my life for good. Please don't turn me away."

Arnath could see from the sincerity of the man's expression that his was a life that had held little promise or hope. Arnath had the man's very dignity in his hands and he was not going to treat that lightly. "It will be sweaty work today, Kewin. You'll ruin your fine shirt."

"No, sir. It's a warm day. Just won't wear it." With that Kewin unlaced and stripped off his shirt, hanging over the courtyard fence.

"Good man. Over there with the others." Arnath said, watching Kewin join the selected work crew for the day and turned back to the table as the last of the payroll was dispersed.

*

The work Arnath and Shrakar had devised for the day was simple: Before the elves arrived with their construction materials, the ruddy soil of the back yard had to be dug out. All of it, and at least a foot deep. After the construction was done, soft sand from around the lake would be spread across the training yard, to soften the blow of frequent falls, but for now all of this refuse infused soil had to go.

It was sweaty work indeed as they worked from the very back of the yard, where the smooth, rocky wall of the mound made a natural back barrier, pushing forward as one long crew, from the fence that touched the mound to the spring pool, whose over-hanging source created another natural enclosure on the opposite side of the yard. They dug forward, a couple of feet at a time, edging closer and closer to the back of the outpost. The dirt was shovelled a huge pile on the opposite side of the yard from where the cooks and washers worked, meant to be carted away by tomorrow's workforce and dumped in the swamplands that lay north-east of town.

As expected, plenty of gold coins were found as the work progressed. Shamuth, who stood guard over the worksite - always keeping one eye on Garthe as he drew up further building plans at the back table - discouraged the men from shouting out with glee every time they found something, and thus disrupting the work. True to his word, Kewin made no fuss when he overturned a large clod of caked-together earth and revealed a veritable mother-load. He simply knelt, gathered up a fistful coins for himself, and then said, "Fellas, come look at this!"

Everyone gathered round, marvelling at Kewin's find, all of them saying how lucky he was. Arnath came over and looked. Even with all the workers hands reaching in and out of the hole, it was easy to see it was indeed a fortune in gold coins. All of it Arkonian.

"Have at it, fellas. I got plenty." Kewin said, smiling as he went to work on another spot. Arnath gave Shamuth a look, wanting to get the excited men and women under control.

"Let's grab a barrow. Divvy it all up later." Shamuth said. Disappointed their free-for-all was abruptly ended, the workers started scooping the gold coins into a wheel barrow. As they got near the bottom, Shamuth shouted out, "Wait!"

Everyone's eyes turned to Shamuth, who called out, "Master Trellith! Over here!"

Trellith bounded over, and looked at the deep divot in the earth. He knelt and swept aside the last of the gold coins, revealing a large map embedded in the mud. "Oh my…" he said, then turned to look up at Shamuth. "This is delicate work. I'll need a couple of trowels and some shoe brushes. "

Garthe joined Trellith, and for the next hour they progressively freed the map while the yard work continued around them. Chipping away like sculptors working marble, they tapped the imprisoning mud away from the edges and folds of the map until they could lift it free. Together, Trellith and Garthe carried it to a newly strung line the washer women had spanned near the counting table. Hanging it over the line, they began to gently sweep over it with dusters and brooms, letting the dried mud fall away. Soon familiar lines began to show.

"Arnath! I think we've found it!" Trellith exclaimed.

"Found what?" Arnath asked, driving his shovel into the ground and stepping over to join them by the line.

"I believe this is the outpost's master map." Trellith said, continued sweep dust off the ornately painted and stitched cloth, using his thick monocle to spy specific markings on the map. "Look here – the borders between the northern and southern kingdoms in both the common and elf tongue."

"And on this side, the rolling forest between Mayhairn and Solmairith." Garthe said, barely seen, his head bobbing back and forth on his side of the line.

"Repairing it will take a mighty bit of work," Trellith said leaning in close to Arnath. "But it will be worth it. This, this is the find, the true gold. Maintaining a map of the known world will be of greatest service to our clients, the heart of our business."

Nodding, Arnath said, "And restoring this will get us half way there." Arnath took a deep breath, and was grateful for their fortune. After days of fires and deaths, this was indeed a blessing. He was just about to turn to head back to his shovel and the work, when he noticed almost the entire work crew looking curiously over at the map. "Well then. I'll guess we'll call that lunch. Come, you all. Grab some food and have a look."

*

After he'd eaten, Arnath stepped through the front corridor intent on crossing the street and speaking with Durnly about the on-coming wave of elf labourers. Right outside the door, he found Illona in an argument with postal worker seated upon a cart. Illona held the outpost's postal pennon like it were a queen's sceptre, punctuating every point of her argument with a wave of it. It turned out, Illona merely had a gripe with the notion that no western-bound postal carts had come in a day or two, and how was that a way to run a postal service?!

Rather than laugh at the plight of the poor young man, Arnath waved him on. With the greatest relief the young postal worker snapped his horse's reigns, and was off down the eastern slope of the main road.

Arnath reminded Illona that all posts bound for Solindar, or the west in general, were to be held until after Lorta and his craftsmen arrived. They themselves would be travelling the king's road west several times a week, so posts could go with them, most of them being orders and supply instructions anyway.

This seemed to deflate Illona. It left her with nothing to do today. Arnath promised as soon as something came up, he would seek her out and set her to the task, which appeased her a great deal.

Arnath found Durnly with his hands full behind the bar. Much of the outpost workforce not engaged today was here at the Briny Sea, whether for luncheon, or just to spend their newly earned coin on an afternoon off. Arnath made note to check on Jaross later and see that he was getting the help he needed. When Arnath stopped in front of the exasperated Durnly, the man merely said, "Not now, your bloody workers are keeping me busy. Fancy man is outside, if you are looking for proper conversation."

Arnath stepped away, strode over to the balcony, and found Heflynn seated at a table by himself, sipping at a goblet of wine. The balcony was full with drinkers and diners, enjoying a view that spanned from the rock formation on the west side of the lake, the fin, to nearly Morley in the Eastern horizon. Arnath saw that Listrelle also sat alone at a nearby table, eyes fixed on the view and refusing to turn his way.

"Don't bother, Captain. I tried." Heflynn said ironically, pointing the captain to the chair next to him. As Arnath sat, Heflynn said, "One would think the charms of a boy from court were wasted on her."

"With this view, can you blame her?" Arnath said putting his feet up and letting the sun shine on his face.

"Indeed." Heflynn agreed, sipping at his wine. "I've seen much of the kingdom, but this view... No wonder you choose to retire here."

"Retire." Arnath laughed. "I've worked more in the last week than I did in the last weeks of the war."

Suddenly, Durnly appeared beside him and roughly set a frothy stein in front of Arnath. "This won't be the end of it either. You've brought money and life into town again. We went from ghosts and cobwebs to hustle and bustle overnight. Try that. It's the red ale from the south."

Arnath took an obliging sip and liked what he tasted. "It's good."

"Good. I'll order more casks. Your workers are gonna drink it all before days end." With that Durnly was off again.

Arnath and Heflynn raised their glasses to each other and drank deeply. "He's not wrong, you know."

"About what?" Arnath asked.

"About you and your men revitalizing the area. Not sure if you knew, but on recent maps it merely shows the northward arcing road, a dot that says "Kroman's" and nothing more. No mention of a natural, recreational lake, the beautiful rock formations off the western tip of the mound. The idyllic look of the town itself. There are no signs on either side of the king's road indicating that all of this is here. A shame really."

Arnath thought between sips of his ale, then said, "I'd hate to be the one who spoils it. Most outposts attract all the wrong sort."

"Spoils it?" Heflynn grinned. "You've told me what you're trying to achieve. Ruffians will take one look at the beautiful Elfin architecture you've commissioned and slink away. Why you'll be the reason the royal seal will be beside every door of every business in town one day. You'll see."

Arnath was taken aback by the notion. He had not even thought that their outpost would merit the royal seal of approval, and thus be included in all official maps. That "TO" for Traveller's Outpost on a map meant steady business for the lifetime of any inn that earned it.

Arnath sipped on this, allowing his eyes to drift over to Listrelle's table and noted that she had gone from staring into the sunlit fields and the lake to listening rather pointedly to their conversation.

That was when a blood-curdling shriek rang out across the street.

Arnath and Heflynn were up immediately, racing for the door. Listrelle was close behind, her unbuckled rapier and belt clenched in her hand.

Illona got out of the doorway as the trio shot through, then sprinted right in after them.

In the back courtyard, as the four of them emerged - Heflynn an arrow nocked in his short bow, Listrell her rapier at ready - they came across an odd site. Shamuth had his arm around one of the few women who were digging out the yard, and was leading her away from a hole that everyone else was looking down into with pained expressions. As Arnath approached, Trellith shook his head, indicating there was no danger. "Was bound to happen. Likely there will be more."

Getting close Arnath, Heflynn, Listrelle and Illona looked curiously into the hole. With one glimpse, Illona buried her face in Garthe's shoulder. Within the hole were a gnarled, mud caked hand and foot.

"Should we find more, we'll take it all down to the graveyard, and say proper blessings over them." Garthe said, turning his cheek toward Illona. "Please go inside and get the drop cloth we used on the table last night."

Not looking again at the grisly sight, Illona slunk away and disappeared into the outpost.

Arnath looked at the hole, and thought again of curses. Heflynn could see his consternation and said quietly to him in a wry tone, "I meant what I said to you. But still, just in case, you might want to plug the bottom of that spring pool, lest a kraken or some other terrible beast emerge from it one day."

*

The work was done as twilight fell over Kroman's Town. The entire yard had been dug up, from the rocky back wall to the back door that led into the main front corridor of the outpost. More gold and maps had been found, along with many weapons and pieces of armour, as had also been more parts of dead persons. It put a decided pall over the work every time a piece of one of the ill-fated outpost guests was found, tinged only slightly with joy when more Arkonian gold was found.

As the day's payroll was doled out – a mere pittance compared to the gold obtained by each of the workers that day – Arnath and Shrakar said their thank you's to each of the workers as they left and asked if they wanted an escort home. Though the fortunes in their pockets was a great temptation for any thief, most felt that there was no one in town who would steal from them. The only strangers in town were Heflynn, who worked for the royal court, and Listrelle and her guardsmen, those who offered up their services to escort workers home to begin with.

Earlier Illona had been dispatched to the mayor's office, to announce the plans to bury and perform proper rites over the remains of the deceased outpost guests. Word was put out that a procession down to the town graveyard would take place in the fullness of night.

As Kewin received his days pay in hand, he swung his hand over the charity box and dumped all of his coins in. Nearby, Arnath gave him an approving nod, saying, "You're sure you want to give it all away?"

"Yes, captain.' Kewin said, lacing up the front of his fine shirt. "The gold I found in the yard today will sustain me for a year, maybe more. And that's only if I do no other work that whole time. It's only right we help Jaross in his time of need."

"What other work would you do?"

"May I show you?" Kewin said, gesturing toward the back door. "We'll be back in time for the procession."

Arnath gestured for Kewin to lead on, then followed him through the back door.

*

They had walked into town, turned at the message board, which was festooned like a ship in a regatta with all the mayor's many notifications regarding recent events. They passed the baker's shop, coming to a darkened shop front. Kewin rattled a heavy key in the door, and opened it for Arnath to peer inside. There were counters, work tables, heavy spools of thread on racks and many upright and quite realistic stuffed models of human, even Orc, hands. Arnath quickly surmised what he was looking at.

"You're a glover."

"My parent's business. They trained me when I was young. But when they died, from illness, both of them, so suddenly... The grief was too much. I thought perhaps now, in my good fortune, I would try it again." Kewin said peering into the darkness. "Far too much room for just me upstairs. Might rent out rooms. Not like at your inn, not to travelling adventurers, but to workers who come to live here for the construction of the outpost."

Noting this wasn't the first time today he'd heard the outpost was shouldering the weight of the town on its back, Arnath said, "A good plan." And left it at that.

*

Later, in the fullness of night, the town had gathered in their most somber attire and began the slow procession down the graveyard. They all fell in behind the cart that had the many remains of the outpost guests in a bundle onboard as it rolled down the main street and continued on the eastern road.

The graveyard of Kroman's Town and the surrounding area was situated to the north-east of town, in a forested patch of land off a road that pointed straight up from the second cut-out in the arcing road connecting Kroman's to the King's Road. The road led up, all the way passed the swamp lands, and then disappeared into a sparse forest. The graveyard was laid out in a large ring, as was traditional, that nearly touched the edges of the small forested area.

The large group encircled nearly the entire road, finally coming to a plot that had been dug with a wooden post marker. It was hoped the elves would make something more dignified whilst they worked on the outpost. The group settled themselves tightly around the grave, whilst Garthe supervised the lowering of the bundle. As the workers then stepped aside, Garthe held aloft his illumination ampule and shook it very lightly, so its bright light only shone briefly.

"We emerge into light, and in the end the light guides us ever away. May the light guide these souls." Said Garthe somberly, to which the crowd repeated, "May the light guide these souls."

A long, quiet period ensued, most having their heads down in prayer. Arnath looked around and noticed many were at a loss as to what to do next. Likely the only man they knew who had died, Roberge, the owner of the outpost, had been well memorialized two years ago when the disaster had first occurred. No one had the words for the strangers they now lay to rest.

Arnath cleared his throat, and began to sing "Let the light guide me always". Though he held no such beliefs, he was raised in such a household and knew all of the words. The town quickly joined in and sang a somber rendition of the entire song. When they'd finished, they all filed away, leaving the workmen to bury the remains.

cHaprer seven

The **he work began** in earnest days later when the elves arrived. Their arrival was a welcomed relief from the dark days that had recently passed.

The first caravan of them, and the supplies they brought, stretched on for nearly a league in length. What would seem a logistical nightmare – The placement of all equipment, supplies and persons – was, it turned out, entirely worked out before the elves had even arrived. They set the majority of their supplies on the two arcing roads that led down to the king's road on either side of town, without blocking the roadways too much at all. The elves set up a huge camp for themselves around the lake, leaving room by the portion closest to town for the citizens of Kroman's to still make use of the beach and lake itself.

Perhaps the most wonderous thing they brought with them were the huge foundation columns with which to build the five stories of the outpost upon. As per the task, each column was five stories tall, made of elf-wood and curved like a gigantic bow. Elves did not always build in straight lines, so the supports were in curves, rather than perfectly-straight columns. And when all was said and done, the last peg hammered into place, the amazing curving beams would never be seen again, having been encased in the grand structure they would support for untold years ahead. Everyone in town came down to marvel at them, like the tusks or rib bones of the most gigantic creature imagined. Listrelle took umbrage at the notion that such gigantic, potentially dangerous obstructions were in the off-shoots of the King's road. Heflynn, who always found a way to be near her whether she liked it or not, would intervene when she made her stuffy protests, dissuading Listrelle from raising any official fuss with a mere pat of the pocket he kept his badge of office in. His way of saying, the King surely approves.

This not only ended all arguments it also garnered a look of frustration entirely unique to her. Heflynn took great amusement in it, giving him another reason to metaphorically pull her pigtails.

Arnath, Trellith, Shrakar and Garthe moved all of their belongings out of the back courtyard of the outpost, and joined the elf encampment around the lake. Their spot was very near the firepit they'd used the night of the fire at the stables, under the largest tree on the eastern side of the lake, therefore not a far walk to the road and the days work.

As the last of supplies found their place on either side of town, supervised by Taishen, who rode a regal horse back and forth over the hump-back road through town to inspect the placement of the multiple dumps of elf-wood and tools and trimmings, the question of where to begin arose. Arnath knew he and his partners were not in charge of this portion of creating their business, so he was very careful in the way that he suggested to Lorta that they first repair and extend the stables. For as long as the construction project went on, there would be an army of horses that would need housing, feeding and grooming. And that would present constant problems during the construction if not handled first. So logical was what Arnath presented, Lorta did not say he agreed, he just shouted to a worker to have Taishen brought to him immediately.

Lorta and Taishen walked the grounds around the stables, pointing at this feature and that for some time, until finally arriving back at the spot where they left Arnath. "It will take two days, and will deplete some of the supplies we brought. To replace those, I'll need to send someone to Solindar immediately." Lorta said, etching a list on a scroll.

Arnath had merely to turn and find Illona, who was never far out of eyeshot in her capacity as the project's runner, ever eagerly awaiting another task to race off to. He waved her over, and asked her to find her uncle. When she raced off, Arnath turned back to the elves and explained who Illona was and that she was too young to go from town to town on her own, relating the anecdote about how she mistook the dashing Heflynn for a cutthroat on the road. Even the normally stoic elves chuckled at this, as she returned, with her uncle Shamuth trotting to keep up. Arnath relayed their instructions, and handed over the scroll Lorta had composed to Illona.

Arnath then accompanied Lorta and Taishen up the road toward the outpost, where Lorta had said there was another matter that needed attending.

It turned out, perhaps the refurbishing of the stables was a good thing to have going on first, because the construction of Trellith's smith could not take place until the last of the old outpost – the entire first and second floor – were ripped down and hauled away. While he was grateful to have seen the floors relatively intact in order to incorporate their layout into the final designs, they would have to be removed in order to install the foundation columns into the very rock of the mound. Two crews could work simultaneously – one updating the stables, the other gutting the last remains of the old outpost. Arnath was saddened by the notion that the old building had to disappear entirely, for it was what inspired them to start this business to begin with.

"We needn't haul it all away." Lorta said. "We could fashion some of the equipment storage and your climbing wall out of the sturdier slats of wood."

"Keep some of the old girl alive?" Arnath said, understanding the spirit of the suggestion.

"Precisely."

Another dilemma was brought up when they went out back to the courtyard, one that heaped no small amount of embarrassment on Arnath's shoulders. "I understand you bundled the debris from the explosion and hauled it through the front corridor." Lorta said, with a hint of inquiry.

"Yes. There was no other way to get it all out. Maybe we could have moved it over the first floor to the street with ropes and pulleys..." Arnath was saying, knowing full-well he was about to be taught a lesson in building he'd wish he had known earlier. Before Arnath even finished speaking Taishen strode over to the back fence, near where it joined the back of the building, and hopped up on one of its crossbeams to peer over the other side. He motioned Arnath over. Arnath grudgingly stepped over and mounted the fence beside Taishen. Looking over, he immediately deflated inside.

The fence, which stood head high and spanned from the back of the outpost to the rising rock wall of the mound, likely only existed for the sake of their nearest neighbour's privacy. To keep Roberge's rowdier customers from peeing on the back of their houses. There were no other fences between the one Arnath stood on, all the way down the slope of the hill, to the sparsely wooded rear of the first cut-out in the eastern road. Arnath immediately understood where Lorta was going with this notion. He also felt an utter fool for having dragged three stories worth of charred, splintering wood through the front hallway of the outpost, when all they needed to do was remove a section of this fence. It was another humbling lesson, indeed. Arnath lit off the fence, and said, "I'll go talk to our neighbours."

For the next hour Arnath went door to door, speaking with the people who lived in the four attached homes next to the old outpost on the eastern side of the sloping road. The last house, the fifth, was an abandoned cottage less than twenty feet from the first cut-out in the eastern road. Arnath explained, that if they, his neighbours, could tolerate the bustle of equipment and more being hauled, rolled and dragged up the hill behind their houses for a month or so, and only during daylight hours, they would always have access to their front doors and most of the street for the duration. While it took some soothing assurances to get most of them to agree, old lady Minidell, who ran the dusty post office in the town hall and was widow to an elf husband, was quite pleased with the notion that she would be able to watch a parade of "fine looking elf gentlemen with their shirts off for a month or more" right outside her window.

This solved no end of problems. Rather than hauling the gigantic, curvy foundation beams up the rising main street, they could be hauled across the grassy lands under the balcony of the Briny Sea, over to the eastern road and then up the back way to be positioned from the back courtyard. Far less dangerous than trying it from the main street, especially since a pully system could be mounted on the top of the mound and each massive beam could be gently set in place without ever hanging them precariously over the pedestrian populace of the town.

The only problem, and only a legal technicality, was that under the laws of the kingdom obstructing one of the King's road cut-outs was a minor offense. Seeking to get around the wait of a posted request, and the potential of dealing with an unruly bureaucrat, Arnath went straight from Old lady Minidell's tiny house back up the hill and across the street to the Briny Sea. There he found a red-faced, sweat drenched Durnly racing this way and that behind the long bar, doing his peg-legged best to keep up with the orders given by his serving women, who themselves were swamped with a full house of drinking and dining elves.

Durnly gave Arnath a sidelong look, as he grabbed up a tankard and quickly poured from the cask of red ale. He slammed the tankard down in front of Arnath as he passed, immediately busying his hands with another drink. "And to think, I thought you were going to ruin my business." Durnly said, shaking his head.

Arnath picked up his tankard of ale, and guilty-faced, asked, "Shall I get you some help?"

"From where? Everyone who can work in our little town is working on your project. There's no young blood left." Durnly grouched in an exasperated tone, and then disappeared down the bar.

Arnath squeezed passed the busy serving girls and found Heflynn alone at the end of the packed balcony, his unofficial perch of late from which to gather intelligence about the necromancer and other dark matters for the crown. He stood, sipping wine and leaning against one of the posts that supported the over-hanging tarp and looked west. Arnath strode down the balcony, exchanging nods with many of the elves who recognized him as one of the four owners of the business they were about to build. He joined Heflynn and turned to see what so held the archer's attention.

The western valley below was a bustle of activity. A full tent city now stood around the lake, from this vantage appearing to be populated with hundreds of tiny people going this way and that, and the road leading away from the stables held a hundred palettes of building supplies, as well as the gigantic monster bones of the foundation columns leaning upright against the fin.

Heflynn toasted in the direction of the giant elf-wood columns, and said, "So the great work begins."

"And all the little, not so great works as well." Said Arnath somewhat sheepishly. Looking away from the west, Arnath sipped from his ale and noted something new to the east. On the western side of the swamplands to the north of the eastern road was a long row of portable commodes stretching almost to the forest. At least they've planned for that, Arnath thought, staring over his ale.

Heflynn, sensing his discomfort, asked "What is it?"

"I hate to bother you with this, but..." Arnath said slowly.

And before Arnath could even finish, Heflynn extended his pinkie finger away from the base of his wine goblet – the finger with the small copy of the royal signet ring on it. There were perhaps twenty-five of the embossed golden rings throughout the kingdom, worn by officers of the crown who needed to affix their seal to requests to the palace or to expedite orders given in the palaces' name. "Ooh. You need to borrow this? Not a problem, captain. I know what pressures this endeavor has you under. What's it for?"

Arnath explained about the first cut-out and what was going to happen with the construction supplies, how they were to be moved into the back courtyard. Heflynn grinned and said, "I'd bet you wish you had thought of that a couple of weeks ago."

"True. But then we did not have the lovely Listrelle marching from one end of town to another enforcing by-laws." Arnath said, wondering if Heflynn could do something about her fastidiousness too.

Catching Arnath's thread, Heflynn said, "Ahhh, there are some things even the royal seal cannot squeak passed."

"No?" asked Arnath, his curiosity piqued.

"No." Heflynn said, looking balefully into his wine. "The woman shows no interest in being on any kind of friendly terms with me, let alone friends at all. That said, a romance is not in the cards, and I shall leave her be. I find her dazzling to my eye, but without her interest... well, I just feel the fool. I always find the romances wherein there is a strong bond in the beginning, beyond lustful fascination, are the best."

Arnath thought on this a moment, his mind immediately going to Lanea, who was his best friend until the fate of misadventure snatched her away, in the highest of adventures, in the drunken revelries that followed, and the tender moments that followed those. Though her body against his was the purest exhilaration, it was her laugh he missed the most. "I couldn't agree more."

Knowing there was a mountain of work to accomplish still this day, and that he had taken all the time he could for talk of love and other things, Arnath threw back his head and swallowed his ale in three deep drafts. He put down his tankard, laid a hand on his chest and exhaled fully to ward off belching loudly in front of a balcony of elf strangers. "I'll send Trellith by to see you when we have documents ready."

Heflynn raised his glass to Arnath as he left, and continued watching the mustering army of workers below.

*

"A posted advertisement? Who would answer it? We've met everyone in town by now, haven't we?" a befuddled Trellith asked as he handed Arnath a wooden plate laden with meat and stewed vegetables. Arnath shook his head as he sat with his food on a log near their firepit.

"Not for here. For Morley. For places, say, west of Solindar." Arnath said, digging in with his spoon. "What's the next near town after Solindar?"

They all thought on it a moment, but it was Garthe who looked up from the anatomy scroll he was copying, his quill to his chin, and said, "Quinhaven."

"Right – Quinhaven." Arnath said, pausing only a second to decide whether or not to tell Garthe about the black spot of ink he'd just dotted his chin with, and deciding against it, continued, "We post the signs in those two towns and get some needed help for Durnly and the others who will be feeding and serving and washing the clothes of this army we have invited to invade this poor town."

Trellith wrung his hands clean on a canvas napkin and dropped it on the wooden plate beside him. He pulled the largest of his ledgers from a nearby leather satchel and opened it in his lap. "And you specifically want me to say young? Why young in particular?"

"So, they can keep up with one hundred elves ordering peach cider and trenchers all at once. You should have seen those poor women up there today." Said Arnath between bites. "I was exhausted just watching them, and we three have been to war."

Garthe ignored that last bit. He knew well what Arnath was talking about. Conversations in the context of life before he came to be in their charge and after had happened daily since he was 9-years old.

Arnath looked around curiously, "Speaking of we three..."

Catching Arnath's meaning, Trellith looked over his shoulder, "Oh, Shrakar is helping Jaross with the horses whilst the hammering is going on. Then I hear later he has been enlisted by Taishen to hammer an anchor for ropes into the top of the mound."

Arnath thought on this for a second, then asked, "To secure the beams from above?"

"Yes, quite so." Trellith said beginning to draft a sign in light charcoal. "Though I myself await Taishen to begin pulling the smith apart, and transport it to our location."

"Sorry, friend. I should have sent word."

"Regarding?" Trellith asked, his full attention on Arnath.

Arnath told him about the need to gut the old outpost down to the foundations, which meant the installation of the smith would have to wait till a new foundation was laid. Arnath could see Trellith's face grow more and more red the longer he spoke, until finally Trellith picked up his ledger and smacked it loudly against his thighs, "That's no way to run a campaign!"

"That's just it, friend." Arnath said, gesturing for him to calm down. "While we might be experts in assembling troops to withstand a dastardly horde, assembling troops to build something that lasts, I'll defer to the experts. And so, should you."

Trellith looked away, his arms crossed. "I did have a profession before I came under your command, you know?"

"As did I," Arnath said, "But still in the passage of time, I became somewhat less than expert in it. Be better to get advice on farming from that woman who lives down the road."

"Merynda." Garthe chimed in without looking away from his scroll. "Her name is Merynda."

"Merynda. Right." Arnath said absently, eyes staring off.

"And that's another way to muddy a campaign. The two of you all star-crossed for your messenger girl and your woman of the fields. Best to concentrate on the task at hand. I'll tell you this much, and I truly mean it," Trellith said, gruffly picking up his charcoal and resuming his lettering. "The next town we start a business in had better be packed to the borders with dwarf women."

*

Illona and Shamuth had made it to Solindar just shortly after noon. With the task being as simple as Illona delivering some instructions to Lorta's business and Shamuth knowing exactly where that was, they were done within minutes of arriving. Shamuth suggested they go to the large inn, have some lunch and maybe shop in the fine clothing stores, so the day wasn't entirely a waste. Illona only agreed if they could first go to the local post office, so she could have a look.

As they rode through the town, Illona did her best to not stare and gape in wonder at the elves. This was their home after all. It was one thing to watch them going about their business in Kroman's where they had come for the great build, but somehow here in their home streets, it seemed ill-mannered.

One elf did catch her eye, however, and it was entirely her uncle's fault. Whilst they dined at the inn, Shamuth had made an off-hand remark upon seeing Shimalena about her being Garthe's girlfriend, and that nearly made Illona's head spin. How could she herself compete with this veritable goddess of a girl if that were true? And if it were true, why was master Garthe being so nice to her of late? He really had gone out of his way to include her in all the goings-on at the outpost. It was all so confusing.

Only when she caught her uncle snickering at her discomfiture out of the corner of her eye did she relax and realize she was being had. Her family had always treated her like an odd duck, a figure of fun. For indeed she was, and she knew it. Dressing in work clothes, obsessing over the work of adults of late was only the latest in a life of eccentric behaviour. When she was much, much younger, she had once chased dragonflies around the swamp for a month. This amused, rather than disturbed her family, and they felt it gave them permission to tease her. It stung her deeply at times.

Watching Shimalena as she went gracefully from table to table, enchanting the customers, leaving them spellbound, Illona wondered what it would be like to be like that. The girl who dazzled all those around her, who wasn't the clumsy creator of calamitous accidents everywhere she went. She resided herself with the notion that she might never know.

This melancholy reverie broke when Illona saw a tall, older elf approach Shimalena, ask something of her, to which she then gestured over at their table.

"Uncle, do you know him?" Illona asked, tapping Shamuth on the elbow.

Shamuth turned, then stood up to welcome Shimar as he approached their table.

"I did not wish to disturb your luncheon, but word was that you were here, and I thought I might impose upon you to relay a message to Master Garthe for me." Illona couldn't help but notice the deep, emotionless tone with which the old elf spoke.

Her uncle replied, "But of course, Master Shimar. And may I present my niece, Illona, who works as the outpost's runner? I actually escort her on business of her own today."

Shimar gave a slight bow, and ignored Illona's outstretched hand. Shamuth gave her a scowl until she put her hand down. Elves did not shake hands, instead they exchanged bows or hand gestures of respect. Illona awkwardly let her hand fall, saying "I'm very pleased to meet you, Master Shimar."

"And I you, young lady." Shimar said, entirely ignoring her social faux pas, then turning back to Shamuth, "Would you please tell Master Garthe I shall be in Kroman's in three days time."

"Of course, I can. You should know they no longer reside at the outpost. They're in the encampment by the lake." Shamuth said.

To which Illona added, "By the largest tree on the east bank."

"At the lake, the east bank." Said Shimar, affixing it in his mind. He then bowed, and said, "Good day to you." And immediately strode away.

As Shamuth resumed his seat, Illona could see he was snickering at her. "They really don't shake hands at all?"

"No dear, they don't" Shamuth said, shaking his head at her piteously.

"We do this…" A gentle, high-pitched voice said right next to the table, startling Illona and Shamuth. They turned and saw Shimalena there. She demonstrated a gesture, taking her hand from her sternum to then letting it fall, palm up in front of her. Illona did it a couple of times, until Shimalena nodded. "Yes."

"Goodness, Shimalena." Shamuth said, "I didn't think you spoke the common tongue."

"I try, learn." Shimalena said, her accent full of rolling L's and R's. "I learn speak for healer Garthe. To talk, know better."

At that, Shamuth did his best not to laugh at the decidedly red glow that overtook his niece's cheeks.

*

Shrakar hiked with Taishen and several other elves up the wooded eastern slope of the mound. This longer hike was much easier, less steep than the opposite side, closest to the outpost, where the mound dropped off like a sheer cliff on all of its rounded sides.

They passed by the campsite where Shrakar and friends had rousted the wedding thieves, the exploded logs still strewn around the site, and continued up toward the top. The top of the mound was level almost all the way around. Those experienced with the sea compared its shaped to that of a whale, with its blunt head and downward sloping body. The top remained wooded on the eastern half, then grew almost entirely bald of greenery on the western half, the portion that Kroman's town was built under. The rock appeared to be smooth from a great distance, from the King's highway and the ground all around it, but standing upon it one could see the crags and layers of different coloured rock. Veins of earth where plants could find purchase and sunken holes where animals sheltered were abundant where they now stood, at the very peak of the mound's height.

From here, they could see the surrounding area for leagues in all directions. Even through the trees on the eastern slope, one could see not-so far away

Morley, and south of there, where the King's road split off into the central kingdom. A couple of the elves pointed to the west, where they could see their family's farmsteads just outside of white, shining Solindar. Shrakar shaded his eyes and looked north. From this height he could see the rolling fields of Isthmar, where the last great battles of the war took place. And then to the far west, the tips of the spires of the once great temples, those allowed to remain standing as reminders of the foolish religious zealotry that nearly damned his species to extinction. Among them, only Taishen was old enough to have known the war, and his eyes met Shrakar's briefly, sharing an understanding, as Shrakar looked away from his troubled homelands.

Shrakar waited for a couple of birds that had taken up residence on his shoulders to fly away, then hauled the heavy coiled rope off his shoulder. He let it fall to the ground where the others had dropped their palette full of equipment. Taishen removed a small, non-retractable scope that had varying degrees etched into its side from his belt pack. He peered through the device, and strode over several steps. There, he pointed at a crevice in the rock. He handed Shrakar the rope, bade him to hold it tight, and then walked to the edge of the mound to a point where he was almost leaning over the side, the rope taut behind him. He looked directly down into the outpost courtyard for a brief moment, and then pulled himself back up along the rope.

Satisfied they were in the right spot to anchor the ropes, Taishen motioned for all to take up their hammers and begin to drill in the pilot spikes.

*

Arnath was just coming down the stairs from Kortell's where Trellith, Lorta and several other elves were beginning to chip apart the smith, when he caught sight of Kewin waving at him from his front stoop. Arnath skirted around the many carts in front of Kortell's door meant to take the entire smithy like puzzle pieces down the road and around the corner to the outpost.

"Can I show you something, Captain?" Kewin said, beckoning Arnath up the stairs. Once inside, Arnath could see by the light of many lamps that Kewin had cleaned the entire first floor, and put his shop to rights. Not only that, there was now a large pile of kid leather work gloves on the edge of one of the work tables. "Try these." Kewin said, offering the nearest pair in the pile to Arnath.

Arnath fitted the soft, yet sturdy feeling gloves to his fingers. Though they were pliable and allowed full range of movement, they felt as though it would take something truly sharp to cut into them. Unable to get them fully onto to his hands, Arnath stripped them off and shook his head. Kewin took them from him and passed him the next pair in the pile, saying, "Bet those will do it."

And Kewin was right. Arnath was able to fit them fully onto his hands, interlacing his fingers all the way to the knuckles. "These will come in handy over the next few days. How much?"

"Nothing for you, captain." Kewin said, waving the notion away. "But I was hoping you would buy the lot for the site. Hand them out to the workers. Surely, they brought their own, many of them..."

"But for those that didn't, you would be the one to supply them." Arnath said, finishing his thought. He nodded at this, and produced a handful of thick coins from a pocket in his vest. He laid them on the table, not spilling a single one, so dextrous were his hands in the gloves.

Kewin pointed up the stairs, gestured for Arnath to follow.

At the top of the stairs, Kewin pointed left, "That's where I live. And down here..."

Down the hall, they came to a split in the hallway towards the back of the building where four doors faced each other. One was the commode, and the other three were good-sized rooms with beds and the regular furnishings. "I cleaned up some. Had new bedding brought in, if you and your men..."

Surprised by the offer, Arnath clapped Kewin on the shoulder, and said, "Not for me and mine. We are enjoying our last nights under the stars before becoming gentlemen. The end of our lives in the rough, you see. I have talked to Trellith about posting about rooms in other towns though."

"Other towns?" Kewin asked, watching Arnath go back down the stairs.

Back in the shop front, Arnath explained about the chaos at the Briny Sea earlier. "Your apartments, and all the others around town should be able to accommodate the many extra persons needed to support the businesses we've swamped with our endeavor."

"Perhaps we should talk to the mayor." Kewin suggested.

*

"Of course, of course." The mayor blustered loudly, trying to be heard over the sound of the echoing hammers on rock from the top of the mound, the sound of wood being pried away from the remaining outpost structure and the raucous crowd at the Briny Sea. Things in Kroman's Town had become so very busy of late. But Bumpol didn't worry too much about it. In a number of weeks, the construction would be done, the last of the wood shavings swept away and things would become as lax as they had been before. Or so he hoped.

Wiping sweat from his brow, Mayor Bumpol said, "I'll post something as soon as it is drawn up."

As he, Arnath and Kewin reached the outpost, they were all surprised to see the charred second story was almost entirely gone. Not wanting to encroach upon the increasingly dangerous site, the mayor touched his hat to them and said, "Looks like there is much work to do. I'll leave you to it."

The mayor tottered off back toward the center of town, as Arnath and Kewin walked into the front corridor of the outpost, the only part of the first floor still covered over.

As they reached end of the corridor, a loud whistle was heard from above, and an elf minding the door to the courtyard gestured for them to halt. Through the door, Arnath and Kewin could see an incredible amount of rope, leagues of it, begin to snake down the rockface of the mound and spilling into the courtyard. Then, as the larger ropes settled, slimmer ropes came down, and with them Shrakar, Taishen and the other elves who drove in the pilot stakes, climbing backwards all the way down from the summit of the mound.

Once they were safely on the ground, the elf minding the door ushered Arnath and Kewin through. They stepped over to the table, where Arnath deposited the satchel of new work gloves for all who needed them to try on. Arnath and Kewin grabbed hot buns from the cooking women, who would very soon have to vacate the worksite, the coming days being far too dangerous to have them directly under the multitude of dangerous materials being readied for installation.

As Shrakar and Taishen approached the table, Arnath noted that a huge gap in the back fence had been created already, where the fence met the back of the outpost, and through the gap he could see palettes of materials piled up all the way to the first cut-out in the road. Along the fence, a couple of neat piles of slightly charred wood were stacked up, next to the temporarily discarded portion of the fence itself. The work was well and truly under way.

Arnath and Kewin noted Shrakar looking disappointedly into the bag, and Kewin immediately said to him, "None your size right now, friend. But come by my shop, and we shall fit you up for a fine pair." Words which pleased Shrakar greatly.

Lorta appeared from the back corridor, with a large number of elves behind him, and a hush fell over the courtyard. He turned to Arnath, Shrakar and Kewin, and asked, "You will be staying?"

While Arnath and Shrakar said they would be, whilst Kewin excused himself and left via the main corridor. Lorta watched him go, and said, "For the sake of safety, that will be the last access or egress from the street. Henceforth, all persons entering the property will do so via the back path from the first cut-out in the road. Ladies, allow us to help you move your works to the bottom of the hill, where the feeding and cleaning stations will reside from now on. After that is cleared, we will set up safety brackets in this spot, and begin to tear down the first floor and basement..."

CHAPTER EIGHT

By the time Shimar came to visit Garthe, many things had happened in Kroman's Town, most of them to do with the building of the outpost.

The refurbishing of the stables had been completed. A long, covered extension now stuck out of the back the building that ran parallel to the western road. It was big enough to house an additional fifty horses, twenty-five on each side.

Once the first floor and basement of the outpost had been entirely ripped away, and the foundation scoured of all debris, the rear was extended by a few feet and the front was drilled through to make room for a much larger drainage pipe. The existing pipe had passed under the street, all the way under the Briny Sea, and then under the overhanging structures on the north side of the main street until it reached its destination – to drain into the swamp. The old pipe would be forced out as they bored through the ground for a larger pipe that would accommodate the waste drainage for the new building.

Once this was done, at the inconvenience of closing the Briny Sea for a whole afternoon to prevent accidents from happening, the ground caving in under customers and such, the new back foundation was shored up, and stones were laid over the mortar foundation of the basement.

A day and a half after the posts advertising the need for many new, and hopefully youthful labourers, went out to Quinhaven and Morley, Illona delivering the latter ones herself in her new Elven riding clothes purchased on a whim in Solindar, a horse drawn cart arrived with several people aboard who were deposited in the town square. This poor group consisting of four woman and two young men floundered about between the fountain and town message board until Kewin, who was enjoying an afternoon pipe on his porch, approached them and asked what each of them sought to do here in Kroman's. One of the girls was a baker's assistant, so Kewin walked her up to the door next to his, knocked, introduced her to Gaila and Hamly and told the girl he had a room for her and there were many others as well in the houses encircling the street, she had but to look for signs.

Another girl said she was an apprentice seamstress, so Kewin walked her to Leina's front door and made introductions, wanting to make sure the poor girl didn't end up working under Illona's grouchy mother, Feila, who's own seamstress and washing business was just one door over.

The two young men said their experience was in cooking, and working as scullery boys, so Kewin walked them, with the remaining group in tow, to the Briny Sea and introduced the boys to Durnly. One of the two remaining girls politely introduced herself to Durnly as well, stating that she cooked and cleaned and served tables. Visible relief washed over Durnly's face as he guided his new charges toward the places they could begin working, so quickly Kewin hardly had time to remind them he had rooms to let, as well as many others in the town.

The last girl, a beauty approaching twenty with blond hair and blue eyes, said she wasn't sure what she'd came to Kroman's to do. Seeing she was a tad lost, perhaps just wanting an escape from her old life, Kewin invited her to lunch and discuss what she thought she might like.

Sitting at a table near the balcony of the Briny Sea, she told Kewin her name was Anya and that she was from just outside Morley. Her parents ran a laundry that also sold bedding, and she was ever so tired of it. As she told Kewin about her life in Morley, Kewin watched her looking curiously around at the many people in the establishment. Though most were elves here for the construction project, he did his best to point out persons he knew from town, and tell her a little bit about them.

"And what, pray tell, do you do, good sir? Other than roll out the welcome carpet for the new citizenry." Kewin could tell Anya was teasing him a bit, but he went on to tell her he was the town glover. Anya seemed interest in this, as she could sew well, but just didn't want to end up in a laundry ever again.

Kewin explained that not only was there his glove shop, there was a lady dress maker, Leina, whom they'd met, and an old tailor of men's clothing, Grovan, though he was not very active these days.

"What's involved in gloving?" she asked in between bites.

Kewin went on to explained the basics of the trade, comparing it greatly to tailoring. It was when he spoke about the details of curving corner seams, Anya perked up, saying, "That's what I do with sheets back home. Mum always had me do the curving corners, 'cause I was best at it."

Hopeful about her abilities, Kewin suggested after lunch they go back to the shop, and he show her the rooms he had to let, and perhaps they try working on a glove pattern together. Anya smiled at this, her directionless feelings draining away.

*

Garthe and Illona sat on a log side by side facing the lake. Garthe had an anatomy scroll unfurled on his lap and was explaining some of the inner workings of a person on display there. For her part, Illona mostly ignored what he was saying for it was making her queasy and just enjoyed being in Garthe's company. Whilst Arnath and the others worked on the outpost, there were no assignments for her and she could not have asked for a better way to spend a lazy day. This was perfect.

Right up until Shimar approached the campsite, with Shimalena at his side.

"Good to see you keeping up with your studies, even at your leisure." Shimar said as he approached the log, setting down the many belted together textbooks and the huge leather tube he carried. "These texts and scrolls shall not only keep you busy, but all are for your reference library as well. I hope you do not mind my bringing my granddaughter along. She has business in town today."

"Master Shimar. Thank you for bringing them." Garthe said standing with a bow and the elfen hand gesture of respect. "Wonderful to see you Shimalena. I had no idea you were Shimar's granddaughter."

Shimalena stepped forward, kissed Garthe on both cheeks, saying "No way to tell you. I try, get better speak common."

Illona arose in a dumbfounded state. The stunning elfen beauty was the granddaughter of Garthe's mentor. She might never get a moment alone with him ever again.

As Illona stiffly performed the hand greeting, Shimalena eased her hand aside, stepped right up and hugged her. After kissing Illona on both cheeks, she said. "I glad seeing you, new sister."

"I...Me...Too." Illona said in a tremulous voice.

Garthe noted that Shimar had rolled his eyes and looked away, perhaps finding this informality of youth a tad distasteful. To help the moment pass, Garthe said, "What all have you brought me, Master Shimar?"

Shimar sat down on the log, his back stiffly straight, and began to unbuckle the thick belt that held the leather-bound tomes together. "This might take some time. Perhaps the young ladies can see about Shimalena's business."

Elated by the suggestion, Shimalena turned to the still-baffled Illona and said, "Where is Briny Sea?"

Illona stiffly pointed across the campsite and up the hill, where the last of the arcing foundation columns could be seen moving across the grasslands under the Briny Sea's balcony. From this distance, it looked as though it crawled under its own power towards the eastern road. Shimalena immediately grabbed Illona by her pointing hand and dragged her away with a peel of angelic laughter.

Garthe was surprised at how quickly the girls had become fast friends, if that was indeed what was happening. Shimar obviously chose to ignore the girls as he pried open the first tome. "Now…" Shimar said, smoothing the pages open. "This text is not only about casting, but about spell histories. Have a look here…"

*

Though she didn't resist being swept along up the hill, Illona trotted after Shimalena on awkward feet. She didn't exactly know what was going on.

As they got closer to the crest of the road, Shimalena stopped, let go of Illona's hand and composed herself. Once again, she was the poised, graceful young lady who held herself like a queen. Illona saw the reason for the change just a few steps further ahead. Several elves were working in the street in front of the outpost. Many were tamping down the cobblestones that were loosened by the boring out of the new drainage pipe under the street. Other elves stood guard at the front of the construction site, which was now basically a large pit that had only few a boards and ropes covering over the potential falling peril from the street, now that the frontage of the old outpost had been completely taken away. The elves who watched over the safety of passersby and those working with iron rods to secure the loosened cobblestones all took the time to give Shimalena the gesture of respect, and some bowed deeply in her direction as she passed.

"You know them all?" Illona asked in wonderment.

"I serve at inn. Know the many families. All families know grandfather." Shimalena said, then checking if any of the elves could see, pulled a funny face at Illona, then turned towards the door of the Briny Sea, assuming her regal façade once more.

It struck Illona that Shimalena's noble bearing and seemingly unattainable nature were a face she presented to the world, be it in her capacity as a serving person or as the grand daughter to a great elder elf, and that underneath that was a lively girl with a spritely sense of humour she kept mostly to herself. But it was something she wanted Illona to know.

As Shimalena came down the steps of the Briny Sea, gliding for all appearances, such was her grace, many heads turned and hush fell over the hall. When she reached the end of the bar, where Durnly stood, she stopped and curtsied to him.

"What can I do for you, good lady?" Durnly asked, a little bit tongue tied.

"I come, Solindar. I wish to serve." Shimalena said in a sing-song voice, that still rolled her R's harshly.

"I just took on a new serving girl. I don't know if I'll need more..." Durnly said, clearly embarrassed by having to turn this beauty away.

"I not wish to take any job from girl. You will need I too." Shimalena said, and plucked an empty drinking flute off the bar. She turned to the hall, and holding the flute aloft said, "Mo'heer Da'oon?"

To her query in the old Elvish tongue, nearly half the hall raised their glasses up. Durnly went a little slack-jawed. Half his customers wanted drinks, and his serving girls didn't even know.

"Also..." Shimalena produced a cloth bag from her satchel. She opened the bag revealing a mound of green leaves, ground down to nearly power. She held the bag up, calling out, "Mo'heer Da'hath'ka?"

Every table where elves were eating raised their hands and waved her over.

She turned back to Durnly, "This be Da'hath'ka. Common spice. All elf like very much on food. You have little cups for on table?"

Durnly reached under the bar, produced a stack of small clay cups and gestured for Shimalena to pass him the spice. He took the bag from her and passed it, and the cups, to one of the serving girls behind the bar with him, saying, "A portion on every table."

"One more thing I have." Shimalena said. Durnly watched as she turned heel, this angelic girl who had just made the following month of serving a foreign workforce ten times easier, and walked away. He and Illona and the serving girls stood at the bar and waited until Shimalena reached the stage at the far end of the hall.

Shimalena took to the stage, sat on a stool and produced a small lute from her satchel and set it on her lap. She ran her nails across the strings, and, satisfied the instrument was in tune, began to play. It was a light, lilting and joyful tune, one the elves all seemed to know, as they bobbed their heads and tapped their fingers on the table to its rhythm. Certain beyond any doubt he had to keep this mysterious elf girl under his employ, Durnly began quickly to pour dozens of fresh flutes of peach cider.

So enrapt and relaxed was everyone as they ate and drank to Shimalena's music, they were uncertain if they should panic when the entire floor of the hall shook underneath them.

*

Seconds earlier, on the grassy land below the balcony of the Briny Sea, the large work gang of elves heaved on the ropes guiding the last of the giant curved support beams on its sled, and all heard the loud, sudden whip-crack of a rope breaking.

The shirtless elves who had held the ropes dove out of the way as the gigantic coil plummeted down around them. Their hands freed, they raced to join the other three gangs holding the intact supporting ropes, all of them straining to guide the huge beam upright again.

Up above, on the balcony of the Briny Sea, Heflynn dove out of the way just as the top of the support pillar, as thick as a large tree trunk, slammed into the balcony, completely crushing the corner of the structure. He quickly rolled to his feet, and began ushering frightened elves off the unstable balcony. As people ran out, Heflynn could see the elves with the tamping rods looking in through the entrance, and he bellowed in their direction, "ROPE !"

The elves sprang into action, racing across the street to the construction site.

Durnly rushed to Heflynn's side, fearfully eyeing the wall that was buckling under the weight of the giant beam. "My! Could lose the whole wall!"

Heflynn looked along the wall and saw an entire row of tables next to it, the customers completely unaware they could be crushed in an instant.

"We've got to brace it." Heflynn said to Durnly, and then turned to Illona, saying over the panicked shouts of the crowd. "Illona! Get everyone out – now! All of them outside!"

As Heflynn and Durnly disappeared onto the balcony, Illona began to wave her arms at the crowd dining against the precarious wall, and tried with a fearful warble to get everyone's attention. "Everyone! Out the door! Outside – quickly!"

From the stage, Shimalena saw what Illona was doing, and also began to wave her arms and cry out, in Elvish. All the diners got to their feet and raced for the door.

Pushing past everyone coming out, Arnath and Shrakar, who had a huge length of rope slung over his shoulder, raced inside and toward the balcony entrance. The two of them got to the threshold, where they could see the floor of the balcony was buckling. They leaned out, peered over and saw Heflynn and Durnly, their bodies braced against the top of the giant leaning beam, their faces tight under the strain. Durnly's peg leg had already been drilled through the wood of the balcony floor by the pressure.

Arnath looked directly at Heflyyn and asked, "How long?"

"Not long. I can feel myself giving."

"If it gets passed us, and through the wall..." Durnly said, left the notion hanging, his entire body straining just to get the words out.

But Arnath knew what he meant. "Through the wall, to the floor and then it drags the entire damned building down the side of the hill."

"I can get the rope through the hole," Heflynn said, nodding up towards the large pilot hole in the column just above his head. "I'll need my hands free, and then once the rope is through..."

Arnath understood what he meant. He turned to Shrakar, asking, "You can catch it?"

"I catch." Shrakar said without hesitating.

"You can fall that distance?"

Shrakar shrugged. "Fall, sure. Land...?" He genuinely wasn't sure about the last part.

"On my count. Good luck, friend." Arnath said, taking one end of the rope, allowing much of it to unspool on the floor.

Shrakar walked down the length of the bar, loosening the rope as he went, coiling one end around his fist. He gestured for Illona, Shimalena and the others to stay outside the door. If this didn't work, Shrakar, Arnath, Heflynn and Durnly would surely die, and the entire Briny Sea could be pulled down the hillside, to crush the elf workers below. Another disaster like the old outpost befalling poor Kroman's Town.

Shrakar could see it in everyone's eyes in the doorway. Illona and Shimalena shed tears as they held hands, their knuckles white with fear. Shrakar and Trellith's eyes met, and they exchanged what could be a final smile.

"Steady, lad" Trellith said, his grimly serious eyes hiding the fear behind them from his friend.

Shrakar nodded, turned toward the balcony, tightening the rope in his fist.

Outside, mere seconds earlier, Arnath had raced onto the balcony, spilling a goodly portion of the thick rope over the side of the railing. He hunkered down and jammed himself into the spot Heflynn had just slipped out of, the wood under their feet straining with the weight of the three men. They had seconds – if that.

Heflynn took the end of the rope from Arnath and grabbed a special arrow from his quiver, an arrow with a leather thong affixed behind the fletching. He fed the rope through the thong, pulled it secure and nodded at Arnath. He nocked the arrow, pulled back the bow, and aimed up, straight through the pilot hole.

"Shrakar – One – Two..." Arnath shouted, straining against the weight of the pillar.

At the count of one, Shrakar was already racing toward the balcony, rope flailing in his hand. At two, he had gained great speed and was nearly at the balcony threshold.

"Three!"

Heflynn loosed the arrow, which plowed through the pilot hole, dragging the snaking rope through and into the air beyond.

Shrakar dove off the balcony, sailing into the air. Nearly twenty feet out from the balcony, he caught the rope as it wiggled through the air behind the arrow.

And instantly began to plummet towards the ground.

Shrakar didn't panic. He had two seconds, maybe. He began to gather both sides of the rope towards him, swiftly collecting it up, hand over hand.

On the ground below him, Taishen and a contingent of strong elves stood ready to catch and steady him, if they could.

As Shrakar grew nearer and nearer to the ground, the rope grew tighter and tighter on the top of the beam, until it had no more give. His body was jerked as he tucked up his feet to avoid hitting the ground. Taishen and the others raced in and grabbed him, then fanned out along the rope, all pulling with all their strength to raise the column away from the building.

Up above, when Shrakar's body weight pulled against the column, it jerked loose from the balcony. Arnath and Heflynn quickly kicked at the wood around the base of Durnly's peg to free him, and the trio raced to safety.

"I think that marks the end of the work day." Arnath said as they made it to the safety of the dining room floor. Cheers met them as they approached the stairs. Reaching them, Arnath collapsed on the top step, right next to where Trellith stood.

"You know, brother. I really thought becoming businessmen meant we weren't risking life and limb on a daily basis anymore."

"Best think again on that." Trellith said, handing Arnath a lit pipe.

Down below, on the grassy field, Taishen guided the work gangs with strong shouts of "Heave!" in Elvish as they forced the curving, behemoth column towards to the eastern road, where it would sit with the other three until morning.

Shrakar stood alone as the work gangs got further and further away, looking this way and that on the ground until he found exactly the thing he was looking for.

*

That night, a celebration took place around the lake. Knowing the Briny Sea would be closed for most of the day tomorrow, not only for repairs but also for safety's sake as the four support columns were locked in place at the outpost, Durnly had brought a good number of casks and kegs to the lake gates by the stables and allowed people to drink them freely. It was going to cost him a great deal of money, but he didn't care. He'd survived. As did a large number of others who could have died this day.

Before the celebration had begun, Heflynn and Shimar were able to speak at length. Heflynn had of course consulted with Shimar on matters arcane for the crown before, and the origin of the live-stone was yet to be investigated in full.

As they paced around the lake, Garthe and Illona watched them from the eastern side of the lake, where Arnath and his companions camped by the largest tree. They were adults, discussing adult matters and the two of them found it fascinating. It was only when Shimalena came to their site with a skin of peach cider for them to enjoy together did they realize how they must have looked, sitting, staring across the lake at the two men, not even talking to each other. Shimalena laughed at them, plopping herself in between them and started passing the skin back and forth. Before long Shimalena tried in slurred words to get them to play a game with her called "Who gets kissed?", the suggestion of which made them both turn red as apples.

Later in the night, having almost forgotten it from all the celebrating, Shrakar gave Heflynn back the unique arrow he'd retrieved in the field. Heflynn rolled the arrow over and over between his fingers, eyes distant.

"What is it, lad?" Trellith said in regards to the prince's distant reverie.

"Strange, this. It's supposed to be a substitute for grappling hooks. A way to get ropes over walls. And yet today it saved the lives of a good twenty or thirty people. Amazing." Heflynn said, still staring down at the arrow.

"Some arrow indeed. Keep it handy." Trellith said, with a fellow archer's appreciation.

Thinking on it, Heflynn said, "I shall. Until your outpost is built, then I'll present it to you again. Could hang it up in the outpost, a kind of symbol, I guess. For luck."

Shrakar and Trellith raised their drinking skins to that, and drank deeply.

Over the course of the night a great many came around their fire pit to visit and at give Shrakar the gesture of respect and the deepest of bows. Arnath had dragged another log over to accommodate their growing number of companions. With their party's original four now sat Shimalena, Shimar, Illona and Heflynn. He kept looking over his shoulder, fully expecting Apaulon and Listrelle to appear and join them. The "we three" in his mind had grown by one years ago, and now it seemed it was growing again. He'd noticed that their usual places around the fire, the ones they fell into naturally on the road, had changed. Garthe, Shimar and the girls had a whole log to themselves. The sight made Arnath's heart swell with pride, seeing his fostered son creating a life for himself now that he was off the road. With that pride came some returning pangs of loss for their time on the road. He knew it was likely the sentiment of too much ale, but he embraced it, as many people had this night. He was alive, and very much felt it.

*

The next day was rife with tension. The four giant columns were going to be moved from the first cut-out in the eastern road, up the hill behind the first of the houses on the rising main street and then set in place in the outpost foundation, via rope and pulley rigs anchored to the top of the mound. Because of the accident the day before, most citizens of Kroman's Town were understandably on edge.

Lorta accepted responsibility for the accident, in as much as it was his notion to bring all four columns into Kroman's via the western road and drag them across the grassy field to the eastern side of town. It was a logical toss up between doing that, or taking all four to the eastern road via the King's road south of Kroman's, where even the slightest accident would have scandalized the kingdom. The court always heard of major incidents along the highways, and frowned greatly on them. They had already carted the monstrous columns here from the forests outside Solindar. Pressing that luck further was asking for trouble. Lorta was indeed stuck between the possibility of an accident happening in Kroman's Town, or one on that particular span of the King's highway, and chose the former. Today, he was going to divide his time between supervising the installation of the columns and effecting repairs on the Briny Sea – replacing the damaged part of the balcony, as well as shoring up the underside of the structure.

The eastern road was entirely closed to traffic, and secured by a contingent of King's guard. Graten had brought in two full squads to halt all traffic attempting to use the road, redirecting them to the western road to get into town, and then only as far as the town square, where a goodly number of guards stood to prevent all but the approved construction workers from using the rising main road. Apaulon, now Lance Corporal Apaulon, his promotion for his actions in catching the murderous thieves having come through, was in charge of the soldiers within the town, so the citizens didn't gripe too much in being told where they could and couldn't go since they were being told by a familiar face. Most of the townsfolk had decided to watch the placement of the columns from the lake, making an outing day of it.

Kewin had put away all of the wares in his shop, and allowed people to come upstairs to his very back lodging room, the one as yet not rented, and watch from the window that had a relatively unobstructed view of the outpost courtyard, the uppermost part of it anyway.

Shimar and Garthe had a station set up by the stables, lest there were any accidents. Illona and Shimalena stayed with them, to lend assistance and also to keep company on a day that mandated they stay out of the way.

Not sure what to do with himself, Heflynn borrowed one of the many canoes from the boathouse beside the lake, and lazily paddled around as he watched the construction site. Should anything happen, he could get to shore quickly.

While Arnath and Shrakar were going to work with the elves to place the columns, Trellith, whose size might make him dangerously underfoot, would work with Lorta to effect repairs at the Briny Sea.

Everyone knew where they needed to be, and the whole town had their fingers crossed as the work began.

*

By the afternoon, almost all the townsfolk not working at feeding those on the construction site had fallen asleep. It was taking near two hours between the placing of each beam, and the watching of it was becoming tedious. They could hear the sound of the pulleys, the groan of the mighty wood, the shouts of the work gang leaders, and then eventually the loud smack of wood and stone locking together as each beam fell into place – which drew a cheer the first couple of times.

Heflynn had abandoned his canoe, and snoozed leaning on a log near Garthe's improvised medical station. Right next to him, Shimalena was doing the same.

Illona had left earlier, had visited with Apaulon for a bit, and then went to the post office where both Mrs Minidell and her uncle Shamuth, who guarded the outpost payroll contained within the post office safe, slept in their chairs. Illona passed the time by sorting what little mail there was, swept the office floor and read many inter-office documents. They were all quite dry and not at all exciting, but for one – a blank application to work for the King's postal service. Though she was a month too young to apply still, she rolled up the application and put it in her pocket.

Garthe had gone to the camp site and retrieved the thick tome on spells and spell lore, so Shimar might teach him more whilst they stood vigil. Thus far the day had had little in the way of injury, but for an elf who badly jammed three of his fingers in the morning. Garthe hoped that was the extent of it, but in the late-afternoon a calamitous crash was heard from the work site.

From the lakeside, the sound they heard was a combination of echoing wood striking rock and a chaotic rattle of metal. Immediately thereafter, the shouts of many people could be heard.

The loud noise was enough to wake everyone by the lake.

Garthe and Shimar turned toward the slope of the main street and immediately saw Shrakar come bounding towards them with someone in his arms. The guardsmen stood aside as he raced down the hill, the cradled figure's arms and legs lolling from side to side. Everyone stood aside when Shrakar reached the table and laid the seething man down on it.

"Tackle come loose and swing down on him hard – here and here." Shrakar said touching his wrist and ribs on the left side. "Still trouble. I go back."

Heflynn and Shimalena, awakened by the crash, were now on their feet and watched Shrakar race away. When they looked down at the man on the table, Shimalena gasped. "Telifarr!"

The elf, clearly a friend of Shimalena's from back home, was one of the rare elves with shiny, long brown hair. Almost immediately after being placed on the table Telifarr seethed and tried to roll into a ball.

"What do we do?" Heflynn implored.

"Help to lay him back. He cannot curl up like this." Shimar said. He, like Garthe, already had his healing stone out, and was passing it over Telifarr's body.

Heflynn grabbed Telifarr's ankles and pulled him flat against the table which produced a seething groan from the injured elf.

"All the ribs on his side are broken." Shimar said matter-of-factly, waving his stone over the area.

"His wrist is not broken, but the muscles are bruised to the bone." Garthe echoed back.

"Concentrate on his ribs."

Garthe moved his hand up nearer to Shimar's. Shimalena could see Telifarr was still in deep agony. "What can I do?" Shimalena ask her grandfather in old elvish.

Shimar pointed at Telifarr's right hand, at the mound of his thumb, and said, "Squeeze there. Though his ribs cry against it, he must take deep full breaths."

Shimalena squeezed Telifarr's hand in the spot she was shown, and the elf immediately spasmed. His whole body outstretched in a rictus of agony. Immediately, Shimar pulled out a flat grey stone and placed it on Telifarr's forehead. Holding the stone down with his first two fingers, Shimar intoned a deep hum, and Telifarr's body instantly went limp.

Shimalena and Heflynn stood away from the table, utterly shocked. "Is he...?" the archer sputtered.

"No, no." Shimar said, pocketing the grey stone. "He is in a deep healing sleep. Garthe and I must work without him fighting us."

Heflynn and Shimalena both expelled sighs of relief.

Just then, Illona came back from up the hill, saw a man who for all appearances was dead on the table, and fainted onto the cobblestones.

*

Shrakar stepped back to the door of the Briny Sea, took a couple of bounding strides for speed and jumped over the chasm that was the unfinished basement of the outpost. He caught one of the many ropes that hung from the three in-place support columns, and swung his weight across the gap.

When he landed in the back courtyard, he could see they were still in trouble.

Though upright, the last column was swinging wildly back and forth. It listed drunkenly from the top, where one of the pulley ropes had broken away, and the pulley had swung down to smash straight into poor Telifarr.

"Shrakar – Grab hold!" The Orc looked up the rock face of the mound and saw most of the workforce were holding onto a thick rope that counter-balanced the listing beam. Near the top, Arnath waved him forward. They needed his greater weight to stop the beam from lolling around.

Shrakar raced up to the wall, jumped up, grabbed the rope and pulled himself into position behind Taishen. Everyone above adjusted as Shrakar's weight pulled their end closer to the ground, thus elevating the column just a tad higher.

Seeing the beam was now only slightly wavering in place, rather than lolling around dangerously, Taishen called out to the elves above manning the pulley ropes, barking in old elvish.

Very slowly, the beam began to move back along the ropes toward the rock-face. When it got very close, close enough for the men hanging down to touch it, a new rope was tossed to them from the top. Arnath and others fed the rope through the top pilot hole, and tossed the rope back up the mound. This rope was then fed through pulleys anchored into the rock of the mound itself, and then given some slack so they could begin to ease the column steadily away from the mound and towards the foundation of the outpost.

At Taishen's command, several elves dropped off the line that ran up the side of the mound, rolled to the ground in the courtyard, and grabbed the guy ropes swaying off of the column. The remaining men, Taishen, Arnath and Shrakar among them, hung as counter-ballast as the column was guided closer and closer to its destination – a column footing in the foundation at the front of the outpost.

Finally, past the point of no return, the column's weight hung entirely on beams at the back of the foundation, and those at the front, near the street. Everyone hanging off the mound came down, and split into equal work gangs, manning the guy ropes to guide the column into place.

Taishen came right up to the lip of the footing dug for the column in the deep basement, and continuously called out commands, ordering the beam be moved slightly this way and that.

Finally, Taishen spread his hands, palms down, and gestured for them to gently lower the beam.

As it settled into the hole, the strained noises of scraping wood on stone threatened another catastrophic accident, but in the last moment the column slammed into the footing with a thunderous wooden clap so loud that hundreds of frightened birds flew away from the top of the mound.

Cheers resounded from the building site, and all around the town.

The hardest part of creating the new outpost was done.

*

Again, that night a party was held for the entire town, this time within the confines of the fully repaired Briny Sea. Arnath had gone into the post office and took a goodly bit of coin out of their saddle bags in the safe, leaving a good-sized wine skin for Amorth who had guard duty and could not attend the festivities, and brought it to Durnly. His generosity had taken care of the town the night before, so tonight the owners of the outpost were returning the favor.

Trellith took Arnath, Shrakar, Garthe and anyone else who would follow out to balcony to show them how the outside had not only been repaired, but also added on to. Both ends of the balcony had been extended to accommodate larger-sized tables. Heflynn jokingly remarked that his spot, his single man's perch, had been taken away from him.

Trellith also assured them that the drainage pipe under the hall had not been damaged by the accident yesterday, having gone down into the pipe with a lantern and his monocle screwed in to look for cracks himself.

Lorta and Taishen made their rounds, extending their respects to all, and receiving just as much. A few peach ciders in and Taishen took to the stage, beckoning Shimalena join him with her lute. He sang a song in old-elvish that all the elves joined in on. The citizens of Kroman's Town didn't understand a word of it, but they could certainly dance to it. This prompted the many musical players of the town to race home and return with their instruments. The stage now full with musicians, songs would strike up either by Shimalena beginning the pluck of a tune, or Kewin on the other side of the stage beating out a rhythm on his bodhran. The tables nearest the stage were cleared away and the dancing did not cease for the rest of the night.

Further cheers resounded when Shimar arrived with Telifarr, who stiffly managed his way down the stairs to join the party.

After Sargeant Graten was relieved that night by the returning Listrelle, she and Apaulon allowed the Guardsmen to join the party in shifts, one or two at a time, with their promise of good behaviour. Though the safety of the construction site was no longer in question, a giant, covered-over scaffolding having been erected across the entire front of the outpost, the guardsmen were still responsible for keeping the dozens upon dozens of palettes of construction materials from being pilfered in the night. Apaulon shook hands with all at the party who knew him and received many a congratulations for his newly attained rank, none making him swell with more pride than when Captain Arnath and his men shook his hand and saluted him.

Mayor Bumpol took to the stage, and asked for quiet. A hush fell over the long hall, and he began to speak. It was his usual speech about the resurging pride in the once floundering Kroman's Town. Most around the hall, the elf workers, made confused faces at his words. To the mayor's relief, Lorta stood up from a nearby table and began to translate his words into Elvish, one statement at a time. Like any politician, the tiny man knew how to work a crowd, and many of his statements drew resounding cheers from the room.

Navigating through the crowd, Listrelle stepped out on the balcony, and found Heflynn there, drinking wine by himself, as she knew he would be. As she settled on the rail near him, she said, "Why am I not surprised, amongst all this celebration, that you are off alone, perpetuating your air of mystery?"

"Is that what I am doing?" He smiled at her, sipping his wine. Since she had never spoken to him so, he sensed a grand duel coming and he liked the prospect.

"What else?"

"Perhaps, but at least I am not masking the unattainable beauty of woman-hood behind a staunch, militaristic façade." Heflynn said turning to face her.

"Perhaps I don't want my beauty to make people exclude the notion that I'm a person with thoughts of her own, not a prize to won, and mounted." Listrelle said, a twinge of bitterness in her voice.

"And perhaps, as a someone who has been on display for an entire kingdom to poke and prod and admire since childhood, now a man, I merely relish my private moments. No air of mystery needed then. " Heflynn replied without the bitter tone, but with equal honesty.

That chasm between them surmounted, Listrelle turned away and gripped the balcony railing tightly. She steeled herself to say more. "Should I have passed my exams and my rank be increased, I shall likely be sent far away."

"It will." Heflynn said matter-of-factly.

"It will?"

"Increase. You will be promoted. I send word on to the capital."

Listrelle's face grew immediately red with anger. "How could you? That was my rank to earn, not to be handed to me like a bouquet from a suitor!"

"And it isn't." Heflynn said, looking her directly in the eye. "No soldier in my travels has proven themselves more dedicated than you. You take your duties for what they are, a duty to the people of the kingdom, not a thing to be pantomimed for political gain. I've seen you in action. Your chief concern is the safety of others, above all else. And that is why I sent my recommendation to the garrison in the capital. Because you are without question a good soldier. I have been surrounded by, guarded by soldiers my whole life. I know the good from the bad, so I stand by my judgement. And yes, you did earn it."

Listrelle stood silently, her head down. Then said in a muted voice, "Thank you."

"You're quite welcome."

"As I said, I imagine a promotion would take me far away…"

"Yes, quite likely."

Listrelle thought for a moment, then said, "Your rooming above the scrivener's store?"

"I am."

Listrelle straightened and turned toward the door, saying as she left, "Then perhaps I shall see you later."

"Only perhaps?" He called after her.

She stopped at the threshold of the balcony, and partially turned back to say, "Yes. Perhaps."

And then she was gone, disappearing among the thick crowd at the bar. Heflynn turned back to the starry night, thinking that perhaps was good enough.

*

Trellith sat on a high stool at the bar, and tried to talk to Shimar about crafting less intrusive spectacles for his eyes over the music and laughter. Periodically, their conversation would halt briefly as they observed the multitude of interactions the teeming life all around them presented. Well in her cups, Anya beckoned Kewin join her on the dance floor. Kewin handed off his bodhran and beater to Hamly the baker, who took his rolly-polly frame up to the stage and marched around, continuing to beat out the song, to much applause. Even from this far away, Shimar could see his granddaughter as she played her lute and watched her new friends Illona and Garthe as they danced together. Mostly Shimalena smiled down at them from the stage, but Shimar caught moments where she watched them through narrowed scheming eyes that bespoke of coming mischief, a look he grew to know from her infancy onwards. Then, passing right in front of them, guardsman Listrelle quickly eased her way through the crowd, up the stairs and into the street. Trellith and Shimar turned their heads the way she had come, and saw Heflynn alone on the balcony.

"One would think the cursed live-stone had cast a love spell over the entire town." Trellith said, shaking his head.

Cocking his head to one side, Shimar replied, "Were that all the only damage that infernal stone was capable of every town in the kingdom would likely want one of their own."

Trellith froze, his ale stein mid-way to his mouth. He wasn't sure but he could have sworn the normally stoic elf had just cracked a joke.

CHapter nine

It took a **full moon cycle** of hammering, sawing, pounding, sanding, trimming, fitting, adjusting, painting and furnishing to get the outpost built. For all the celebration around it, when the construction of the outpost, and all the noise that came with it, had been going on for more than a fortnight, some of the citizens of Kroman's Town were starting their collective mornings with an irritated scowl.

The day after the party for the column setting, the components for Trellith's smith were moved into the back courtyard and set in place with both Lorta and Trellith supervising. The smithy had to be tall enough to accommodate customers of many sizes, yet its workings had to be built at a height for Trellith to ply his craft. This meant carefully modifying the many pieces brought over from the now retired Kortell's smithy.

While this progressed, wood workers in the courtyard built the steps to the basement, and the doors that would be used in it. Several large cabinets for storage were lowered into the basement by pulley, and a huge safe was carefully lowered down and then mortared into one corner. Everything they could think of that should go into the basement was placed in it before the actual flooring over the first floor was installed.

And, so it went...

Many of the tall, strong beams used to guide the support columns in place were carefully sawed apart, and then were installed to span the floors as load-bearing beams. Heavy clay piping was interlaced amongst the beams, all feeding downwards to the drainage pipe in the basement. Other clay pipes rose up to where the roof would eventually be. A pipe was installed that ran from the roof down the side of the building, becoming hidden away behind Trellith's smithy, then ran all the way back to dip into the spring pool, which would serve as the source of all water that was used for drinking, washing and flushing away at the outpost. To be sure the pipe seals, and the pipes themselves had integrity, water was flushed through the large pipe on the roof that would eventually connect to the tank that the spring pool water would be pumped into. Once it was established that all the pipes were sturdy and had no cracks, then the rest of the building that would encase the piping within the walls and floors could resume.

As the first floor was laid, Garthe became busy, consulting with the elves on his designs for the tiny clinic that would be situated next to the front door of the outpost. It would jut out slightly from the building, have a separate door onto the street from the main front door, and have stairs down into it, much like the first floor of the outpost itself.

The reason for this was simple – The first floor was going to be recessed into the foundation by a few feet. Entering the front door, one would have to take a few steps down onto the floor. This allowed for the ceiling's extra height, a ceiling that accommodated visitors of all heights, including Orcs. The main stairs and the corridors upstairs would all be constructed in the same way, to give headroom to the tallest of guests.

Shimalena overheard these details and more as she flitted around the table where Garthe and Shimar were having a kind-of goodbye lunch. Certainly, Shimar would be back to help guide young Garthe, but he was needed in Solindar, and so was returning home. Not a tearful goodbye, just a polite send-off luncheon. Shimalena herself would be staying in Kroman's Town, working at the Briny Sea until the construction was completed. Knowing this, Shimar wanted to speak to Garthe on the matter of his mischievous granddaughter, but couldn't seem to get the right moment, as she kept flitting by their table. Shimar hoped he could speak privately with Garthe on the matter, being near certain the boy had no clue regarding the pairing customs of the kind of traditionalist elf family Shimalena came from. The old mage feared his granddaughter would spring it upon Garthe, and Illona as well, by surprise, before either of them could decide it was something they wanted.

*

Though busy as everyone else on the project, Shrakar had managed to take the time to visit Kewin's shop and get measured for a properly fitting pair of gloves. Orc skin was known to be notoriously tough, but he still found himself being punctured by splinters and nail heads daily on the job. Kewin and Anya had him lay his hand on a large sheet of drawing paper, and they traced around the span of his hands. They also measured the width of his fingers and the length of the back of his hand, both flat and with his fingers bent. Shortly, within a day and half, Kewin and Anya came to the construction site and gave Shrakar a pair of perfect fitting tan work gloves, with the promise they would retain his pattern should adventuring ever call again and he need some proper battle gloves.

Floor by floor, up the new outpost went, the furnishings begin installed by the pulley system from outside after the finishing on the floors had dried. For the lower floors, they merely finished the back wall last. For the upper ones, the ones Arnath and company would be living on, the furniture was fed through each apartment's large balcony doorways before the doors themselves were installed.

With Trellith's smithy installed, he fired it up for a test run almost as soon as the mortar was dry. Once the works were tested, Trellith began work with the elves to manufacture metal fittings for the construction. This came in handy when certain supplies ran out, and things could be created on site, rather than to have to send to Solindar for them.

Things were needed still, so Illona made regular message and supply runs back and forth to Solindar. She accompanied Shimar on his journey back, the elder elf not minding keeping up with her brisk messenger's pace as long as it kept her from asking too many questions about his granddaughter. Though he felt the need to discuss Shimalena with Garthe, he was entirely uncomfortable talking about such notions with their strange girl companion. What he did matter-of-factly impart to her was that traditional elf families did not restrict their family units to two parents, as more modern elves and human folk did. Even modern elf law did not limit the number of people who could be involved in wedlock. Soon Shimar realized he had opened a floodgate, especially after explaining he was not Shimalena's grandfather by way of birth, which was impossible for a mage, but by a married familial relationship. Illona spent the rest of the excruciating trip asking no end of questions about the kinds of combinations of families he knew of. Though in her late teens, the poor girl seemed to have no idea about mating, other than that was where children came from. Everything involved was a mystifying as sorcery to her.

Having gleaned what little she could from the elder elf, Illona's ride back was a veritable storm of confusion. She had asked Shimar questions right up to his very door, which he practically dashed through upon arriving. Illona went about her business, delivering further instructions and orders to Lorta's company. She also checked in with a few of the wood workers creating the ornate outer doors for the outpost and fake weaponry for the training center. She gave all of them a time estimate on the completion of the construction, when their materials would be needed. Illona ate lunch at the large inn, thought on buying a couple more of the rugged, yet elegant elven travelling shirts and couldn't make up her mind. She was absolutely distracted by the notions Elder

Shimar had brought up. Since Shimalena was from one of those Traditionalist elf families, did she have strange notions of what coupling was? Illona had seen Shimalena's wild, rebellious side and could not help but think that that streak in her extended to experimenting in those traditional elf values with human folk. Shimalena clearly could have had her pick of the eligible bachelors like Taishen from Solindar. Instead she chose to spend all her time with Garthe and herself. The idea of being with Garthe she understood. He was a natural born healer, therefore would never be without profession, and as an apprentice mage would be dedicated to lifelong study. His home would have such a library. Any girl could only dream of a partner with such a sprawling library. To her that imagined collection of books made up for the notion that Garthe could never father children. Almost, anyway. As for how she fit into the mix, Illona was entirely perplexed as to how Shimalena had chosen her for this strange triangle. It felt wonderful to have a friend, a girl her age who she could just be herself around. But it also felt wonderful when the three of them had had too much to drink, and would affectionately paw at each other. In the moment, it felt harmless, but now, thinking on it, knowing what she now knew, the confusion was somewhat unbearable. Who could she ask about it? Illona admired and trusted Captain Arnath, but he was a full-grown man. He might just laugh at her for asking. Heflynn, whom she was learning to be comfortable around, would likely laugh louder than Arnath. Maybe Listrelle, who was closer to her age, but was also quite prim in her manner, and might find an impromptu discussion of girlish topics unseemly. Besides, she hadn't seen Listrelle since the morning after the big party at the Briny Sea, when she was leaving the rooms above the Scribe's storefront.

Illona ate her food mechanically, and sighed. She took solace in thoughts of new shirts and a postal service application practically burning a hole in her top drawer at home.

*

As the outpost neared reaching its intended five-stories, Arnath found himself working in the early part of the day and merely helping to coordinate, sometimes merely watching the work in the second half. The young elves were running circles around him all day long, and when he first noticed he felt truly ashamed. Still to this day he had the stamina for quick bursts of battle, doling out his energy like a strategist, knowing how long a fight would be. But a construction project from dawn until dusk... Come lunchtime, Arnath felt spent and defeated. Lorta had discounted them some money, due to all the work he and Shrakar were putting in, particularly Shrakar, whose Orc body would not feel the crush of age for perhaps decades to come. Guilt for the discount and letting his workmates down pressed hard on him, despite the fact that when he reached the part of the day when he could work no more, there was truly no fighting against it. His body could not be pushed any further.

On one such day, where Arnath had found himself underfoot in the back courtyard, he stood by front scaffolding, staying out of the way of the door and he smoked a pipe, watching the goings-on in the back courtyard. Hunching a bit over to watch the movement of people and equipment, he missed the approach of a woman and her children from the rising west side of the main street until they were nearly upon him. Standing straight, he took a long haul on the pipe, and then noticed the approach of Merynda and her children. Arnath nearly choked on his smoke, but quickly composed himself.

"Captain Arnath." Merynda said, not questioning. She knew who he was.

"That's right. And you are?" Arnath asked, know full-well who she was.

"I'm Merynda." She extended a hand to him, and he took it. Their eyes meeting. "My farm made a contribution to the purchase order here at Briny Sea this afternoon. I thought we would come into town and see how your outpost was coming along."

The entire time she spoke, neither she nor Arnath noticed they continued to clasp each other's hands, their friendly handshake having been long over. It took Arnath a moment, looking into her eyes from so close, for the words she had said to sink in. When they did, he eased his hand away, fearing he might start to perspire on her palm.

"Quite well as you can see." Arnath pointed upwards, saying, "Nearly complete."

"Oh. Good." Merynda said, and they both felt the panic of having hit a stumbling block in their first conversation.

Arnath wasn't going to let her get away so easily. He said, "And who do we have here?"

Merynda wrapped her arm around her son's shoulder, a haunted-looking boy of about twelve who stood behind the protection of her hip the entire time. "This is Jarthow."

"Hello, young man." Arnath said, extending his hand.

The boy stood entirely still, looking up at Arnath with both distant and judging eyes. It wasn't until his mother gave his shoulder a squeeze, did he extend his hand, allowing Arnath to shake it. "Hello, sir."

Not meeting Arnath's eye, perhaps to simply not see the effect the terrible impression her dour son had made on him, Merynda indicated her daughter, a bouncy girl of seven. "And this is Perrin."

Without prompting, Perrin wrapped her arms around Arnath's thigh and hugged it. "Hello Mr Captain."

"I'm afraid I've acquired a passenger." Arnath said, a laugh in his voice.

"You might be stuck with her for a while." Merynda said, a smile in her eyes.

"Well, since I've grown a third leg, I feel somewhat hungry. Shall we eat?" Arnath asked, gesturing toward the door of the Briny Sea.

Merynda turned her head awkwardly, saying, "We've not been paid for our wares as yet..."

Arnath shook his head, not letting her hang for single a moment, "I wouldn't dream of having you pay. Besides, we have an account. So, don't trouble yourself. Let's eat."

That settled, Arnath motioned for them to follow him across the street.

*

After sunset, as the last of the elves were putting their tools away and leaving for the night, Arnath brought Merynda and her family across the street for a look at the outpost. He led them through the main corridor to show them the progress in the back courtyard, not feeling it was quite safe enough to take the children upstairs just yet. Much to both the children's delight, Shrakar was testing the ropes on the training wall built against the rise of the mound. Jarthow and Perrin raced up to the wooden wall that was bolted to the rock face, rising more than twenty feet up in the curved shape of a clam shell. Ropes and hand holds were built into the wall, so a warrior might train to take on the mightiest mountain, or the deepest crevasse. Seeing the children below, Shrakar eased himself down his rope, winked across the courtyard at Arnath and began to show the children the many features of the yard.

Grateful for a moment alone, Arnath and Merynda leaned against the door-frame and watched Shrakar play with the children. Arnath looked at the ground, unsure how to broach the delicate subject. Seeing his discomfort, Merynda said, "He was six when his father died. Perrin has no memory of him, but Jarthow ... He was in the room when my Corrin passed. His father took a piece of his son with him, I'm afraid."

Arnath nodded. "What was it?"

"Our last battle, Heshtro." She said showing him the scar on her forearm, slightly healed by her first encounter with Garthe. The scar and the battle she named raised Arnath's eyebrows. He did not participate in that one particular battle at the close of the war, having been elsewhere, but he knew of the brutality of the crushing loss. That Merynda even stood here alive was impressive. "Corrin was wounded, quite severely. And all of our mages were dead. He was stitched together and survived. I nursed him back to health after the war, we married, established our farm, had the children but he never fully healed."

"No mage could...?" Arnath asked, letting it hang.

"No. You were in the war, and now travel with a mage. You know those things, the deep internal injuries, must be tended to early for the body to fully heal. Otherwise, you're just fighting the wounds over time."

"And time always wins." Arnath said, quoting their old drill sergeants.

"Yes, it does."

"And since, no men from the nearby farms have taken the boy in hand?"

"No. No one." Merynda said, knowing she was answering two important questions for Arnath. "It's too bad really. He could have used an influence like yours."

"Could have?" Arnath asked, not understanding her.

"Once this place is opened you will be up to your chin in rough customers, brigands and thieves. That's no place for a boy who has already been wounded by the world."

Arnath turned to face her and pointed aggressively at the ground. "Not here. Not ever. Like you, I swore an oath to protect this kingdom and its people. I have no intention of letting this place be a flophouse for criminal scum. I don't want them in my town, let alone under my roof. One can certainly go where the scent of gold takes you without letting it turn you into a cut throat. Take my companions and I as an example. I've learned all about the type you revile in my travels, and they won't be lodging here."

"I see." Merynda said as Arnath turned back toward the yard, perhaps a tad embarrassed his convictions led him to speak with such fervor. Merynda took advantage of his awkward feelings, and stole an extra moment to just look at him admiringly, the most important question about him now answered.

*

That night, Arnath walked the three of them down to the stables, where their cart and horses were put up. Arnath made sure to shake Jarthow's hand, look him in the eye and tell him what a pleasure it was to meet him. The boy seemed more befuddled by the gesture than pleased. Arnath took this an improvement, as perplexed could lead in all sorts of directions, whereas dour and dismissive was only that. Perrin was much easier to please. She stood up on the front seat of the cart, wrapped her arms around Arnath's neck and let herself dangle off of him, giggling the whole time.

Finally, after prying the wriggling girl off his neck and setting her back on the long seat next to her brother, Arnath rounded the cart to stand with Merynda. He asked if she would come for the opening day of the outpost. She said she would if she could, making no promises. She did say she would come the first opportunity the work of her farm eased. Then, holding his hand, Merynda kissed Arnath on the cheek. Insides all aflutter, Arnath helped her up onto the wagon, and watched them go down the western road toward the King's highway.

When they finally got out of his sight, Arnath crossed the road and walked through the gates to the lakeside. The tent city was shrinking ever smaller as the days went on. Workers under Lorta's employ returned to Solindar upon completing their given skill's contribution to the growing structure. Most of the remaining tents housed those skilled in the decorative arts, those who would put the finishing touches on the building once the doors and windows arrived from Solindar.

Arnath strode with his head in the clouds, cheerfully nodding to those he knew until reaching the tent by the big tree. Trellith, Shrakar and Garthe were there. Shrakar was dead asleep, his head lolled back, jaw wide open. Everyday on the project he had been utilized for his great strength, alongside Taishen. No matter the job, if it required someone who could handle heavy materials, Shrakar stepped up to the task. Most days, after work, Shrakar would head to the lake with some food from the Briny Sea, eat and then immediately fall asleep without so much as a swig from his wineskin. On top of his work day today, he'd just served as a play companion for two energetic children. Eventually, he had to bid the children goodnight and head away to sleep. Trellith and Garthe, were very much awake and beamed at Arnath, awaiting any word on his evening with the farm maiden and her children. Arnath merely sat against the log, next to Trellith and grabbed his skin and took a long haul on it.

"So, the lady farmer came a-calling?" Trellith asked, more as a prod, since he knew the answer already.

"She did indeed." Arnath said, looking more than a little satisfied.

"Will she return soon?" Garthe asked, pointing his quill pointedly.

"She may come for our opening day. If she can get away."

"And what of her children? Are they good little children or unholy brats?" Trellith asked, fully expecting the latter to be so.

Arnath explained to them about the boy, and about the untimely death of his father. Arnath stated he was fully confident that the boy's dour disposition was something that would fade with time. He knew so because they had seen it before, he said looking directly at Garthe.

"I remember." Garthe said, recalling that strange and painful time. "Morgosh had only taken me as his apprentice from my parents a year or so before. To wave goodbye to one's family, then shortly to lose your master, your whole world... "

Garthe let the last hang, the memories still raw, even after a full seven years.

"We too were at a loss as to how to be of help." Trellith said, nodding as he did, eyes on the fire, gazing into the past.

"But you did. Help, that is. Day by day, little by little. I could have disappeared into a shell of grief." Grathe said. "But our adventures helped me rise out of it. I'm very grateful still."

"Think not on it." Arnath said, passing the skin back to Trellith. "I imagine myself dead, many times over, had you not been there with us."

"Myself as well." Trellith said, finishing a swig.

"Indeed, you've snatched us from the jaws of death repeatedly. Perhaps mourning for Morgosh together, we created our own bonds, our own family." Arnath said, his tone growing serious.

Grathe nodded, and said, "But this boy sees nothing but the jaws of death. Has thought of nothing since. His father being swallowed by them. I shall keep an eye out for him, see if his inner spark lies within medicines."

"As will I." Trellith said. "I've never known a young man who wasn't fascinated by the ring of the forge."

"Thank you, gentlemen. If I am to pay proper court to Merynda, her children are a responsibility I must also tackle in kind. Your help is more than appreciated, with the boy in particular. The little girl is no problem, boundless energy though she has." Arnath said with sincerity, but then looked at Garthe, an impish twinkle in his eye. "Mayhaps you can teach me how to handle that aspect."

Garthe looked at them both, ignorant as to what part of that notion drew such a chuckle from Arnath and Trellith. "I had no sisters. I can't see what you mean."

"Come now, lad. You've paid court to two beautiful young women in front of the entire town for weeks." Trellith said, joined in with Arnath's baiting with a humourously scolding tone. "Or didn't you think the hundreds of people coming and going of late would notice?"

"But I haven't. Shimalena and Illona are my friends!" Garthe protested, only adding to Arnath and Trellith's enjoyment of his awkward predicament. "Surely the whole town, all the labourers from Solindar, don't think that we three..."

"What else are they to think, lad?" Trellith said, poking his pipe toward Garthe. "The three of you are of marrying age in some communities. My, in some farming communities, you'd be well past the acceptable time, might even have children."

"But I have no intent towards marrying them. Either of them. I can't have children anyway. I have my studies!" Garthe exclaimed, burying his face in his hands.

Arnath traded a quick look at Trellith, a silent confirmation they'd teased the boy long enough. Arnath then sat forward and said, quietly, "As long you haven't sullied either of these girls..."

"I haven't. I wouldn't." Garthe blurted, then thought on it. "Even though I'd like to. Be intimate with them, I mean. Something might happen... were there not two of them. Fathers, what should I do?"

"No matter what happens, be honest. And no matter what, don't be hurtful." Arnath said. "To be involved with someone, then spurn them because you got what you wanted... It's not something a man with good heart does."

Trellith nodded at this, and said, "Agreed. I'd say also, be extra careful for our messenger girl's heart. She seems somewhat arrested in her growing. Living in this isolated place, surrounded by the elderly... I don't think she's had the experiences you and the elf-girl have. She may never even have seen animals rutting on a farm. Perhaps has no idea of the mechanics of it all."

"Why does that matter?" Garthe said, utterly perplexed.

"Because," Arnath said, picking up from the dwarf. "She may not understand that your closeness will lead to huddling, coupling. She might even be terrified of the very idea. Let her lead the way when it comes to that."

"Your elf-girl, on the other hand, I think knows her business regarding romance. Again, whatever happens, be honest. It not just your life, it's theirs too." Trellith said, with a degree of finality.

Garthe only had a moment to think on all of it, staring into the fire, when the sound of footsteps on the grass could be heard. Shimalena emerged from the darkness, the golden light of the fire cast upon her from head to toe. She shook a skin, presumably of peach cider, at her side and eyed Garthe with a wicked smiled. That smile went away in an instant as she curtsied to Arnath and Trellith. "Good evening, gentlemen of outpost. Garthe can come for walking?"

"Of course, he can." Arnath said, suppressing laughter. "Off you go, lad."

Garthe rose, crossed over to Shimalena, who kissed him despite the older men's presence, and the two disappeared into the night.

Arnath snatched the skin from Trellith and drank deeply. Handing it back, he said, "Were it at all possible, I would feel no surprise if one day we were the grandfathers of a young half-elf mage."

"Or a towny boy who was swift on his feet like his mother." Trellith added.

"Mere months ago, we were tomb raiding adventurers who drank and whored our prize money away. Now we sit around the fire giving the boy we raised advice so he does not become the heartless town letch. My younger self balks at who we've become at times."

Trellith drank deeply and handed the skin back. "Gave the boy we raised advice on how to be a good man, within sight of the tallest building in town, a business we fools for-any-damned-adventure built from the ground up with our own hands and money. Who have we become indeed?"

For the rest of the night, the two old warriors passed the skin back and forth until was dry.

*

Garthe and Shimalena emerged into the outpost courtyard, and found Amorth there, tending his security duties. Seeing the two youngsters there, holding hands, Amorth took the hint quickly. Being that Garthe was one of the owners of the establishment he guarded, he strolled out of the yard, stepped past them, heading for the front door, where he would mind his post from afar for as long as they needed. "Master Garthe, M'Lady." Amorth said, disappearing down the outpost corridor.

Garthe and Shimalena crossed the courtyard and sat on the natural bench of flat shale rocks that surrounded the spring pool.

Settling close together in the moonlight that reflected off the pool, Shimalena unslung the skin from her shoulder and placed it in Garthe's lap. She then partially unlaced the front of her shirt, parting it slightly from him to see. Garthe swallowed hard, determined to talk over the serious matters as quickly as he could, for he knew he couldn't control himself for long.

"You don't have to do that." Garthe said, not daring to reach and close her shirt.

"You no want to see me? I want to see all of you." Shimalena stated, holding back her usually teasing tone. The innocence both he and Illona displayed charmed her so. Something in her wished this part of it could last forever, but she knew it couldn't. She reached for the wine skin, making sure to leave the back of her hand in his lap for an extra second before picking the skin up and uncorking it.

As she held her head back, drinking deeply from the skin, Garthe composed himself and thought on what Arnath and Trellith had said. Finally, swallowing his fear, said, "I don't want to hurt you. Either of you. You or Illona. I didn't know desires could lead this way. To more than one person at once. And now, I don't know what to do."

"You are not virgin. You've said." Shimalena said, passing him the wine skin, from which Garthe quickly gulped down several swallows. He now completely regretted telling Shimalena, after too many ales during the last big party held across the street, that almost two years ago his adventuring fathers had questionably made the drunken decision to take him to a house where ladies of the night plied their trade for his sixteenth birthday.

"What is your fear?" She asked, genuinely not understanding why her handsome mage was so restrained in his desires.

"Illona is. She must be treated... delicately. I'm afraid if you and I are together, she will be heartbroken and will spurn us as friends forever."

"And if we three were together?" Shimalena asked flatly.

Garthe swallowed down some cider, and repeated her words, "We three?"

"Not so strange. Look at this, the town. All the old person. Over years and years, you not think they have relations and do business, and be friends, with different couple making different children from each, but all together in same place?"

"Of course, over time..." He said, not finding fault in her logic.

"And when do time start? Tomorrow? A year? Twenty years?" Shimalena said, edging closer to him. "For me, time, all time, is now."

Then, she leaned in and kissed him.

*

Heflynn rode into town via the eastern road, the sun on his face, keeping to the far right so as to avoid the elf craftsmen who were pulling materials from the last of the palettes and darting in and out of the first cut-out.

He'd only been gone for a few days, investigating a haunting in the north woods. It turned out to be merely a clever old woman who wanted people to leave her alone. Since no one was actually harmed, Heflynn did not have her arrested and warned the nearby townsfolk to just let the old crone be. Such was the nature of his work investigating the arcane for the crown. More often than not there were very human explanations for the dread things people reported.

Heflynn was happy to be called away. As swept up as he was watching his friend's outpost being built, he was also more than a little crestfallen that Listrelle had been ordered elsewhere to fulfill her duties under her new rank, as she had correctly guessed she might be. Since their first night together, they had spent no nights apart. They had made love and talked of possible futures until dawn. In the day, Listrelle was her usual prim, stoic, soldierly self, as befit her new rank, a sergeant major in the King's Guard. The moments of joy they had in each other's arms at night had a minute pall hanging over them. Both he and Listrelle knew she would be called away soon, and duty would separate them. Knowing in advance made it no less painful to separate, that pain doubled by the notion that their pairing might be frowned upon by the Guard – A lower ranked King's guard and a direct relative of the King. Not exactly a scandal, but some might call into question her rank and so begin the spoiling of her career in the guard.

It made a public goodbye out of the question.

Since she was sent south-west, to quell some disturbance reported near Sol-mairyth, Heflynn choose to lessen the distance between by officially making his headquarters in Kroman's Town. In truth, his headquarters were wherever the post could reach him but Kroman's was beginning to feel like home to him – He'd found true companions here, he'd found love here – and it was close enough that he could ride to the palace in a matter of days if he was needed for an official palace function.

Riding up the east side of the rising road, Heflynn could see little of the details of the outpost frontage, but still was impressed. The apex of the roof was nearly as tall as the peak of the mound, and jutted over the street by quite a distance at the top. Getting closer, he could see many elves working under the protective canvas stretched over the scaffolding, some installing windows, many painting and varnishing. The main doors had yet to be installed, he guessed as he passed by, catching a wink of light from the back courtyard through the front door. The medical clinic could be plainly seen at the bottom of the scaffold, jutting out into the street far enough to press right against the gossamer canvas. Heflynn could just spy a hint of the white painted interior as he finished his ride by.

Crossing the town square, beginning the dip down towards the stables, a swift movement caught the corner of Heflynn's eye and turning, he saw Illona speeding towards him. He slowed his regal black horse to allow her to catch up. Dismounting, he took the bridle in hand and waited for her. "You wished to speak, Illona?"

"Yes. Yes, I did. Do, I mean." Illona said, catching her breath.

"What is it?" Heflynn said, starting to lead his horse to the stable gate.

"I was hoping... I mean, I wanted..." Still out of breath, she gave up trying to speak and simply pull a scroll from her pocket and unfurled it to show it to him.

"You are applying to the king's postal service." He said looking down at the document. Then it dawned on him. "Ahh, you wish an endorsement."

"Yes, if you'd be so kind." Illona said, red in her cheeks. "I'm not old enough yet, but when I turn of age..."

"Oh no." Heflynn interrupted Illona, her heart sank a moment, thinking he had changed his mind. "You can file this application at any time. They will inform you of their decision after your eighteenth birthday."

"I can?" Illona asked, seemingly astounded by the notion.

"Yes. Let's get my charger away, and we'll go straight to the post office."

*

That night, a celebratory dinner was held to commemorate Heflynn's becoming a resident of Kroman's Town. What was supposed to be a small friendly dinner with his friends from the outpost, ended up being somewhat hijacked by Mayor Bumpol, who was bursting with pride that a member of the royal family was going to be living in his town.

Word had spread quickly after Heflynn had made queries of Lorta and Taishen about how much work it would take to refurbish the old, octagonal shaped cottage that sat a stone's throw from the first cut-out in the eastern road.

The first whispers became a whirlwind, and by the time Heflynn and his fellows settled at their table on the balcony, the entire town knew.

To avoid disappointing the mayor, who likely would have fallen into a pit of despair had he not, Heflynn gave a short speech. He thanked everyone for being so welcoming, and asked that everyone keep the gossip around him to a minimum, as his role as the kingdom's arcane investigator brought him into contact with multiple unsavory things from the beyond and Kroman's already had an outpost destroyed by one of them.

When he went back to the table he was greeted by many exaggerated dour faces. "That surely threw a bucket of cold water onto the festivities." Trellith declared, a little too loudly.

"Yes. Why not tell these poor, old folk you'll be opening a demon portal next to your cottage?" Arnath asked, unable to contain his snickering.

"Come now, gentlemen." Heflynn said with a dismissive hand wave. "Are you not hosting a town-wide celebration in a couple of days? Any revels in regards to where my saddlebag gets hung should be decidedly low key in comparison."

That notion, parties, low key or otherwise, stuck in Arnath's mind for a moment. They'd been drawn into many a celebration since arriving in this quaint little town. He couldn't recall if they had imbibed and revelled as much on the road. They must have, for there was no money to show for the last twenty-odd years of his life. They'd find a treasure haul and celebrate the lean times being over until they were entirely skint of coin and the lean times began again. Not exactly the path to prosperity. Here, at least, they celebrated life-affirming things, not just the coins in their pockets.

That last thought drew Arnath's gaze down the table, to the far corner where Garthe sat next to Illona, in one of her stylish new elvish riding frocks, giggling about who knows what. The young mage's laughter stopped immediately when he saw Arnath stand and raised his glass, looking Garthe in the eye the entire time.

"Oh, please don't." Garthe said across the table, his face becoming red as an apple.

"Pipe down, boy. It only happens once a year." Arnath then looked around the table, and to everyone said, "This week marked the fourth full moon of summer. That is the time of year when we three – Trellith, Shrakar and I - celebrate the birthday of our esteemed colleague. Since his long-gone master dealt with his family when he first joined us on the road, and he being a boy of nine at the time with no mind for such things, once Morgosh had died we had no way to know exactly when his birthday was. It has become our tradition to celebrate his birthday on the anniversary of his joining our company – The fourth moon of summer every year. So, I ask you to raised your glasses in toast and tribute, in celebration of Garthe the mage, on this, his eighteenth birthday."

The entire table stood, and shouted, "Garthe the mage!" in the direction of the thoroughly embarrassed lad hiding behind the rim of his goblet.

And, of course, Mayor Bumpol overheard and that gave him excuse to make a speech and begin the celebration anew.

*

Later, when the Briny Sea was mostly closed down, Arnath borrowed a lantern from Durnly, and walked across the street with Heflynn. He lit the lantern as they passed through the veil of canvas that enshrouded the front scaffolding and stepped down the short steps into the main corridor of the outpost. Almost immediately, a figure filled the back door, and shouted, "Who's that? Who goes there?"

"It's me, Shamuth. Thought I'd show the prince our little establishment." Arnath said, raising the lantern so Shamuth could see them.

"Very good, captain. My prince." Shamuth said, his salute and bow barely visible in the lamplight. Then, he disappeared into the darkness of the court-yard, returning to his guard duties.

"Come see this." Arnath said, taking a few steps into the corridor and raising the lantern higher.

The front corridor of the outpost was set up exactly as it had been before, but for the floor dipping down and therefore the ceiling was now nine feet above. As before, the main corridor was in the center, if slightly to the left. When first coming down the stairs, there was a section of wall that had racks for coats of all heights, big and small. The coat pegs were not screwed in yet, but Heflynn got the idea.

Next to the coat racks on the wall was a wooden case that was unoccupied presently. "For our license, and local maps and such." Arnath said, turning further down the corridor with the lamp.

Next to the case, a long, waist-high counter ran for near ten feet. Where the counter met the wall, sat a criss-crossing cupboard of open nooks, which Heflynn figured was for the post and messages for their guests. Arnath walked down to the end of the long counter, lifted up a hinged barrier and stood behind it. "My new position in life." He said with a smile, and began to point at various things behind the counter. "These empty racks here will hold small kegs and casks from the Briny Sea. Ones we can replace by merely walking across the street. This free space on the wall next to them will have a scaled down version of the master map. One for quick conferring of information. The real maps will be upstairs."

"What about that rack above the map space?" Heflynn asked.

After a brief pause, Arnath said, "For my sword."

"Ah. A place to truly hang it up forever." Heflynn said, nodding.

"The whole place is really for that, I'd say. Come look at this." Arnath said, motioning Heflynn to join him behind the counter. As Heflynn came around, Arnath shone the lamp under the counter, saying "You have some coin? Small coins, this is only a demonstration."

Heflynn reached into the purse at his waist and handed Arnath a few coppers, a most curious look on his face. Leaning to look under the counter, Heflynn could see a large, carved wooden funnel topping a pipe that disappeared into the floor. Arnath spilled the coins into the funnel, where they circled crazily around for a moment and then disappeared into the pipe.

"Where do they go?" Heflynn asked, a look of wonder on his face.

"Down to a hidden lockbox in the basement."

"So, you can't be robbed." Heflynn surmised.

"Because all coin that comes our way never stays on this floor." Arnath said, finishing the thought.

"What if someone makes it into the basement?" Heflynn only half-asked. He could guess what Arnath might say.

"Then they are trapped. One way up, one way down."

"And a Captain of the King's guard, a dead shot Dwarf, a mage and seven-foot half-Orc waiting for them if they try to come back up." Heflynn said, snickering at the notion. Most outpost owners were fat, old inn keepers. Any ruffian that dared to raise a stink in this outpost was in for a huge surprise, and face full of missing teeth.

Arnath turned and opened two wide cabinet doors beside the space for the map. Inside were racks for swords, hangers for quivers and shields. "Weapons cupboard. For the customers. As proprietors, we haven't come to a decision on weaponry within the outpost."

"'Tis rather personnel, asking someone to strip of their weaponry." Heflynn said, inwardly balking at the mere notion of the request.

"We know. Might end up being a case by case basis." Arnath said, closing the cupboard and motioning Heflynn onwards.

After stepping out from behind the counter, Arnath crossed the corridor that exactly mimicked in dimensions the one that a short time ago was ripped to shreds by the debris bundles from out back. This newly constructed version was lacquered in a dark brown shade, deep enough to fool the eye that it was black. The recent varnishing of all the wood surfaces made them shine in the lamplight. As they stepped into the outpost's common room, Heflynn stepped beside him, to take advantage of the lamplight and looked around.

All in all, it was large enough for some twenty persons to enjoy, without jostling each other. Though there was a larger dining table, nearer the front of the building, most were better suited to groups of two to four.

At the rear of the room, which extended nearly to the rear of the building, was a large fireplace, the recessed stone innards capped over by an ornately carved wood mantle. Several chairs surrounded it, high-backed with subtle patterns in the cushioning, even one that was Orc-sized.

The wall the common room shared with the main corridor had a pass-through cut in it at elbow height, allowing a full view from the counter into the corner area and vice versa. The ledge on the wall was tooled wider than the rest of the pass-through's frame, to act as a place for food and drink for customers who stood. Centered under the pass-through ledge was a small round table and two comfortable chairs. The table was for playing pegs on, and had the snaking course of playing holes for the pegs drilled into it. One side of the table was slightly recessed and covered in green velvet, a space for the dice to be rolled. A brass-handled drawer was underneath the table top, presumably to store the pegs and dice.

The opposite far corner near the fire place had small tables for food and drink, and more ledges built into the very corners for one to lean and put their drinks down, at the same height as the ledge in the pass-through. Right next to that corner stood an empty book shelf. Standing next to that was a tall rack, criss-crossed like X'es, for scrolls.

"We have no reading material yet." Arnath said.

"I can send for some. The palace is replete with books, as you'd imagine." Heflynn said.

"Excellent."

After the book and scroll shelves, the support beams created a natural divide in the room. The upper spanning beams had extra-large hand-holds craved in them, and Heflynn surmised these were for Orc guests to hold onto rather than be uncomfortably crouched over at all times. At the base of the support beam was a small upraised, semi-circular dais wide enough across for perhaps two performers, musicians or orating bards, to perform for the room. The small dining tables fanned out from the platform so everyone in the room could see the performers.

The wall next to the beam with its small stage spread wide to the front of the building. At elbow level a jutting ledge, wide enough for plates, ran from the beam to the front of the room. Unlike the rest of the room, with its polished, dark lacquered surfaces this portion of the wall was a textured spackle of plaster. Pointing at it, Arnath said, "We have a tapestry coming from Quinhaven. A depiction of the battle of Isthmar."

"Fitting." Heflynn said, knowing all-too-well that Arnath, Shrakar and Trellith had distinguished themselves beside his father and uncle in that last great battle of the war. His father never failed to bring it up.

"Speaking of fitting, do you have that arrow? The special one with the thong attached?"

Somewhat taken aback, Heflynn took the quiver from his shoulder, plucked out the arrow and handed it to Arnath, who turned and strode across the room. In the corner, at the end of the plastered portion of the wall, the support beam had a brass hook affixed to it at eye level. Arnath took the thong and hung the arrow on the hook. He then knocked twice on the beam, and said, "Unlucky bastard."

"Unlucky? One would think my arrow was quite lucky." Heflynn said, with an ironic half-scowl.

"Not your arrow, mate." Arnath said, knocking once again on the support beam. "Deep inside this wall, in this corner is the very support beam we struggled against, not once but twice."

"You mean to say the beam that nearly destroyed the Briny Sea was the same one that cause the accident, injured Shimalena's friend?" Heflynn inquired, somewhat agog.

"The very same."

Heflynn strode over to where the arrow hung, and gave a couple strong knocks on the wood. "Unlucky bastard, indeed."

"We'll leave your arrow there to remind us of how lucky we were, and would hope to continue to be." Arnath said, then turned to the front of the room. "See here, this is Garthe's clinic."

The front wall of the room had frosted glass windows from waist-level up, and a door at its center. Arnath opened the door, swung it wide open and held the lantern inside. Heflynn leaned in the doorway, and saw the room was completely white-washed. It was large enough for perhaps four persons and an upraised bed in the center. Counters and shelving filled the corner opposite the short flight of stairs to the street.

"Tight space. What if Garthe gets an Orc patient?" Heflynn inquired.

"We'll treat them out here on the big dinner table, I suppose." Arnath said, having not thought of it before. "Or out back in the courtyard. This is a good start for a town with an aging populace. I'm sure, in time, his practice will grow."

*

Arnath and Heflynn climbed the high-ceilinged stairs to the first floor above the entry corridor. The corridor on their right that stretched out before them was long and narrow. Like downstairs, the wood of the floors, walls and ceiling was darkly stained. Affixed brass candle holders hung at head level up and down the hallway.

Arnath knocked on the wall to his right, saying, "These will be Orc quarters."

They reached a very tall door several paces down the hall, and went inside. The room was long and had an upraised iron fireplace, a wash station and privy in one corner. There was ample shelving, all of it set high on the walls. Two huge beds, each some ten feet long, were set up side by side in the room. "For a couple of Orcs travelling together, or in a party."

"They'll be happy with those beds." Heflynn said, wide-eyed at their massive size.

"Come look at this one." Arnath said exiting the room. In the corridor, right beside the door they had just left was another door of the exact same dimensions. Beyond it was another room that stretched all the way to the front of the building, where a window that would eventually look out into the street was installed. It had a privy and high shelving like the other, but only a single bed – one that was twelve feet long and eight feet wide. "My goodness!" Heflynn said upon seeing it in the lamp light.

"For a travelling Orc couple. Or a really big fellow." Arnath said with a smile.

"A big fellow indeed."

"Should see Shrakar's bed. With all that stuffing, I imagine every goose from Solindar to Quinhaven is running about naked." Arnath joked, and Heflynn laughed as they left the room. Crossing the narrow hall, there were two doors to choose from. Arnath strode a bit down the hall, choosing the door closest to the front window.

Inside was a room appointed like the others, but designed for smaller-sized customers – humans and elves. The ceiling was lower than across the hall, and all the furnishings and shelving were for average-sized persons. A large, comfortable looking bed sat inside the room, just across from the doorway. In the far corner from the door were a wash basin and privy. The privy was shielded from view by a screen, much like a dressing screen, but mounted on the wall. Heflynn checked all this over, and asked, "Have you tried the system yet? Running the water to the basins, flushing the privies?"

"The pipes, yes. But we haven't filled the tank on the roof yet. We will soon. Once the two doors for the front and courtyard are installed, we ourselves will be moving in, so we'd better have running water by then." Arnath said, turning on the tap over the brass bath basin to show it was dry.

Heflynn looked at all the appointments of the room thoughtfully, and moved to the window. He looked out, having to peer through the small gaps in the canvas covering the scaffolding outside to get a look at the view beyond. He could just make out the roof of the Briny Sea, and the lake to the far left.

"I'll take this one." Heflynn said, turning from the window.

"You'll do what now?" Arnath asked, somewhat befuddled.

"Master Lorta says it will take some time to fix that sagging old cottage at the end of the street. Until then, I'd rather room with you fellows. No chance to ply my trade rooming over the scrivener's."

"Ply your trade? Here? How?" Arnath asked.

"Since you plan to house and train free adventurers, many of their parties will be seeking to plunder ancient sites that may have some lore behind them that their parties might be unaware of. We don't want another deadly live-stone unearthed now, do we?" Heflynn explained.

"Next you'll say the crown will be issuing permits for such adventures." Arnath said jokingly.

"It has been contemplated." Heflynn said without any sense of whimsy. "Whilst men are free to plunder whatever riches they can from the ruins of the myriad ancient kingdoms that ours are built upon; some constraint is required to stop hapless treasure seekers from unleashing ancient terrors upon our present-day world. By the light, emissaries from Kruendaal have sent complaints to the palace stating that adventurers they suspect were from here unleashed a curse that destroyed the entire Ulgrew mountain range, if you can believe it."

Arnath looked at Heflynn wide-eyed and said nothing. He made a mental note to tell the others to be silent about where the fortune that built this structure came from. Arnath agreed with, but was also deeply disturbed by what Heflynn said. He and his party had adventured across the three kingdoms unfettered by governance for more than twenty years. At times they ran afoul of the law, particularly the western guard of the neighbouring kingdom, Kruendaal, otherwise they lived as free as the wind itself. To hear that adventuring such as they had done might some day be regulated was disheartening. It could mean the end of the appeal of a once-free lifestyle that Arnath and his companions had enjoyed to the fullest, and had now chosen to be in service of. Their whole business depended on people's desire to seek fortunes at risk of life and limb. To be told that wasn't allowed by some bureaucrat, a post office clerk even, rendered that entire life path pointless.

Not wanting to spoil the tour, Arnath held his tongue and smiled, clapped Heflynn on the shoulder, saying, "Our first customer."

Returning to the end of the hall by the stairs, they came to a door and went inside. By the lamplight, Heflynn could see the furnishings were a tad smaller and the shelving was set lower on the walls. "Trellith's?" he asked.

"Exactly. He asked to be on the lowest residential floor. Dwarves are not fond of stairs, as you can imagine. And if he does not wish to be underfoot of Orc customers in the morning, there's this." Arnath said, then marched to the back of the room where a windowed wall had a door in its center.

One could see the back courtyard through the rippled glass of the door. Arnath had to reach low to turn the knob that was positioned on the door for Trellith's use.

They stepped out onto the balcony, into the cool air of the night. Heflynn stepped to the rail to look, but didn't get too close – It only came to his knees, and he could easily imagine himself spilling over it. From here, he could see the entire back courtyard – The smithy, the spring pool, the wall of the mound, the climbing wall built onto it, the long, huge cabinet that almost ran the entire length of the fence. The cabinet, which was as tall as a man, had huge doors interspersed along its length, and was painted a deep crimson and was decorated with brass fittings and knobs.

Arnath made note of Heflynn's interest in the cabinet, and said, "It will house all the training equipment – wooden shields and swords, arrows, padding for mock combats, ropes for the wall. Anything you can think of. As promised, Lorta made it from the remaining, usable wood from the old outpost. Mostly."

The cabinet stopped just short of the gap that remained in the fence. Palettes of materials could be seen on the other side, in the wooded area sloping down to the first cut-out.

Standing next to the gap that in the fence was Shamuth, who gave a nod when he saw Arnath and Heflynn looking down from the balcony.

"We'll close that up eventually. Lorta suggested the fence be hinged at that point, so we can bring in larger materials again. Renovations, and such."

"Good idea." Heflynn said nodding. Turning away from the fence, Heflynn noted a curiously thick rope dangling just away from the balcony. It was not quite girthy enough to anchor a ship, but it was close. He had to lean out from the balcony to grab it. "What's this for?"

"What else? For all of us who live here to get down in a hurry without the bother of the stairs. Trellith had the idea to give his poor knees a break in the mornings, but Garthe really liked the notion too. He figured we could put a bell on a string that could be rung from outside the clinic door at night. The bell would ring next to Garthe's window, all the way at the top floor, and he could come quickly sliding down to attend a late-night patient without waking all of our guests, tromping on the stairs."

"Brilliant. You've thought of everything." Heflynn said, impressed.

"We can only hope. Shrakar liked the idea too. He can get downstairs swiftly, lest we have any fights amongst the patrons that require breaking up, and what have you. Want to see more?"

"Of course."

"Alright. Up you go." Arnath said, waving his hand at the rope.

Heflynn leaned out and grabbed the rope again, and, getting a two-hand grip on it, hiked himself over the railing. He began to rise quickly, hand-over-hand, up to the next balcony. Arnath waited for Heflynn to disappear onto the balcony above and followed, the lantern slung over the back of his hand.

Arnath swung his legs over the second-floor balcony railing, and took a few moments to catch his breath. "I shall be glad to have the training yard all to myself in the mornings."

Still somewhat winded, Arnath pointed to the door, and Heflynn opened it and went inside.

The room they entered was the same size as Trellith's but was furnished more like a library. By the lantern light, Heflynn could discern several racks spanned with dowels along the walls, both short and quite long. An enormous table stood in the center of the room, strewn with maps of all types and sizes. Unopened boxes of quills and ink sat ready atop the table too. Around the room, four of the tall, criss-crossed racks for scrolls were interspersed along the walls.

Much of one wall was occupied by a rack with a long, thick dowel spanning it. Hung over the dowel was a map of a least ten feet wide. As Heflynn approached it, he asked, "The master map?"

"Yes, the one we found in the yard." Arnath said, approaching with the lamp.

As the light grew closer, Heflynn could begin to make out the details of the ornate map. Only within the libraries of the palace had the prince seen a map so dedicated to pointing out the subtleties of foliage and landscape.

"We had Feila, Illona's mother, run it through some cleaning solution after the mud was flaked away. Worry was the inks would disappear when the mud washed out, but they stayed. Colours still look somewhat bright too." Arnath said, moving the lamp closely around the cloth map's surface.

As the light passed over, Heflynn could make out forests created with delicate green thread, rivers in the lightest blue and an interweaving of gold and grey throughout the span of the king's roads in all three kingdoms.

"Incredible." Said Heflynn, running his fingers over the rippling surface of the map.

Arnath turned, casting the light over the table. "Here we can brief our guests on the nuances of the terrain they will be taking on. We can create smaller, more detailed maps of the places we know already. Eventually this whole room will be crammed to the ceiling with maps of all shapes and sizes. We'll create copies, send them on with our clients in the hopes they will experience less in the way of pitfalls than we did."

"I say again, once the royal inspectors see what you have achieved here, you will be awarded the TO marking on all new maps. You'll see." Heflynn said without mirth. He'd seen a great many outposts in his time, travelling about the kingdom as he had, and the further Arnath took him into this one, the more impressed he was.

They stepped out into the corridor near the staircase, and Arnath pointed down the hall. There were two doors on both sides of the hall. Arnath stepped forward to the nearest door on the same side as the map room, and opened in it.

Inside was a long room with many beds in it, six bunk beds in all with cloak pegs and mounted wooden cupboards next to each. They were set length-wise against the wall, and spaced around the room so as to give the most leg room. A common table with chairs was in the center of the room. A wash station and privy were set up in the corner, this privy having a hinged door on its privacy wall. An upraised wood stove stood near the brass washing tub, which had a folding dressing screen nearby.

"For large parties to stay together." Arnath said.

"Excellent." Heflynn said, nodding.

Back in the corridor, Arnath pointed at the two doors on the opposite side, and said, "More Orc-sized quarters, a single and a double. But should we be full-up, few Orc customers say, we can put up couples or families in these rooms too."

Stepping down to the end of the hall, and the door nearest the window, Arnath opened the door and ushered Heflynn in. Inside was very similar to the room Heflynn said he'd take but for more shelving and a larger brass tub in the corner.

Arnath saw Heflynn admiring the tub, and asked, jokingly, "Will you be wanting to switch rooms?"

"No, I want to be close to the ground for the same reasons you fellows have that rope out back. But if you could switch out the tubs, I'd appreciate it." Heflynn said.

"Very well. Done." Arnath said, and looked around the room. "This single is much like yours, but since it is next to the larger, the flop room, I figured it could be for female members of a party, or for a party leader who is not so close to their men. Or single traveller."

"You'll be serving all kinds here, I imagine."

"One can only hope." Arnath said, and left the room.

When they reached the top of the stairs to the fourth floor, Heflynn noted there were four differently configured doors in the corridor. Upon lighting the top step, he saw a tall door directly to his left with large marbled glass panels in it. Moonlight was shiny through it from outside. On the right, where the Orc quarters were on the other floors was a singular, over-sized door for the entire wall. Directly in front of them was a regular sized door, and all the way down the hall, next to the window, was another door like those on the other floors. Heflynn noted as well that this corridor was longer than the floor below, which accounted for the front of the building over-hanging the street below.

Arnath pointed at each door in turn. "The glass door leads again to the balcony, which is longer on this floor. We had it built so, otherwise Shrakar would have to come into my quarters to get outside in a hurry. So that door there is mine, down the hall is another luxury-sized single and behind the big door is Shrakar's. Come see this."

Arnath strode down to the big door, opened it and shone the lamp in. Heflynn peeked inside and saw what Arnath was talking about. All the way down at the end of the room was a bed that filled the entire dimensions of the corner, perhaps twelve feet by twelve feet. Shrakar could lay sprawled like a starfish on it and perhaps not have a single toe over the side. The image made Heflynn give a snort of laughter. "By the light, what a bed."

"See what I mean about the naked geese?" Arnath joked again. Then he turned and went to his door across the hall. Opening it, he ushered Heflynn inside and followed, casting the lamp light about. Heflynn noted the room was decidedly longer than Trellith's, with the shelving and furnishings at a man's height.

"You and the others have no personal items in your rooms. Are you waiting for the doors to be installed to move things in?" Heflynn said, truly curious.

"Oh no. We don't really have any personal items. We three, now four, have travelled on foot and horseback for more than twenty years. We've only owned the weapons at our sides and the clothes on our backs that entire time." Arnath smiled and looked around the room. "It'll be nice to collect clothes and trinkets the way others have done their whole lives for once."

Heflynn nodded at this, thinking on how he had chosen the nomadic job he had exactly because of the trappings of the palace, the over-abundance of luxury, and the fawning of courtiers. He envied Arnath and his companions for their twenty plus years of unbridled freedom.

About to turn from the undecorated room, Heflynn noticed something. "Your bed. It's quite large too. One might think big enough for two people."

Arnath smiled and said again, a wry gleam in his eye, "One can only hope."

Heflynn could see as they turned at the last upward landing that the stairs did not end in a corridor, but rather a singular door instead. Above them the roof sloped at an angle. They had reached the top of the building.

Heading inside of the apex-shaped space, Heflynn saw many work benches, as well as a scrivener's desk and multiple racks for books and scrolls. "Garthe's lab. Unlike the rest of us, he has started to fill his quarters up." Arnath said, indicating the many books and scrolls that Shimar had provided. "We got him all these mixing beakers for potions and such for his birthday."

Arnath walked away from the work table that was stacked high with many different shapes and sizes of glass wear employed in the conjuring arts and went over to a wall that divided this top story of the building in half, and opened the door. Inside was a room that went all the way to the front of the building. A sizeable bed sat next to a semi-circular window that looked out on the grassy fields, the lake and the forests beyond. "As I said, a bell will hang there by the window, then Garthe can go down the rope and see to his nighttime patients."

Heflynn cocked his head to one side, and said wryly, "Do you think that bed is big enough for three?"

"Goodness, not you too." Arnath said, rolling his eyes. "The poor lad is already celebrated enough, being a skilled healing mage at his age. Imagine as well the eyes of all his elders on him and his companions as though they were romantic players in a travelling mummer's show."

"I only jest." Heflynn said, then pointed back to the lab, "However, a more serious thought, considering how the last outpost met its demise, how safe do you feel with all that will be going on in there, right above your quarters?"

Arnath strode through the door again and walked to the back of the laboratory room. On the right side of the windowed door that faced the mound, was a large hatch in the wood of the slanting ceiling. Arnath set his lamp down on a work table, unlocked the heavy clasps at the top, and eased the thick hatch in and down on its hinges. Heflynn stepped forward to see the revealed space outside.

Beyond the hatch opening was a huge cylindrical water tank, one nearly the width of a grain silo. Standing as tall as a man, it was topped off by a conical lid. "This will supply all of our wash basins, tubs and privies. Now you see there..."

Arnath was pointing at a rectangular shaped pattern of screws embedded in the wood that faced the hatch opening. "One axe strike in the center of that, and this whole room gets flooded by the tank. Hopefully the boy won't be creating too many fiery experiments up here, but if one does get out of control..."

"Ingenious. How do you refill that monstrosity?" Heflynn asked.

Arnath bade him follow as he stepped through the door and onto the uppermost balcony on the back of the outpost. Outside, Arnath pointed up to the roof just beside the water tank. A pump very much like those one would use at a well was attached to the tank via a large pipe. Arnath traced the point of his finger, following the pipe, all the way down the side of the building, across the yard and to the spring pool.

"The spring pool supplies the water?" Heflynn asked, agog.

"Yes. A never-ending supply. Every morning one of us will have to come up and pump the tank full, and the spring pool will refill itself."

Heflynn raised his eyebrows, a smirk on his lips. "Natural spring water to flush away the leavings in the privies? Not even the palace is so opulent."

Arnath laughed, as he donned the gloves tucked in his belt. "Only the best for our customers. Tour's over. Come on – Over you go."

Arnath grabbed the rope that dangled from the heavy metal frame embedded in the apex of the roof, and passed it to Heflynn, who tightened his gloves, gripped the rope and jumped over the side.

*

The last little finishing touches to the magnificent new outpost trickled in to Kroman's Town as the scaffolding was being taken down. The windows had been polished, and a clay tube that ran from Garthe's window all the way down to the clinic door had been installed. Garthe had tied a weighty key to a chord and dropped it down the tube. Together, he and Illona measured out the length needed to keep the bell affixed next to his window ready to chime, and hung a brass ring from the chord, one that people could pull to summon Garthe at night. Another short tube was embedded in the wall, and its chord led to a bell just inside the door, that could be heard from the outpost common room for regular hours, when Garthe could do his reading sitting by the inside door. Illona tested the night bell, giving the cheerful bell a chime, and Garthe dashed from his room high above, through his laboratory, put on his sturdy gloves and slid down the balcony rope. He was in the back doorway of the outpost, and at the inner doorway of his little clinic within seconds, though rushing as he did winded him. Illona and Garthe found, much to their chagrin since they had planned to spend the day together, that people approached Garthe about their many maladies as soon as he emerged from the clinic door. It seemed even though the outpost was not quite open, the clinic now was.

Once the face of the building was revealed, the whole town came by to marvel at it. Though the tall building could be seen all the way from the far side of the lake, people came to stand right under it and gape, their necks craned all the way back to take in the off-set, top heavy upper floors. It was indeed worth a close look, another architectural marvel by the master builder Lorta and right here in their hometown. A couple of gawkers had to be rescued from plummeting backwards down the stairs of the Briny Sea, so far had they backed up across the street whilst looking up.

Because of the gaping crowds, a family matter put intensely private emotions on display right in the street for all to see and cluck about thereafter. Illona's mother Feila was helping inventory the bedding that had arrived from Morley. Feila would be washing it all on a weekly basis, so she knew where it all had to go, to which beds and which storage cupboards. The bedding was heaped high in the back of a large cart parked in front of the outpost's front doorway.

Shrakar was in and out of the front doorway, taking what bundles Feila indicated to the rooms she directed him to. She instructed Illona to follow Shrakar, lest a sheet or towels fall off the piles on the stairs, and the lose track of where they should go. This left Garthe without an assistant, and a cue had now formed, stretching away form the clinic door. Feila felt no chagrin in inconveniencing the boy about whom so many rumors swirled regarding her daughter.

At the front of the cart, Arnath was haggling the price with the old couple who had brought the big load from Morley, and who were quite upset they were not getting a contract to regularly wash the wares they had brought. Like the outpost, Feila's backyard had a spring pool fed by the mound. It was the very heart of her washing business. It also made the carting back and forth of the outpost's laundry from Kroman's to Morley on a weekly basis entirely unnecessary, and this was something that the old couple from Morley were having a hard time understanding. They felt creating the linens somehow meant they had an automatic contract to be the washers thereof forever. The husband was getting quite heated with Arnath about it.

Between this quibbling, the unloading of the cart, the in and out patients at the clinic and those who came to gawk at the intricacies of the outpost frontage, no one noticed Kewin and Anya as they strolled, arm in arm, having come themselves to look at the grand new building. No one would have been surprised by the two of them walking so close together. Since the last big celebration at the Briny Sea, where Anya had summoned Kewin off the stage to dance with her in front of the entire town, everyone knew theirs was a love in bloom. Not exactly the subject of gossip, but everyone in Kroman's knew of how Kewin had let himself get swallowed by a life of drink after his parents had died and had let their business squander. But via working for the outpost and investing his found Arkonian gold, he'd reinvigorated his life and business for the better, like an entirely new man. The work gloves he gave away to the construction workers opened the floodgate of new customers for his glove shop. He and Anya had not had a free day since, so numerous were the orders they needed to fill. Anya's skill in creating decorative stitching only created greater demand.

Together, they represented the kind of prosperity and hope, a hope that included the possibility of growing families, that had returned to the town since the outpost project had begun.

Arnath had kept his calm the entire time the linen man from Morley barked and snarled at him. This was merely business, and no blood was ever going to be drawn. Weighing these day-to-day hurdles in business against the corpse strewn carnage of the life he and his fellows had previously led helped him shrug off such minor aggravations. He was taking the man's bluster in stride, when something strange happened.

The man's eyes glassed over and he just stopped mid-shout. He stared down the street, slack-jawed.

Certain they were not done dickering, Arnath turned to see what the old man was looking at. He turned and there was Kewin and Anya wandering up the street, pointing up at the eye-catching features of the outpost.

When Arnath turned back, the old man roughly shouldered his way past him, and stormed towards Anya, an accusing finger pointed in her direction.

"Oi, there girl! This is where you been?! I ought to whallop you here in the street for what you put your poor mother through!"

The instant the man's voice boomed in her direction, Anya shrank into Kewin's side, under the protection of his arm. She buried her face in his chest, not even wanting to look at the raging man. Kewin put his arm around her, and scowled at the man, saying, "Who might you be, to accost a lady in the street so?"

"Who am I?!" The man angrily bellowed in his thick southern accent. "I'm only the girl's father, I am. Thought I raised her with more respect than to abandon her poor mother, to throw away her apprenticeship in our business. You'd think a girl would be grateful to inherit a business like mine. But no, she has to run off and play trollop with the likes of you. The tears her mother cried, I says."

"Hold your tongue, old goat. Anya has been nothing but a lady in my presence. I won't have you besmirch her in front of me." Kewin said, his anger rising.

Arnath had strode quietly up behind the confrontation, and stood ready to intervene. While it looked as though the older man had a few powerful punches in him, it would not serve Kewin's honour at all to been seen beating up an old man in the street.

Arnath wasn't the only one who stepped closer. Whether it was out of concern, or to enjoy the tawdry spectacle, a crowd now fully surrounded the confrontation.

"A lady?! My Anya. Tosh, I say! The quim of Morley she was..."

"Because you made me so!" Anya's explosive outburst shocked everyone around, but the old man seemed to take pleasure in it, like a combative challenge.

The man's wife had slid to his side, unable to look at Anya, and said quietly, "Del, let's leave her in peace. We best go from here."

"Are you mad, Magra? She owes us. A lifetime of feeding and a roof over her head we gave her. And what does she do? Leaves you with a broken heart? What daughter does that to her poor mother?"

"Stop bringing mother into this! I left because of you, you monster!" Anya shrieked, tears flowing down her face.

Taking his arm from around Anya, and stepping protectively in front of her, Kewin asked in a seething tone, "Is what she said true? Did you turn out your own daughter?"

Rather than shrink in shame, Del puffed out his chest, saying, "She's my daughter, it's my right. Our washer's business fell on hard times, we did what we needed to. Where's harm in that?"

"The harm?! You slobbering cur!" Kewin shouted. Before he could swing his balled-up fists, Arnath stepped in between the two men.

"Take Anya home, Kewin." Arnath said quietly.

"But he...!"

"I know. Let us deal with it. You get her inside, away from prying eyes." Arnath said. Kewin nodded, his rage sloughing away and put his arm again around the weeping Anya.

The defiant Del reached out for her as Anya and Kewin disappeared into the crowd. "Hold on now, she's coming with us!"

Arnath looked past Del and saw the cart was now empty of all of his wares. His use for this barking troll of a man was at its end. Arnath's face was passive as he placed his fingers on the nape of Del's neck and then forcefully drove his thumb into his Adam's apple. Del tried to jerk away, but Arnath dug his fingers into the man's neck, and held him firm. Arnath stood close and stared in the man's eyes until all defiance bled out of them, and he could see the man fully realized that he could be killed right where he stood. All of his bluster was absolutely powerless against it.

"Hear me as the air is choked from your lungs, and know that I am serious. Get on your cart, leave this town, never to come back. Should you set foot in Kroman's Town again, you'll be killed. I'll spare your life today, but on no other. I've slayed many a monster in my time, and I know them well, but none so vicious as one who would turn his own daughter into the street for coin. That requires a unique breed of evil. One that will never be welcome here – ever."

With that, Arnath thrust the man away, hard enough that Del had to struggle to stay on his feet. Steadying himself, Del looked at Arnath through watery eyes, and caught his breath, his defiant sneer already returning. "You'll not do me like that, you lunk. I'll have the sheriff on you, and see what he says about your rough tactics."

"Perhaps not rough enough for you to get the message." Sheriff Daruun said as he emerged from the crowd, being careful his sheathed rapier did not rake anyone across the knees in such a tight gathering. He had clearly been nearby long enough to know what the trouble was, and his look stated wordlessly his disgust in Del's very presence. "I second the Captain's edict. If you have your money, then take your wife and go. Making me ask a second time will be a mistake you will regret for the rest of your life."

Though his face was contorted with rage, Del merely gestured for his wife to mount the cart and turned away.

Magra stood at the end of the cart, her eyes on the cobblestones. "Our only daughter... What shall we do? We'll grow old, too old for our labours. How are we to survive now?"

Her words brought Arnath back to the time when he'd returned home from the wars, only to tell his parents he was setting out on the adventuring road, likely for good. His mother had the exact same worries, until Arnath gave them a huge portion of his back-pay and encouraged them to hire reliable hands, which they promised him they would before tearful goodbyes. Arnath could tell the woman standing next to him knew no such sorrow and had this routine down pat – Deflecting people's ire and disgust at her husband's behaviour by eliciting sympathy from those who would give it. Arnath's stern look let her know he was not falling for it, as he said, "That question was for a time long passed. Did you truly think she could not find love outside the cold disregard of your home?"

"How could I know...?" Magra said blankly.

Arnath turned from her in disgust. Her ploy for his sympathy was completely transparent, and he'd have no part in it. Arnath moved to join the sheriff and they walked away from the crowd. "I apologize for usurping your role."

"No bother. You were quite right to do so in this case. Vile man." Daruun said as they walked side by side. "And that poor girl. Imagine coming to an entirely new place to escape a horrid past, only to have it come right to your door to haunt you. Terrible."

"Indeed. I hope this does not sour her on staying here. Both she and Kewin have had dark days in their pasts, and their pairing could be a balm for each other's reflections on them."

Daruun nodded, turning his head to one side. "Or a reminder. See you at the celebration, Captain."

Sheriff Daruun walked on, leaving Arnath in the street, stewing. After such a horrid display of raw emotion in front of the outpost door, he didn't much feel like celebrating.

*

Once the practice weapons, curtains and decorative tapestries, and also the many fine toiletries that would stock every room had arrived, the only finishing touch the outpost needed was the installation of the front and back doors.

They had arrived the day before, and were brought up the back way. Arnath and the others unwrapped them from their cloth coverings and marvelled at how beautiful they were. Throughout the kingdom of Vallasen, doors meant a great deal for every business and home. Arnath remembered his childhood home had three upright bars embedded in it, representing the strength of he, his mother and his father, over a painted depiction of the sun shining down on an ever-flowing field of wheat. Such was the art on the multitude of doors throughout the kingdom. Temples of the light had a large sun on them, sometimes spanning across two doors. The Briny Sea had no doors at all, signalling that all were welcome.

The new front door for the outpost had four inlaid panels. One depicted a hand holding a sword aloft for Arnath, another an axe for Shrakar, another a nocked arrow for Trellith and the last a hand the center of which had a glowing stone for Garthe. It stood some nine feet tall and had a knob of gold affixed to one side. The backside had the panels without decorations and iron slots for a barricade to be inserted into.

The back door had similar carvings in the panels but were placed in different order, to show the unity of the party, who now owned this fine establishment.

As was traditional, a hanging curtain was placed over the doorway of the outpost until the opening day. Shrakar and Arnath steadied the doors as they were installed by elves from Solindar. Once secured in place, they all tried opening and closing them, and marvelled at how light and quiet the doors were, despite being made of materials strong enough to repel an army for a short turn.

Arnath opened the front door from the inside and gestured to his fellows to follow him. "There is one more thing left to do before our opening ceremony tomorrow."

Moments later, Arnath, Trellith, Garthe and Shrakar stood before the tiny counter in the town registrar's office that occupied the floor above the post office in the town hall. Heflynn and Illona stood behind them, standing on tip toes and craning their necks to see around Shrakar's broad back in such a small space.

On the other side of the counter Mayor Bumpol himself emerged from the many cabinets stacked high with papers and unfurled a large sheet of parchment. "Here we are gentlemen, one business license for display in your outpost. There are a few details to fill in and you are ready to start earning coin. So first off, what is the name of your business?"

Bumpol waited, a toothy smile on his face, whilst Arnath, Shrakar, Trellith and Garthe exchanged uncomfortable looks. At no point in time had they ever discussed, from the rough terrain away from the Ulgrew mountains to this very moment, a name for their business.

"Something to do with Isthmar, maybe. To go with the tapestry..." Trellith proposed limply.

Arnath and Shrakar scowled at this, Arnath saying, "And invite furious arguments from all who pass by from the losing side of the war? No!"

The four of them argued back and forth on it, deflecting each other's suggestions. Heflynn, Illona and Mayor Bumpol blurted out many as well. Kroman's Spring got a kind of shrugging approval, but no real yays or nays.

Garthe briefly stayed out of the argument, allowing himself to think. Then he blurted out, "Arnath's"

"What's that lad?" Trellith asked, everyone else having hushed up.

"You all came together under the Captain's command. You chose to adventure at his behest after the war. Then we chose together to end those adventures, and open our outpost. Why not call it Arnath's?" Garthe said, looking from person to person.

"Arnath's" Trellith said, looking away as though at an imagined sign.

"Arnath's Outpost." Heflynn said. "Has a ring to it."

"Gentlemen, you honour me. If no one objects..." Arnath said.

And no one did.

"Excellent. Arnath's. Traveller's outpost at Kroman's Town." Bumpol said, filling in the parchment sheet. "Sign here, good proprietors."

Each of them took a turn, squeezing past each other, bellying up to the counter and signing their name – Arnath knelt down and let Trellith kneel on his knee to get high enough.

"Terrific! Who will witness?" Bumpol said.

Heflynn peeked around, displaying his signet ring, and said, "Perhaps I should."

Arnath and Shrakar shuffled out of the kiosk to allow Heflynn in. Heflynn signed the witness line with flourish, then dabbed his signet ring with ink from the quill and rolled it next to his signature on the page, leaving behind the royal crest in fresh black ink.

Mayor Bumpol delicately picked up the document, blowing on the wet ink as he said, "Magnificent. Congratulations, gentlemen! That leaves only the ten gold, and we're done."

Illona had jumped into Garthe's arms for celebratory embrace and a kiss. The two parted immediately upon hearing the hefty sum said aloud. Arnath, Trellith, Shrakar and Garthe looked at each, wide-eyed. "Ten gold pieces?!" Trellith choked.

"Why, yes, gentlemen. You have paid no taxes or for your business license whilst the lengthy construction period was going on. But you've owned the land that whole time. I presume you wish to open tomorrow, so you are required to pay those fees now." The mayor said with his usual enthusiasm, despite delivering a sour message.

Arnath turned to Illona, saying, "Can you let me into the post office?"

Downstairs, Illona used the key given to her by old Mrs Minidell, who was happy to have an energetic apprentice to oversee the post office, to get inside. Illona then opened the safe for Arnath, who reached in and pulled out the last of the saddlebags secured there. "I suppose we should keep our money in our own safe from now on."

"The post office will miss your visits, Captain." Illona said, trying to sound official and closed the safe back up.

*

Once back at the outpost so recently named for himself, Arnath stood behind the counter and doled out pints he'd poured from the kegs mounted behind the counter. Everyone took up a stein and raised them again and again for each of the many toasts everyone gave in turn.

In between the re-filling of drinks, Arnath dumped the rest of the contents of the saddlebag into the funnel under the counter. Arnath and Trellith exchanged a dismayed look over the counter at how unimpressive the sound of it was. "Is that...? Trellith asked, knowing what the answer would be.

"The last of the spoils of the Ulgrew mountains." Arnath said in a low voice, so as to not put a damper on the small celebration. "We still have our account in Solindar, and some credit with our contractors there as well, otherwise..."

"And still some local labour to pay. And after that..." Trellith said, eyebrows raised, emulating Arnath's mood. The two of them drank deeply, both knowing that whatever was in the strongbox downstairs, paired with the account in Solindar, was all the money they had. And with a business to run, it wasn't going to last long.

Heflynn stepped over, catching them mid-drink, entirely missing the somber mood the two shared. He placed his wine goblet on the counter, and said, "They should be here soon."

Heflynn turned to Shrakar, and asked, "Would you give me a hand?"

Shrakar shrugged and followed Heflynn out the back door, taking his big stein with him.

A knock at the door gave everyone a start, even Garthe and Illona, who had been sitting away by the fireplace in the common room, playing footsies in front of the fire.

"Did someone actually go around the curtain?" Arnath asked, aghast at the breach of etiquette. He lifted the hinged counter, passed through and walk down the corridor to the front steps.

Expecting to give someone a piece of his mind, he opened the door and found a nervous Kewin on the other side. Doubly embarrassed, Arnath opened the door, saying, "Kewin, please, come inside."

"Thank you." Kewin said with downcast eyes, still utterly shamed by the revelations of two days past. He stepped down the steps, and awaited Arnath at the bottom.

Joining him, Arnath asked, "How is Anya?"

"Beside herself." Kewin said, somewhat lost. "She's taken to our bed, inconsolable."

"She should know we all stand with her. We all feel terrible to have been involved in something so personal." Arnath motioned Kewin to follow him down to the counter. "Come, have a drink."

"Actually, Captain, I came to speak with Master Trellith. if that is alright."

"Of course." Arnath gestured toward the end of the counter.

Kewin moved down the corridor, and to the end of the counter, where he had a brief, quiet conversation with Trellith. Trellith then hopped off the stool he sat on and said, "This way."

Arnath watched them head out the back door, curiously, as did Illona and Garthe through the cut out in the common room wall. Just as Arnath was about to return behind the counter, a knock sounded from the door yet again.

Arnath was up the steps like a shot, ready to rage at the uncouth person who dared trespass the curtain outside. He opened the door on a radiantly smiling Shimalena. She patted the cask under her arm, and said, "Delivery, Captain."

Knowing well the cask of peach cider Shimalena brought was going to be drunk by herself and her young friends, Arnath shrugged inwardly and ushered her inside.

*

Outside Heflynn and Shrakar stepped over to the fence and unfastened the locks, Shrakar the ones up high, Heflynn the ones below. They swung the big section of fence aside on the recently installed hinges, and latched it in place against training gear cupboard. Heflynn pulled out his pipe and began to thumb leaf into it from his poke. "Shouldn't be long now."

They both watched the wooded gap between the fence opening and the back of the first cut out for a moment, then Shrakar was struck with a thought, "We have guest. Need water."

"Indeed, we do." Heflynn said, as Shrakar turned away and crossed the yard to where the thick rope hung near the balconies. Shrakar leapt up, grabbed the rope, and flew up it, hand over hand at incredible speed. When Shrakar disappear over the lip of the roof, Heflynn, mightily impressed at the speed of the climb, lit his pipe and turned back to watch the gap.

Up on the roof, Shrakar began to pump the handpump next to the water supply cylinder. He kept one hand on the cylinder, feeling the wood for the rising level as he pumped away.

Down below, Trellith and Kewin stepped outside, and went over to the smithy. Trellith turned a lantern's wheel up high, so they could see, and gestured for Kewin to sit on a stool. Trellith then sat on a stool that was a tad taller than Kewin's so they could see eye to eye. Getting himself settled, Trellith asked, "Do you know her size, lad?"

"I think so. I have measured her for gloves." Kewin said.

"Fair enough. What about materials?"

Kewin reached into his waistcoat, pulled out a gold coin and passed it to Trellith.

Even without his monocle in, Trellith recognized it as one of the Arkonian gold coins found right here in the courtyard. "Oh my. You're sure about this?"

"I am. Make them from that. Keep the rest for yourself."

Trellith shook his head. "I'll not need so much. Perhaps I could fashion a pendant as well..."

Trellith was interrupted midsentence by swooping sound of Shrakar sailing down from above on the rope. As his big sandaled feet dug into the earth of the yard, Heflynn turned from the fence, and said in an urgent whisper, "They're coming!"

"Who's coming?" Kewin said, utterly confused.

"Stand up, lad. Best behaviour now." Trellith said, hopping off his stool.

*

Moments earlier, a carriage escorted by a dozen horses rolled down the darkness of the curved eastern road from the King's Highway. They all maintained a quiet gallop until they came to a stop at the first cut-out.

Astride the horses where men and women of the King's guard, all in formal dress uniforms. In front were Sergeant Graten and Lance corporal Apaulon, who dismounted their horses, approached the carriage, opened the door and helped two finely dressed figures, whose faces were hidden by draping hoods, down from the carriage to stand on the road.

Graten made a great many hand gestures at the troops, and then gestured for his charges to head into the darkness behind the first cut out. Apaulon brought up the rear, his dirk drawn and a large dressing bag he'd hoisted out of the carriage in his other hand. The carriage turned around in a large, arcing turn, half the soldiers escorting it followed it back down the eastern road, whilst the rest of the guards rode into town.

In the back courtyard of the outpost, Heflynn saw the figures approaching and stepped in front of the gap in the fence, his arms wide. Graten stepped passed him, with no greeting other than, "You vouch for that man?" pointing at Kewin.

"I do." Heflynn said, without pause.

As the two hooded figures approached with Apaulon, they removed their concealing hoods to reveal a short older man with dark skin and a thick moustache that curled upwards at the corners. The woman next to him was close to his age, had ornately coiffed black and grey hair, and had sharp eyebrows that pointed in the corners, just like Heflynn's.

"Mother." Heflynn said, embracing the woman.

"My son. It has been too long." She said returning his embrace.

Releasing the woman, he stepped over to the man that he was a least a head taller than and embraced him. "Father."

"You mother is right. You've abandoned us, my boy." The man said in a mock chiding tone.

"Oh, nonsense, father." Heflynn said, stepping away from the embrace. "I was at the palace giving a report but a month ago."

"Too long, my boy, far too long." Heflynn's father said, stepping away from his son, his eyes landing on Shrakar. Immediately the man put his arms up, and approached the big half-Orc. "Shrakar! Mighty Shrakar! Look at you. You were but a boy when I last saw you."

Shrakar bowed as the man approached, and embraced him. Stepping aside, the man gestured to his wife to come closer. She stepped forward, eyes bright and a smile on her face, saying, "Shrakar, our saviour."

Whilst his wife embraced Shrakar, the man turned to Heflynn and said, "Shrakar saved my life during the war."

"I know, father. You tell the tale every time you have too much wine." Heflynn said, rolling his eyes.

Stepping away from Shrakar's embrace, the woman said, "Because it is a tale worth telling. Imagine a life without your father, and know this great warrior is the reason why he is here to embarrass you with old tales."

"Of course, mother."

Stepping into the moonlight with Kewin at his side, Trellith said, "You make out like he was the only hero on that terrible day."

"Ah, Trellith. Here we are, old men now." The man said, stepping over to Trellith, his arms wide. He knelt down and embraced the dwarf warmly.

"Old? Speak for yourself." Trellith said in a mock-serious tone.

As the man resumed his full height, his wife approached and Trellith gestured grandly at Kewin. "Majesties, may I present Master Kewin, friend and companion to the outpost, and glover of Kroman's Town. Kewin, this is Prince Domar, brother of King Kordollon, heir apparent to the throne of Vallasen, and his wife Princess Terj'wan, duchess of Pantosh and Prince Heflynn's mother."

Kewin stood stiffly, then gave a proper bow, saying, "Majesties, I am greatly honoured to meet you both."

"And we you, my good man." Terj'wan said, offering her hand for Kewin to bow over once again.

Domar stepped close, saying, "A glover, you say?"

"Indeed, sir."

"Have a look at this. They are most uncomfortable." Domar stripped off one of his gloves and passed it to Kewin.

Kewin gave the glove a cursory glance, and sneered at it. "Oh, that's not right, my prince. Stitching is all wrong."

"I thought so."

Terj'wan scowled at her husband. "Don't make the man ply his trade out here in the dark of night."

"Say we all head inside for some libation, and further company." Trellith said, ushering everyone towards the door.

Shrakar went to the fence and swung it closed, locking it against the wall of the outpost. He turned and found everyone was on their way inside, but for Graten and Apualon, who stood on either side of the back door. As he went inside, Shrakar picked up the dressing bag Apaulon had carried and pointed to a door to the left of the bottom of the stairs in the hall leading to the long counter, saying, "Privies there."

"Thank you, Shrakar." Apualon said as Shrakar disappeared inside.

*

Arnath had heard the royal's arrival, and the tones of playful banter outside. He checked his Captain's clasp, making sure it was upright on his tunic. He then gave a "psst" over to Garthe, Illona and Shimalena in the common room. "They're here. Best behaviour, children. Try not to fondle each other too much in front of our guests."

The trio giggled at this, but Arnath scowled and said, "I mean it."

Absorbing Arnath serious tone, Garthe, Illona and Shimalena stood up and straightened their clothes, trying to look as serious as teenagers could for the royals now coming down the corridor.

Arnath opened the hinged counter, fastened it up against the wall and stepped out just as Domar and Terj'wan came down the corridor. Arnath gave a bow, his hand across his chest and covering his Captain's clasp. "Prince, princess – It is an honour to host you."

When Arnath arose, Domar embraced him. "Arnath. Captain. So many years it has been."

"Too long, my prince." Arnath said, returning the embrace. When they parted, Terj'wan offered her hand, which Arnath took, bow and kissed her knuckles lightly. Even after he stood tall again, the princess held onto his hand, enjoying the feel of his thick, strong warrior's fingers in hers.

"Look at you. The prince and I grow old, and you look ever the robust warrior, ready to take to the field. How did twenty years not wear on you as it did us?" Terj'wan said in a near-teasing tone.

Arnath turned a little red, saying, "We ran around the kingdom like fools searching for gold, not knowing the time was getting away from us."

"Oh, that must be it."

Arnath guided Terj'wan by the hand, and gestured for Domar to follow, as he stepped across to the common room. "May I present the rest of our party. You will have heard of Garthe the mage, member of our party for many years on and an owner of this establishment."

Garthe bowed, saying, "I am greatly honoured, your highnesses."

"As are we young man." Terj'wan said, eyeing the girls more than Garthe himself.

"You travel in esteemed company, as I am sure you know." Domar said, somewhat ceremoniously. Meeting a new mage was an occasion to be marked for anyone in the kingdom, regardless of rank.

"I do, majesty. They have been my guides, my fathers, lo these many years."

"Illona is the runner for our outpost, and a hopeful for his majesty's post service." Arnath said, moving on to the nervous Illona who fumbled a bow and curtsy combination, as she wore pants instead of a skirt.

"Charmed, dear girl." Domar said.

"Thank you, your majesty." Illona said, her voice warbling with nervous energy.

"And this is Shimalena, who works here and across at the Briny Sea. She is the grand daughter of the great elven mage Shimar, with whom Garthe studies." Arnath said, after which Shimalena gave a graceful curtsy in her flowing skirt.

"My – such a beautiful young elf I have never laid eyes upon." Domar said.

Unable to resist, Terj'wan said, "And which of you ladies have stolen the heart of the promising young mage?"

To which Garthe and Illona blushed deeply, but Shimalena merely cocked her head and said, "We have not decided yet."

This drew a burst of laughter from the room, breaking the ice for those still unnerved in the royal presences.

"Drinks?" Shimalena asked, crossing the room, then the corridor to slink behind the counter. Everyone nodded and spoke their agreement as Shimalena began to skillfully pour from the casks of ale, wine and cider.

"Perhaps you would like a tour of the..." Arnath began to say, until Domar's hand gripped his forearm.

Utterly entranced, Domar said, "Is that...?" and then crossed the common room to the broad tapestry that now hung over the plastered wall.

"It is indeed, my prince." Arnath said, joining alongside the prince and turning the flame higher on the nearest lantern.

The tapestry was some six feet across and hung down some three feet from the brass bar mounted up on the wall. Embroidered upon it was an intricate depiction of the last heroic and bloody day of the battle of Isthmar. On the left was a rampaging hoard of Orc zealots that stretched from the closest embroidered border to the far horizon and, across a carnage-strewn battlefield, on the right were the lines of the three kingdoms. In the front of those lines, amongst the intricately armoured soldiers, were clear depictions of Arnath, Shrakar, Trellith, Dalgar, Morgosh, Lanea and Prince Domar. On a rocky ridge above them, surrounded by soldiers and fellow archers stood King Kordollan, his and the soldiers many long bows aimed into the Orc front lines. In the background, further down the lines from the heroes that drew the eye, were Orc clerics and opposite them human and elf mages, exchanging powerful blasts of lightning and explosive magic spells across the bloody battlefield. Interspersed amongst the flashing explosions were silhouettes of singular combats – humans and elves fighting to take down giant Orcs, the new Orc allies grappling with their zealot brethren. The sky overhead threatened the darkest of clouds over the Orc lines and brightest of hopeful sunshine over the forces of Vallasen, Farsuum and Kruendaal.

The fresco that wrapped the second floor of the palace must have been a direct reference for this piece, for, even giving the most savage of battle cries, the facial features of all those present were clearly recognizable.

Prince Domar spilled quite a bit of ale down the front of his tunic as he gazed in slack-jawed wonder at the tapestry. "There we are... And General Scopar... even my squire, Quinley. So horrible a death I have never seen. Oh, what a great and terrible day."

Terj'wan flopped down in a chair opposite the tapestry, and said, "Please don't get him started. We'll be subjected to tales of his heroism on that fateful day, told in the minutest of detail for hours on end."

"Well, mother, we are in the exact company for it." Heflynn said, shrugging at her.

"My poor head. I shall need another drink." Terj'wan said, fingers to her furrowed brow. And as soon as she was done speaking, Shimalena was there, taking away her empty flute and handing her another full one. As quickly as she appeared, Shimalena was away again, grabbing a tray from the counter top and disappearing down the back corridor.

Outside, Shimalena emerged into the courtyard, two steins upon her tray. She handed one each to Graten and Apaulon, saying "Gentlemen."

"Thank you, dear girl." Graten said raising the stein to his mouth. Over the rim, he could swear he saw the elf girl run her fingers scintillatingly across Apaulon's abdomen as she went back inside. Choking down his ale, Graten said, "Lovely girl, the elf is. You know her well?"

"No, sir. Hardly at all." Apaulon said, taking a deep sip on his ale to cover a rakish smile.

Utterly confused, Graten drank his ale in steady sips, and thought worried thoughts about the future of the kingdom's youth.

In the common room, Illona could see Princess Terj'wan growing steadily bored of the back and forth between all the men, each expounding enthusiastically over the details of the tapestry. She stepped forward, uncertain if she was breaking any kind of protocol, and said, "Would the princess be interested in seeing Master Garthe's healing clinic?"

The princess perked up at this, saying, "Yes, dear, I very much would."

Garthe stepped around the huddle of old soldiers at the tapestry, and produced a key from his purse. He opened the black painted door at the front of the room, and stepped inside. Princess Terj'wan followed, just as the lamps began to brighten inside.

Illona stepped in to find the princess turning on heel to look around the bright, clean room.

"Is it not quite small?" the princess asked as her eyes landed on Garthe.

"Certainly, majesty. But so is Kroman's Town. I imagine if my reputation grew, like Master Shimar's, people will come from further away to see me."

"And then you will need a bigger space." Terj'wan said, finishing his thought. After another cursory glance around, she hoisted herself up on the table and looked at the two of them, one eyebrow cocked. "I can trust in your discretion?"

"Of course, majesty. What ails you?" Garthe said.

Illona closed the door to the common room, saying, "You may trust in us, your grace."

"I have been plagued by the most terrible headaches for some time now, Years, in fact. No potions or solutions the healers at the palace have provided have had any effect." Terj'wan said, dropping a little of her regal bearing.

"Can you show me where they hurt the most?" Garthe said, as he approached the table and withdrew his healing stone from its pouch.

The princess pointed to the right side of her head, and traced her finger down towards the back of her neck. Garthe held up the healing stone in front of her, a silent gesture for permission, to which Terj'wan nodded and said, "Go ahead."

Illona stepped in and held Terj'wan's hand as Garthe closed his eyes and began to run the stone over her head, then her neck and finally down her back.

The stone glowed brighter as his silent communion with it continued on, until Garthe opened his eyes, and the stone's luminescence dimmed away.

Garthe inhaled deeply as he collected his thoughts, readying to put his communion with the stone into words. Finally, he said, "May I see your feet?"

Perplexed, the princess lifted her legs up, letting the orange and gold skirt fall away, to reveal her feet in a pair of beautifully crafted high-heeled shoes.

Garthe nodded, and said, "The shoes you prefer force you to stand in such a way that it put pressure on muscles in your lower back. Those muscles, which are linked as though in a chain, are pulling on the muscles in your neck and head. Until you abandon the wearing of these high heels, your headaches will not go away."

"No!" Terj'wan cried, flinging Illona's hand away and burying her face in her hands. She must have been truly loud, for the clinic door flung open, revealing the concerned warriors in the common room on the other side. Domar stepped in, stood close to Terj'wan and put his hands on her shoulders. "What is it, my darling? Whatever it is, we can face it together."

Terj'wan took her hands from her tear-strewn face, and said in an anguished tone, "The healer said my headaches are caused by the shoes I wear. How can I abandon my regal bearing? How?!"

"Darling, you will still be more than half a head taller than me." Domar said, trying to keep reason in his tone, despite his growing amusement.

"But all the charm and elegance and beauty, it will all be gone."

"People will still think that way of you, no matter how tall you are." Domar said, looking to the others for help.

"Not me, you fool. My beautiful shoes!" Terj'wan cried in anguish, burying her head in his shoulder.

Domar looked over at the others, then shook his head. "A true palace crisis."

*

The next day at around noon, the number of guardsmen on either side of the upraised curtain mounted in front of the outpost doors doubled. This drew whispers of excitement from the gathered crowd. Surely, they would open soon.

All whispers and excited chattering abruptly stopped when the top of the door, which could be seen opening above the ceremonial curtain rack. The racks that held the curtains for these opening ceremonies did not take into account Orc-sized doors. Fully expecting Arnath or Trellith, the two who most often acted as spokesmen for the outpost, to appear, the crowd gasped loudly in unison when Prince Domar emerged from behind one side of the rack, and Princess Terj'wan emerged from the other. As the gasp died, it was replaced with thunderous applause from the crowd.

The prince and princess waved and bowed to the crowd until the applause died down. Then, having done this hundreds of times before in hundreds of towns throughout the kingdom, took up positions in the center of the curtain, each gripping one closed curtain, their hands laid over each other's.

"Ladies and gentlemen, good people of Kroman's Town, and all who have travelled from afar for the occasion..." Terj'wan started, her voice carrying all the way to the back of the crowd. Domar continued as his wife's last word faded, "Behold the stirring wonder of another triumph of the master builder Lorta – Welcome one and all to Arnath's – the traveller's outpost of Kroman's Town!"

With that pronouncement, both Domar and Terj'wan stepped backward towards the frame of the rack, holding onto their sides of the curtain and revealed Arnath, Trellith, Shrakar and Garthe, dressed as finely as men who had lived as battling vagabonds could, in the doorway.

They waved at the crowd, bowed for the cheers they gave and then waved everyone inside.

The guards formed up on either side of the prince and princess, and this created a kind of human corridor for people to pass through as they shuffled toward the door, shaking the hands of the royals enthusiastically as they went. As was fitting, honoured guests went in first – Lorta and Taishen, Mayor Bumpol – who seemed somewhat cross he was not let in on the secret of the royals attending the opening and that he was not asked to give a speech, Illona and her mother, Durnly and his staff, Jaross and the many, many more waiting to get a look inside.

The proud owners manned their places throughout the outpost; Arnath behind the counter, Garthe at the common room door of his clinic, Trellith out back at his smithy and nearby Shrakar showed the visitors the many features of the training yard. As the hundred or so people filed through, Arnath dispensed drinks and greeted people, Garthe showed people the clinic and made sure they saw the privacy curtains and knew where the night bell was. Trellith demonstrated the works of the smith whilst working on some gold jewellery, narrating each step as he did. Shrakar set up a few of the practice targets and let people take shots with blunted arrows from their arsenal of practice weapons, host duties that were interrupted a couple of times over the course of the day when he had to climb up to the roof and refill the water tank. It seemed many people were running water through the basins and flushing the privies just for the sake of watching them at work.

When Arnath grew tired of serving behind the counter, he beckoned Shimalena over to take his place. Arnath, ale stein in hand, walked from room to room, talking about the features of the outpost and humbly receiving compliments. All the while he was searching over people's heads, scanning each room for a certain someone.

Garthe did his best not to get roped into treating people this particular day. Illona kept an appointment log for him, quill and ledger in hand, one that filled up quite quickly. The gaggles of potential patients were at least polite enough to step aside when Shimar stepped in, and approached Garthe with two large satchels. He set them down and said, "This one is for the shelves down here, and this one is for your learning library."

Garthe and Illona ignored Shimar's lack of greeting, as was his way, and Garthe said, "Thank you, master. Would you like to see the laboratory?"

"Most definitely, but later." Turning away, Shimar finished by saying, "I have something else to deliver."

Shimar then glided away through the crowd, intercepted the flute of cider Shimalena held out for him as he passed, then disappeared down the hall. Trying to be gentlemanly, Garthe offered to take the satchel that went up to his room and instantly regretted it as soon as he tried to pick it up. Illona could at least drag her charge across the floor to the library shelves. Along with the trunk of books the guard had brought from the palace in the morning, the shelves would be stuffed once Shimar's texts where unpacked. Within a few awkward steps, her uncle Shamuth saw Illona struggling and lent a hand, leaving Garthe to wrestle with his satchel and the long climb ahead.

Taishen and many elf craftsmen watched as Trellith beat and tapped heated gold around an iron peg. Shimar stepped through the crowd, saying "Surely that cannot be comfortable."

Trellith turned to him, the clear monocle screwed into his eye socket. "You've come bearing a solution?"

"I have indeed." Shimar said, and pulled a pouch from his waistcoat. He passed it to Trellith, who unfurled it, revealing a set of eye glasses and set of darkened goggles. Trellith took the monocle from his eye, let it hang from the chord on his neck and put the glasses on. He turned to everyone with an elated smile.

"Ahh, that's more like it!" Trellith looked at the gold affixed to his iron template rod, and did not even have to squint. "My thanks, Master Shimar."

"No bother, Master Trellith. You'll also find a pair of spare lenses inside the pounch, should these get broken, or you wish to fashion some new frames for yourself." With that, Shimar turned away and disappeared. Trellith put on the darkened goggles and held the gold over the fire to soften it up again.

Arnath watched the townsfolk being put through their archery paces by Shrakar, and tried not to laugh as the harmless blunted arrows flew this way and that, bouncing off the climbing wall, landing anywhere but their targets. Arnath and the others thought it would be a good thing to show the locals what the training center would be doing. And if they ended up thinking it was altogether silly, all the better. Having their neighbours live in fear of their customers was the furthest thing from their minds.

As Arnath watched Shrakar flinch when yet another volley of wayward arrows flew, an elderly couple approached him. It took Arnath a near minute to recognize them and then it dawned on him. "Nestar? Gilea? So good of you to come."

The old farming couple who lived west of Solindar smiled at Arnath, and returned his toast with their cups. "We wouldn't miss it." Nestar said. "Had some goods for you and the Briny Sea to deliver. Timed it so as we could make your opening. Magnificent place. Truly."

"Thank you." Arnath said, raising his glass to them again.

"On our way here, we were entreated with another delivery for you." Gilea reached into her shawl, and pulled out small square envelope, which she handed to Arnath. He took it curiously, opened it and read the small note within. As he did, his expression fell with disappointment.

"Merynda. She wanted to be here but her boy, Jarthow, has taken ill."

"Aww, the poor lad." Gilea said.

"The fall is coming. Change in the weather affects us all different." Nestar said, nodding.

"True, love. I feel it in my bones already." Gilea said, adjusting her shawl to ward off future chills.

"Is that what that is?" Arnath asked, having felt pains in one of his war injured knees of late.

Before anyone could even respond, Arnath caught a whipping movement in the corner of his eye, reached out his hand and snatched one of the blunted arrows out of the air before it could strike Gilea in the face.

Arnath turned, held the offending arrow up, and found everyone in front of the practice targets staring back at him, slack-jawed. Many were already wincing in anticipation of Arnath's wrath. But he merely threw the arrow in their direction and said, "That's enough target practice for one day."

A crowd had gathered by the smithy, as Trellith continued to shape the gold blobs that wrapped around the iron rod pinched in his tongs. Prince Domar stood watching, two guardsmen nearby. Kewin approached him from the back door, had to wait while Domar waved the guards away from him. He then took a brand-new pair of soft-looking kid gloves from his belt and presented them to the prince. "See if those are more to your liking, majesty."

Domar slipped the gloves on, interlaced his fingers to tighten them, then flexed his fingers quickly. "Excellent, my good man."

All around the elf craftsmen, many of whom already had gloves made by Kewin, nodded their approval.

"Where did you get those?" Terj'wan's barked question seemed to come from out of nowhere, and startled many around the smithy.

Domar turned to see her approaching from the back door, her eyes locked on his new gloves. "Why from our new friend, Kewin the glover, of course."

The princess snatched up one of Domar's hands and rolled it over in hers as she examined the glove. "I would like some too."

Domar had found that, despite performing her officiating duties today with aplomb, Terj'wan had become quite abrupt and demanding since learning of the solution to her headaches. If one of her favorite things in life were going to be taken away forever, she would have everything else she wanted and wasn't going to ask politely.

"Perhaps we could swing by your shop when the party moves to the lakeside...?" Domar asked, clearly seeking Kewin's aid more than his service.

"Of course, my prince. There is one thing I need before returning home however." Kewin said, eyeing the two gold rings that Trellith and an elf craftsman were molding patterns onto with thin but red-hot tools.

Terj'wan saw the rings, her mood brightening and asked, "For your lady?"

"She's not been herself. Her terrible past has shattered the peace she came here for. But I want her to know I don't care about her origins, however grim." Kewin said, eyes watching the rings being crafted.

"I think we can be of help, my good man." Domar said, his eyes sharing a conspiratorial look with Terj'wan.

*

Anya laid in the bed, the covers up to her chin, a soaked kerchief for her never-ending sniffles clutched in her hand. She'd dowsed the lamps after Kewin, her beloved Kewin, had left to attend the outpost opening. No matter how much he pled, she could not bring herself to go. To face an entire town that now knew her dark secret.

She felt as though it would be quite alright if the whole world went on whilst she laid here in the dusky light and cried forever.

Kewin must have come home early, for she heard the keys in the door downstairs. Then she heard several people. Anya hoped that the people who rented from Kewin had not come home drunk, still wanting to celebrate. Her fragile state was nightmare enough already.

Any hope for peace she had was shattered when she heard heeled feet tromping determinately up the stairs. Then those feet marched straight down the hall!

Anya flinched under the blankets when the door flung open, and room was suddenly bathed in lamplight. She peeked over the hem of the quilt to see the most regal-looking woman she'd ever seen standing in her doorway, staring down at her.

"Do you know who I am, girl?"

"No... ma'am." Anya said, quiet as a temple mouse.

"Ma'am? That's highness or majesty to you girl. For I am Princess Terj'wan, wife of prince Domar, sister-in-law to our king, mother of the handsome princes Korduul, Ilfien and Heflynn. And I command you, good seamstress, arise from your bed so we may dress you finely, and do your hair finer. Up, I say – Now!"

Anya leapt out of the bed, as though compelled by the sheer power of the princesses' will.

Downstairs, Kewin and Prince Domar could each hear fearful step Anya took coming down. When she did step into the lamplight, she looked lovely as could be, if perhaps a bit shocked yet again to another royal before her. Anya stepped aside from the shop doorway to allow Terj'wan to skirt around her as she reached the bottom of the stairs, and then bowed deeply to the prince. "'Tis my greatest pleasure to meet you, majesty."

"And I you, Anya. Now feel free to ignore us. Your man has something to ask of you."

Anya looked at Kewin, her face befuddled. That is until he got down on one knee and opened his hand, revealing the rings he held within. Then her face brightened, infused with new life, and her tears began to flow again – this time with joy.

*

The party had moved outside, to the side of the lake in the evening. A large tent had been set up, and Durnly's people served food and drink to all who came. Two of the lakeside firepits had been lit and covered over with metal grates, so many large slabs of beef and ribs could be grilled. Extra barrels and casks had been ordered for the day and brought down from the Briny Sea to the lakeside.

Word travelled quickly of Kewin and Anya's engagement, bringing further mirth to an already joyous day. The difficult question of what would become of poor Anya and Kewin had changed to the much livelier one of whatever shall we wear to the wedding.

Arnath, for one, was glad to move the celebration, and the celebrants, outside. He was relieved to have taken Feila's advice, and locked the bedding and towels away before opening up the outpost to the public. The whole town and more had been through the outpost, and had gone out of their way to touch just about everything. Though he was accustomed to sleeping with the dirt of the road right next to his head, the notion that his bedding and that of his guests had been manhandled by perhaps hundreds of people gave him an uncomfortable shiver.

As he made his rounds, shaking the hands of those who had congratulations for him and those he wished to thank for helping to build their business, Arnath felt a continual pang of disappointment. If only Merynda were here. He knew well that her son should come first. Any good parent would feel that way. Once, long ago when Garthe was only twelve, a group of fellow travelling adventurers had kidnapped him for his healing ability. He, Trellith and Shrakar would have hewn down mountains to get the boy back. They eventually did, no mountains destroyed, however some ten corpses were left in their wake.

Maybe these feelings wouldn't be so cloying if he found Merynda's boy easier to like. It was one of the many challenges involved in finding such a natural pairing at his age. There was the distance as well. Her farm was not that far away, but it was far enough.

"You seem very far away from here."

Arnath looked up to see Heflynn approaching holding a goblet for himself and a fresh stein for him, which Arnath accepted and took a long, deep swallow from. Shrugging, he then said, "The day is both exactly how I pictured it, and not at all. Just doing some reconciling before I start circulating again."

"I understand." Heflynn said, settling on the bench next to Arnath. "I'm happy for you fellows. It's a momentous day. This reunion is something my father will go on about for the rest of his life, trust me. The outpost is built and operating, the town will prosper, but still, without Listrelle here, it lacks a sense of..."

"Completion?"

"Yes. Completion." Heflynn said, nodding and taking a deep sip of wine.

The two of them sat for a time, silently, meditating on the notion of completion and the women they pined to have at their sides right now.

That is until crack of violent thunder resounded in the sky, several leagues to the south-west.

Arnath and Heflynn both looked and saw the darkest of cloud formations moving at a threateningly fast pace toward the town. The black blot in the sky was simply too massive to miss Kroman's Town.

"Will you look at that. Fall has truly announced itself."

"At least it gave us some warning." Heflynn said.

All around them, panicked people began to gather up the accoutrements of the party – The chairs, Tables, Kegs and mini-bars – and started to rush them towards the main street, up to the Briny Sea.

Out of the crowd, Apaulon came rushing towards them. "My prince – Your parents want to get on the road. They said they want to try and outrun the storm. Staying here overnight isn't an option, not with your father's impending duties."

"Understood." Heflynn said, rising off the bench. He then turned to Arnath and said, "Coming to see them off?"

"I will. I should help with some of this, since I'm heading that way."

Heflynn raced off with Apaulon. Arnath grabbed chair after chair, stacking up as many as he could carry. As he leaned back and hoisted them up, Arnath looked again at the ever-blackening horizon, with its flashes of lightning and loudly encroaching claps of thunder.

It was a sorely disappointing end to what was up until then an auspicious day. Arnath turned away from the gathering storm, began to trot with his burden into town, hoping it would pass quickly.

END OF PART TWO

PART THREE: THE GATHERING STORM

CHAPTER TEN

The storm that had started on the day the outpost opened persisted in fits and starts for another three weeks after, the sky never becoming any friendlier than a slate grey.

And, in that time, not a single customer had come to eat, drink, train or spend the night at the outpost.

Arnath stood bent across on the counter, leaning on his elbows and looked down the corridor out the open back door into the courtyard. The sound of the rain outside was amplified by the giant, white tarp he and Shrakar had hung over the entire yard from the anchor point on top of the mound. Made of a thin, silken material Lorta had said there was no pronounceable human word for, it allowed not a single drop through its surface, keeping the smithy and the training yard entirely dry. They had anchored it in such a way that its high apex was over the smithy, and thus all the rain would drain over the far fence, into the wooded area behind the last houses on the main street. In the direst of emergencies, times when the outpost was entirely full-up, they could keep the tarp up and allow customers to sleep under it on bed rolls in the yard. That seemed such a wistful idea now.

Once again Heflynn had said, "You've thought of everything" upon seeing the ingeniously engineered rain covering over the courtyard.

Arnath grated at the compliment. They hadn't thought of the one thing that now hung like a lodestone around their necks – What if they'd spent absolutely every penny they had carried away from the raid on the Ulgrew mountains on an incredibly expensive building, and no one showed up to stay there?

Though they had money enough in their account with the Briny Sea to feed themselves daily, eventually their purchased casks of ales, cider and wine would run dry. What good was a warm common room without libations for the guests? The coin collected from Garthe's clinic and Heflynn's lodging were basically keeping the outpost in drink and, feeling utterly despondent in their encroaching destitution, the proprietors were the ones drinking it all.

Tonight was no different. Arnath leaned on the counter, looking blankly outside, a stein at his elbow. Shrakar sat near the fireplace, opposite Trellith, both of whom drank from large steins in silence. The words had run out of them. Mere attempts at enthused speculating about the storm passing had fizzled out a week ago. All that was left was the silent contemplation of failure over much drink.

Heflynn, while not a proprietor, had mostly joined in the melancholic ritual. It was a gut-punch to see one's friends shoot for the heavens, only to fall so unceremoniously low. When Illona brought a post from the palace that required his investigative skills elsewhere, he jumped at it and rode out of town.

Even Garthe, the only somewhat successful member of their quartet, joined in the melancholy observance. His clinic would always be needed, but it seemed he and his adventuring patriarchs had built themselves an incredibly expensive retirement home in which to grow poor in. It was all so sad. Garthe knew they had hung up their swords out of necessity – adventuring not favoring men their age. Out of sympathy, he joined in their joyless drinking, with only the occasional chime of his clinic bell or nights with Illona and Shimalena serving as much needed interruptions.

This night had stretched on, filled with only rain and melancholy sighs. Arnath had seen enough of this, yet another grey day. He picked up his stein and swallowed its contents, then put the stein in a bin meant to be picked up by a Briny Sea staffer for washing several times a day. "That's it. I'm locking up."

Trellith, Shrakar and Garthe watched him stride for the door, their faces dour.

Just as Arnath reached the bottom step, the door whipped open, letting in a blast of wind and rain. From outside the roughest of voices said, "Are you receiving tonight?"

*

After Arnath had ushered them in, beckoning them to go through to the back courtyard, Garthe, Trellith and Shrakar watched the covered shapes of five individuals of very different sizes in concealing rain cloaks slosh down the corridor.

Making to follow them, Trellith stopped long enough to say to Garthe, "Go and tell Durnly to keep the kitchen open long enough to serve our guests food. And summon Shimalena to serve them."

With that Trellith and Shrakar disappeared down the corridor.

In the back courtyard, Arnath had managed to get a couple of their soaked cloaks off. Shrakar stepped in to help with the rest. He picked the largest of the party and found himself face to face with another Half-Orc who also wore the allied sigil on his shoulder armour. They exchanged knowing nods and polite greetings in Okreen. As Shrakar threw the wet cloak over his shoulder with a splat, and moved on to collect from the next person in the party, the Orc said his name was Ogron and he was pleased to meet one of his own. Shrakar collected up the rest of the cloaks, taking the ones Arnath had, and unstrung a heavy line from the top of the smithy, pulled it all the way to the tree next to the spring pool and tied it off as tautly as he could. He flung each cloak over, and straightened them along the line, all the while barking and croaking in Okreen at Ogron, telling him about himself, his companions and their new outpost.

Meanwhile, Trellith had stepped outside and unclasped a table bolted on hinges to the wall outside the smith. He eased it down, and extended folding legs out from under it. He looked across the table at their customers, who he could see now were an older man, a warrior woman, an Orc, two slight young men of perhaps Garthe's age and an ancient looking old mage. He cleared his throat and said, "If you so please, lay all of your weapons on the table and we'll take care of them."

"What's this?" said the man, perhaps their leader, who was Arnath's height and size, but maybe ten years older. He had long grey hair and a leather patch over his left eye. His right eye was squinting down at Trellith in anger.

"We need surrender our weapons to stay here?" barked a tall well-muscled woman in revealing warrior's leather armour, her hand possessively gripping the hilt of her sword.

Trellith immediately put up calming hands, "No! No. It is part of the services we offer here at Arnath's. I am a master smith, and will check the integrity of all your weaponry during your stay. Anything in need of repairs will get repaired. Anything needing mending, and so on. We can also order you special items from Solindar or Morley, if you so desire."

Not sure they were convinced of the innocence of the strategy he and Trellith had cooked up to render their guests less deadly, Arnath stepped forward and said, "Ours is a different kind of outpost. We specialize in the needs and training of ranging adventurers, as we once were. When you leave us, your weaponry will be in far better shape than now. Blades sharpened, arrows re-fletched, grips rebound. Whatever is needed. Please, place your trust in us."

The older man and the powerful woman exchanged a look and then a shrug, and began to unstrap their various weaponry. Their party followed suit, and soon the table was nearly spilling over with all kinds of implements of death. Trellith went down the line of them, making quick notes in a ledger with a flicking quill. He then showed the inventory to the old warrior and the woman for their approval.

The man with the eyepatch stepped away from the table and approached Arnath, asking, "Training, you said? What kind of training?"

"All kinds. Sword. Axe. Archery. Spears. Fighting staff. Climbing. Group melee. Group melee against specific creatures. It all really depends on the nature of your quest."

"I don't think we need training in any of that." The old man said.

"And the younger ones?" Arnath said looking at the two slight boys, who Arnath thought might be brothers, so close was their appearance. "Born after the wars, and not trained soldiers. Have they been with you long enough to know you can fight back-to-back and trust to survive?"

The older man looked at the boys, his jaw working from side to side, calculating. He finally enquired, almost inwardly, "The nature of our quest, you say?"

"Let's get you all warmed up by the fire. We can discuss it after you've eaten."

The older man and his party all nodded in agreement at that idea.

In the common room, after several trays of food from the Briny Sea had been consumed, and a couple of steins had been drunk by each party member, the party had separated into groups. The young men, Trenth and Mego, sat close together at the small table by the fire, and played a game of pegs noisily. Garthe and the mage Grentoss talked for a while in front of the clinic door and then disappeared upstairs, presumably to Garthe's lab. Ogron and Shrakar drank from huge steins and stood in front of the tapestry. Ogron marvelled at it, stating that any one of the Orc silhouettes fighting on the allied lines in the background could well be him.

Both Arnath and Havanth, the old leader of the party, leaned on either side of the counter. Shimalena had returned from the Briny Sea, bringing back replacement snacks and casks, and was now on the small stage in the center of the common room, lightly strumming her lute. Her lilting music covered over the contentious conversation over the counter.

"You swear, you and your staff will maintain absolute secrecy?" Havanth said quietly to Arnath, for the third time now.

Arnath nodded across the counter at Havanth, keenly aware he was being watched by Valdara, the warrior woman who served as second to Havanth in the party, as she leaned on the nearby support pillar at the edge of the common room. In their travels this was likely a common defensive stance, she standing ready to step in quickly and kill anyone who moved aggressively against Havanth. Still, Arnath wondered if the way she looked across the corridor at him, impassively through squinted eyes, was a readiness to kill, or perhaps pounce on him in some friendlier way, having experienced both after that kind of look.

"You have our word, as fellow adventurers, no other guest who comes through this door will know the nature of what you seek and where it is." In that moment, Arnath could not have made his voice or eyes more honest. He sincerely hoped this was not going to be the way of it with all of their in-coming guests, dickering at length just to discern their individual quests from them.

Havanth moved his hand slowly into his leather waistcoat, finally withdrawing a map fragment so small it could not roll into a proper scroll. He placed it on the countertop and spread his hands across it to flatten curved fragment as much as it could be, saying, "We're going here."

Arnath straightened up as he looked down at the fragment, eyes wide, as though he had seen a ghost. He shouted, "Trellith!"

In a moment, Trellith could be heard from the outside door. "What is it?"

"Light the lamps in the map room." Arnath said, staring down at the map fragment as though it were something foul.

Depicted in the multicoloured inks of the parchment, was the exact spot where their companion Dalgar had horribly perished a decade ago.

*

Arnath held his hands up for quiet, and waited for the all shouting in the map room to cease. When it did, he calmly said, "We are not saying you can't go. We are saying that if you do decide to undertake it, expect the caverns to be underwater this time of year. I'll say it again – We have attempted this very raid before ourselves."

Trellith interjected, "And lost a great warrior trying to escape the caverns before the flooding."

"Yes, yes. One of the heroes of Isthmar." Havanth said, waving the words away as though his action could swat away the truth of them.

Trellith could see the man's dismissiveness was angering Arnath deeply, so he sought to bring reason to the room by saying, "Yes – exactly. A great warrior, an archer of renown. And he died, swept away by the torrents under the waterfall. All we are saying is if it were late spring or summer, you'd able to breach the walls within the cave system without much problem. But now, after we've had rain for three solid weeks? Impossible. Those caves will be completely underwater."

"So, you said!" Havanth sniped. Trellith was absolutely sure the man was angered more by looking a fool in front of his party, than by having embarked on an adventure at the entirely wrong time of year.

As Garthe handily scribbled away, copying a map of the area, alternating quills for different coloured inks as he went, he said, "We could train you to climb, and to swim, and to tread water at length before you go. It will increase your chances, should there be flooding, especially if the interior excursion is still something you do want to attempt when you get there."

Valdara looked at Trenth and Mego, then said, "Yes, that makes sound sense."

Both she and Arnath looked to Havanth for his approval on the notion, both of them hoping he was not such a fool for gold that he would recklessly kill his own party by running blindly into a quest unprepared. After a moment of staring blankly at Garthe's map, Havanth finally nodded, saying quietly, "Yes. We could do that."

Like everyone else, Trellith was relieved the argument would go no further for the night. He motioned for everyone to gather around him, and picked up a quill. "Now, I will draw what I remember of the cliffs surrounding the caves. Imagine a giant horseshoe, with a waterfall at its center..."

*

Arnath came downstairs in the morning, and stepped out to the courtyard to find Shrakar hanging off the climbing wall in an unusual way. As he stepped closer, Arnath could see Shrakar was some six feet off the ground, entirely parallel to it. His feet were planted flat against the climbing wall, as he held his back rigid and used only one arm to defy gravity.

Seeing Arnath, Shrakar said, "Good for back, shoulder, axe swinging muscle."

"Alright." Arnath said, grabbing up a rope, gripping it tightly and marching slowly up the wall until he was hanging parallel to the ground. He eased his grip and then hung by one arm. "I see what you mean."

Looking straight up the face of the mound, Arnath noted that Shrakar must have stowed the training yard's covering tarp away. Though the air had that distinctive moist fall nip to it, the sky above them was blue and clear for the first time in weeks. Arnath hoped this weather would hold, not only during the party's training but also when they attempted their treasure raid under the falls as well.

The tingle of a bell resounded in the distance, and within seconds Garthe slid down the balcony rope, landed in the courtyard saying, "Morning!" and disappeared into the outpost.

"Early morning patient." Arnath said, a strain in his voice.

"Switch arm." Shrakar said, doing just that.

Arnath switched the arm gripping the rope, with a sharp exhale. "That's better. Oh, maybe not. Starting to burn already."

"That's good. Make stronger."

"May I join you?"

Arnath and Shrakar turned their heads awkwardly around and saw Valdara, dressed in one of the woolen morning robes they provided to guests.

"Grab a rope." Arnath said, trying his best not to sound like his breath was too strained. For just the tiniest moment Arnath swore he saw a flash of long, white-blond hair as it whirled over the last step inside the outpost, then disappeared down the corridor. The clinic bell must have woken Shimalena as well.

Valdara approached the wall, kicked her loose sandals off and tied her freshly washed hair back with a leather thong. Valdara then plucked the rope on Arnath's left off the wall, stepped a bit away and walked up the wall. Hanging parallel as she was, her muscular legs were fully revealed as the robe gave in to gravity. She snatched up the robe, allowing a part of each side to fall between her legs for a more modest covering. Only then did she hang by one arm, letting her breath seethe between her teeth.

"Will there be breakfast soon?" Valdera said, trying not to sound strained.

Thinking Shimalena would head to the Briny Sea straight away, Arnath said, his jaw muscles straining, "I imagine so."

"Switch arms." Shrakar said, and they all did.

Valdara inhaled deeply, and said, "I don't want you to think Havanth is a fool. He has an old soldier's pride, that's all."

"I meant no disrespect." Arnath said, straining. "We only want success for those who stay here. And success in our game means survival. He must know that."

"I'm sure he does." Valdara said, straining even harder for breath. "But I'm sure he feels surviving sometimes is not a victory. As the last surviving member of the seventh..."

Both Arnath and Shrakar turned towards her and said, "The seventh!"

And both of them jumped down from the wall, and faced her. Valdara, utterly confused, took the time to ease herself down. Standing upright, she cracked her thick neck and said, "Yes, the seventh. Why is that such a surprise?"

"It is we who shall have quite a surprise for your captain by the end of the day. Trust me." Arnath said, almost beaming at her.

*

Later, after everyone had breakfasted on eggs and sausage and potato and turnips stuffed with eggs – for the Orcs - they assembled in the courtyard and were divided into groups. Shrakar was going to take the young archers down to the lake, whilst Arnath worked with Orgon, Valdara and Havanth on the climbing wall. Garthe sat with Grentoss near the smithy, and would study the spells the old mage uniquely knew, and Trellith would do a full run down on all the weapons the party had.

Arnath stood at the bottom of the wall, looking up at his trio of charges as they hung by their fingers from high hand-holds. While Valdara and Ogron seemed fine to hang their whole bodyweight by just their hands, Havanth was not adept – always shifting his weight, his breath seething the entire time.

"Ropes!" Arnath called out like a command across a battlefield. Ogron and Valdara immediately snatched the climbing ropes in front of them, and hung off of the wall. Havanth took three tries to grab his rope, and transfer his weight off the wall. Arnath did his best not to let his face reflect his opinion, which was increasingly leaning toward the notion that if Havanth did try to descend down the cliffs under the Kolifarii waterfalls, he would likely be killed.

After a few minutes, Arnath shouted, "Holds!" and the trio transferred from their ropes to the handholds once again, Havanth once again taking several clumsy attempts.

Garthe sat next to Grentoss, who had one of the large tomes Shimar had brought on their opening day across his lap. The old mage ran a thin, boney finger down the page as he read. "See here – It says the treasure of the last Kolifarii king was hidden away under the falls by his soldiers a fortnight before the Arkonian invasion. It does not state if the invasion ever came, however it says the bricked-up passageways were guarded, even long after the king had died. So long in fact, that the knowledge of what was being guarded was lost. And eventually the kingdom itself collapsed into ruin."

Grentoss looked away from the arcane lettering and gave Garthe an impish smile. "Imagine that. A kingdom spoiled by riches that fell to ruin because they forgot where those riches were."

Garthe laughed at this, and then looked up as Trellith cleared his throat from across the weapons table. "We had even less information than that when we made our attempt. We knew the passages were bricked across, but knew nothing of where to look. Does the ancient writing mention anything like that, levels, chambers, anything of the sort?"

"There's some drawings on the next page." Garthe said, motioning toward the book. Grentoss turned the page slowly, and looked over the drawings with raised eyebrows.

From inside the outpost, a muted chime sounded and Garthe was immediately on his feet, saying, "Excuse me, Master Grentoss." Then, he disappeared inside the outpost.

"No, no, see to your patients." Grentoss said, not taking his eyes off the ancient text. After a moment, he took his finger off the page and waved it in Trellith's direction. "This might be something."

Trellith rounded the table, and stood beside the old mage, pushing his spectacles up his nose as he looked down at the ancient text. "A great many passages branch off of the large one hidden behind the falls, but only one leans downward after a time, and it appears, according to this drawing, that is where the cache is walled up." Grentoss said, pointing out features of the near-indiscernible illustration.

Trellith peered down at the drawing, and then, a decision made, looked over at the climbing wall. "Arnath – Havanth and his party need to look at this."

*

Down at the lake, Shrakar had been putting Trenth and Mego, both decidedly non-swimmers, through their paces. The sky had gone grey again, though it didn't seem like any rain would fall, Shrakar guessed, remembering to keep an eye out for clouds that would threaten lightning. At first, he tried to get them to cross the width of the oval lake, and ended up having to rescue the both of them. Then he tried moving them down the lake, closer to town, where the lake was more tapered, but the result was the same. Finally, he picked a sliver of a corner of the lake near the large tree he and his friends favoured, and had them try to traverse that, all the while remaining in the water with them.

Of the two, Mego seemed to take to the water better than Trenth. This struck Shrakar as strange because of the two slight young men, Trenth seemed the more athletic. And it appeared Trenth thought so of himself as well. Every time Shrakar had to splash over and save the boy from drowning, he would strike at the surface of cold water in frustration and cast an angry glance Mego's way. Close as they appeared, there was an unhealthy competition between the two, and Trenth, it seemed, took all victories over him to heart.

After a time, Shrakar decided it was best to try to acclimate them to water another way and suggested they go back to the outpost.

*

Trellith found himself once again surrounded by looming observers as he sketched out a clearer copy of the drawing in the ancient text of the inner cave system under the Kolifarii Falls. This time the map room only had Ogron, Valdara, Havanth – all of them having bathed away the sweat of training and wearing the thick bathing robes the outpost provided – and Arnath, who observed the diagrams in the ancient text and Trellith's re-creation with a stern grimace.

The death of Dalgar had stung Arnath hard, a pain he carried still. To find now, all these years later, handy blueprints with a knowledge that might have saved his life re-opened that old wound, made it raw again.

"You will approach from the north, of course. Then make your way to the west side of the river. There are bridges to cross, meant to take travellers to

Solmairyth, but you will cross and then turn off the dirt road to follow the river bank all the way to the rise of the cliffs." Trellith was saying as he drew, pointing occasionally to the map Garthe had made.

"When we made our attempt, we approached from the east bank." Arnath said, his voice softer than usual, his thoughts roaming back in time. "It was the wrong way to go."

"What do you think is the difference?" Valdara asked Arnath.

Arnath approached the table and pointed to Garthe's map. "We climbed down here and tried to navigate across the side of the cliff, attempting to reach the underside of the falls. The difficulties we encountered on this curving cliff-side were too numerous to count. We got only a half of the way to the waterfall, and then decided to go back. Our lives were in peril, and we sought to save ourselves and rethink our strategy. But the rains had other ideas. A deluge swept over the falls, and caught up Dalgar in it. After that, we were too disheartened to try from the other side. You see these trees, on the west bank? On the east side they stop short of the horseshoe by more than two hundred feet. On the west, the trees nearly meet the bank next to the falls. You can anchor your ropes there, and descend nearly straight down. The distance to the cave wouldn't be too far, depending on the width of the falls at the time."

Picturing the climb, Havanth nodded, saying, "Thirty feet, perhaps fifty if the falls are engorged." Then a dark look overcame his face. He'd imagined his own demise.

Seeing this, Valadara asked, "What is it?"

"Those falls." Havanth said, his head shaking slightly. "Should we spill from the rock face, and get swept under... I can't see a way of surviving that."

Arnath said plainly, "This afternoon we shall train again on the wall, only this time we shall work from side to side, as you will on the craggy rocks. You'll need rope and hammers and pitons, which we'll supply you. You can secure ropes along the cliff on the way in, to ease your ascent on the way out. Shrakar has a kind of training in mind, a way to master breath control, lest you get pulled under by raging currents under the falls."

"Training for breath control? What do you mean?" Havanth asked, entirely puzzled.

"You're not going to like it." Trellith said, keeping his eyes on his diagram.

*

Sitting beside the spring pool, Shrakar was just finishing up with a large stone, wrapping and knotting a rope around its center, the second of which he'd prepared for this new training exercise. Trenth and Mego watched him, turning occasionally to check that rickety Grentoss was okay on the climbing wall. The old mage was moving at turtle speed from hand hold to hand hold.

Shrakar put on one of his work gloves, dropped the stone into the spring pool and let the length of rope snake through his hands. Eventually he had to let the rope go, and then pointed down into the pool.

Trenth and Mego looked down into the clear waters of the spring pool and saw the tops of two ropes floating side by side a good span apart. Trenth looked away from the pool, saying, "Oh no, you don't really expect us to..."

"Whatever he wants you fellows to do, do it."

Shrakar, Trenth and Mego turned to see Arnath, Trellith, Valdara and Havanth approaching from the back door. Havanth looked at the boys quite grim-faced.

"He wants us to submerge in the pool, and hold onto the ropes until we cannot breathe!"

Reaching the spring pool, Havanth looked into it, and saw the tops of the undulating ropes that floated some four feet under the water. Havanth got the principal of the exercise right away. He stripped off his thick robe, revealing he wore long underclothes from the waist down. His old warrior's trunk was a saggy mass of battle scars. "I'm not letting that waterfall kill me."

Havanth sat down at the edge of the spring pool, and Shrakar slung a short circlet of rope over his shoulder and under one arm, saying, "So I can get you up."

"Right." Havanth nodded, then turned to Arnath. "Looking at the map of the inner cave system, I began to see what you've been driving at. The cliffs, the falls, the currents – Any one of those things could kill us, as they did your friend. Well, we won't be going out like that. None of us. We'll stay here and train until you and your men say we are ready to go."

A look of understanding passed between the two men, and Arnath said, "Well then, off you go."

Havanth heaved his bottom off the lip of the spring pool and, raising his arms over his head, and disappeared under the water.

Leaving room for Shrakar to reach in and rescue him, everyone leaned in to look into the pool. Havanth held the top of the rope, his body floating upright a mere three feet beneath the surface. Be it the cold of the water, or the lack of air, the struggle on his face was plain, and grew with each passing moment. The cringe on his face became the most agonized of rictuses and he let out a silent scream accompanied by a blast of bubbles.

Instantly Shrakar knifed his arm into the water, and, standing up, emerged with Havanth hanging from his circlet of rope. Shrakar eased the sputtering Havanth to the cool flat stone surrounding the spring pool.

Between coughs, Havanth could be heard saying, "So terrible. Not me. Not dying like that."

Eventually, his coughs subsided and he sat up, allowing Valdara to cover his shoulders with his robe. Havanth looked up at Arnath, and said, "I've seen entire columns of men ripped apart by the dark magics of the Orc clerics, and still I cannot imagine a more horrible death."

"Let us make certain that never occurs then."

"Your word?" Havanth implored, eyeing Arnath gravely.

"You have my word." Arnath replied, inwardly pledging to Dalgar's memory that he would do everything he could to keep it.

*

That night, after every member of Havanth's party had tried the torturous test in the spring pool, they sat in the common room, doing their best to relax. Now that Havanth had taken to heart the need for dedicated preparation as though their very survival depended on it, there would be little leisure until they mounted their horses to leave Kroman's Town. Until sunset each day, they would be put through their paces by a group of hardened veterans, until their screaming muscles quivered like jelly. None of them looked forward to the prospect.

Having already eaten, Havanth's people sat in groups of two and sipped at their drinks in morose silence. Exhaling from his pipe behind the counter, Arnath noticed that their numbers seemed off. He couldn't place the discrepancy until he heard the distinctive thunk of an arrow striking home from outside.

In the yard, Arnath found Trenth alone, nocking and firing arrows at one of the thick, straw-filled practice targets in the moonlight. Though it was dark, Arnath was impressed by the young man's ability to land the center of the target near every shot. As Arnath got closer, he heard the young man sniffle, and saw him wipe tears from his face. He could have turned, and left the boy in private, but Arnath thought perhaps since Trenth was under his roof that he should try to be of some help. Arnath stepped closer, and the young man turned his face away, making as though he were busying himself with his next arrow.

"The exercise in the spring pool isn't meant to be cruel. At the heart of it, we want you to train your mind to be calm whilst submerged. It's key to survival. So, I think, anyway."

Trenth, embarrassed to have been caught in such a vulnerable state, only slightly turned toward Arnath. "He doesn't have to be so cruel about it."

Arnath thought on the tone the words were spoken with – An angry despair. He could tell the boy was stung to his core.

"Havanth only wants all of you to survive. I assure you; He means no harm."

As soon as the words were out, Trenth whipped his rage-filled eyes toward Arnath, seething, "Not him – Mego. He thinks it's funny that I take longer to master skills than him. He never fails to bring it up. Ever since we met, he's done it. Now, with this training... He knows I've feared the water, but still he..."

The words were choked off as Trenth was racked with sobs. Near as soon as they came, Trenth inhaled sharply and stood tall, cutting off his tears. Overcome with emotion as he was, he had no wish to blubber in front of an admirable warrior like Captain Arnath.

Arnath thought on what Trenth had said, and the words "Ever since we met" stuck in his mind. Despite their matching appearances, and the closeness they displayed, Trenth and Mego were not brothers. It now occurred to Arnath that these two young men loved each other.

This way of being was not strange to Arnath by this point in his life. He had, in fact, learned of it as a young man, first out into the world, a fresh recruit in the King's guard. As an inexperienced youth with only a farm upbringing and education, Arnath had poked fun at the couples of the same sex amongst the ranks. Soon however, he found this led to severe ostracization from the other soldiers, who pointedly made it clear he was an ignorant farm boy and knew nothing of the workings of the world. Was he going to go through life pointing and laughing at every new, until then unknown, sight before his eyes for the rest of his days? Would he see an unknown range of mountains and laugh like a jester at it? Why not wear a mummer's foolscap then? For surely only a fool would go through life that way. Arnath took the lesson to heart. He had grown up on an isolated farmstead, and what little knowledge he'd acquired there represented but a kernel of what could be seen throughout the greater world. From then on, he set aside much of his judgement of people and their ways, allowing himself to absorb more via experience.

Knowing what he did now, Arnath felt a pang of guilt for not surmising it before. Looking back, he realized that Trenth and Mego had nearly no reaction to Shimalena as she served them and played music in the common room. Others, elves, men and women alike, would gape at her in a kind entranced awe. Not these fellows. They only saw each other. Dalgar, Arnath's closest boon companion and the one whom they all sought to honour by helping Havanth's party survive their travails, was such a man. Though they didn't speak of it much, Dalgar once described an aspect of his way of being to Arnath by asking him to imagine the desire to please and be pleased in a coupling, but also retaining all the will of competition against one's brethren, even with those closest to your heart. Arnath thought perhaps that this problem was rearing its head for Trenth and Mego.

Mego was a tad slighter than Trenth. Perhaps before they met, none had ever marked him as an athlete or a potential warrior. Having attained it in life, after a painful early life of goading, Mego might have become entirely insensitive about how he revelled in his accomplishments, even when speaking to someone he held dear, like Trenth. For his part, Trenth didn't seem to be someone who allowed himself to be bested, despite his slight size. In all things, he was the victor. He had to be, lest he disappear into the stature of a small man. Of the two, Trenth had decidedly angry eyes, and Arnath guessed he solved many problems with his fists. In the case of Mego, who he loved and would never harm, he could not lash out violently, and the pain of these defeats, however small, compounded and nagged at him, eating him up inside.

"I ask this, not at all to chide you, lad, but perhaps to help you see your way to the truth. Why is it you can tell me that his actions pain you so, and not him? Is your relationship such that you need keep your deepest feelings secret?"

Trenth's eyes creased at the corners, as though Arnath's question was about to prompt an angry outburst. But as he made to speak, Trenth's eyes softened and he slumped, sighing. "I don't know."

Arnath let that hang, hoping he was able to help the young man see to the heart of the matter as Trenth nocked another arrow and readied to fire.

*

In the middle of the night, Illona dashed down the front steps, into the cloak area of the front corridor, peered into the common room and dashed out again without saying a word. Her sudden appearance and disappearance, drew strange glances from around the common room. Before anyone could ask about it, the outpost door opened again and the sound of many boots on the stairs could be heard.

Havanth looked up from the table where he sat and played a languid game of pegs with Valdara, fully expecting, from the sound of the heavy boots, that another group of adventuring patrons had arrived. What he did see emerging down the corridor made him intake his breath sharply.

There they stood, though aged twenty odd years, were men of his old regiment, most certainly alive.

"Light take me." Havanth said, rising from his chair, awestruck.

In the front corridor stood Shamuth, Fernlow, Tindall and Amorth in their finest leathers, rank insignia on their left breasts. Shamuth smiled, reacting to Havanth's dumbstruck visage, and said, "What's the matter, captain? You look like you've seen a bunch of ghosts."

Havanth, the look of disbelief still upon his face cross the room with open arms and embraced Shamuth. "I'd not thought it possible." Haventh said, his voice trembling. "How is this possible?"

"Quite simple, Captain." Tindall said, grinning like a fool. "We live here."

Still holding Shamuth's shoulder, Haventh turned as Arnath entered with Trenth and asked, "You did this?"

"Of course. Valdara said you were the last of the seventh, I knew she was wrong about that. Thought perhaps a reunion was I order." Arnath said as he moved behind the counter, and began to pour stein after stein.

"Well, bless you for it then, Captain. You've given me the surprise of my life."

Havanth embraced each of his men in turn, but only shook Amorth's hand, for he was of the Eleventh and had to remind Havanth of how they had met when their two regiments were briefly attached. That was the beginning of many in-depth reminiscences of their time in the field, and a night of joyous drinking ensued.

Arnath stayed behind the counter and poured drinks freely, staying out of the way of the festivities, as did Trellith and Shrakar. They had no wish to over-shadow the reunion, and, as men of the first regiment – The King's regiment – they tended to do that everywhere they went. No, tonight was for Havanth and the men of the Seventh.

As the night wore on, and the stories took on a more maudlin tone, since the seventh was indeed a regiment doomed to a bloody fate. Shimalena played from the dais and the men would occasionally sing songs of honour and glory. Shamuth, with his deep bass voice, sang a rendition of "The hill I will die on" that brought everyone to tears.

Later, after Havanth had introduced his current travelling party to his former soldiers, and the festivities were fully inter-mingled, Arnath pretended not to notice when Trenth and Mego slipped away upstairs by themselves, turning his back to pour more ale as they went by him. When Arnath turned back to place freshly filled steins on the counter, Valdara was there, eyeing him coyly from across the counter.

"You've given the captain a tremendous gift." She said, taking the stein as he nudged it towards her. "I find myself surprised daily by the kindness you show."

"Despite nearly drowning you all every day?" Arnath said wryly, sipping on an ale he'd poured for himself.

"Yes, in spite of that." Valdara said, returning his smile.

"Well, we are here to serve."

Valdara eyed him with the same narrowed lids she had the night she arrived, and said, "Speaking of your kind service, I was hoping you could show me how to heat my bath. It has been a quandary since we got here."

"Of course." Arnath slipped through the hinged counter and gestured to-wards the stairs. "After you."

Upstairs, in her second-floor room, the single that faced the main street, Arnath placed some more logs in the fire of her elevated stove. Kneeling in front of it, he picked up a small coal shovel and shovelled hot coals from the bottom of the fire into a brassy-coloured metal box and closed its lid. Then, he turned to the nearby tub and used tongs to slide the already burning hot box into a slot under the tub designed to hold it in snugly place.

Arnath rose up, and turned on the faucet, allowing water to cascade into the tub. He turned to Valdara, saying, "There you have it. Easy as..."

Seeing Valdara, Arnath was dumbstruck, as she had stripped her clothing and now only wore one of the morning robes, which was open in the front. She rose from the bed, and moved towards him, allowing him to see even more of her nakedness under the robe.

"Would you care to join me in the bath?" She said, standing very close to him.

Arnath looked aside, for the merest glimpse of her naked, well-muscled body had stirred him to his core. It had been some time since he was alone with a woman. Swallowing deeply, he said, "I wish that I could, for you are lovely, a tantalizing sight to behold. But I cannot. There is... someone."

Valdara stepped away and closed her robed, her eyes downcast. "Know that I envy this woman, Arnath. She is lucky to have the heart of such a fine man, a man of your character. To think I, a maiden of steel, cannot even seduce you..."

"Maiden of steel, you say?" Arnath said, not hiding his surprise.

"Yes."

"You fought at Heshthro?"

"I did."

Arnath smiled at her, and said, "Then do not feel bad you could not charm me. It is one of your sisters who has my heart. And like Captain Havanth and his brothers in arms, you shall see her very soon."

*

The next morning, as Arnath made his way down to the exercise yard, he could hear voices outside already. Reaching the bottom of the stairs, he stepped out and found Grentoss on the climbing wall, with Garthe standing to spot him on the ground below. Grentoss had one of the loops of rope that Shrakar used to quickly extract people from the spring pool slung around his bottom and one of the climbing ropes knotted around the top of that, near his chest. His bony hips were bent and his lower legs hung free as he pulled himself across the wall one hand hold at a time.

As Arnath got closer to the climbing wall, he heard the patter of fleet feet on the stairs and wasn't at all surprised to see the whirl of Shimalena's silver hair again as she sped down from the stairs and into the main corridor. At least Garthe received some affections last night, he thought, exchanging a knowing look with the young mage across the yard. Much as he chided himself inside for not fulfilling his manly needs last night, Arnath knew he'd chosen wisely. Valdara was alluring and even a bit mysterious, but wanted other things in a partner now. He wanted only Merynda, and that was that.

In the yard, as well were Trenth and Mego. They stood side by side and would alternately fire the special thonged-arrows with ropes affixed to them over the back fence into the trees. They'd been fascinated by the thonged-arrows since arriving and having been told the story of how Heflynn's arrow had saved many lives during the construction of the outpost. Trellith had made them each a grouping of the special arrows for their quivers, and it seemed they were working at becoming adept at their use. Arnath gathered their goal was to fire at a heavier tree branch, and get the rope lashed around it. So far, they'd only managed to get a bunch of arrows and several lengths of rope over the fence, all of which would need to be retrieved and the process started all over again.

As Arnath approached the climbing wall, Garthe said, "Good morning. What do you think?"

"Think? What is it exactly?"

"Master Grentoss will likely not be able to withstand the climb down and then crossing the wall under the deluge of the waterfall. He will, however be needed inside the caves."

Arnath nodded, understanding what Garthe meant. "Any magic seals on the chambers will absolutely require his attention."

"So, rather than have him climb across," Garthe continued, "I devised this, to help him swing across the gap from where their ropes fall to the mouth of the caves."

"Not exactly swinging though, is he?"

From his position up on the wall, Grentoss turned slightly to Arnath. "I'm building up to it. It takes some coaxing to get the fear out of these old bones."

"Besides, we should wait until Shrakar or Ogron are awake. They can keep Grentoss safer whilst he swings, better than we could."

"True. Very true." Arnath nodded at the notion, and felt some pride in Garthe for yet another ingenious idea. On the adventuring road, his sparks of imagination had proved invaluable and often were key to their survival. It seemed that would continue here in the training yard, even though he had a busy healing clinic to run.

Arnath's thoughts were interrupted by the loud thump of feet in the sand. He turned to see Shrakar stripping his gloves off by the dangling balcony rope.

"Oh good. We find ourselves in need of your help." Arnath said.

*

Over the next few days, the outpost owners trained Havanth's party to exhaustion from daybreak to sunset. Arnath and the others concentrated on the climbing and swimming aspects of their training, for it was highly unlikely they would have to fight anything, man or creature, inside or outside the cave system. Shrakar had one edict across the board: Anyone who fell from the climbing wall had to immediately march over and jump into the spring pool. Eventually, the entire party got quite good at relaxing their bodies and holding their breath in the cold water of the spring pool.

With Shrakar and Orgon's help Grentoss got better at the long right to left swing that would propel him from the cliffside to the mouth of the cave. After Arnath had coached him to keep his legs stiff, his knees pointed in the direction he was going, and to not flail them in the air, his flight got smoother and truer with each practice.

Both Trenth and Mego were eventually able to swim the width of the lake twice without need of Shrakar rescuing them. By the springpool, Arnath had overheard Mego giving Trenth words of encouragement and suggestions for breath-holding tricks to try, and was pleased. It seemed his advice was having a positive effect.

A general plan was forming – Valdara would descend the cliff next to the waterfalls first, and as she crossed, would hammer in pitons to hold a guiding rope into the rock face. At Garthe's suggestion, the rope that they would descend down would be long enough to dip far into the roiling waters under the falls, so anyone who fell might grab it and climb their way back out of danger. Ogron would go next, carrying much of their equipment. Grentoss would follow, swinging across the rock face to be caught by Ogron, then Havanth, then Mego and lastly Trenth would guard their upper position with his bow until they were all inside the cave system.

They had consulted the maps with Trellith, and found the third highway cut out to the west of Solindar was the best place to start their trek south to the falls. Taking the King's road that led south to Solmairyth would take them leagues out of their way, and add unwanted days to their journey. Arnath would accompany them to the cut out, to make sure they made it into the King's wood without detection, as it was frowned on for large parties to travel the woods off of the King's Road without permission. And he'd get to see Merynda on the way back.

Arnath kept that last part a secret from Havanth's party. Though Valdara was embarrassed by her failed attempt to seduce Arnath, her intrigue over which of her sisters from the maidens of steel regiments she would be reunited with outweighed those feelings of embarrassment and she hung close to him, always prodding him for clues.

As the sun set every day, Shimalena and one of the others from the Briny Sea would bring steaming trays of food across the street and leave them on the long counter. In the line that formed along the counter for everyone to fill their bowls and plates, Grentoss stood behind Garthe and asked, "Would you join me outside Master Garthe? I have something to show you."

They settled outside on small stools, their plates on their knees, bowls on the ground beside them. Shimalena came out and deposited a goblet of wine and a stein of ale next to the bowls and, after delivery a kiss on top of Garthe's head, disappeared back inside.

"I've noted you only carry the one stone." Grentoss said between bites. "A green healing stone."

"Yes, it's the only one I have." Garthe said, and eyed Grentoss over the rim of his stein curiously.

"While these things are never certain, I do have a feeling about the coming quest. I think it shall be the last I shall undertake."

Taken aback, Garthe enquired, "You don't think...?"

"Oh no, Master Garthe." Grentoss snickered as he put his plate on the ground, realizing how ominous his statement must have sounded. "What I mean is age has caught up with me, and I fear my time on the road is at an end. I should have taken up a post, like yourself, ages ago."

"I see." Garthe said, entirely relieved. Grentoss could well have had a prescient ability for all he knew, and had actually foreseen his death. "What will you do?"

"I had thought to teach. Once we have divvied up whatever gold we may find from under the falls, I should like to come back here and tutor you for a time."

"I would like that."

"Then, I shall move on to, nearer to the capital. There I can teach sciences and histories until another young mage presents themselves." Grentoss sipped his wine, and then put his goblet down. He reached around his neck, and pulled a thong over his head, one that had a small leather pouch on it very similar to the one Garthe wore. He poked his fingers inside and pulled out a teardrop-shaped gem of the deepest crimson. "Do you know what this is?"

"No, Master Grentoss." Garthe said, leaning in closer to examine the smooth-surfaced stone.

"This is a power stone." Grentos said, rolling it between his fingers. "It is designed to focus the will, to give a boost, say, to any spell or intent you are casting. I should like to instruct you some in its use, before I leave it with you."

"Leave it with me? I couldn't!" Garthe blanched at the notion.

"Oh yes, you could. Squander no talent – remember?" Grentoss said, invoking the first oath of all magical practitioners. "I shall not be in need of such a gem to focus my power in a classroom. You, however, young Garthe, are only beginning your journey."

"I seem to have settled in here."

"Oh, nonsense." Grentoss said waving a dismissive hand and taking a deep sip of his wine. "Having a place to come home to is the best way to adventure. I have lived as you and yours did until you built this place, and I must tell you

– Having a home to venture forth from and return to after any kind of folly is the much better way to live. A tub of hot water, clothes that are clean – Ahhh. Much better indeed. One could find all the gold in the world, and still stink to the mountaintops from being in the dust of the road too long. Mark me – There is no glory in that."

Garthe snickered at Grentoss words, one of the rare occasions when he knew exactly what his elders were talking about. There were times on the road with Arnath, Shrakar and Trellith where a bath had been weeks in the past. Too many times, really.

Grentoss ambled over to the huge practice weapons cabinet along the fence, and began to open the large doors one by one. Finally came an "Aaah" from within one cabinet, and Grentoss stepped out with an archery target awkwardly in his arms. He shuffled it over, away from the cabinet, and lowered it to the ground.

"What will we do with that?" Garthe asked.

"Like I said, I shall show you some of the properties of the stone." Grentoss said, hobbling back to his stool and easing himself down. "The rest you can practice yourself. Shimar provided you with an excellent book on casting, the one bound in green leather, a copy of something I myself learned from many, many years ago."

Grentoss gestured for Garthe to put out his hand and then reached out, placing the crimson stone in the young mage's palm.

*

"Would you say she had long hair, light, like mine?"

Arnath snickered at Valdara, his spoon half way to his mouth. Ever since he sat down at the larger dining table in the common room, she had sidled up next to him and needled him with a barrage of requests for hints. Around the common room, all those dining listened to her girlish prods for info as though it were part of their dinner entertainment.

"A couple of days. You cannot wait a couple of mere days?" Arnath asked, knowing she was dying to know the identity of the woman they were going to see on the road to the Kolifarii Falls.

Valdara threw up her hands, a spoon in one of them, and remarked in a frustrated tone, "This is a child's game. You plan this reunion hoping for the same result as the one you arranged for Havanth and his men the other night, but you leave out one notion, lest it spoil your fun."

"Which is?" Arnath asked, actually interested to know what she meant.

"Havanth was the captain to the men you invited here. A superior who had the reverence of his men."

"And?"

"You presume all we maidens of steel liked each other. We were sisters in battle, no doubt, but not all of us bonded as comrades in arms. How would you feel if you roped me into a reunion with someone I despised or perhaps despised me?" Valdara asked, and then eyed Arnath for an answer, her face frozen somewhere between query and accusation.

Arnath thought on this, taking a couple of bites from his plate, and then said, "I shall let you know how I feel when that moment comes a couple of days from now."

This drew a peel of laughter from around the room, and got him punched in the shoulder by Valdara. Arnath thought her punch for more powerful than reason allowed, for the floor beneath them shook ever so subtly. In that same moment, a noise as loud as thunder resounded from the courtyard.

All of them – Arnath, Valdara, Shrakar, Trellith, Havanth, Ogron, Mego and Trenth – clambered down the main corridor and raced up the short steps to the courtyard to find Garthe and Grentoss on their backsides and small tufts of burning hay fluttering down all around the training yard.

"What happened?" Arnath enquired loudly, as he approached Garthe, stamping out little hay fires all the way.

"The boy is just too powerful." Grentoss said as Havanth and Valdara dusted him off and helped him to his feet. "I told him to try and set the center of the target on fire. Then fwooosh!"

At Trellith's urging Shrakar, Ogron, Mego and Trenth grabbed buckets kept behind the tree next to the spring pool, filled them and began to race about the yard, putting out the larger of the fires. Shrakar peered over the fence, searching the ground and trees for little fires.

As he knelt beside Garthe, readying to help him up, Arnath looked at the blackened spot on the ground. Where Grentoss had indicated the target once stood, was now only occupied by the charred remains of the wooden stand and a radiating sun-shape of char on the ground.

"Lucky you didn't blow a hole in the climbing wall and through to the mound." Arnath said in a joking tone as he helped Garthe up.

"Do not jest. He could likely do just that, with very little effort." Grentoss said, shaking the dirt from his robe.

Arnath had learned over the years, from his time in the trenches with battling mages, to travelling with Morgosh, that the stones mages carried were not the source of their power, only a tool through which their power was focussed. No matter what kind of stone – be they healing, power, weather or other single purpose stones, like Shimar's sleep stone – the magnitude of the effect they produced depended entirely on the innate power of the mage who wielded them. Arnath had also known that Garthe was an incredibly strong mage for some time. He'd seen the boy bring people back from the brink of death since he was 9 years old. Once fully trained in the other magical arts, there was no telling how powerful he would be.

"Perhaps you should take the power stone back." Garthe said, reaching his hand toward Grentoss. Arnath looked at the dark red stone in between Garthe's fingers, and he thought of the humility of Garthe's approach to the untrained power he had within. He had always feared the possibility of his power harming others.

"No, no." The old mage said, his hand waving Garthe's away. "It is yours to wield now. And mastering the discipline of control along with it."

Just then, having heard the explosion from all the way across the street, Shimalena emerged from the back door. She saw the little fires everywhere and the patch of scorched earth and ran straight into Garthe's arms.

Assured he was in good hands, Arnath left Garthe's side walked over to the spring pool, grabbed up a bucket and filled it to join the others as they put out the many tiny fires around the yard.

CHAPTER ELEVEN

Havanth and his party left Kroman's Town two days after Garthe had so surprisingly blown the archery target to smithereens in the training yard. The party had become as expert as they could at every skill they'd need in order to tackle the Kolifarii Falls and the daunting cave system below. Horses packed heavy with supplies, Arnath rode out of town with them, after having his companions create a distraction for Mayor Bumpol, who seemed determined the departing party should serve as guests of honour in a goodbye parade wherein the townsfolk would come and wave and cheer at as they left.

Arnath wanted to keep the goodbyes as short and as secret as possible. Havanth had asked for privacy, and as his host, that's exactly what Arnath was going to provide. Dozens of waving people, all yelling "Good luck on your secret mission that a great many cutthroats along the road would be willing to kill you in order just to know where you're going" seemed like something from a nightmare to Arnath. Like those he had as a young soldier, dreaming fitfully about showing up to morning muster without leggings and boots.

Much as he cherished the welcoming people of Kroman's Town, there were certain aspects of his business that did not align with the pastoral nature of the sleepy town. Arnath knew well from his time adventuring that even possessing a map fragment that might possibly lead to hidden treasure was enough to get someone killed on the road. The elderly tradespeople of Kroman's could never begin to understand such a thing.

Avoiding a ceremonious exit was not the only hiccup in the party's departure. Trellith had done a fine job of refurbishing each of the party's weapons – sharpening blades, rebinding scabbards, replacing arrow fletching – but for one.

He had found a flaw in the blade of Valdara's sword that would take much work to repair, so much so that replacement was indeed a better solution. Trellith brought her over to the smithy, and gently explained to Valdara that he had found two dark spots when he heated the metal. These spots, that sat near each other on either side of the blade, showed through as darker than the rest of the surface when the sword was heated in the forge. Over them, the surface of the blade took on the aspect of an oily, rainbow colouration and that could only mean one thing. The flaws in the folding of the metal were cracked underneath, and the blade itself could shatter at anytime she used it in battle.

Unlike Arnath and his companions, Valdara was greatly attached to her sword, having purchased it almost directly after the wars. She at first refused to believe Trellith and hurled the crudest of obscenities at him for even suggesting there was a flaw with her beloved weapon.

Eventually, after she'd expressed as much rage as anyone could, Valdara settled on the flat rocks beside the spring pool and cried. A true warrior at heart, she was losing a part of her very identity. Trellith came to her and gently suggested two solutions. He could shorten the blade, for there was nothing wrong with the metal between the flawed section and the blade guard, and it would from then on serve as an excellent short sword. Or he could remove the blade and she could take the hilt to a craft person in Solindar, and get a new Elven-steel blade molded onto the hilt.

After she put her mind to it, Valdara decided to have the blade removed. She was not a short sword fighter, and the notion of new Elven-steel appealed to her. Valadara sat and watched mournfully as Trellith disassembled the hilt, removed the blade and then re-assembled it. He turned it over to her and Valdara cradled it to her chest as Trellith placed the blade into a trough and set it into the forge to melt.

As the party were being helped carrying their things down to the stables to load up their horses, Havanth and Arnath had the most awkward of exchanges. Arnath pushed the party's bill across the counter toward Havanth, who saw the number and blanched.

"It's a fair price for the services provided. Not only did you stay and eat and drink and train, your weapons were serviced, your horses were billeted and cared for. See here – we did not charge you for Grentoss room and board, as he did teach Garthe quite a bit whilst here." Arnath said as gently as he could. This was the first time he had ever had this conversation with one of their departing customers, and did not wish to bark his reasons for the charges at Haventh like ransom demands.

"Of course, of course. It's just that…" Havanth reached into his waistcoat and pulled out his purse. He unlaced it, single eye downcast the whole time, and overturned it on top of the counter. The clink of coins Arnath heard was far from impressive.

When Havanth lifted his purse away, there was a mere two gold pieces and some silver and coppers. The bill was for three gold.

Arnath picked up one of the gold pieces and worried it between his fingers on the counter. He tried to forget all of Havanth's obstinate bluster when his party first arrived, and instead thought on the many times when he and his men had had to rely on kind strangers just to eat when they fell upon hard times on the road.

"I swear to you, Captain Arnath, if we find anything, anything at all in those caves, a goodly portion of it will come back here to you and yours." Havanth said, upraised palms before him.

"As is right, but I will not hold you to it." Arnath said quietly. He had no wish to bind Havanth to that commitment, lest it curse their quest and then the party die in the waters of the falls. He did not want that on his conscience. Turning the coin in his fingers he said, "What will your party do if there is nothing to be found? How will you even feed yourselves?"

"I... I do not know." Havanth said, his shoulders slumping, as though he had heard the awful question nipping at the edges of his mind for as long as he could remember, but it had never been asked by another person until now.

It took until this moment for Arnath to realize it, but Havanth's party were just like his had been up until a couple of months ago. An adventuring party of old warriors and new blood, travelling the aimless roads in search of gold and, more often than not, being rewarded with starvation, a rocky bed of dirt and more regrets to count than coin. It took a mountain crashing down on their heads to awaken Arnath and his companions to the fact that their adventures had to be over and done with. Only they came to that realization with a fortune in their possession, and a plan formed around that fact. Havanth and his companions just might let their search for fortune kill them, for there was no alternate life laid out before them, none their adventurer's eyes could see.

Arnath set the gold coin he'd been fumbling with on the counter, and slid it across toward Havanth. He then swiftly swept up all the other coins with the edge of his hand and reached down to drop them in the funnel under the counter. Havanth looked down at the gold coin and blanched, "Captain, I couldn't..."

Arnath pushed it further towards him and said, "You will."

After a moment's hesitation, Havanth, shame-faced, picked up the coin and dropped it into his purse and then stowed that away in his vest.

"Now," Arnath said as he stepped through the gap in the counter. "Let's get your party on its way."

*

On the King's Road, less than a half days ride from Kroman's Town, Valdara rode beside Arnath, giddy with anticipation. With each new farm they passed, she would scan his expression, searching for a sign they had arrived at the home of her sister from the maidens of steel.

Seeing Merynda's on-coming property, Arnath steeled his face against the breezy feelings he felt growing inside. He had not seen her in such a long time, and was ready to burst with emotion, despite needing to keep up the façade for Valdara's benefit just a little longer.

As they passed Merynda's farm, Arnath tried to keep the deception going for as long as possible, but Merynda's daughter Perrin emerged from the high stacked tuffets of raked hay and corn stalks near the road and squealed, "Hello, Mister Captain!"

With the game up, Arnath reigned in his horse and jumped down to the ground to scoop the already giggling little girl up in his arms. "Good afternoon, Perrin. I see you're busy at work. Is your mommy at home today, or has she left you in charge?"

"Don't be silly, Mister Captain. I'm always in charge, even if mommy is here."

"I imagine you would be." Arnath said walking with her in his arms, trying to get a view of the front of the house. The fields had been completely harvested since he was last this way. The onset of the severe fall rains would demand it. All that remained in the fields were tall, conical bundles of cornstalks and hay, a tight maze worth of them that prevented the sight of the house from all but a few angles.

Arnath peered down the sloping field toward the house, and heard a crunch of hay right beside him. He turned and Merynda was there, having emerged from behind one of the stacks. "I spied you coming a half-league away. The way you stoop in the saddle, I knew it was you."

Arnath set Perrin down, wriggling her entire descent, and stepped towards Merynda. She stepped in close, encircling her arms around his neck. The kiss they exchanged occurred so naturally, neither of them gave a thought on how long it was in the coming. And neither of them could have even guessed how long they had been kissing when little Perrin said, "Eww, you're making smacking noises like the horses drinking from a bucket."

Merynda and Arnath parted, and, looking down at Perrin, laughed.

Recovering from the euphoria of their first kiss, Arnath said to Merynda, "I have a surprise for you."

"More than just a visit out of the blue. I'm intrigued." Merynda said, and took Arnath's offered hand, allowing herself to be led to the roadside.

"Merynda!" Valdara was heard shouting, and nearly toppled Merynda with an embrace before she could see who had grabbed her. Only when Valdara broke away and stood before her, a wide smile under her watering eyes, did Merynda realize who had just hugged her.

"Sister!" Merynda exclaimed, and this time was the one who initiated a warm embrace.

The two women hugged, both of them starting to laugh at the revelation that they were both alive after all this time, even after the carnage they had witnessed. Arnath turned to see Havanth making an impatient grimace. Ogron was none too pleased either, as Perrin was tickling his feet in the stirrups, trying to get him to play. Arnath ventured a guess that Ogron might not be as comfortable with human children as Shrakar was.

He turned back to the two veteran maidens of steel, and said, "You ladies have a full day to catch up. We must be on our way to Solindar." Arnath then reached his palm toward Valdara, fingers beckoning.

Valdara looked at him dumbstruck, but only for a moment. Realizing what he was waiting for, she detached a heavy pouch from her belt and opened it to take one last look at the hilt of her sword. Arnath received the pouch from her, saying, "Your sword should be fully ready by tomorrow afternoon. You'll find us in the common room of the largest inn."

"You're not staying?" Merynda said, entirely crestfallen.

"I have to get this to a smith in Solindar, then see these people on their way." Arnath said, seeing the disappointment on Merynda's face. "But I shall return in a day's time, if that is alright by you."

"Alright? You had better!" Merynda said punching him in the chest with an audible thump, that drew a laugh from all around.

Arnath feigned defeat as he stepped in close to her, taking her in his arms. "Very well – I surrender."

They parted after kissing once again, but Arnath stayed close, quietly asking, "Jarthow – Is he well?"

"Better." Merynda said, matching his intimate tone. "He was quite weak for a time."

"We should have Garthe take a look at him, after I am done with my customers."

"Alright." Merynda said, glad of his concern. Then he kissed her once more and strode away to his horse.

Havanth nodded at Valdara from his horseback, and said, "Behave ladies. We wouldn't want to have to come back and bail a couple of wayward maidens of steel out of the Guardsman's poke."

*

Arnath rode into Solindar with Havanth's party just after sunset, making it in time to reach the forge of P'sheinar - a lady smith whom Trellith had connected with the first time they passed through town intent on making such alliances - before she closed for the night.

Though a Traditionalist elf, P'sheinar spoke enough of the common tongue to easily discern what was needed for Valdara's new blade. And, yes, it could be ready for tomorrow afternoon. That taken care of, there was nothing else to do until the bank opened in the morning, so Arnath suggested they go to the ale house.

Havanth and his party were somewhat taken aback by the number of waves and hails Arnath received since arriving the common room of the inn. They still kept coming, even long after Arnath explained that the majority of the building had been done by local craftsmen and Arnath and his companions were the employers of the majority of the elf artisans of Solindar for more than a month. He knew them all and they all knew him.

Equally surprising to Havanth and his company were the number of drinks that arrived at their table without being asked for. Surprising, but not unwelcome.

The next morning Arnath rose early, did his exercises, bathed and went to the bank. It had turned out that things were not so grim after all in terms of the business account the outpost companions held. It had been more than a month since the last of the work had been done on the outpost, and all of their creditors here in Solindar had been paid out. There was still a decent amount of money left over. They might never have starved, but short of coming here to Solindar during those rainy weeks, they had no way of knowing that.

Arnath obtained several rolls of coppers and silvers, enough for both his establishment and the Briny Sea to make change for their patrons, and got a receipt to take back to Trellith. He found Havanth and his men down in the common room of the ale house. Since all they had to do was await Valdara's arrival, they ordered food and passed the time having an informal pegs tournament over drink, one that drew a crowd of interested elves who customarily played it somewhat differently than the human folk. Even Ogron pointed out, in his heavily accented croak, that Orc-kind played by different rules at certain key points in the game as well.

Valdara arrived at the common room in the afternoon to find a crowd around her companion's table, one that would transition from the quietest whispers to the loudest, sometimes startling, roars with every single move Trenth and Mego made. Having been thoroughly trounced in the game by the young men, Arnath and Havanth were free to stroll with Valdara over to P'sheinar's smith.

They walked into the back area of the smithy as P'sheinar was rebinding the leather around the grip of Valdara's sword. She bade them sit and talked through what she was doing in her best accented common tongue. When she finished, tapping the last pin into place, she handed the sword over to Valdara.

When she pulled the blade from the scabbard, the ringing shing of the steal surprised Valadara. P'sheinar smiled and nodded proudly at Valdara's expression. Her customer liked her new sword.

And she did indeed. Valdara gave the long narrow blade a few swooping, practice swings, before raising it up close to her face. The steel had a rippling green sheen to it that could only be seen this close up. Though it was not as wide as her original broadsword, this one felt it had a weighty power of its own.

Arnath could see by the squint in the corner of Valadara's eye she was mightily pleased. He stepped over to P'sheinar and presented her with a note to take to the bank, which the old elf woman received with a smile, and squirrelled it away in her shawl.

Valdara, who had belted on her scabbard, slid the sword home and glared inquisitively at Arnath. "What are you doing?" she asked in a somewhat indignant tone.

"I'm taking care of the bill." Arnath said, not understanding Valdara's ire.

"You can't do that. This is my sword to pay for!" Valdara seethed fervently as she strode up to stand face to face with him. She must have been very pleased with her new sword indeed to want to start a brawl over the bill, Arnath thought.

"And your old blade?"

"What about it?" Valdara barked the question like a harsh retort.

"I imagine right now Trellith is melting it into several dozen arrowheads. Once we've sold off all those arrows, do you expect some kind of consignment pay?" Arnath asked playfully.

Valdara's mood shifted completely away from righteous indignation, to befuddlement. "Well, no. I suppose not."

"You've paid us for this blade already. Now P'sheinar needs to be paid. It's that simple."

Not wishing to cause herself further embarrassment, Valdara gave P'sheinar the gesture of respect with her left hand and exited her work yard.

Arnath and Havanth exchanged an amused glance, and then gestured their respect and goodbyes to P'sheinar themselves.

Later, after collecting Grentoss, Orgon, Trenth and Mego from the inn, the entire party rode out of town. As they moved onto the King's road, their horses at a walking pace, Valdara rode up alongside Arnath's horse. "Havanth told me what you did for us? And still you paid for my new blade. I don't quite understand it."

"What's to understand?" Arnath asked, not at all being coy. Though Valdara may have found his behaviour mysterious, he himself didn't.

"You arranged the reunion between Havanth and his men. You got Trenth and Mego to start treating each other as beloved instead of athletic competitors. You let us away without paying our full bill. You arranged my reunion with Merynda. You paid out for my new blade, when I was willing to do so. I just don't understand. To what do we owe this...? This...?"

"Kindness." Arnath said when he saw she was searching for the right word. "Has no one ever been kind to you before, Valdara?"

After a moment's thought, she said, "Not like that, no. You know the road. And the old soldier's life on it. Occasions when someone surprises you with that sort of behaviour... Well, it has been rare."

"Same for my companions and I." He said, taking his eyes from her, and looking down the road, whilst inwardly thinking of the many long roads behind him. "The many inns and outposts we stayed in over the years, not one of the proprietors seemed to care if we survived what we embarked on. My friends and I want no one to depart feeling that way. We want you to not only succeed, but to survive, to thrive in your path. We see reflections of ourselves in you and your companions. But for the prince, who you didn't get to meet, you are our first guests. Our first try at playing genuine hosts, not bill collectors. The people that surprised us the most in our travels were the ones who offered us food, perhaps a bed when we had nothing to offer in return. They offered us kindness, despite our roughshod appearance, or the fact that we travelled with one who many still see as an enemy. They saw people in need and stepped forward to be of help. Our goal wasn't just to leave the dust of the road behind. It was to provide a lodging, a sanctuary for those of the same minds as we. Those who perhaps haven't known the kindnesses we did on the occasions we had needed them most. Maybe that is the source of my kindness; I hold a hope for you, that your long journey would end with a hearth by which to put your feet and sword up instead of an untimely death. Not just you and your companions, all those who would come through our door."

They rode in silence for a time, until Arnath noticed Valdara was watching him with narrowed eyes, and smile in one corner of her mouth.

"What is it? Do my notions of hospitality seem quaint to you?"

"No. They are in line with all else that is good in you. I think I may have returned your kindness. Unknowingly, but I did." Valdara said.

"How so?"

"We got to talking about you, Merynda and I, and I mentioned that you spurned my advances." Valdara said, holding back laughter.

"And how does that repay my kindness?" Arnath asked, wondering what was so funny.

"I believe the word she mentioned more than once about your next meeting was "ravage"." Valdara said wryly, and then, not waiting for Arnath's reaction to that titillating news, pointed across the road. "Oh, look – Is that the third cut-out?"

They waited for a cart filled with farm goods to pass and then crossed the road into the cut-out. Just as Arnath had suspected two mounted guardsmen saw them and guided their horses over. Havanth's party did as Arnath had earlier instructed, and feigned tiredness from a lengthy journey on the road, with exaggerated yawns and slumping poses on the logs by the unlit firepit.

Arnath placed himself closest to road, and pretended surprise when he heard, "You crossed the road against traffic. Isn't it a bit early to make camp?"

"Camp for the night? Certainly, good guardsmen." Arnath said in his friendliest of voices, and then he took one pivoting step towards them, so as to reveal the battered captain's clasp over his left breast. "We merely wish to get out of the sun for a time, and to refresh our horses."

"Understood, captain. Very good, sir." Said the young guardsman who lost all tone of authority from his voice.

The guardsmen rode off toward Solindar, and Arnath busied himself with his horse, watching them over his saddle the entire time. As soon as they took a bend into the city streets, Arnath nodded to Havanth.

Haventh and his people quickly gathered up the things they had removed from their horses to support their pantomime and readied the horses once again to go. Valdara checked the road heading into Solindar, saw it was empty and nodded to the others. She stepped away from the roadside, approached Arnath and kissed his cheek, saying, "Thank you."

Havanth stepped over to Arnath and held out his hand to be shaken.

"I gave you my word, and I mean to keep it." Haventh said, shaking Arnath's hand and looking him in the eye.

Arnath looked back into Havanth's one, saying, "You would honour me and mine best by keeping all of your people alive. By keeping them safe."

"And I shall." Havanth then turned away towards the others – Valdara, Ogron, Grentoss, Trenth and Mego - who waited at the threshold of the forest. In turn they all either waved or saluted at Arnath and then disappeared, leading their horses into the thickness of the forest.

On his way back through Solindar, Arnath paid courtesy calls on Lorta and Taishen – to see if all was right with the billing and payroll – though he knew the money was withdrawn already. It was the soldier's discipline in him that sought to detect any financial pitfalls before they tripped-up he and his partners. Arnath then rode to Shimar's and paid him a short visit to ask if he had any reading materials that he wanted to pass on to Garthe. Arnath related the story of the amazingly kinetic power stone Garthe had acquired, and wondered aloud if there was any text Shimar might have to help him train with such a volatile artifact. Shimar thought on it a moment, then disappeared upstairs briefly. He returned with a thick volume that he said he did not need returned. Before leaving, Arnath asked about the live-stone, and what came of the investigation into it.

Shimar said he had not heard from Shinthala in some time, and that he was truly concerned. Rumors rippled throughout the inn and the trading posts regarding the area down her way, near Solmairyth. Shimar gathered there was a disturbance in that area, one that involved a dark magician. Arnath said that this made sense, and that it may be serious, as Listrelle had been called that way more than a month ago, and Heflynn had been gone for almost three weeks without word. He was likely investigating the phenomenon, if word of it had become so widespread people discussed it freely in the public houses. Disturbances like this did occur, from time to time, when untrained mages dabbled in dark magics and in doing so, were consumed by them. It was one of the primary reasons that the mage's first oath existed.

Arnath bade Shimar farewell, and rode out of Solindar. Trotting onto the King's road, he got sidelong looks from the patrolling King's Guard, who could have sworn they saw the older captain travelling with a large party of motley adventurers earlier that day.

As he rode the short distance to Merynda's farm, Arnath had pendulous thoughts that swung between the swoon of seeing Merynda again and his discussion with Shimar.

Arriving at Merynda's, he crossed the highway and trotted down the dirt road to her farmstead. Turning toward his left, he could see the sky in the far south-west was blackened. A rim of dark clouds sat over the area he and Shimar had discussed, the southern elf city of Solmairyth, far darker than those clouds that had rolled in to thunderously announce the coming of the fall.

Reaching the front of the farmhouse, Arnath tied his horse to the porch near the water trough. When he looked up, she was there. Merynda had emerged whilst he tended to his horse, a mischievous smile on her face.

"What is it?" Arnath asked, noting there was no giggling little girl-child anywhere near him. "Where are the children?"

As he strode up the steps, Merynda said, "Nestar and Gilea are getting on in years. I sent the children to assist them for a day or so."

"A day or so." Arnath said, imagining the possibilities.

"That's right." Merynda said, as she took up his hand and began to pull him into the house. "We are all on our own."

CHAPTER TWELVE

Illona awoke before dawn on the morning of her eighteenth birthday, washed, dressed and raced to let herself into the post office. Once there, she excitedly awaited the arrival of the morning postal cart.

Shortly after giving Illona the keys to the office, Mrs Minidell simply stopped showing up. At first it was because she was so enjoying the month-long display of young, shirtless elf workers that passed by her window, titillating reminders of her own elf husband, long gone. Then, after the outpost was built and the show was over, she realized she simply did not wish to run the office anymore.

Illona could see herself running the office for her whole life, and that was why she was up early and waiting. The response to her application to the King's postal service was overdue.

She busied herself with little tasks around the office while she waited. Soon, there was nothing left that could be made any tidier. Illona had done a full day's work in quite a short time, and her impatience was giving way to boredom. She took up a position with her elbows on the counter, facing the door to the street, getting entirely lost in thought.

Foremost on her mind was the possibility that she would have to leave Kroman's Town. The large yard she had seen behind the impressive post office in Morley would likely be where she would be trained in the many intricate details of the job. Would that mean she would have to live there? Would she have to live in a rooming house, or did the post service have a barracks like the Kings guard? Would her mother even allow that? She was already adamant that Illona never stay the night at the outpost. And how could she travel to Morley if her training did allow for her to keep living with her mother? All those questions, the logistical ones involved in the possibility of being accepted by the post service, roiled over and over in her mind. And underneath those were the more personal issues involved. What would happen to her friendships with Garthe and Shimalena in her absence? Would they carry on as a couple without her? Would their special bond be broken by the distance, however short?

Distracted by all those tumultuous thoughts, Illona completely missed the arrival of the postal cart, and remained utterly unaware of it until the delivery boy roughly opened the door, arms laden with packages. Thoroughly embarrassed, she snapped out of her reverie and raced around the counter to help him.

After the young man in the postal baldric had left, Illona dutifully sorted the packages behind the counter. It took a great deal of concentration, as she had set aside the scroll addressed to herself early on in the process of helping to empty the delivery cart. Finishing up her sorting, Illona continually snuck glances at the scroll, her excitement growing. Then, her official tasks finally done, she plucked the scroll from the countertop and broke the seal.

Illona's eye only flickered over the open scroll for an instant before she let out a gasp and dashed from behind the counter.

In the street, she sprinted wildly around the corner from town square, narrowly avoiding bowling over a few people going about their business. Illona raced up the hump of the main street until she reached the door of the outpost, which she ripped open and leapt inside.

Illona sailed over the three steps, her sturdy boots hitting the floor with a thump and continued on at her frantic pace across the corridor. She passed Trellith who was behind the counter on a high stool, examining a map and enjoying a pipe.

"Oh, Illona – I was hoping to see you today. Since it is your b –"

Before he could even finish, she was gone, boots stamping up the stairs like rapid hammers. Trellith shook his head at the fading sound, saying grumpily to himself, "Well, happy birthday, then."

Illona reached the top of the stairs and pushed through the door. She crossed Garthe's lab, not slowing at all, and burst through the door of Garthe's room, holding the scroll aloft, shouting, "They said yes!"

Her elated smile and upraised hand both began to come down at the pace of a slowly deflating balloon.

On the bed before her lay Garthe and Shimalena, both deeply asleep, so much so her shout did not wake them. They were clearly naked under the blanket that had fallen partially away from them. So had slumber embraced them, they looked like the images of cherubs that guided people into the light in the temples.

Illona covered her mouth as the first sniffle of an onslaught of tears overtook her. Quickly she turned for the door, opened it...

And froze in place.

Even her on-coming tears ceased. She stood still and wondered why she was upset in the first place. What was it about the sight that bothered her so? They were her two absolute favourite people in the world, those closest to her heart. Why would the sight of them contently together cause her anguish? It shouldn't, she knew.

Then it occurred to her that it might just be what wasn't there that caused her emotions to burst forth as they did.

Illona closed the door and placed the scroll on the chair next to it. She reached down and slid her boots off. Then she undressed, folding her clothes carefully, for it was her birthday and she imagined she'd see many people later in the day, including her mother. She laid them on the chair and turned toward the bed.

Seeing that Garthe and Shimalena had still not yet awakened, she padded quietly across the room, crawled onto the bed and slid her body between theirs.

*

Arnath rode into town in the early afternoon. He waved as he passed Shrakar, who was sitting on one of the many ledges of the fin that overlooked the western side lake. Arnath thought he might join Shrakar for a swim after he put his horse away and changed at the outpost. It was a warm day for the fall. He'd even had to take off his cloak and stow it behind his saddle on the ride from Merynda's.

He felt warmed inside too. His night and morning with Merynda had been perfect. It was what they both needed to solidify the beginning of their relationship. And it was what he needed – a last baptismal into his life off of the adventuring road. He was a businessman with partners, ties to a community and now a family-type of relationship. All of his dark thoughts of failure had been quelled in Merynda's arms.

As he turned toward the stable entrance, Arnath saw Trellith and Illona approaching from the main road. He dismounted and awaited them by the stable gates. Arnath noticed Illona, who was courteous enough to slow her usual rapid pace to accommodate Trellith, had a glow about her, a twinkle in her eye he couldn't quite pin down.

Trellith said as they approached, "You've arrived just in time to join me in giving Illona her birthday present."

That must have been it – her birthday! Arnath felt a fool for forgetting but he had had a mountain of things on his mind over these last weeks. He covered his forgetfulness with a smile and a hearty, "Happy Birthday, Illona."

Arnath gestured for them to go on ahead. As she passed, Illona said, "Thank you, captain."

Trailing behind them as they entered the stables, another important detail about Illona's birthday crept forward in Arnath's mind. "And what of your application, Illona? Have you heard from the post?"

As Arnath tied the reigns of his horse in its stall, Illona said, "They said yes!"

Arnath embraced her, saying, "I'm very proud of you. We lose our runner to a great institution; one I know you'll serve with greatness."

Illona embraced him tightly, saying, "You'll never lose me, captain. I'll be there whenever your outpost needs me."

Arnath felt the warmth in her embrace, and hoped his words had filled in minutely for the absence of her long-gone father on this, her birthday.

"You'll have me in tears before her actual present is given." Trellith said, in his dry tone.

Arnath and Illona took his gruff hint, broke apart and faced him.

Satisfied he'd be heard, Trellith went over to the next stall, the one where his chestnut mare was billeted. He untied the horses' reigns from the peg and, holding them, said, "You cannot be Illona of the King's Post without a horse of your own. It's likely, after training you'll be assigned to the post office here, but you will still need a steed to ride in case of emergencies and such. That being said, here, she is yours."

The entire time Trellith spoke Illona's lower lip began to tremble, a little at first and then reaching near fluttering by the time he was done. When Trellith reached forward, to pass the reigns to her, Illona burst into tears.

"Oh, Master Trellith, I couldn't."

"You can, dear, and you will. I'd only ask you let me ride her from time to time. I have occasional errands to run too, you know. So here – Happy Birthday." Trellith said, passing her the reigns.

Illona took the reigns in hand and stepped in to embrace her new horse around her neck.

Arnath pointed to a saddle that lay on the pen barrier near them. "That is also for you. A gift from all of us at the outpost. We had the leather artisans in Solindar make it especially for you."

The saddle was fit for a human, though customized. It was unlike Trellith's in that his had extra stirrups and handles to help him up and down to the ground. The custom element were two quite large saddle bags, tooled with decorative Elfin floral knotwork.

"They're both beautiful. The best birthday gifts I have ever received. Thank you." Illona said, wiping tears from her eyes with one hand and stroking her mare under the chin with the other.

Arnath helped her put the saddle on, leaving the saddle bags on the wall, and Illona set out for a ride. Whilst Arnath tended to his horse, Trellith said, "She came down from Garthe's room a short time ago."

Arnath thought on it a moment, then shrugged. "So? Everyone likes to... you know, on their birthday."

By Arnath's thinking, Illona was family already. Turning her time alone with Garthe into some stern lecture about responsibility, especially if it was her first time, was to turn something beautiful into something tawdry and embarrassing. His fatherly feelings for the girl halted at the instinct to scold her for enjoying her life. He himself had brawled and whored his way across the three kingdoms. Who was he to lecture anyone on how they lived?

Trellith followed along with Arnath as he left the stables, a saddlebag across his shoulder.

"Besides, Garthe and Illona, perhaps Shimalena as well, were not the only ones enjoying good company last night." Arnath said, wistfully.

"Ah, you and Merynda finally jumped each other's bones. Good. I'm glad for you, captain. Not glad for me in my lonely state, but glad for you." Trellith said as they crossed the town square and began the rise up the main road.

They stopped into the Briny Sea for a quick drink and to give over the rolls of changing silver and coppers to Durnly, who remarked they might make that part of their arrangement – to pay for their kegs with the coin he needed for his business, but, having only one leg, was horribly inconvenienced to have to go and get it. Arnath said they would discuss it further as they left.

Rising up the stairs to the street, they saw the door of their outpost was blocked by a trio of King's Guardsmen. Arnath and Trellith stopped in their tracks for a heartbeat, the habit of being just outside the law for decades. They grinned at each other, pleased their rascal's instincts hadn't entirely disappeared. When the guards turned from the outpost door, they saw that their leader was their friend Apaulon.

"Ah, captain, master Trellith, there you are. We bring communications from the palace. There didn't seem to be anyone about to receive them." Apaulon said, a scroll with the royal seal on it in his hand and a rather official looking wooden box under that same arm.

"My fault. I let Garthe sleep while I took Illona to the stables." Trellith said as he opened the outpost door and ushered the soldiers inside.

When only Arnath and himself remained on the street, Trellith winked at Arnath and trundled over to the clinic door. He reached up, pulled the brass ring several times, sounding the bell high above.

They came down the steps just in time to hear the sharp sound of Garthe zipping down the rope out back, and see him blindly sprint into the corridor, so fast that Arnath had to stop one of the startled, young guardsmen from drawing his sword.

Seeing everyone in the corridor, Garthe halted, his hair wildly tussled from sleep and closed his night robe, not awake enough to know what is going on.

"There's no patients, boy. It is just fit time for you to get up." Trellith said.

Garthe nodded, said a few words that made no sense to anyone present, and then turned and began the long trek back upstairs.

Arnath and Trellith laughed to themselves as Arnath rounded the counter, closing the hinged portion behind him. "So, corporal, to what do we owe this visit?"

Apaulon stepped forward and presented the scroll to Arnath, who received it and broke the royal seal open. Arnath scanned over it silently as Trellith came down the counter, saying, "Well, what is it?"

"It says, I, we really, have been imparted reserve rank of captain by the king. My fellows, you and Shrakar, I suppose, will also be given reserve ranks, the same as those when you last served, lieutenant and sergeant as before. These reserve ranks are honorary until we are called upon by a member of the crown or the King's guard in the name of the crown to defend the kingdom or our region of the kingdom. Something we would do anyway."

"Somehow, I think Illona got better presents today." Trellith said, rolling his eyes.

"Wait, there is more." Arnath said, reading further. "A portion of these reserve duties will include the training of King's Guard in your region, for which we, the outpost I suppose, receive a monthly sum of... one hundred gold."

When Arnath said the amount, one of the guardsmen gasped.

Arnath looked down at the letter, his brows knit. Trellith looked across the counter at Arnath, asking, "This is a good thing, is it not?"

"This has to be Domar and T'erj'wan. They were impressed with the training yard, and are looking to use it as a way to protect their son."

"How do you mean?" Trellith asked, confused by Arnath's statement.

"The wording of this would allow Heflynn to enlist us in his arcane pursuits far and wide. By the dark, this would allow any mere private to walk in here and enlist us to chase bandits on the road." Sneered Arnath down at the document. "This isn't what I want."

The corridor drew tense, everyone seeing how grimly angered Arnath had become. The guardsmen exchanged furtive glances, uncertain if Arnath's rejection of the royal order amounted to treason.

Trellith placed a calming hand on the counters edge, and asked gently, "And what of the rest of us?"

"What of you?" Arnath seethed, still blinded by anger.

"We spent this last month afraid we would starve to death in this opulent tomb we'd built. Our first guests didn't pay us enough to cover the food they ate." Trellith tapped the letter with his forefinger. "This, this guarantees we never starve, never worry about whether what we did here was right. And think on this, captain - This puts us on the map."

Arnath's head turned slightly, as he thought on it. It was a guarantee that their outpost would be royally endorsed on all future maps. But the cost...

"I'd grown accustomed to the picture in my mind. That of a businessman with family, the dust and blood and indignities of the road behind me." Arnath said, his eyes averted from everyone.

"And so, they are. What in this decree says your desires for the future are negated? It insures them. In following this edict, we become rich men. Name a month, one month, other than the one after we fell from the mountain, wherein we had a hundred gold between us. You can't because there wasn't one. This doesn't call us back to the road, Arnath. It gives us sanctuary from it for good."

Arnath thought on Trellith's words, straightened and allowed a smile to cross his face. He then turned to Apaulon, and said, "What else do you have for us there?"

Apaulon broke the seal on the box, and cracked it open. He pushed it towards Arnath, who looked curiously inside.

"What have we here – three new rank clasps, one for each of us. A jot for one hundred gold." Arnath said as he placed the items on the counter.

"I'll take that." Trellith said, sweeping the valuable jot off the counter and heading for the door next to the stairs. He disappeared inside, the sound of his feet descending down the short steps into the basement fading away.

Arnath picked up the last item from the box. It was a plaque in the shape of a shield, the writing embossed in the black metal plate mounted on the wood stating that Arnath's the outpost of Kroman's Town served the crown with the training of the King's Guard with many more flowery words to describe the overall idea.

The front door opened as Arnath cradled the ornate plaque. Shrakar stepped inside, a towel around his neck, his look becoming curious as he did a quick inventory of the items on the counter. The guardsman stood aside to allow his bulk to pass them in the corridor. When he reached the counter, Arnath handed him a Sergeant's clasp, saying, "It appears we are soldiers again. In a reserve sense, anyway."

"We train the guardsmen now?" Shrakar asked, barely understanding what the writing on the shield meant.

"That's right."

Shrakar grinned at Arnath, after noting his clasp was not one that indicated he was an Orc ally, like the one he still had from the war, but a full reserve sergeant in the King's Guard.

"We train now?" Shrakar asked.

"I don't see why not. We've no customers, and nothing to do until the birthday party tonight." Trellith said from behind them in the hall, having come back up from putting the valuable jot in the basement safe.

Arnath gestured at the guardsmen, motioning them down the corridor. "Alright, lads. To the yard. We'll put you through your paces."

*

It was five days after the night of Illona's birthday party at the Briny Sea, wherein the whole town came out to celebrate her birthday and congratulate her on her acceptance into the ranks of the King's post. Arnath and the others were again training a trio of King's guard, this time under the giant tarp in the yard.

The rains had started the night of the party, and had not let up since.

And Arnath's mood grew ever sourer as the days passed. Trellith at first thought he still rankled against the burden placed upon them by the crown. It surely seemed that way as Arnath put any guardsmen who showed up at the outpost through punishing, repeated drills that left them not only exhausted, but also sore to the bone. Today was no different.

Three young guardsmen were standing on the climbing wall, doing the one-armed perpendicular hang. All three of them were holding aloft weighted practice swords from the training cupboard with their free hands. Arnath marched back and forth by the top of their heads, speaking low tones that sometimes gave way to barked commands.

"It will feel at times as thought your muscles could tear free from your body. You must feel that pain to the fullest, to then know how to ignore it. In battle, your very lives depend on pushing beyond those limits, for as long as the battle lasts, not as long as you think you can. The length of the battle dictates how long you spurn the pain, nothing else."

One of the guardsmen groaned, and let his elbow bend, the fake sword flapping against his chest.

"Raise that sword up, boy!" Barked Arnath, but it was too late. All three young guardsmen let out pathetic groans of pain and fell from their ropes. The three of them rolled on the wooden platform under the climbing wall, cradling their sore arms and moaning like a chorus of ghosts.

"Get up, you fools!"

"All right – That is enough for today. Once you can stand, go inside and get some food and drink. Sore muscles need a hearty meal." Trellith said as he approached. Once he was done speaking, he looked pointedly at Arnath, his eyes accusing over the rims of his glasses.

Knowing fully that he was being judged harshly, and deservedly so, Arnath turned his back and slammed the butt of his fist against the climbing wall. After he'd helped the last of the guardsmen to their feet, Trellith stepped closer to Arnath. "You may not like our services being usurped by the crown, but you needn't take it out on these boys. What shall you do when a lady guardsman comes to train? See if you can make her cry?"

Arnath hit the wall again, and fiercely said, "It's too long! Six days, and in this..."

Arnath gestured angrily at the rain pattering on the tarp. Trellith looked up, and then nodded, piecing together the true source of Arnath's fiery mood. "There was no guarantee Havanth and his people were going to come back and share what they'd found."

Arnath turn back to face Trellith, saying, "That is not the source of my concern. Six days, Trellith. Six days. Two to get from the road outside Solindar to the falls, perhaps a half day or more added for rest. On the third day, the rain would have started. But if they were inside the cave system when it started, they wouldn't know."

"You think they are trapped." Trellith stated more than asked, and in his mind, he was now seeing the same scenario. The timeline fit, by his calculations. And it didn't take much calculating to figure Arnath was going to do about it. "I suppose you'll be wanting to mount a rescue."

"I'll take Shrakar. We'll grab Merynda and Taishen on the way." Arnath said, already heading for the back door of the outpost. "You and Garthe should mind the outpost..."

Arnath's last word was nearly cut off by the ripping sound of Garthe's gloves on the rope from above. As soon as his feet touched down, Garthe said, "I want to come. I could be of help."

"I know you could," Arnath said putting his hands on Garthe's shoulders as he approached them, "But you are needed here, by your patients and by those who might be injured here in the yard."

"No! I won't have it!" Arnath and Garthe were startled by Trellith's shout and turning, saw his determined expression. "If we go, we go together. Just like before. The four of us. We four. They are all of our customers. We shall rescue them together."

"What of the outpost, our royal contract?" Arnath asked not in argument but more to understand the logistics of their absence.

Trellith, ever the strategist, waved away any difficulty those notions presented. As he went to the smith and gathered up his bow and a quiver of arrows, he said, "We leave the keys with Shamuth and his men. They can watch the outpost, and keep it safe. If they absolutely have to open, then they can deal with our customers, and Shimalena and Illona can help out."

"Well, then, that solves that." Arnath said, patting Garthe on the shoulder. "We four, indeed."

CHAPTER THIRTEEN

They got organized and were on the road to Kolifarii Falls quite quickly. The details fell into place as Trellith had said.

Shamuth, Tindall, Amorth and Fernlow agreed to watch over the outpost, only opening it to the public if a serious of influx of customers were to be spurned if they didn't. They also said they would train with guardsmen who came by, all being experienced, mid-ranking veterans themselves. Shamuth remarked that he and his men were quite jealous – A dangerous rescue mission involving a treasure of the ancient empire. Who wouldn't want to join such an expedition?

Trellith, though thoroughly embarrassed to have to ask just days after her birthday, needed to borrow the horse that now belonged to Illona. She didn't mind, understanding how important the need to rescue Havanth and his party was. She assured Trellith that Princess Dragonfly, as Illona had christened the mare, would be happy to join him on another adventure. Trellith said nothing when he heard the ridiculous name that had been bestowed on his former horse, though his cheeks did turn the colour of boiled beets.

Illona would need to borrow another horse from the stables, as Arnath had asked her to search the eastern roads, to find either Graten or Apaulon and let them know of their absence. And their need of impending rescue if they did not resurface within four days.

They rode quickly to Solindar, stopping only to allow Arnath a few brief moments with Merynda. She was out her door, and near the side of the road by the time Arnath had dismounted. They exchanged a quick kiss and embrace, breaking apart quickly as the cold, pelting rain was an unfit environ even for the warmth of romance. Holding each other close she looked into his eyes, saw the deep concern there, and without being asked, said, "Valdara."

"It's been too long. Something has to have happened to them." Arnath said, the rain streaking his face despite his hood.

"Well, I'm coming with you. I'll get my things." Merynda said, about to turn away toward the house, but Arnath held her arm fast.

"No – please. I need you to stay here. And in four days time, if you have not seen hide nor hare of us, go to Solindar and recruit Taishen and some others."

"Four days." Merynda said, nodding.

"No sight of us in four days, and we ourselves shall be in need of rescue." Arnath reiterated.

He then kissed and embraced her again, then left once more for the road. Merynda waved to them all as they got underway, calling, "Good luck!" at their backs.

In Solindar, they delivered the same message to Lorta and Taishen, who nodded gravely and began to discuss on who best of the capable adventuring elves in the town should comprise a potential rescue party. Garthe suggested they contact Shimar, stating that magics had been the cause of a few of the tragic ends of their quests and could well be the problem this time as well. Garthe didn't mention the death of his master, Morgosh, though the lesson of his passing applied to this situation. Garthe did not like to think on it, and recounting it to others only brought it all back to the fore. It was just too horrible a way to die.

Unlike the last time he'd come, Arnath beckoned the patrolling King's Guard to follow them to the third cut out in the road, showing them his new reserve captain's clasp. He told them because of an emergency, they were going to violate the King's forest beyond the cut out, and that in four days time other rescue parties might come and do the same.

Then, thankful for the sparse cover the canopy of the forest would give them from the rains, Arnath and his companions rode into the back of the cut out and disappeared into the forest beyond.

*

They were within sight of the falls come sunrise a day and half later. The rains had stopped and the sky was clearing. Two things were easy to discern in the wide vista afforded them from their vantage in the rolling hills above the falls. One was that the heavy rains had indeed caused the river below the falls to flood, and the other was that the mouth of the cave beneath the falls was completely submerged under water. Arnath, Trellith and Shrakar exchanged a grim look as they all thought the same thing – That was exactly how Dalgar had died; Sucked into the cave, and spat out again a corpse with the flow of the river.

Trellith looked through his long spyglass and, yes, several ropes were bound around the tree trunks above the falls that snaked down into the water right next to them. If Havanth's party had made it into the cave system, they were either trapped within, or were already long drowned.

Another sight that demanded the eye was further south. A near pitch black cloud formation hung like a wide stationary tornado over the land to the south west. Though it tapered to a thin column where it disappeared behind the forest, the top of it spread ominously across the sky in all directions and just hung there. Trellith thought he could see a kind of undulation occurring throughout the disc-like capital of the threatening formation as he looked at it through the spyglass. "What in the name of the blessed-light is that?"

Arnath looked at the understandable awe on his companions faces, and scowled to himself. He'd been so excited to get back to Merynda, he'd not paid the phenomenon proper mind. The area it hung over had to be Solmairyth, the place where the elder mage Shinthala had taken the live-stone for further investigation. Where Listrelle had been dispatched, and presumably Heflynn followed. "I've seen it before, on the road from Solindar. I thought it was the beginnings of those blasted rains."

"You might have been right in your thinking, given the dark maelstrom that rolled in from the same direction the night we opened the outpost." Trellith said, not taking his eyes off the malevolent plume that hung in the sky. "But that... That is no cloud formation I've ever seen."

Arnath saw that Garthe had his eyes closed and held his hand up, facing the hanging disc-shaped plateau in the sky. Though his eyes were closed, Arnath saw the contact with the phenomenon, even at this great distance, pained Garthe to his core. Then, with a shiver that encompassed his entire body, Garthe broke contact and opened his eyes. He took a deep breath and said, "It is the same energy as that I felt in our training yard. But the power is amplified, incredibly so. It has to be the work of the necromancer."

Shaking his head, Arnath imagined just how powerful the dark mage Garthe spoke of must have been. Garthe was indeed a sensitive mage, despite the gaps in his training, but for him to feel the pull of the necromancer's energies from this distance...

Arnath went to his horse and mounted in one swift move. "We learn the fate of Havanth's party quickly, before sunset if possible. Then we ride like the wind to get as much distance between ourselves and... whatever that is as we can."

In silent agreement, Shrakar, Trellith and Garthe mounted their horses and followed Arnath down the mountainside.

*

Reaching the river valley under the mountain forest, Arnath and his companions found the flooding caused by the rains engorging the lake above the falls to be far worse than they'd estimated from above. The bridge across the river was completely washed away. Without the bridge, getting to the other side, where Havanth and his party had made their climb down under the falls, was impossible, save for travelling back to the King's road to the north. It was a day and half's ride they did not have time for.

They tossed ideas back and forth until their frustration turned into argument, and that didn't last long. Each of them knew that urgency required them to solve this dilemma and fast. Quibbling would not help.

After a time, each of them silently stewing on the problem, it was Shrakar who sprung into action. He withdrew his great axe from the scabbard on his back and marched over to the nearest trees, those at the beginning of the rise of the mountain. He scanned the trees and then approached one with low slung, but thick branches. He picked a long, thick straight branch and began to chop at its base on the tree trunk.

Arnath saw what Shrakar was doing, and immediately surmised what the clever Orc's plan was. If the branch was long enough to reach the river bed, Shrakar could vault across. Arnath went to his horse and pulled a goodly length of strong rope from his saddle.

Once Shrakar had freed the branch and cleaved the twigs from its length, he approached the riverbank, and Arnath loaned him a shoulder to brace against the drag of the current as he dipped the branch into the river. Shrakar felt the branch touch bottom with perhaps half its length submerged. He pulled it back out and set it down. Arnath handed Shrakar the rope that he had tied a large loop in. Shrakar put it over one shoulder and picked up the branch again.

Arnath picked up Shrakar's axe with some effort and stood away with Garthe and Trellith as Shrakar strode away from the bank several paces and hefted up the branch on his shoulder. With a sharp inhale, Shrakar surged forward, running at the bank at top speed. Only when his feet neared the edge of the bank did he lower the branch, piercing the water nearer to the opposite side. He heaved the branch forward, and it caught in the river bed, his momentum catapulting him into the air. As the branch became upright in the air, Shrakar shoved his weight away from it. His brief airborne arc flung him well over the edge of the opposite bank, where he touched down and rolled.

Regaining his feet, Shrakar stood and waved to his companions – He was alright. Shrakar took the rope from his body and walked over the remaining support struts of the washed-out bridge and tied the rope tautly off.

Even from across the river, as he tied off the other end of the rope, Arnath could see that something had occurred to Shrakar. The Orc stood away from the bridge support, gestured for his companions to wait and bounded down the riverbank toward the rise above the falls. With his great height and power, it took no time at all for Shrakar to traverse the distance.

Trellith once again pulled out his long spyglass and pointed it toward the rocky forest's edge above the falls. Shrakar had reached the trees where Havanth and his party had secured their ropes.

"What's he doing? Has he found anything?" Arnath asked, standing at Trellith's shoulder.

"He's reached the base. Several ropes are tied off. I think he means to climb down for a look at the mouth of the cave." Trellith said, one eye squinting into the spyglass. He tilted the long tube up for a look at the area around the rocky cliffs. "Wait! Their horses! Their horses are still tied off in the woods near the cliff."

Arnath spat out a silent curse, and then said, "Then they are still trapped below or worse."

Trellith tilted the glass down again to reacquire sight of Shrakar, and blurted, "Wait! Shrakar is pointing at something. I think there is something on our side of the falls. Oh! He's coming back."

Trellith took the glass away from his eye. He and the others didn't need it to see Shrakar come bounding back down the opposite bank.

Shrakar reached the remains of the bridge on his side, and eased himself into the rushing waters. He let the powerful current take his body, fOrcing him nearly flat against the surface of the water, like a bird in flight, as he worked his way, hand beside hand, along the rope he and Arnath had tied across the river.

In a short time, he reached the opposite bank and Arnath helped him out of the water. Shrakar caught his breath, then said, "Up there. On the shore near falls. Someone. Think one of the archers."

They mounted their horses and rode at a furious gallop along the riverbank, racing for the shore of the lake above the falls. Their pace had to slow as they climbed up the base of the mountain and were once again fully immersed in the forest. Soon, they had rounded the base at a point that took them above the falls, and descended again, towards the shore of the lake.

As they left the forest and emerged onto the rocky shore of the western side of the lake, he was there...

Mego.

He sat shivering next to a large, natural pool of water in the rocky surface, a dozen feet from the shore. A rope rose out of the water of the pool and was affixed in the trees at the edge of the forest.

Arnath pulled a blanket from his saddle and ran to the boy. Placing the blanket around his shoulders, Arnath could feel Mego's skin was ice cold to the touch. Shivers rippled violently throughout his body, especially in his jaw muscles. Arnath heard the chatter of the young man's teeth even with the roar of the falls so nearby.

"Allow me." Garthe said, kneeling beside Mego, his green healing stone already in his hand. Arnath stood aside and let the young healer do his work.

Arnath looked at their surroundings, trying to guess how Mego came to be here. The pool beside them was three times the size of the spring pool in the outpost yard. From what he could tell, the rope that rose diagonally out of the pool was tied off to something far down below. Just how far down the pool went was hard to guess. The waters grew very dark about twenty feet down.

Shrakar jumped down from the trees above, where he'd left the rope tied. In his hand was one of the arrows with a thong affixed behind the fletching that so fascinated Trenth and Mego. Shrakar showed the arrow to Arnath and Trellith and narrative was beginning to form.

Turning to kneel next to Garthe as the mage continued his ministrations over Mego, Arnath again saw the giant black disc in the sky on the southern horizon. Not only did its disc-shaped summit seem wider, the column that descended to the ground seemed closer to the lake somehow. As though it had moved during their journey through the King's forest.

Arnath shook off his worry over the ominous sight, and knelt beside Mego, whom Garthe had bundled from head to foot in the blanket, and laid him on the ground. His shivering persisted, even as Garthe passed the glowing green healer stone over Mego's body. Arnath looked to Garthe, asking, "Will he live?"

"He will live. It is good we arrived when we did. He was frozen and exhausted to the point of near death. Any later, a half day, an hour, he would not be with us. He might be able to speak, but be gentle. He is still very fragile."

Arnath nodded. bending at the waist to get close to Mego's blanket-covered ear. "Mego, can you speak?"

The young man's teeth chattered, but he managed, "Yes"

"Can you tell us what happened, Mego? Take your time, do not exert yourself."

Mego did his best, getting the stuttering words out between the chatter of his teeth and fits of hastily taken breaths. When his party had arrived, the rains had long begun but the waters of the lake had not yet risen to the point where the falls had flooded the river below. The cave opening was fully accessible. Just as they had trained at the outpost, they descended and crossed under the falls, one at a time. Because of the extensive training, even elderly Grentoss was able to swing across in one go, caught by Ogron and Valdara. Trenth and Mego went last, and once they were all securely in the cave behind the falls, they ventured forth.

They turned left from the mouth of the cave, as was suggested by the ancient maps in the texts Shimar provided. That direction soon found them descending on a steep path that then led them to the right for a time and then left again. They were all fairly certain they were no where near the falls anymore. Soon, the natural, curving formations of the rock gave way to a man-made wall with a door in it. They could not budge it, not even with might Ogron's powerful shoulder heaving at full strength. Only after Grentoss cast a spell that would dissipate all magics imbued upon the structure did it begin to budge.

With great effort, they got the ancient door fully open and went inside. It was indeed the treasure room of the ancient Kolifarii King. The stacked treasures ran along the walls, piled on high for several meters deep. Havanth and his party could not believe their luck – A map fragment from a merchant and the aid of Arnath and his companions had made them as rich as kings themselves. They were still laughing and celebrating, when they heard it – the rush of millions of gallons of water coming towards them.

Only after Ogron applied his shoulder to the door, this time from the inside, heaving it shut and then Grentoss re-applied a spell to seal the door did they realize they were trapped. They heard a wave of water slam into the door, rapidly cooling the stone all the way to the ceiling. The rains had swelled the lake, causing the falls to overflow and the river below to rise and flood into the cave system. A lake that size, that much water, it could take weeks for the waters to drain away. Surely, they were as rich as kings and now, just as assuredly, they were going to die surrounded by their riches within a matter of days.

Mego continued on to say that in their search for ways out of the room, they found a small pool behind the stacks of treasure. Within the pool they could see twinkles of reflected light that had to be sunlight. The pool must have connected to a shaft that led to the surface.

Of the party, only Trenth and Mego would fit into the pool at all. Trenth made the attempt several times, eeling on his back into the pool, disappearing up to his ankles. Then, at panicked speed, he would wriggle back out again, coughing up water, gasping for breath. He shivered uncontrollably. The water was unbelievably cold.

Yes, there was a shaft to the surface, but the initial neck of it, the section right behind the cave wall, was so narrow only he or Mego could make it through. After that, a wide diagonal shaft appeared to reach all the way to the surface, some distance above. Trenth was convinced that just getting past the initial bottle neck was enough to drown him.

Mego then made the attempt. Unlike his partner, he managed to get his feet all the way in and disappeared for some time. When he came back, he did so head first, crawling out of the little pool onto the cave floor in a fit of spasmodic coughs.

Mego had an idea. He'd get past the choke point and fire a rope, using one of the thonged climbing arrows, up to the surface. With hope, it would not be too slowed by the water and catch on something. He could then try to quickly climb to the surface.

Havanth had balked at the notion, calling it suicide. As desperate as their situation was, he had no intention of sending the boy to die for them. No one could hold their breath for that long.

Valdara had a thought that might make reaching the surface possible. What if Mego fired the arrow and then came back into the cave for breath? That way his next foray into the flooded vent would have a rope ready for him to make the ascent.

They all agreed this way was better, and readied the tools Mego would need. They put small knots in the end of several of the thin, strong climbing ropes they had. Trenth volunteered to once again go into the flooded cave, to place the equipment, so Mego would have less time in the frozen waters. He shoved Mego's bow and a quiver of arrows into the pool, along with the knotted ropes, as far as he could without going in. He then got on his back and once again shovered into the pool, disappearing up to his ankles. After a short pause, Trenth wriggled back out, once again coughing and sputtering.

Regaining himself, Trenth explained he'd set the bow, arrows and rope on the far side of the slim cavern. He'd threaded the knotted rope into the thong attached to the arrow, which he'd pulled slightly from the quiver. All Mego needed to do was nock the arrow, get upright and fire it.

Everyone wished Mego good luck. Trenth and Mego exchanged an embrace and a kiss. Mego then gulped in deep breaths and slid into the pool.

Havanth and his party stood over the pool, waiting, for what must have felt like an eternity.

For Mego it was worse. The cold water was chilling his muscles and his fingers straight away. Just nocking the arrow on the bow was what took the all the time. Finally, the arrow in place, he stood, pulled the bow string back to the fullest of its span and released the arrow. The power of the bow's release negated the resistance of the water and the rope eeled speedily up the cylindrical cavern. Mego was near out of breath when the rope stopped feeding out of the water.

He gave it a hard tug, felt resistance and then bent down to the pool's entrance.

Inside the treasure vault, Mego re-emerged. His skin and lips were blue. It took some time, nestled within Ogron's huge cloak, before he could speak well enough to say his arrow had found purchase.

Havanth and the others discussed what best Mego do once he made it to the surface. Should he go back up to Solindar? Wasn't Solmairyth closer? Could it be as simple as Mego buying bottled provisions and sending them down until the waters once again abated?

Unfortunately, Mego could not accomplish any of those things. By the time he broke the surface of the pool, he was almost drowned and frozen to a point near death's door. Until Arnath and his companions arrived, Mego could do nothing more than sit and shiver, and hope somehow that he'd survive.

*

The whole while Mego told his stuttering tale Arnath, Trellith, Shrakar and Garthe quipped ideas back and forth as to a method of rescue. With each detail Mego filled in, ideas were bolstered or quashed.

Now that Mego was done talking, and sat drinking a healing tea Garthe had made, Arnath and the others had free reign to discuss the logistics of freeing the trapped treasure hunters.

But nothing, no useful idea came regarding getting past the bottleneck at the bottom of the deep pool. Not even Garthe, the smallest of them could go down and offer assistance. Now eighteen, Garthe might have been somewhat slight, but not like Trenth and Mego, who had near child-like builds.

It was the discussion of him not being able to make the descent that gave Garthe an idea. He himself didn't need to go down for the assistance he planned to offer.

Arnath, Trellith and Shrakar looked him like he was quite mad for a moment.

"Is there some great magic that Shimar has taught you we don't know of yet?" Trellith asked, eyeing the lad over the rims of his glasses.

"Magic, yes – But of a kind you are all familiar with." Garthe said, and then turned to his horse. Garthe rummaged for a moment inside his saddle bag, leaving Arnath, Trellith and Shrakar to exchange curious looks.

When he came back to them, he had a glass jar in his hand, one slightly smaller than a stein. Inside he had placed several of his cloth-wrapped combat grenades and Grentoss' power stone. He demonstrably sealed the glass jar with a thick cork. "I brought a couple of my birthday presents. I was going to use them to collect plants for potions. If we weight this one properly, we can guide it to the bottom of the pool."

Arnath looked at the ingredients in the jar, saying wearily, "An explosion that size within a contained space could kill them all. Not to mention the water from this pool rushing in all at once."

"I believe Grentoss can control that with the stone." Garthe said.

"Let's leave it to them to decide." Trellith said, sitting down cross-legged and taking one of his notebooks from his pouch. He immediately began to sketch a diagram of how the little bombs should be placed, based on what Mego had said.

Shrakar came to stand over Trellith's shoulder and said, "Make big enough for Ogron."

Ogron was not quite as large as Shrakar, but from Mego's description the blast would need to blow away a considerable chunk of the upper wall and ceiling to create a hole big enough to accommodate his size. Trellith nodded over his shoulder at Shrakar, indicating on the paper how widely the little explosives were going to be placed.

Pleased, Shrakar stood up to full height as Arnath waved him over to the horses. "We'll need to secure these ropes to the trees. We'll throw them down once the blast has occurred. Dropping them in before might sheer them off too high for the party to reach them."

Shrakar nodded at this. It made sense. He grabbed a long coil from the back of Trellith's borrowed former horse and followed Arnath to the treeline.

"Place these explosives on the wall as shown in the sketch, and take best cover at a distance along the same wall when Grentoss uses the stone to set them off. The in-coming water may be up to your heads, but climbing ropes with be ready for you inside the pool once the debris and water settle. Your hosts from Arnath's" Garthe read aloud, and then rolled the scroll and placed it inside the jar. He forced the cork down hard.

Arnath took the long travelling scarf from his neck and began to coil it loosely around the jar. He then took the dirk from his belt, tied a rope to the blade guard and slid the blade through the folds of the scarf, and then tightened it all together as securely as he could.

"Try from here." Trellith said on the opposite side of the wide pool. Arnath strode over, the rope and wrapped rescue package in hand, and saw what Trellith meant. Because the deep cave rose at an angle, the side Trellith indicated was the place when the jar was less likely to bump against the side during its watery descent. Perhaps this was once the lava vent of an ancient volcano, that had unleashed its fury diagonally from the angry depths and created this crag-filled rocky shore.

Arnath lowered his short sword grip into the water, feeling that weight of the dirk indeed outmatched the buoyancy of the jar, and began to feed the rope into the water, hand over hand. He moved his shoulders slowly back and forth, controlling the descent through the water as best he could.

Everyone, including Mego, stood around the pool, gesturing this way and that, signalling which way Arnath should try to steer the submerged rescue package to prevent the jar from being damaged by the sides of the diagonal tunnel. For his part, Arnath ignored them, he had little control over the struggle between the buoyant jar, the heavy sword and their relationship to the ebb and flow of the waters below.

Despite the chill in the air, sweat was pouring from Arnath's brow by the time the package reached the point where the density of the water enveloped it in darkness. By his estimation, this is where the thin bottleneck started, and he knew from Mego's tale that there was only a short distance to go. Then, after a few more rolls over his shoulders, feeding the rope down, he felt the tip of the sword hit rock.

Arnath eased his shoulders back and forth, raising and lowering the rope, hoping those below would hear the tip of the sword on the rocky bottom of the pool.

Tap-Tap-Tap. Tap-Tap-Tap. Tap-Tap…!

The rope became suddenly tense and Arnath opened his hands and let it spool through. He set the rope on the edge of the pool, and they all watched as it disappeared over the side and sink into the depths.

"Alright – they have it. Let us clear away from the pool, and be ready when the explosion sounds with the ropes." Arnath said motioning everyone away from edge.

Shrakar moved the horses down the shore, and everyone helped ready the ropes. Soon they all waited, laying on their bellies on the jagged rocky ground a good distance from the pool. It began to feel as though they were lying there for some time, and nothing was happening.

"What's taking so long?" Garthe said, irritated by the wait.

"Imagine if it was us down there, lad." Trellith said, in a dryly humourous tone. "Would the argument we had when presented with this solution be a short one?"

"I suppose not."

"They talk of the choice between smothering under the earth, or being dashed by flying boulders and drowned." Arnath said, imagining the conversation himself. "We will give them all the time they need."

As soon as the words were out of Arnath's mouth the ground under them shuddered violently. Then, a giant plume shot out of the pool, blowing water in all directions.

"Go!" Arnath shouted, and sprang to his feet. Together, they all dashed for the pool and threw their ropes over the side.

They reached the side of the pool in time to witness the incredible sight of the pool draining into itself. The water dropped away, down and down, letting out the loudest of gurgling noises, like the world's largest tub of bath water draining, until it reached the place where the bottleneck used to be. Now, there was a sizeable chunk of it gone, and the last of the water drained into the jagged gap, taking the ends of the ropes inside the cave with it.

For what felt like another long span of time, the water burbled at the bottom of the chasm, the ropes that disappeared into the chamber floating listlessly in the water.

Then one of the ropes grew taught. Then another!

"Wait 'til you see them to pull! Let them get clear the roof of the cave!" Arnath said, kneeling to grip one of the tight ropes, eyes fixed on where it floated on the surface of the water.

And then he was there – Orgron! And with Grentoss clinging around his neck!

"Shrakar! Here!" Arnath waved Shrakar over to his rope, to help with the Orc's heavier weight.

And then, from the surface under the second tightened rope emerged Valdara, with Trenth clinging onto her back. When her legs had cleared the water, Havanth emerged, and began the arduous diagonal climb up the shaft.

On the rim of the now empty pool, Arnath and his companions steadied the ropes. Trying to pull the survivors up might cause fatal slips on the wet, rocky surface of the drained cavern, so they did their best to hold the ropes fast as Havanth's bedraggled party made their way sluggishly up the slope to the surface. In turn each of the rescuers noticed that Orgron, Valadara and Havanth were further slowed by the burdens slung over their shoulders – Saddlebags bulging with extra weight. Arnath thought it was utterly foolhardy to try and escape with riches whilst having their very lives saved, but he did not blame them. Only a mere few months ago, he and his companions had done the exact same thing, plummeting down a mountain with more of a mind toward the straps that held treasure than to protecting their own skulls.

Ogron's great strength got him to the surface first. Garthe helped the drenched and dishevelled Grentoss to the ground, and Ogron, both exhausted and relieved to be alive, flopped to the ground once freed of the old mage's weight. The jingle of coins that resounded when he hit the rocky surface might well have been heard in Morley, it so echoed off the lake.

"Many thanks, my boy. We owe you our very..." Grentoss gravelly voice gave way to fit of coughing, and Garthe patted his back lightly to help clear the last of the water from his lungs.

Then Valdara was over the rim, and Trenth jumped from her back and raced into Mego's arms. The two stood locked in an embrace and wept. Valdara let the saddlebag slide from her shoulder fall free, and it impacted with the hard stone as loudly as Ogron's had. She flung her arms around Arnath's neck and said, "The light be upon you, Arnath."

Nearing the rim, Havanth slipped off the slick stone surface. One arm flailed away from the rope, as he tried to regain his footing, wide-eyed. With a step forward and twist of his waist, Shrakar got a hand behind Havanth's back and muscled him over the top.

Havanth fell to the stone surface, one saddle bag spilling forth as he roughly landed.

Arnath and his men looked down at the coins in awe. The gold coins were wide as the palm of one's hand and perhaps as thick as the handle of a butter knife. The volume of gold in each would have made them likely worth five that of the standard one gold of the kingdom. And it was easy to estimate by the bulging saddlebags that Havanth and his party had a thousand of the coins. They were indeed wealthy as kings.

Havanth scrambled to his feet and embraced Arnath. "He got you. I knew Mego would get to you."

Returning his embrace, Arnath said, "We actually came on our own. And luckily so, since poor Mego…"

Everyone was startled by a sudden blood-curdling moan.

They turned and saw Grentoss on the ground, Garthe still kneeling beside him, his eyes closed as he held his palm towards the sky to the south. His sudden wail died away, as he began to shake. "We must be away. Away from here at once!"

Havanth and the rest of his rescued party turned in that direction, and their jaws dropped. The black plume and the ominous over-hanging capital that topped it were now closer than it had been before. It was a void of blackness in the afternoon sky, impossible now to mistake for angry weather.

Shaking his head, Havanth asked, "What in the infernal dark is that?"

"Remember the tale I told you of the stone we found in the training yard and the lurking necromancer that was hunting for it?" Arnath said, pointing at the blackened portion of the southern sky. "Well, we think that's him. Gather your things, everyone. We'll make for our rope bridge and collect your horses, and then be gone from here."

Haventh knelt to scoop his gold back into his saddlebag and with great effort hoisted it once again across his shoulder. As he stood, Havanth looked down, into the circular chasm they'd just been rescued from, and then across the span of the falls to spot where their poor horses had been tied without food or water for days. He wasn't sure, but he thought he saw movement. Then he saw someone on one of the saddles and was completely certain. "Look there! Someone is stealing our horses!"

Everyone looked. Reflexively, Trellith whipped the spyglass from his belt and pulled it open. It took him a moment to focus on the spot, but when he did, he let out, "It can't be! It's the prince - Prince Heflynn!"

CHAPTER FOURTEEN

It took everyone rushing to the edge of the falls opposite the rising forest to get Heflynn's attention. Though a there was a span of distance between them, everyone could see the normally elegant prince was disoriented and completely dishevelled. His clothes were torn as though someone had tried to violently strip him. Despite the chill of the fall air, he did not shiver against it, so unaware of his surroundings was he. Heflynn appeared to be focussed on a singular task, and the voices shouting at him from across the falls were an intrusion.

What drew Havanth's eye in the first place was the flicker of white in the sun when Heflynn had slung the body of a woman in torn underclothes across one of the saddles. Even from the great distance, Havanth could see the woman's skin was incredibly pale, and stippled with burns and wounds. Her flame of red haired hung like a bright pennant over the side of the horse. When he described her to Arnath and his companions, they all exchanged a grim look, hoping to the light that their friend from the King's guard and Heflynn's lady love Listrelle was still alive.

Upon achieving the prince's bleary-eyed attention, they motioned for him to join them down the river where the bridge supports still stood on the banks. He seemed to understand the chaotic directions shouted at him by the multitude across the water and proceeded down from the hills over the falls. On their side, Arnath and Havanth's parties together ventured up into the woods that would take them around the base of the mountain and back to the riverbank.

When they reached the broken bridge struts, both Arnath and Shrakar did the chilling crossing, hand over hand, their bodies forced flat like fluttering flags on the surface by the strength of the current. Soaking wet, they raced to meet Heflynn as he lolled precariously in the saddle, holding the reins of the second horse that Listrelle laid prone across. The prince practically fell into Arnath's arms attempting to dismount. Arnath caught and steadied him, and Shrakar checked over Listrelle.

"What happened, man?" Arnath said, his face close to Heflynn's, which was almost chalky compared to his normal brown, swarthy visage. The prince swayed against Arnath's grip on his shoulders, his arms draped limply over the captain's providing little support. He had seen the prince less than a month ago, and now he looked as though he had somehow just been transported from the front lines of Isthmar. The blanching of his skin made the black lighting scars running up and around his neck look very pronounced. Arnath knew they could mean only one thing.

Arnath looked over the prince's shoulder, to the spot where Shrakar was checking on Listrelle. After a cursory exam, his hand on her back and a thumb gently resting on her neck, Shrakar turned to Arnath and nodded. Listrelle still lived.

"Go retrieve their horses. We'll need them." Arnath called to Shrakar, lifting his chin in the direction of the falls.

As Shrakar bounded off, Arnath thought he heard something from Heflynn, the faintest of words. Arnath leaned in close, and said, "Say again. What is it?"

At first all that came from Heflynn's mouth was a ragged exhalation, then he found his voice, saying, "He knows where we'll go."

The words chilled Arnath to the bone, but he still managed to ask, "Even if we flee, into the distant hills?"

"What it wants is in..." Was all Heflynn could get out before he fainted away. Arnath supported his weight, his arm under the princes to keep him from falling.

Arnath looked down the path that ran along the riverbank. Shrakar was on his way back, on Ogron's stout horse and the other four following along, roped together by their reins. The numbers of horses and riders and the divide of the river presented a problem that Arnath immediately put his military mind to. They needed to ride at speed to the King's road, where they could all rearrange who rode what horse, but for now there were too many people for the number of horses on one side of the river.

He thought it over, ignoring the black disc in the sky that once again looked closer than last he dared glance its way, and finally came upon a solution. Turning his head from the lolling prince's ears, Arnath called across the river to Valdara, telling her to come across as he and Shrakar had. Not at all pleased to have to take a second chilling soak within the same hour, Valdara griped to herself as she dipped into the river, and began the floating journey along the rope across.

Arnath called to Havanth, "You take my horse. Trellith and Garthe will ride together, as will Trent and Mego. Ogron will of course take Shrakar's horse."

Havanth waved he understood, not wishing to shout over the river, and everyone arranged themselves as Arnath had dictated.

On their side of the river, Valdara emerged from the water and ran to her approaching horse. From the roll behind the saddle, she whipped out a heavy cloak and wrapped it around her shivering body.

As the group of five horses merged together, Arnath asked Valdara, "Will you take Listrelle in your lap?"

The warrior woman said, "Of course." And walked over to mount up, gently easing herself under Listrelle in the saddle. Arnath helped the lolling Heflynn into his saddle and mounted another of the horses Shrakar had guided over. With Shrakar then on Ogron's horse, there was only one free that would need leading until they reached the King's road.

Arnath looked across the bank and saw the other half of their party had already galloped off. Turning back, Arnath saw why. The looming disc of blackness in the sky was perhaps an hour away from crossing over the falls. They had to be away, and fast.

It took them until sunrise the next day at the fiercest pace to make it to the King's road. There, exhausted and road ragged, they switched to their proper horses, and took a break in the nearest cut out to water and feed them.

Garthe was able to minister to Listrelle and Heflynn, who had been awakened by the vigorous ride. As Garthe waved his healing stone back and forth over the two of them, the colour returned to Heflynn's skin and the black lightning scars began to fade. Listrelle, however remained unconscious, still heaving ragged breaths.

Arnath, Trellith, Havanth, Valdara, Shrakar and Ogron stood away from the others, quietly conferring on a strategy, if one was indeed to be found.

"It doesn't matter where you go." Heflynn called over, his voice once again at full strength.

Arnath and the others came closer, and stood over where Garthe ministered over him. "What do you mean?"

"You can all run for the hills. The necromancer believes what it is after is in Kroman's Town. And if you go somewhere else, it will pluck people off the ground and drain their minds to find out where you've gone."

"What it wants is in Kroman's Town?" Arnath asked, fear in his voice. "And what exactly is that?"

Looked at each of them, and then pointed right at Garthe. "Him."

"Me!" Garthe said, utterly horrified. "What does it want with me?!"

"I do not know. My contact with it was far from a two-way exchange. But I can say this – It is now convinced that Garthe is in Kroman's Town and it may likely rip the town apart to find him."

"What in the blazes would an ancient Arkonian necromancer want with our young mage? How could it even know master Garthe existed? That doesn't make any sense." Trellith said, frustrated with the lack of information.

"It pulled the knowledge from mage Shinthala's mind. And then it started slowly probing the people of Solmairyth for more, sifting through a million individual thoughts and memories like grains of sand. Once Listrelle and I were there, I'm afraid it eventually got what it wanted." With the last anguished words, the prince hung his head shamefully. "I'm sorry. We couldn't stop it from taking our thoughts. We are lucky to be alive."

Arnath stepped forward, and placed a hand on the prince's shoulder. "Indeed, you are. If it sapped the minds an entire Elven town in its dark quest, killing them without regard, there is nothing to stop it from doing so again. Almost everyone in Solindar knows Garthe, or knows of him."

"We need to get there, and warn everyone." Trellith declared.

"That's right. We ride for Solindar, stopping only to warn the farmsteads along the way." Arnath said turning to the others. "We paid visit to almost every farm from here to Kroman's before and during the building the outpost, all of them know us and have knowledge of Garthe. We need to save them along with the people of Solindar."

Everyone could see it in Arnath's eyes – A full military campaign was forming in his mind.

"and what of Kroman's Town?" Valdara asked.

"If that is its destination, then that is where we make our stand."

*

They thundered down the King's road all morning, stopping only to warn farmers they knew like Nester and Gilea and their many other suppliers. The warning was simple – the necromancer that destroyed the original outpost of Kroman's Town was headed this way, and if they could not get on the road to Kroman's within the hour, they'd best take shelter in the far north woods beyond their fields until it passed.

They also stopped to inform any King's guard they met of the impending doom at their heels. People would need to be halted along the highway from trying to reach Solindar or from getting past the borders of Kroman's Town. The eastern side of the road beyond Kroman's would need to be barricaded and manned by hundreds of King's guards, to prevent the murderous necromancer from getting further into the heart of the kingdom.

These occasional stops, with water and feeding were not enough for all of the poor horses. They had already been tied to trees and starved whilst Havanth's party awaited rescue. The horses that carried Trenth and Mego, and later Ogron, keeled over and died mid-gallop, spilling their charges into the road. Havanth and Valdara quickly hoisted Trenth and Mego on the backs of their horses, and the furious ride continued on. When Ogron's steed collapsed, there was nothing for him to do but secure his axe and saddle bags on his shoulders and race along after the party. The stout breed that carried Orcs like he and Shrakar were indeed strong, but not enough for the weight of two Orcs on their backs. Trellith offered prayer to the light that Princess Dragonfly, as her silly name had taken root in his mind, would survive the mad dash. As desperate as their mission was, he could not bear the notion of having to tell Illona her mare had died right under him.

Since they had taken the King's road from the river, instead of riding up through the King's wood to the cut out outside of Solindar, Arnath had initially thought they might take more than a day to reach the elf city. But because they had avoided the obstacles within the King's forest, and tore straight across the land at breakneck speed, they made it to Solindar in half that time.

Once there, the noonday sun over their heads, they rode at speed through the streets, shouting for all to make way, straight to Shimar's house. After Heflynn carried Listrelle inside, Arnath ordered the party to ride for the stables, where the horses were put up and instructed to be cared for.

Arnath bade the party to split up, other than Shrakar who was to remain at Garthe's side at all times, and start warning the townsfolk about the approaching threat. He then told Havanth, Valadara and Ogron - who had just made it into town on foot - to follow him.

They went to the bank, where Arnath was immediately recognized, and he bade Havanth and his fellows to drop their saddlebags, pocket some coins and leave the bags here. Havanth balked at leaving his fortune with strangers, likely having little to no experience with banking in his adventuring life. It was only when Arnath said, pointedly, "You're slowing us down" did Havanth begin to understand. Havanth, Valdara and Ogron squirreled many coins securely away amongst their clothes and set their bags by the counter. Havanth then turned to Arnath, three gold coins in his hand.

"You don't have to... That's much more than you owe, my man." Arnath said.

"No, Arnath – We owe you our very lives." Havanth said, again pushing the coins toward Arnath, his good eye giving an insistent glare. Arnath took the coins from Havanth with a humble nod.

Arnath then instructed the bankers to weight each bag, produce a receipt for each one and be ready to close the bank when they returned. When the confused bankers asked why the bank should close, Arnath merely pointed to the sky outside the high windows, and at the threatening black disc that hung there. The bankers immediately came out from behind the counter and grabbed the saddlebags, wanting to finish their task as quickly as they could.

Outside, Arnath could see that the word had gotten out. Groups of elf families ran panicked through the streets. Already members of the King's guard were directing people to the road leading east out of town. Arnath led Havanth, Valdara and Ogron through the chaos to the main inn, where he could see quite a crowd had gathered.

Inside the main hall, Garthe stood with Shrakar near the table he and his companions had often used as he spoke to the packed ale room of listening elves. Lorta stood near him and translated for the traditionalist elves who understood none of the common tongue. Arnath and his companions hung back, closer to the long bar, where Arnath ordered food and drink for he and his companions. He then disappeared to the back where the privies were. During this time of crisis, he followed his old sergeant's training to the letter – Eat and relieve yourself whenever time allowed. Sleep was a privilege and best not thought about until all fighting was done.

Returning from the back of the inn, Arnath could hear Garthe continuing to instruct the elves to escape whilst they could, to make it to the far side of Kroman's Town, where the deadly necromancer would likely halt his destructive progress. Satisfied the boy had things well in hand - for every ear heeded his words, this the young mage apprentice of the great Shimar who was also beloved of Shimalena, the beauty of Solindar - Arnath rejoined the others and filled himself with food and drink.

Only when the elves began to ask questions about strategy, about how to fight the powerful dark magician, did Arnath wipe his face and hands with a cloth napkin and step forward to join Garthe.

"I do not know what form the necromancer takes – is it a man, or perhaps only a spirit?" Arnath began, looking at all those around who hung on his words. "But I say this – my strategy is to harry this creature until we do know. And then we can know how it is we can destroy it. As to your citizens, those that can should make for the eastern side of the mound, where the King's guard will be in force. Those that cannot should make for the woods to the north and stay hidden until the danger passes. I'd ask that you form up a sizable number of the former soldiers and hide in force in the elf-wood forest to the south of the city. Once the necromancer passes, bring up the rear and we shall box it in at Kroman's."

Arnath was glad to see warrior elves like Taishen and Tellifar nod and confer with each other and those around them. With reliable elf warriors like that covering the rear, he had little to worry about. He was about to suggest to Garthe and Shrakar that they go, then a thought struck him and he turned back to the crowd.

"One other thing! Garthe is here now. And you mustn't be caught by the necromancer, and be psychically drained by it, as Prince Heflynn has attested, knowing that he was here. I want you all to think this, and spread the word to others – "The mage Garthe is by the lake outside Kroman's Town".

The elves repeated it, some in the common tongue, some in the traditional translation. Arnath hoped it was enough to keep the necromancer from getting hold of the citizens of Solindar who had seen Garthe this day and that kernel of knowledge giving the creature reason to lay waste to Solindar looking for him.

Arnath and his party bade the elves good-bye and good luck, and they left the inn for Shimar's. They dashed down the chaotic streets, frightened elves running this way and that, reaching the front doors of the bank. The three elf clerks were waiting outside for them. They handed Havanth, Valdara and Ogron receipts for the weight in gold they had deposited, then locked the bank shut and ran for their lives. Taking a cue from the bankers, they all ran down the street and turned the corner to the residential area where Shimar's house was. A squad of King's guard patrolled outside, guarding the member of the royal family, Heflynn, within. They knew Arnath and his companions from their hectic arrival in town and let them pass. Havanth motioned for his people to wait outside, as did Shrakar, not wanting to crowd up the space. The last in the door, Arnath stopped to look at the western horizon.

The vast black disc and the column underneath were now following the path of the King's road and much like the tornadoes is so appeared like, was kicking up wind all around it, as well unleashing bolts of bright lighting upon anything in its path. Further down the road, it appeared as though many farmsteads it had passed were fully ablaze.

Looking away from the encroaching disaster, Arnath's eyes met Havanth's, who said, "Hurry" and Arnath turned to step inside.

Arnath stepped in and saw Heflynn kneeling beside Listrelle, who lay limply on her back on Shimar's living room table, her body covered up to her neck with a white sheet. Both Shimar and Garthe ran their healing stones closely over her, from head to toe. As he reached Heflynn's side, Arnath put a hand on his shoulder, and whispered, "Anything?"

The prince shook his head and quietly said, "Nothing."

The quiet of the room was immediately shattered, as Listrelle sat up, with a horrifically loud shriek. Her face was up close with Garthe's when she said in a frightening tone, "He knows you! He knows your power. It's what only you can give he seeks."

With that she flopped back against the table, her head turned away, eyes falling on Heflynn's. Her voice was more like herself as she said, in a coy fashion, "Your clothes are in tatters, fancy boy. That's no way to appear in front of your lady."

"Forgive me, my sweet." Heflynn said, kissing her lips lightly.

"If you command me so…" Listrelle said, taking incredible effort to maintain the playful tone of their banter, despite her obvious pain. But as soon as the words were out, she was gone. Heflynn clutched her hand and hung his head, weeping.

Arnath made the traditional gesture of respect for the dead, his right hand over his eyes, and then looked across the table at Shimar, saying, "Gather what you need."

Without asking permission, Arnath picked up Prince Heflynn, reaching an arm around his back and hoisting him off his knees, and made for the door. Outside, Arnath shouted, "Escorts, mount your horses!" As the guardsmen scattered, Arnath noted everyone else was gone – both his and Havanth's parties.

Heflynn overcame his shock, and resisted Arnath's pull toward the street. "No! We cannot leave her here!"

Arnath turned, his face close to Heflynn and said, "We can and we will. She will be buried with the full honours she deserves, but first…" Arnath said turning towards the west. "We have to destroy the evil that killed her."

Heflynn followed Arnath's eyes. The tower of blackness nearly blotted out the entire western sky. Where it touched down, near the edge of town, it was tearing buildings apart with cyclonic winds and lightning.

The neighing of several frightened horses drew their eyes away from the terror in the sky. Coming up the street at speed was Trellith aboard a large two-horse cart, one of those horses being Princess Dragonfly. Ogron sat in the back of the cart his head peeking up behind Trellith. Behind them was the entirety of their combined parties on horseback, with spares for those now exiting Shimar's.

Garthe and Shimar exited his house, each of them carrying a very large tome, research for the coming fight against the necromancer.

"Get aboard, master mage." Arnath said, striding towards his horse. As Arnath mounted, he saw all of his companions were settled either on horseback or in the cart. He took one last look at the approaching monstrosity, and shouted over the whipping winds, "Ride as you never have. No stops until we reach Kroman's Town!"

CHAPTER FIFTEEN

With her fields fully harvested and tilled for the coming winter, Merynda had little to do but take care of her children and watch the road. She'd been doing that quite a bit of late. Since pairing with Captain Arnath, she'd stop to watch the road for brief moments throughout her day, from her windows or porch.

After the last time he came by, her vigil became somewhat constant, having been given a mandate to rescue him and his colleagues. It would be nice, she thought to herself ironically, if Arnath just came by to go for a walk sometime.

Merynda's nerves were on edge already, waiting for the captain and his band of adventuring business partners to come back, when the road in front of her house exploded into utter chaos.

At first it was just a trickle – The occasional cart bearing old farmers she recognized from the markets. Then the occasional King's Guard on horseback, racing by faster than any post worker she'd ever seen. Then a mad dash of elves – whole families astride carts, horses and on foot, all of them looking desperate and distressed. Soon the entire width of the road was packed with them.

Merynda didn't have to guess the cause of the mass exodus. She'd seen it hanging in the south-western horizon for near a month, mistaking it for a persistent bad weather system. For the past few days, it had begun to slowly creep in the direction of her farm, and against her better nature thought this had to have something to do with Arnath and his companions. Of course, it did. As kind as his heart was, trouble followed him. Like a plateau of darkness in the sky, it followed him.

Her thoughts were confirmed when she enlisted the children to place troughs by the road and fill them with water for the passing horses. The first of the carts to come by after that belonged to her friends from the far side of Solindar, Nester and his wife, Gilea. They waved her over, their eyes desperate, as their horses slopped in the troughs.

"What is it?" Merynda asked, reaching their cart.

"Get the children. Bring some things for them." Nester said, turning his chin toward the back of the cart. "We have to get to the far side of Kroman's before that gets here."

"Any idea what it is?" Merynda asked, desperate for answers.

"Arnath said it was the necromancer that destroyed the old outpost in Kroman's" Gilea said from the far side of the cart. "The captain and his companions should be here soon. They were heading to Solindar, to start the evacuation."

"Well under way, from the looks of things." Merynda said, turning towards the front of the house, shouting, "Jarthow – Get your packs! Under clothes, a few days warm changes for you and your sister."

Once the children were safely away with Nester and Gilea, Merynda went inside the house and changed into the quilted under clothes that fit under her armour. Taking it all from a chest she seldom opened, she donned her armour, belted on her sword and throwing axes and went to the barn to ready her horse. Merynda led her lightly armoured horse to the side of the road, and watched the troubled farmers and elves pass while she waited.

She did not have to wait long. Merynda could see the cavalcade of armoured King's guard and ragged adventurers racing down the road, and hear the shouts for the refugees to clear the way, approaching for miles.

Merynda estimated the time of their arrival, and turned back towards the farm. She marched to the water pump, drank her fill and then filled her largest bucket, hauling it up her farm's roadway to the side of the King's road. She dumped the water, dividing it evenly amongst the two troughs on either side of her roadway and tossed the bucket aside. Then, she mounted her horse.

With a thunder of hooves on the cobblestones of the King's road they came – Arnath and his friends, along with Valdara and the rogues she travelled with, Prince Heflynn looking quite wan and heart-broken in the saddle, and a troop of guardsmen, most likely there to ensure the safety of the prince. Arnath saw Merynda as soon as she mounted her horse. She signalled they need not stop, and kicked her horse forward onto the road.

Merynda kept her horse's speed a pace slower than the on-coming party, and in no time, they caught up with her. As Arnath rode along side her, she urged her horse onward, to keep up with the desperate pace.

Despite the dire state of things, Merynda and Arnath exchanged an affectionate smile. Keeping some humour in her voice, Merynda called out to Arnath, "Please tell me this isn't your fault."

"Only partially, from what we know of it thus far." Arnath said, off-handedly.

"What do we know? What is it?" Merynda implored.

"Oh, just the dark forces of the ancient world come back to destroy us all."

"Wonderful." Merynda called Arnath's way. "Just like the old days."

From behind them in the phalanx of thundering horses, Valdara leaned forward on her horse and called out, "The old days for true, sister. Glad to see you can still fit into your armour!"

*

Even from the protection deep within the forest of elf-wood trees, they could hear the crackles of lighting and terrible winds ripping up the roofs of houses in nearby Solindar as the giant black column approached.

After Garthe and Arnath had spoken at the inn, Taishen and Tellifar rallied together all the elves with warrior's experience and training in Solindar. They each raced to their homes, saw their families on their way to the King's road, gathered their equipment and met where the edge of the elf city gave way to the massive growth of elf-wood trees that covered the land for leagues to the south.

Within the forest, they gathered around the All-Father, the greatest of the elf-wood trees, the trunk of which thirty elves would have to stretch to hold hands around. This tree was central to their spiritual lives, was part of their spring festival, when its seeds where picked up off the ground and taken to the south and planted – Thus making this tree the father of all trees that future generations would hew.

Around the great trunk, they tied many ropes together securely, making a linked rope line that they could cling to if the terrifying, whipping winds made it this far south. Taishen feared they just might, considering how they howled from within the city. He and Tellifar exchanged a fearful glance when they heard the first crackle of branches and creak of trunks at the edge of the forest. The sound of the leaves went from a sporadic rustle to full cacophony in an instant.

Taishen signalled to all he could see, and they signalled all those he couldn't in turn. Everyone hitched an arm over the rope around the all-father tree. Crouched and ready, they waited.

They didn't have to wait long. All around them, the winds whipped up, blasting in all directions. So strong were the gales, maintaining their footing and holding onto the rope was a concentrated struggle. Even squinting against the leaves and bracken that now sliced through the air, Taishen could see those around him straining, legs blown aloft by the force of the powerful gusts.

"Remember what was said!" Taishen called out in the tradition elf language. "Keep it in the forefront of your minds – The mage Garthe is in Kroman's Town!"

"The mage Garthe is in Kroman's Town! By the lake in Kroman's Town!" the elves shouted in elvish and the common tongue, voices muted by the howling winds.

Then, as quickly as the maelstrom began, it passed.

Those closest to the edge of the forest on the encircling rope flopped roughly to the ground, the strong winds no longer pulling their bodies into the air.

Taishen dusted the leaves from himself, and did a quick count – No one had been lost, pulled into the passing spire of blackness. Their equipment, however, was strewn literally everywhere.

"Gather your things up. We must keep pace with it." Taishen called to everyone, and began to trot towards the edge of the forest.

*

Illona paced between the tall stable yard fence and the decorative lake gates. Her friends, and Princess Dragonfly, had been gone for days now. And for the past couple of hours, hundreds of people had been streaming by on the western road or coming into town seeking provisions and shelter from some approaching doom. It was all very worrisome.

Earlier, Shimalena, in a gesture of sympathy and support, had brought her food and drink from the Briny Sea. She told Illona that the elves that fled Solindar had done so because of an approaching dark magical threat. How was knowing that ever supposed to be of comfort to her?

Finally, when the afternoon was giving way to sunset, a calamity reached her ears from the highway. Above the sound of the panicked families, and their rickety carts of possessions, she could hear shouting, thundering hoofbeats and the jangle of armour. Avoiding the many horses and carts on the road, Illona ran to the tip of the lake and, looking past the rocky sides of the fin, she saw them.

The tightly packed group of twenty people were racing down the road, shouting for the fleeing refugees to make way. As they thundered closer, Illona began to be able to pick out her friends amongst the group. Soon, she could make out that Trellith was not astride her horse, but driving a cart. And Princess Dragonfly was one of the horses hooked up to the cart!

When they disappeared behind the fin, Illona ran from the lake, back to the road, once again avoiding the many horses, carts and people as she crossed. She jumped up on the stable yard fence and there waited until the thundering troop ground to a halt.

Illona ignored the cloud of thrown up dust and ran straight to nuzzle her horse's neck. Stepping down from the cart, as many of the other riders too dismounted, Trellith said to her, "See, girl, I brought her back, as promised."

"You did!" Illona exclaimed and leaned over to tightly embrace the dwarf.

"Come now. I couldn't return home and face you if I didn't." Trellith said, when Illona finally let him go. "Now be a good girl, and get these two horses inside. Leave the cart in the street, I have no idea whose it is, but we'll need to return it someday, I imagine."

Seeing that Ogron and Shimar had stepped off the cart, Trellith took Illona's hand and guided her up to the seat. Illona snapped the reins and the cart rolled away, Illona babbling happily at her horse the entire time, making room for the rest of the horses and riders to start loping towards the stables.

Crossing paths with Trellith, Garthe said, "I can't help but feel somewhat replaced."

Trellith rolled his eyes, teasing, "And your other companion is not handful enough?" He then jerked a thumb towards the western horizon. "We have far bigger fish to fry at the moment."

Arnath and Merynda chuckled at the exchange, and then stopped leading their horses long enough to enjoy a passionate kiss. Behind them, Havanth held his horse, and said, "You know, Captain, your entire town is crazy for love."

Breaking apart, Merynda and Arnath looked back at Havanth, Arnath saying, "Makes life worth living, friend."

As they all rounded the fence, Lorta came striding down the slope of the main road. Reaching the front gate of the stables at the same time as Lorta, Arnath and Merynda handed their reins over to Jaross, who had opened the stable doors and began guiding the many animals inside. Lorta said to Arnath, "The King's Guard commanders on the end of the eastern road would like to confer with you."

"Good. How are things looking?" Arnath said, as they began the slow rise up the main road.

"Hundreds of families have made it to the far side of town, beyond the barriers set up by the King's Guard. There are many here in town. They've stayed to find out the fate of their family members they left behind in Solindar, and to help fight, if they can. They are all in the training yard."

"And my children?" Merynda asked the architect.

"They are there as well." Lorta replied.

Merynda kissed Arnath's cheek and ran up the road, saying "I'll see you shortly."

"You will." Arnath waved, and then turned to Lorta, asking, "The tarp you gave us for the rains, is it fireproof?"

"It is indeed."

Arnath nodded, saying, "Good."

As they walked together up the slope of the main road, Arnath noticed a great many carts had been left there, presumably by elf and farming families that had come into town for refuge and simply had no place to put them other than to leave them haphazardly abandoned on the main street. That gave Arnath an idea, but it would have to wait. He gestured for Lorta to follow him down the steps into the Briny Sea, and then disappeared inside.

In the large, but near-empty ale hall, Arnath strode down the bar, to find Durnly at the end, an ironic scowl on his face. "I knew when you and yours moved into town, things were going to get interesting. Re-started the wars with the Orcs, have you?"

"No." Arnath said, picking up the stein Durnly had poured for him and the flute he had poured for Lorta. Arnath passed Lorta his cider and beckoned him toward the balcony. The three of them stepped out onto the balcony and Arnath pointed to the west. "We are up against that."

With the setting sun behind it, the pillar of black shadow and its wide, topping capital looked even more ominous than in the noonday sun. Where the smoky column touched the ground, it whipped up dust and thick clods of earth, whirling them around in all directions. As it inched down the King's highway, flashes of lightning bolted out of it, hammering people and buildings on the ground, dispatching them with showers of sparks and flame.

"What in the utter bowels of darkness is that?" Durnly implored, his jaw slack.

"You used to be neighbours with it." Said Arnath, finishing up his stein. "It destroyed the outpost all those years ago."

"The necromancer!" Durnly exclaimed. "What do we do?"

Arnath ignored the question, turning to Lorta and asking, "How long?"

Lorta squinted his keen, measuring eyes into the distance, and shook his head, saying, "Perhaps a little more than an hour. At the outside."

Arnath clapped his hands on Durnly shoulders and said, "What you can do is cook food. All the food you have. Every scrap. We have refugees across the way. And, in approximately one hour, this entire town and the King's Guard will be fighting that thing. Doing it on an empty stomach is not a good idea."

"That will ruin me!" Durnly, ever practical, had run the figures in his head in seconds.

Arnath shook his head, reached into his pocket and took out one of the huge gold coins Havanth had given him. "No, it will not. Your pantry might be empty, but you will not go poor. Food, man. All of it. And fast."

Arnath pressed the coin against Durnly's chest until the barkeep reached up and grabbed it, rolling it between his fingers in awe. He then turned to his staff, who had been peaking out from the service doorway. Durnly flailed a hand at them, saying, "You heard him – Food! Cook it all!"

Turning again toward the exit, Arnath and Lorta saw Shimalena flit down the stairs with one of the slim cider casks on her shoulder. It was clearly empty, as it took her no effort to hoist it from her shoulder onto the end of the bar. Seeing Arnath, she dashed to him, throwing her arms around his chest. Surprised by the greeting, Arnath returned her embrace. Breaking away, Shimalena asked, "Garthe is home?"

"Yes, dear. He should be home shortly." Arnath said, unsurprised that was the cause of her elation.

Then Shimalena turned to Lorta, and flicked her eyes at a presumably full cask of cider sitting next the empty one she'd just brought in, her eyes expectant. Lorta bowed slightly, saying, "Of course" and tipped the cask onto his shoulder.

Satisfied, Shimalena disappeared up the stairs. Arnath and Lorta exchanged an amused look. Even in the face of impending doom, the lovely girl could get men to do just about anything for her.

As Arnath and Lorta climbed the stairs back to the street, Arnath asked, "Just how many of the King's Guard are at the end of the eastern road?"

"I didn't see the barricade on the King's Highway proper, but I'd guess there was an entire legion here." Lorta answered.

"Good." Said Arnath, coming to a halt across the street from the outpost door. "I need you to do something for me."

"Anything." Lorta said, adjusting the weight of the cask on his shoulder.

"Send Shrakar and Ogron up to gather the rain canvas. Tell them I want it draped over the stables."

"To prevent the lightning from catching the stables on fire. Good thinking, captain." Lorta said, impressed.

"He's tried to distract us by burning them before. This time, we won't give him the chance. I'll be back." With that, Arnath turned and marched down the slope of the street, heading for the hundreds of soldiers he could see at the end of the eastern road.

Passing the first cut-out, Arnath could see a dozen horses had been tied to the trees, buckets of water near them on the ground. In the second, several elf families sat around a fire, their eyes full of fear.

As he passed the stretch of road that led into the northern forest and the town cemetery, he noted the road was manned by widely interspersed guardsmen, all of whom watched westward with long spyglasses, like Trellith's.

Reaching the third cut-out, Arnath came to a criss-crossing wooden barricade that spanned the road. Behind it were hundreds of soldiers, most barely out of their teens, looking just as frightened as the elf refugees.

An unfamiliar bark ordered the barricades open, and when they parted a large man with grey hair and full armour came through, flanked on both sides by Apaulon and Sergeant Graten. As he got closer, Arnath felt a fleeting recognition for the old soldier from the wars. The older man had the clasp of a field commander on his cloak. Arnath saluted, bowing slightly. Arnath flung the left side of his cloak over his shoulder, to reveal the captain's clasp on his chest.

"Captain Arnath? Good. I'm Commander Kylus. This is for you." The commander reached into his cassock, and his hand returned with a small scroll in it.

Arnath took the scroll and Apaulon held up a lantern so it could be read in encroaching dark. Arnath scanned it and said, "I'm to take command of all forces and volunteers within the confines of Kroman's Town."

"We will maintain a perimeter."

"Right." Arnath said, his voice formal.

"You've fought this kind of threat before?" The commander asked, looking as though he might disbelieve any answer Arnath gave him.

"Several times. With varying degrees of success." Arnath said, hoping the commander did not press him for further details. Arnath had come to hate dark magics and the curses they brought over the course of his life with good reason. He'd seen too many of his friends killed by forces that no sword could cut down. In most cases, victory meant merely escaping with one's life. On this night, with the life of the boy he'd raised and the town he now called home hanging in the balance, escape was not even an option. He and those who'd stand by him would have to face whatever was coming.

Another man appeared from deep within the crowd, the soldiers parting for him. He was an elderly mage, bald on the top of his pate, giving way to flowing white hair from the crown of his head that cascaded over his shoulders. His face was covered in a pointed white beard. His robes were of the courtly colours, and around his neck was a medallion similar to the royal badge of office, but also had many arcane symbols incorporated within and around it. Those that stood aside for him regarded him with unabashed awe. Arnath, who remembered the aloof mage from the wars, did not need to be told who he was. He saluted and bowed.

"Mage Orpha." Arnath said respectfully, mid-bow.

The elder mage bowed his head slightly, saying, "Captain Arnath." And then, "How many of my kind stand with you this night?"

"We have the elf mage Shimar. And master Grentoss. And of course, Master Garthe."

"Ahh, the young healer. I have tracked his progress some over the years. You and your men have done well by him, despite not having magical abilities. With he, and the great Shimar, I think you shall do fine. And Grentoss is still alive you say? His activities have been entirely undocumented as of late."

"He's been on the adventurer's road, sir." Arnath said to the great mage, who smiled at the notion.

"Ahh, to take to the road again. The confines of the palace have been most comfortable, lo these many years, but to feel the wind in my hair again." Mage Orpha's eyes glossed over for a brief moment, lost in a reverie of a time long gone. He shook off the thoughts, saying, "Give Grentoss my regards. Light be upon you, Captain."

"And upon you, sir," Arnath said as the great mage was about to turn away. "Especially if the necromancer should get past us. I'm glad you are here to take it on, should it try to head for the inner kingdom."

Hearing this, Grand Mage Orpha and Commander Kylus exchanged an uncomfortable look. Arnath immediately knew that using beleaguered Kroman's Town as a sacrificial barrier was about the extent of the strategic plans the higher ranks had thought up, plans that inadvertently included the callous sacrifice of three of the kingdom's precious mages. And Arnath was the one who strategized bringing the necromancer here to confront it in the first place. If Arnath and his companions failed, the entire kingdom might be at risk, for lack of any real plan or experience in these matters in recent times. Arnath surmised it was the two-fold purpose of the guardsmen who would observe with the spyglasses from the forest road, not only to observe the necromancer's approach, but also to formulate some kind of battle plan after watching it plow through the defenses within the confines of Kroman's Town.

"I see." Arnath said, a cynical edge undisguised in his voice.

Mage Orpha faced him, realizing his air of authority had been openly called into question, and said, "Well, see also that the kingdom has placed a great deal of trust in you and yours, Captain Arnath. The consequences for being incorrect in that judgement would be quite grave for the kingdom."

With that, the great mage of the royal court disappeared again, gliding away into the mass of troops.

Arnath shook off his ire, knowing full-well of the sacrifices that might need to be made in this dire of circumstance. His thoughts returned to the last formality he'd have to square away before the battle. He turned to the commander, asking, "And what of the prince?"

"The prince?" The commander returned, entirely confused.

"Prince Heflynn, sir." Apaulon said.

"Third son of Domar, the prince presumptive, sir." Graten followed on from Apaulon.

"What of him?" the commander asked, growing annoyed.

"He's here, sir. He's a citizen of Kroman's Town. And before you order me to whisk him to safety, sir, I'd have you know he is a willful man who will not want to leave." Arnath, speaking as plainly as he could. He knew exactly what the commander was going to say next, and wanted to prepare him to be rebuffed.

"You must bring him to the safety beyond this barrier at once!" Commmander Kylus ordered.

"I should also add, Commander, the prince carries a badge of royal office. He can contravene your orders and mine. I can ask him if he wants to leave, but I don't expect he will."

While he remained tight-lipped, the commander's frustrated eyes bored into Arnath's for a moment, and then he said, "Very well. I'll leave it at your discretion."

Arnath turned his head from side to side, looking at both Apaulon and Graten. "You're with me?"

"Yes, sir!" Apaulon returned, and saluted.

"I am, sir." Graten said, saluting as well.

"Good. Time is against us. Gather your platoons, and we'll be about it."

The sergeant and corporal turned and waved over the barrier, Graten's wave accompanied by a shrill whistle. A force of young men and women twenty-four strong came through the barrier and formed up beside the road. Arnath looked at their fresh faces, knowing that patrolling the highway was all the soldiering they'd experienced.

Commander Kylus noted Arnath's assessment of the young soldiers, and stepped close to his shoulder, quietly saying, "The light be upon you, captain."

"Thank you, sir." Arnath responded quietly, then turning again towards the troops, made a chopping motion in the air, and shouted, "Forwards!"

Together, they marched down the road until arriving at the first cut out, where they eased their way around the horses, and made their way up through the wooded back way to the open outpost fence.

When Arnath arrived in the training yard, he stood to one side, allowing the guardsmen to filter into the yard past him whilst he took a long, assessing look around. Up on the mound, the large canvas yard cover was gone from its place, Shrakar and Ogron having taken it away. In the center of the yard, a long table had been set up, and Shimalena was serving from trays of steaming food.

As the last of the Guardsmen entered the yard, Shamuth and his men – Tindall, Fernlow and Amorth – approached Arnath. They'd kept watch over the outpost for the days that Arnath and company embarked on their rescue mission, and clearly weren't expecting a veritable onslaught of refugees to be dropped in their laps before the proprietors returned.

"Gentlemen, my thanks for minding the store in our absence." Arnath said, knowing he needed to clear up a great deal of confusion for the old soldiers before he moved on to other pressing matters.

"Anytime, Captain." Shamuth said, speaking for his men. "I understand we've got a fight coming. Where do you want us?"

Arnath said, "I want you here, guarding the refugees and townsfolk. You'll serve as a rear-guard that will get everyone to safety should there be a retreat."

"Really, sir? You know we can stand with you on the front lines?" Tindall said, disappointment clear in his voice.

"I know, gentlemen. And were it not for the great many civilians caught up in this maelstrom, I would be honoured to have you at my side. We have a responsibility to them, to see to their safety, no matter what happens. That's why I need men I can trust to see to it."

Reading their faces, Arnath could tell this helped serve as a balm for the old soldiers' egos. And he meant it. He'd be too busy to mind the elves and citizenry once the battle commenced. Arnath asked Shamuth to take charge of this post, using the training yard as last refuge, and the first cut out as a means of escape from town if the necromancer got past their forces.

Shamuth nodded, saying, "You can count on me, sir."

With that, Shamuth led his men away, closely conferring with them as they walked.

Arnath approached the food laden table, spotted a suitably full tray and signalled to two nearby guardsmen. They trotted over, saying "Sir!" in unison.

"Take this tray to the refugees in the second cut out. Mind the heat, wear your gloves." Arnath ordered, beginning to fill a wooden bowl for himself. As the guardsmen carefully carried the tray away, Arnath eyed the other guardsmen, and said, "Everyone get a quick bite. We go into battle within the hour. It will be hard work, and your next meal only comes when it is over."

Arnath made room for the guardsmen to line up by the trays, and walked over to the smith, eating spoonfuls from his bowl as he went. Smoke poured from the smith as Trellith and Valadara worked together, pouring hot metal into a wide tray. Arnath recognized it as a large mold for shot pellets. As soon as every little mold indented in the large tray was filled, Valdara and Trellith side-stepped over to another tray on the ground, a deep one filled with water and dropped the tray into it. An immediately squeal of metal stress was accompanied the blast of steam from the tray.

"They'll not be pretty. Cracked by not letting them cool at all. But we're short of time." Trellith said, removing his goggles. "Should have a few hundred by the time it gets here."

Valdara turned from where she shook the pellets into the water, saying, "My broken sword will be of some use after all."

"It will indeed." Arnath said, walking onwards. Benches had been set up between the smith and the spring pool, and many of the town's craftspeople and elves sat diligently working away with needles and hide. There was Kewin and Anya, the bakers Gaila and Hamly, Grovan – the old tailor - and Feila and Liena sitting side by side and chatting whilst they sewed, which was a rare sight indeed, because they normally had absolutely nothing to say to one another.

Stepping over near a basket on the ground where Kewin and Anya worked, Arnath looked inside and saw an ever-growing pile of slings. Tossing a newly finished one in, Kewin looked up at Arnath, and asked, "Do you really think this will work?"

Eating from their bowls, Apaulon and Graten stepped over in time to hear Arnath's reply. "In our time on the road, we'd found the only way to either defeat or escape a dark mage was to keep them at bay and continually harass them with shot and missiles. They either let you know what it is they want, which opens the door to reasoning with them, or they become enraged and will try to destroy you. At which point there is nothing to do but run."

Feila, Illona's dour-faced mother, scowled down at her stitching and said, "That doesn't sound like a plan."

Arnath merely shrugged and said, "We know the being is fixated on Garthe for whatever reason. We just don't know why. Until we do, we must hold it off. Within its desire is the means to its defeat."

Everyone seemed satisfied by Arnath's answer, except for Feila, who was never satisfied with anything ever anyway.

Arnath turned to Apaulon and Graten, and cocked his chin toward the back door of the outpost. They followed him as he strode toward the door, setting his bowl and spoon on the serving table along the way. Reaching the door, he began to speak over his shoulder, "Once your troops have supped, I want them to grab all the practice bows, arrows and shields from the training locker and set up caches all around the lake."

Arnath was able to give Merynda, who consoled her frightened children by the fire in the common room, a quick wink as he passed, heading toward the front stairs.

"We know it uses the winds," Arnath continued, "And we can only assume the bolts it throws are similar to regular storm lightning. Therefore, it can catch wood on fire, but not shock anyone holding a wooden shield to death. We can hope, anyway."

As he finished speaking, their feet were on the cobblestones outside and Arnath immediately pointed down to the lake. "We'll set up shields, all around the lake. Use the canoes and paddle boats in the boathouse too. Small groups can intermittently harry the necromancer and hopefully avoid the sting of his bolts. If we can keep it confined on the fin side of the lake, or over the lake itself, for a time, we may be able to discern a weakness. I'll take command at the far end, by the large tree. Everyone should hear my orders from there."

"What of the necromancer taking holding of people and draining their lives away, like the refugees spoke of?" Graten asked, somewhat afraid of Arnath's answer.

"That's true, unfortunately. It is how your comrade Listrelle met her eventual fate. But after it had taken hold of Listrelle and the prince, who knew Garthe's location, it no longer needed to drain any more minds. It got what it wanted." Arnath could tell by their faces his answer wasn't much comfort. Being completely honest with himself, he wasn't entirely sure if the necromancer had been draining the lives out of the people of Solmairyth for reasons entirely different than the learning of Garthe's location. There was something missing, something that only getting the necromancer to communicate might reveal. But they had to get it to halt its path of destruction first.

Arnath pointed down the slope of the road, to the place where Shrakar and Orgon were returning from the stables. "Take all those carts, and create a choke point near here. A small number of our force will remain sheltered by the carts and fire from this position if it makes it across the lake. If it does make it this far, we'll hold this point to allow the civilians to make it to the barriers at the highway." As soon as he said it, Arnath also knew the nearest shelter from the barrier would be the outpost itself, and that the necromancer might destroy their hard-won business to get at anyone who sheltered within. He shook off the thought, knowing it would serve no good in the coming battle. Many, many people, the entire city of Solmairyth likely, had lost their lives already. In the face of that loss, Arnath felt no remorse in having to sacrifice the outpost to give the refugees and citizen's of Kroman's Town a few extra minutes with which to make their escape.

As Shrakar and Ogron approached, Arnath nodded, indicating to Apaulon and Graten to carry out their orders. The soldiers disappeared back inside the outpost. Shrakar pointed over his shoulder and said, "Choke point?"

"Exactly. I have one more thing for the two of you to do before our time is up." Arnath said.

"What dat?" Shrakar asked, sounding ready for anything but looking tired as could be. Arnath didn't even think on it until he saw it on his companion's face. How long had they been awake, tearing across the countryside on horseback, performing arduous rescues? Was it three days? Four? He'd sleep when life allowed, but, by the light, let that be soon. This wasn't exactly the last days at Isthmar, but he wasn't exactly the young man who survived those days anymore either.

Arnath shook off the dark thoughts, and said to the waiting Orcs, "Use the water in our water tower, our spring pool, Feila's pool, the public fountain, the lake if you must and soak every roof in town. The necromancer may take us, but Kroman's will not burn this night."

Ogron saluted and Shrakar patted his shoulder as they went inside the outpost. Before turning to go back inside himself, Arnath allowed himself a quiet moment and immediately felt the flutter of the wind picking up. It was close enough to unsettle the wind here, within the town. That meant there was little time left to organize the last details. Arnath snorted out a long breath, and went back inside.

Arnath made his way into the corner of the common room by the fireplace. Merynda knelt there, in front of the big, Orc-sized chair Jarthow and Perrin sat side-by-side in. Arnath knelt down right beside her, to be at eye level with her children as well. Merynda leaned close to him, saying quietly, "They are afraid of what's coming."

Arnath looked them both in the eye, and, nodding, said, "So am I."

"You are?" Perrin said, utterly astonished. How could a big man be afraid like she was?

"I am. In cases like this, fear is a good thing." Arnath said, taking both of their hands, though Jarthow just let his hang limply in the large warrior's. "Fear tells us when to run and hide. When we are not safe. It also tells us how brave we need to be if we can't run. Like now. We are all afraid because everything we know about the dark force coming toward us is terrible. And that's why we need to be brave for each other. I'm afraid, but I can be brave for your mother and you. If each of us is brave for the others, then we can stand and face what makes us all afraid."

Merynda and Perrin appeared appeased, even inspired by his words, but Jarthow looked at Arnath with cinched eyebrows, and said, "In tales I've read, warriors say they have no fear."

"Well, I am a warrior, and I do." Arnath said, smiling at the boy. "Those who write tales do so from comfy chairs like this one and seldom face the kind of dangers the harshness of the road amply supplies. Anyone who said to me that they had no fear, that they laughed in the face of that which terrifies the rest of us I would think a fool, and would never go into battle with. They race into danger without assessing it, and die badly. Always."

Satisfied, Jarthow finally squeezed Arnath's hand and nodded. Perrin leaned forward and hugged around Arnath's neck, and began to giggle.

This time, Merynda interceded, and peeled the little girl's arms off of Arnath. "The captain must go. He can't have you hanging off him all night."

Disappointed, Perrin sat back in the chair as Arnath stood, saying, "Be safe children. Listen to those around you. When they say run, do it."

Then Arnath turned and left the common room. In the corridor, as Arnath made for the stairs, Merynda caught up with him, turned him by his arm and kissed him. Breaking away, finally, Merynda said, "Know that I love you, Arnath."

"And I you." He returned, and meant it. A sudden thought intruded on their tender moment, and Arnath said, hesitantly, "Listen – In the field…"

"You bark your orders like a vicious dog. I know. I won't take it personally." Merynda interrupted, kissing him again. Then, taking her arms from his neck, said, "Go. There isn't much time left. Change your clothes. You smell."

"You're right." Arnath said, kissed her forehead and then disappeared up the stairs.

Arnath turned on the first floor and strode down the hall, stopping to knock at the door closest to the front window.

"Come in." a voice said from inside, and Arnath stepped in to find Prince Heflynn fully dressed and armoured. A far sight different than the bedraggled state he was in an hour ago. Arnath noted the small apartment was packed to the walls with cases and trunks, likely sent by his parents after their last visit. Maintaining a wardrobe like his certainly took up a lot of space.

Despite his opulent raiment, Heflynn looked in no mood for company. An immovable scowl sat in the corner of his mouth to match the faded lightning scars that poked up from his collar. Garthe could likely heal them away with time, but the wound of losing Listrelle would surely stay with him forever.

"I don't suppose I could convince you to take refuge amongst the King's Guard at the end of the eastern road." Arnath said, fully expecting an argument in reply.

"No. You could not." Heflynn said, adjusting his furred cape, which had armoured pauldrons at the shoulders. He then turned away from Arnath, and began the process of tightly packing arrows into two quivers, one for his short bow and one for his long. Arnath guessed he had replacements amongst the many things sent by his parents, Heflynn's original bows being surely lost in the chaos of Solmairyth.

Arnath wondered if he should even press the argument. The orders given to him were given by a commander who would stay safely snug amongst a thousand troops whilst poor Kroman's Town would yet again confront the necromancer that had scarred its face before. If Heflynn, a prince of the realm, chose to defend this quaint hamlet, their home, with his life, Arnath felt no real need to argue the point. Besides, there just wasn't time for any kind of debate about it.

Opening the door again, Arnath asked, "You'll stand with me in the field?"

Heflynn turned, meeting his eye for the first time, and said, "Of course, I will."

Arnath left it at that, nodding and headed back into the hallway. At the end, he stepped out onto the first balcony. His appearance caught the eye of Graten and Apaulon, who were mustering the guardsmen burdened with near everything from inside the training cabinet. Arnath called down, "Meeting in the map room shortly."

Arnath went back inside and took to the stairs again. On the next floor, he stepped into the map room and found only Shimar and Havanth there, eyes scanning the large tomes Shimar had brought. Havanth looked up from the dusty book and grunted, "Cutting things close, aren't you?"

Arnath rounded the table and stood between Havanth and Shimar, saying, "We'll have a quick meeting in here shortly. Then take to the field."

Looking over his shoulder, Arnath was struck by fact that the tome Havanth studied was written in Okreen, the spoken and written language of the Orcs. Unlike the common human script, the Orc's language was written in vertical lines that bounced from side to side as they descended. Noting Arnath's up-raised eyebrows, Havanth said, "I studied it fervently during the war. They were always sending bats over our heads with messages, orders tied to their legs. Got pretty good at it too."

"I remember. Must have been your unit that received all the parchments from the ones we shot down." Arnath said, still engrossed by the aggressive, descending characters on the page.

"Maybe." Havanth said, allowing himself a moment of reverie, casting his mind back to the old times. But his eye did not remain unfocused for long. He pointed at the text, saying, "The adventurers who were killed here when the live-stone destroyed the old outpost obtained their treasure in the ruins of Arkonia. During that empire's reign, their nearest neighbours were the Orcs, so I am checking for any references in their histories. Like many of the ancient kingdoms, our long-held belief was that Arkonia was destroyed by one of its own mages. Whether by dabbling in the dark, or just wanting the power of the throne for themselves, we may never know."

"And the Orcs would not know from within their kingdom how the Arko-nians chose to combat such a threat, I imagine."

"Nothing on it yet." Havanth said, turning back to the thick book.

Arnath turned to Shimar, saying, "I expected Garthe to be here with you. Where is he?"

"In his laboratory. I think he wanted to be alone for a time." The old elf said, only looking up from his book for the briefest second.

Arnath nodded and then said, "As I said, we'll have a brief meeting to strate-gize here shortly."

Havanth and Shimar, noses in their books, both harrumphed mumbled responses as Arnath left.

Once again mounting the stairs, Arnath thought perhaps climbing them to the top floor might kill him long before the necromancer could. Arnath knew however, that to surrender to his bed one floor above was to surrender to death at the hands of a dark magician. All that he had left had to be given to this fight.

Arnath stepped inside his apartment and made sure to not so much as glance at his bed. Starting with his captain's clasp and boots, he undressed fully, then re-dressed in fresh clothes and affixed his clasp to the left side of his covering cloak, the only amour he'd wear this night. Foggy thoughts of having something made in Solindar, some ceremonial armour perhaps, passed through his mind as he took to the stairs once more.

Reaching the door in the apex of the building, Arnath rapped lightly on it. Though he heard no direct response, he heard the quietest whimper from the other side of the door. Arnath turned the knob and stepped inside the lab.

Garthe sat on a stool next to his long work table, and wept with his head hung low. Arnath stepped further in and saw what Garthe was working on. All across the table were the makings of his little cloth-wrapped grenades, more than a dozen. From the looks of the piles on each little square of cloth, they just needed to be sewn closed. On the table in front of Garthe stood a tall glass jar that had another dozen already prepared.

Arnath picked up a stool and set it beside Garthe's. As he sat down, he placed his hands on the distraught young mage's shoulders.

"I cannot... cannot at all think of what I did that could bring all this down upon everyone." Garthe said through sniffles and tears.

At first Arnath wasn't sure what he could say to be of comfort. He himself had no idea why the destructive necromancer was fixated on the boy. Rare as mage births were, he'd heard of a few born in the years Garthe was alive. In their travels on the road, both before and after Garthe became part of their company, he and his companions had never come across any fool religion's prophecy about a young healing mage. Perhaps that was it – the healing part?

"You said you showed the stoned to Shimar when you first took it to Solindar?" Arnath asked, knowing the answer already.

"Yes, I did."

"And that was the second time you were exposed to it? The first being here in our back yard."

"Yes. That's right." Garthe answered, uncertain of Arnath's thought behind his queries.

"Did you feel drained at all by the encounters?" Arnath asked, pointedly.

Garthe's eyes grew wide, and he exclaimed, "Yes!"

"I know little of this type of magic, but would it be possible that the stone drained just enough of you to awaken something within, something that needs more of what only you have to in order to attain its goal?" Arnath asked, his eyes darting back and forth.

"Entirely possible." Garthe said, his tears now dried. "But what could that be?"

"Once, long before you joined our party, we came across a necromancer in an already plundered tomb. It had no form, was merely smoke and shadow, but was very much alive and could do harm to the living. Incredible harm. But once we were away from those tombs, it could hurt us no more. You see, Garthe – It couldn't leave the tombs. Its magic was entirely tied to the curse within the tomb. Whether the curse was the disembodied mage itself, or a curse was in place to keep it from leaving the tomb, it had no effect beyond its bounds."

Garthe gasped, and exclaimed, "The live-stone!"

"Yes." Arnath said, hammering the side of his fist on the table. "The stone gave it mobility. The darkly cloaked man who the sheriff ran off on multiple occasions was not a man, but the disembodied essence, some portion of the necromancer."

"And the activation of the live-stone, the power that destroyed the old outpost, acted as a beacon. It called the necromancer to its pilfered source of power; it is the thing that allows the spirit to move beyond the ruins of Arkonia." Garthe said, now fully understanding Arnath's train of thought.

Arnath shook his head. He knew their notions were on the proper path, but something bothered him about it all. "The stone released a surge of great power when the two mages fought over it here. But what would awaken it after so long before, after perhaps thousands of years in those tombs?"

It took them only a moment for the realization to hit them, and, eyes meeting they, said the name at the same time.

"Morgosh".

*

They stood crowded around the map room table – Arnath, Trellith, Shrakar, Garthe, Havanth, Valdara, Heflynn, Shimar, Grentoss, Ogron, Trenth, Mego, Merynda, Apaulon and Graten.

"There is a distinct possibility," Arnath said to all as he stood near Trellith, who drew up a rough map of the town on a blank piece of mapping paper. "That our party awoke this menace more than seven years ago. Morgosh, the mage we travelled with at the time, Garthe's first master, was killed, entirely absorbed by a curse within the tombs that likely revitalized the live-stone that gives the necromancer's essence continuance. As guilty as we might feel for setting this monstrosity on its destructive path, the fact of our involvement might give us a tactical advantage."

"How?" Trenth asked with a scowl.

"My master might still be present within the stone. We may be able to call upon him to aid us." Garthe said.

"And if he can't help, or just is no longer there? Then what? That seems an awfully hopeful strategy to take into battle against something that likely destroyed an entire empire." Havanth said, his eye darting between Garthe and Arnath.

"You've learned something?" Arnath asked, struck curious by the last part of Havanth's statement.

Havanth ran his hand over the Orc text, and said, "The Orcs wrote of the Arkonian mage Alathuum being banished from the kingdom for turning towards the dark magics."

"The fragmented records from within the kingdom confirm the last court mage was named Alathuum." Shimar interjected. "I don't think they were even able to banish him. He simply rained destruction down upon his own kingdom for the insult."

"And tonight, we fight him with shot and arrows. Perhaps I shall return to the palace." Heflynn ironically quipped, and it drew only a smattering of nervous laughter. Too many minds around the table echoed his desire to run.

Sensing the prevailing mood of doom overtaking the room, Arnath said, "We also have its desire for Garthe. Whether it be his healing abilities, perhaps to once again join the dark phantasm with the essence within the stone or for some other dark purpose, we can use that obsession to whatever advantage we can."

Scribbling on the map, Trellith said, "Perhaps there is a way to convince it Garthe is dead."

"And anger it further?" Merynda asked, utterly appalled by the notion.

"A potion of some kind?" Garthe said, looking from Grentoss to Shimar.

Grentoss merely shook his head, and Shimar elaborated, "Not in the time we have. Such concoctions exist but take days to brew."

Sensing the prevailing doom was once again about to overtake the room, Arnath pointed at Trellith's quickly drawn map and said, "Battle it is, then. You all have your positions. I'm hoping I can be heard from this position by the lake, otherwise things may fall to chaos."

As his last word was spoken, everyone cocked their head and listened. There was shouting from outside and the chiming of a bell. As Arnath had instructed, Illona had come from her lookout by the fin, to warn them of the black spire's approach.

Arnath looked at everyone, companions and friends, one and all, and said, "It seems our hour of preparation is at an end. To your posts everyone."

*

Illona stopped ringing the clinic bell as soon as the war party emerged from the outpost. Upon Arnath's exit, the wiry girl near pounced on him, bleating, "It's here! It's here!"

Arnath looked down at the silly girl who'd become such a part of their lives over the last few months. He patted her shoulder and asked, "and the basket?"

"It's there where they can find it." Illona nodded vigorously, awaiting more orders. Before the meeting in the map room, Arnath had asked her to place a basket full of slings and shot at the foot of the fin where Taishen and the other elves could find it. Taking in her eagerness, Arnath wondered if it was a foolhardy dimness about her, or the fact she was raised in a town full of old war veterans, that shielded her against the dread everyone else was fighting.

Arnath pointed to the clinic door, seeing the lanterns had been lit inside. "Assist Garthe and Shimar to set up their triage clinic. Then do what I asked before – Stay in the training yard with Shimalena and the others, lest you have to flee."

"I don't want to run away. I want to stay and fight with you." Arnath could tell from her tone she meant it. He'd have to outthink her to get her to stay put.

"Would you leave Kroman's Town without its post master? Because that's who you will be one day, should we survive this."

Illona swelled at his words, standing taller, and said, "No, I wouldn't. I never would."

"Good. Now help Garthe prepare." Arnath watched her disappear into the clinic and then moved further down the cobblestone street until he reached the high barricade of piled together carts that had been built where the road began to slope toward the town square. There he found Kewin and Anya, and several others roping the barricade together and setting the baskets of slings and shot all around.

"Think this will work?" Kewin asked, as Arnath approached.

"It's more to protect your backs from the bolts it flings. If it reaches this point, you should have all run by then." Arnath said the last, looking Sheriff Daruun in the eye, by way of telling him what he'd like to see happen without directly ordering him in front of people.

Daruun gave a somber nod, and ceased his hammering. "I wish there was more I could do. A fencing swordsman can't put up much of a fight against a dark magician."

"Nonsense." Arnath said to the sheriff. "You're right where you need to be. Should it get passed us, you'll be responsible for protecting the citizens of this town. Just as you always have."

Arnath was about to leave the man with those kind words, when a notion struck him. "From your arrests, the thieves from the road and such, did you ever take any slingshots off them?"

"A great many actually." The sheriff said, turning to hand his hammer to Durnly, and then gestured for Arnath to follow him beyond the barricade.

As soon as they got to the other side, Mayor Bumpol was there and fell into step with them. "Everyone is on the other side of the barricade. I leave my town in your capable hands, captain. My, this is exciting, like the battles of old! Perhaps we can build a monument afterward, to commemorate our heroism."

And with that the mayor turned and marched away toward the barricade. Daruun and Arnath exchanged a look, but made no comment. Arnath knew from experience that monuments did little to cover the scars of battle, let alone serve as attractions for the visitors the mayor wanted. No one took time off from their working life and deliberately visited Isthmar. No one.

Shimar, Garthe and Illona arrived just as the sheriff disappeared inside his precinct. The triage area would be set up on the cobblestones between the stables and the sheriff's office. The stables jutted out just a bit further than the sheriff's, creating a natural barrier to shield the wounded from the necromancer's lightning, or whatever else it might cast by line of sight. Illona laid out bedrolls whilst Shimar and Garthe spread out many items on a clean sheet on the paving stones – tools of the healing trade.

When Daruun re-emerged from the sheriff's office, he had a decent-sized wooden box under his arm, one that was piled high with weaponry. "I hope these can help."

Taking the box from the sheriff, Arnath looked into it and, even in the shade of the buildings and the growing dark of night, could see there were many useful flinging and throwing weapons. He reached in and pulled out a combat slingshot, gesturing at Garthe. "You have yours?"

"I have mine." Garthe said, continuing to lay out medical supplies on the sheet, stopping only to pat the weapon tucked into his belt.

A flicker of lightning and a threatening crackle came from around the corner. Arnath turned to the Sheriff, and said, "Go."

Without hesitating, Daruun ran from his office porch up toward the barricade of mashed-together carts. When he looked down at Illona, she avoided his gaze, and said, "We're not done yet."

"But you'll go as soon as this is fully set up?" Arnath asked, his voice dour.

Illona hesitated, then said, "Yes" her voice a mousy whisper.

Arnath didn't believe her for a second, but had no seconds to spare. He exchanged a quick glance with Garthe and Shimar, saying, "The light be with us."

As he strode towards the gates to the lake, Arnath found himself walking alongside Grentoss, who had Garthe's jar of grenades under his arm. Arnath reached into the box, and passed one of the many slingshots to the old mage. "Ahh, very handy. Thank you." Grentoss said, pulling back on the slingshots' pouch.

Arnath stopped on the road, and waved toward the boathouse. Shrakar, Ogron and Graten sheltered there with a small force of King's guard. Shrakar looked over as Arnath left two combat slingshots and a stack of thin, clipped together throwing axes on the road. Seeing Shrakar bounding over for them, Arnath continued on.

As Arnath crossed the field by the eastern shore of the lake, he turned and looked to the west. It was there alright. Perhaps not as close as Illona's panic had led on, but it was surely coming. With each duo of King's Guard he passed by, situated behind a large rectangular and a small circular shield, he handed over a slingshot and whatever throwing weapons he could.

When he reached the underside of the large tree he and his companions favoured, Arnath found a large shield leaning against the big log that faced their firepit. Behind the log, Heflynn and Trellith knelt behind their shields and were placing arrows upright in the ground. Nearby, Merynda and Valdara knelt behind their shields, a basket of shot between them and a dozen spears each beside them. Lorta leant against the tree trunk, a basket of shot at his feet, and a sling in his hand.

Havanth, Trenth, Mego and Grentoss had taken up position on the other side of the tree. Along the lake, many of the guardsmen had dug out the firepits, and were using them as covering trenches to further conceal themselves behind their tall shields. All around this side of the lake was dotted with tiny two and four person encampments, hunkering behind their shields, awaiting orders.

Arnath set the box of small weapons and projectiles down on the ground behind the log, within reach of his friends if they needed further ammunition.

He then sat on the log and pulled the long shield up over his knees. He turned over his left shoulder and said, "Down the road-are they coming?"

Behind Arnath, Trellith plucked the spyglass from his belt and pulled it open. He peered through it for a few moments, swaying it back and forth to get focus past the swirling black spire in the road. And then he saw them in the settling dust behind the passing maelstrom, a force of forty armed elves, led by Taishen. "They're coming." Trellith said to Arnath's back.

"Good." Arnath said, looking over toward Lorta. "How long?"

Lorta peered around the tree, and said, "Perhaps ten minutes."

"Good. Wake me when it is here." Arnath said, crossing his arms and surrendering to his exhaustion for a few merciful minutes.

But for Trellith, Havanth, Valdara and Merynda, who had all seen commanders do this many times in the field before, everyone awaiting his orders were utterly dumbstruck that Arnath had just nodded off in the face of their impending doom.

CHaPTer SIXTeen

A **decidedly sharp poke** awoke Arnath. He figured it was from the tip of Heflynn's longbow, so tiny was the concentrated sting to his shoulder muscles. Arnath jumped to his feet immediately, stepped behind the log he'd been sitting on, keeping the shield in front of his body, and barked, "Shields!"

His command echoed off the lake, was immediately obeyed and then swallowed by the shrieking sound of the black, swirling pillar that had just passed the fin on the northern side. Arnath was grateful for that small mercy; The spire arriving at the field of battle where they needed to it to, where they where somewhat prepared for it.

Arnath looked at their great and terrible foe from the ground up. Where the black swirl touched the ground, it whipped up the wind and tore up the earth and grass, flinging it everywhere. As he looked up the swirling shaft, he noticed there were hints of purple and sometimes a bright crimson hidden within the smoky folds of the column. It looked as though the places where the blackness parted revealed some other place, beyond this natural realm. These undulations continued along the entire height of the swirling staff. The flat disc at the top of the column appeared to have shrunken, no long reaching out a half a league in all directions. Like the column itself, the disc appeared to be two or three layers, swirling like the shaft, at different speeds and in different directions, the outer edges intermingling like tendrils or gnashing teeth.

Under the sound of the howling wind and the occasional lightning crackle, the approaching column seemed to emit a sound unto itself. To Arnath, it sounded both high-pitched screams and the deepest basso wailing at the same time. He found it truly unnerving.

As it crept past the fin and upon the curved shore of the western side of the lake, Arnath thought it had moved close enough, and roared, "Volley!"

From all around the lake, metal shot and arrows streaked through the air, all of which seemed to disappear upon contact with the smoky, swirling column.

Even though their instructions were clear, "Fire your shot and get behind your shield", a good many choose to keep looking, to see if they had any effect on the dark magical phenomenon. And many of them paid the price.

The instant the arrows and shot penetrated the smoky black surface, white-hot bolts of lightning flashed out of the shaft and underside of the capital. The light temporarily blinded anyone who was not behind their shield, and the high-pitched crackle must have stung every ear for leagues.

The saving grace, Arnath noted as he squinted from behind his shield, was that the lightning did not seem altogether guided, or if it was, was not very accurate. Still, he saw no less than six, all guardsmen, fall after the onslaught. Some were the shield partners of the guardsmen who fired the volley, huddled too close and caught the spire's wrath.

All around the lake, shields and bodies smoked.

Arnath turned his head around both ways, saw those he cared for most still lived, and then poked his head over his shield. When he did, he noticed right away the capital of the spire was smaller, like it was shrinking into the spire itself. Arnath didn't know what it meant, only that there would be less lightning from above them.

"Mark my words – volley, then shields. Do not hesitate and look at it! Now – Volley!" Arnath barked across the lake.

This time, only two thirds of the arrows and shot fired at the black spire reached it before it let out another searing burst of lightning. Everyone ducked down after their shot, but some not quickly enough. Sparks and fiery blasts flew from a dozen impacted shields, some even blasted apart. Screams and cries of the injured could be heard from all points around the lake. The top of the boathouse was on fire, as were points along the fence around the stables.

Arnath looked around, assessing the casualties. Already, guardsmen were hunkered down behind shields and dragging their fellows around the lake to medical aid behind the stables. To his shock, the spire lashed out bolts at the running guardsmen, sending huge plumes of sparks off their shields. Arnath peaked over his shield and yelled, "Volley!"

While their arrows and shots soared, Arnath watched through squinted eyes. This time the responding lightning blast didn't come until the last arrow arced into the spire. He ducked down when it did, the sound of the crashing, sparking impacts resounding all around him.

Arnath heard a pained shriek from directly behind him, and several more from all around the lake. He turned and saw Merynda was tending to Valdara, who had a sizeable burn streaking up her thigh. Despite her seething expression, Valdara waved her hand at Arnath, indicating she was alright to stay in the field. Merynda's expression, which was directed at him, was not so reassuring. It wasn't until he felt the stabbing pain on his forehead, and the warm sting of blood in his left eye, that he knew what concerned her.

The mere act of wiping the blood away with the back of his hand drew a piercing pain from over his left brow. Arnath looked at his shield and saw that a small chunk of the corner had been blasted away. Though the pain over his eye grew, he didn't have time for it.

Keeping his shield high, Arnath stood and scanned around the lake. Two things were easy to see – Their forces were once again reduced by the burning blasts of lightning, and the capital topping the deadly spire was once more reduced in size. Arnath seized upon the notion that the lightning blasts required energy the essence within the spire needed to replenish. Thinking on how huge the spire was, how far reaching its top was after Solmairyth, Arnath reasoned they may have to perform a mass retreat quickly if the spire starting plucking people off the ground and sapping their very life energies away. Surviving the night was the goal, but as long as people lived around it, the necromancer's manifestation would have the energy to strike out against them. Lives would continue to be lost until he figured out some way to stop this juggernaut.

*

The first of the lightning blasts were so numerous and far-reaching that Kewin and the others behind the barrier of piled carts quickly ducked down, fearing their shelter would be struck. When he ducked, Kewin had his head back, his eyes skyward, and witnessed a great bolt lashing through the air over the roof of the outpost.

He heard the jolting crack of rock nearby, followed by a great many screams. Kewin squeezed Anya's hand, a quick reassurance, and then dashed into the outpost. Running through the front corridor, he could already see people gathered around a spot in the yard. Once outside, Kewin joined the ring of people and cringed at what they were looking at.

The lightning strike had struck the mound, so devastatingly that a large chunk broke off the mound and had tumbled into the training yard. And had landed on someone.

Kewin stepped forward, braving to investigate where the elf refugees and women of the town stood in a wide circle, away from the terrible aftermath. He could see legs shod in knee high leather boots sticking out from the veritable boulder embedded in the yard. It had to be Fernlow, the veteran of the seventh who Arnath posted here in the rear to see to the safety of the civilians. Though a quick death, it was an awful way for an old veteran to go.

Kewin stood and found himself beside Shamuth, whose wide eyes were locked on his fallen friend.

Another flash of lightning crackled overhead, and Shamuth lifted his head up and shouted, "Into the trees!"

Everyone ran through the open back gate, Kewin and Shimalena ushering them through, taking shelter under the trees in the little wooded area that led to the first cut out. Here, at least any plummeting debris would be buffered by the canopy of branches above.

Anya turned her worried eyes away from the outpost's front door, and looked down the slope of the main road. As the lightning flashed, she could see soldiers being dragged from the lakeside, to the spot Garthe and the elf mage had set up to treat them. The young soldiers who braved across the field seemed to hesitate to go back, however briefly. Even from her perch here, behind the barrier, Anya could see how horribly burned their fellow King's Guard were.

Garthe and Shimar had to work fast once the injured started being brought to them. So powerful were the dark magician's bolts, many of the guardsmen's clothes were burnt all the way through to the skin, which itself was burnt black in the radiating lightning pattern. The two would assess the injured, treating those who had been burnt first, leaving those who suffered wounds from the explosive effect the lightning had on their wooden shields for later. As Shimar and Garthe passed their stones over the bodies of the wounded, Shimar having to ease some of their pain by knocking them out with his flat sleep stone, Illona provided covering bandages for those who had grievous, but not life-threatening wounds. She knew she had defied Arnath in staying, but felt strongly it was here she could do some real good. She had gotten much better, working with Garthe over time, at not being sickened by the sight of blood, or of broken limbs. It was only when a guardsman arrived whose entire hand had been shorn off when his shield took a direct blast that she started to feel queasy and regretted her decision. Illona did her best to quell the uneasy feelings in the pit of her stomach, remembering she was there to help. Besides, from here she could be near Princess Dragonfly if the stables needed to be evacuated. Illona felt a sting of pain every time the horses cried out in fear as the walls of the stables were battered with crashing bolts.

Shrakar had dumped their basket of arms on the ground and filled it with sand and earth from around the base of the boathouse. With the quickest glance over the top of the boathouse at the undulating spire, he gauged his window and leapt up, tossing the full basket of loose earth across the fires that dotted the roof of the boathouse. They went out immediately, and he jumped down, ducking away from another volley of the shrieking hot blasts emanating from across the lake. Shrakar looked up when he heard Ogron say something, though the bolts were too loud to tell what. Then he understood when Ogron gestured for the basket. Shrakar tossed it over, and Ogron began to paw earth into it.

Shrakar didn't know what Ogron planned to do until he ran over and did it, and by then it was too late. Ogron began dumping the dirt from the basket on the little fires that dotted the top of the fence that ran around the stable yard. But that fence sat slightly above the western road out of town and therefore was a prime target for the necromancer's volleys. Shrakar's roared warning was drowned out by the whip-crack sting of several bolts that went searing Ogron's way. Ogron managed to dive away in time, but the missile-like splinters from the fenceposts that exploded behind him caught him in the leg. Shrakar raced over to where Ogron fell, reeling in agony, his left calf deeply penetrated several times over by thick splinters. Shrakar got an arm under Ogron's and dragged him back to the safety of the rear of the boathouse. Graten acted quickly, pulling off his belt and knotting it tightly just under Ogron's knee to staunch the bleeding. Shrakar turned and gauged the distance from the edge of the boathouse to the shelter of the front of the stable. It was too far to run, even with a shield on his back. When he'd reach the corner of the stable fence, he'd have to turn the corner, running exposed still until the stable wall covered them. Seeing how easy it was for the dark mage to nearly kill Ogron from this distance, getting over the fence to the back of the stables wasn't a viable option either. Trying to get Ogron to Garthe could kill them both. Turning back, Shrakar meant to check on Ogron, but something further down the road caught his eye…

The Elves!

Sheltered by the western side of the fin, Taishen and the elves snuck across the King's Road and began to climb up the back side of the fin. Just before he started his ascent, Tellifar spotted the basket of slings and shot left by Illona. He secured it over his shoulder, and began to make his climb.

Shrakar told Ogron what he had in mind. They would wait until the elves started to harry the necromancer and then make their attempt to get him off the field of battle.

It didn't take long. One more round after Arnath yelled across the lake for a volley, and the deadly spire returned fire with blinding bolts, the elves emerged on the top of the fin, arrows already nocked.

All around the tiny lake valley, the defenders saw the elves and hearts swelled. Taishen, Tellifar and a line of elves fired down from the top of the fin. Then, Arnath called out for another volley from below.

So inspired was Mayor Bumpol, utterly convinced that the arrival of the elves meant certain victory, that he rounded the barrier of piled carts and began to call out encouragements to the troops and chastising remarks in the direction of the spire.

Sheriff Daruun called out behind him, "Come back, you're making a target of us, man!"

Seeing his words had no effect, Daruun turned to Anya and the others there, and ordered, "Get inside! Quickly!"

Anya grabbed Durnly's hand, and helped him hobble as quickly as he could for the outpost door.

As he passed the little man, rounding the corner of the stable fence, dragging Ogron on a shield, Shrakar tried to reach out and grab him, but the little mayor raced on past.

"You see! You cannot defeat the noble folk of Kroman's Town, villain!" The mayor called out, standing just inside the lake gates, shaking his fist toward the spire across the lake.

He was about to shout another harangue at the undulating black column when it lashed out with salvo of deadly bolts in several directions. One bolt went up the street where Bumpol had emerged and struck the barricade of carts, blowing them apart, catching the debris alight. Another struck just under the peak of the fin, blasting the rock away and striking Tellifar in the process. The elf tumbled to the ground, a hail of broken-away boulders all around him. The last bolt lashed directly across the lake at Mayor Bumpol, striking him in the chest, driving the little man right into one of the decorative lake gates. The mayor disappeared, swallowed by the explosion as the decorative gate blasted into a million fiery pieces.

Between the explosions just up the road and now right by them at the lake gates, Illona could do little more than curl up on the cobblestones in a ball and cover her head. As Garthe rushed over to shelter her with his body, he peered up the road, looking at the smoking ruin of the cart barricade. Anyone who sheltered behind it was surely dead.

Arnath, like everyone around him, was dumbstruck. One second ago his instincts told him to race across the field and save the silly, but well-meaning, little mayor from his own folly, and the next he was quite dead. There was no doubt, the gate where he stood a moment ago was a pile of smoking rubble now.

Arnath turned toward the spire, his face set in a hardened battle scowl. This had to end.

He stepped over the sheltering log, his shield barely covering his body and drew his sword, barking, "Alathuum! Face me, Alathuum!"

As he reached the edge of the lake, Arnath saw the spire, which had shrunken down to twenty feet tall with no over-reaching capital atop it at all after its last volley, had begun to move.

The spire crept slowly across the lake, its ghostly internal purple and red lights eerily illuminating the entire lake beneath. The bottom of the spire, which floated above the surface of the water, began to expand, forming a disc-like base similar to the now-gone capital. As the base spread away from the spire, the spire itself lost solidity near its peak, its cylindrical shape reducing in on itself.

Then, having reached the center of the lake, the spire floated, topped now in the ghostly shape of a man. Though made of the cloud-like tendrils of blackness, the basic features of human form could easily be made out. Its "head" turned toward Arnath and it spoke his name aloud, the voice a deep chill-inducing gravel from the netherworld that echoed off the mound. Arnath ventured they heard it all the way at the end of the eastern road.

"Aaaaarrrnaaaaaath."

"You know me?" Arnath asked, defiantly.

"I do." The crackling voice said, echoing everywhere - off the fin, the stables, the very town itself.

Arnath nodded. He and Garthe had been right. "Because Morgosh knew me."

"That is correct. My, you are clever for a warrior."

Arnath did not rankle at the jibe. He had to remember he was speaking to the court mage of a once-sprawling empire. A man who a thousand years ago was one of the most important people in the world. "I travel in good company."

"Speaking of which..." The specter let it hang, and Arnath nodded.

"Yes. And what is it exactly you want of master Garthe?" Arnath asked knowing any answer he got would not be worth the price they paid to get it.

"Yours is not to question me, warrior. Just bring the boy before me." The ghost figured said angrily, the spire beneath it undulating shakily. As it did so, Arnath noticed something for the first time...

Within the misty folds of the spectral being's "chest", a distinctive red light would appear whenever his black, misty body moved quickly – Like just now, when it was caught in the throes of anger.

Sensing his fellows had moved close behind him, Arnath turned to his left and found Trellith there. "You saw that?"

"I did." The dwarf said, eyes locked on the human-shaped spire. "It seems the ghostly form and the live-stone are once again united."

"Can you hit that?" Arnath asked quietly.

"Not even with my goggles on, I'm afraid." Trellith said, tapping the rims of his glasses, then turned to the prince, who stood off of Arnath's right shoulder.

"I can." Heflynn nodded, meeting Arnath's gaze for a second.

"Perhaps I should." Came Grentoss voice from Heflynn's right. The old mage clutched the dangling pouch where he kept his formidable power stone. "I do have the weapon for it."

"Both of you. Be ready." Arnath said, hearing the strain of Heflynn's bow string behind him.

Arnath turned back toward the specter floating over the lake, and called out, "And what happens if we don't present the young mage to you?"

"Then you will all die!" Alathuum's disembodied voice thundered off the lake and echoed into the sky. "I shall drain you all of your very life force and take what I want anyway!"

Then, as though to prove its point, a lightning tendril flashed out of the spire and shot toward the first fire pit near the large tree. There, Apaulon lay still, having been knocked unconscious by the impact of his shield taking a hard hit a couple of interchanges back. The lightning tendril smacked the large shield aside and grasped the young soldier around his neck. The luminous tendril lifted Apaulon aloft, and started carrying him slowly toward the center of the lake. Arnath could see Apaulon's body had gone stiff, as though shocked with instantaneous agony over every single part of him.

"It is just like in Solmairyth." Heflynn spoke over Arnath's shoulder. "But the dark mage needs no information, has no reason to keep Apaulon alive. He won't last long."

Without even thinking that they might hit their young friend, Arnath barked, "Volley!"

Everyone within striking distance let loose with arrows and shot. As the pellets and shafts penetrated the necromancer's smoky visage its form crumpled, protecting the center of its non-corporeal body. The effort caused the lightning tendril to weaken and disappear. Apaulon's body fell limply into the lake.

Without hesitating, Havanth ran from the protection of the great tree and into the water. He dashed to where Apaulon floated and, getting an arm under him, dragged the young guardsmen back to the shore.

And it was then that the specter unleashed its retaliatory blast of lightning.

Whether infused by what little energy it had sapped from Apaulon, or just spurred on by unbridled fury, the necromancer unleashed the greatest of its blasts thus far. The deadly energy bolts shot in all directions, most toward those nearest to its floating position over the lake. The lightning reflected off the lake so brightly it lit up the sky above, all the buildings in town, even the treeline of the forest to the north.

The roof exploded off of the boathouse, chunks of rock were blasted away from the fin and the great tree at the lakeside was impacted at the top of its trunk, sending up a furious cloud of sparks, fire and splinters. One of the branches groaned and fell to the ground.

All around the cries of the injured and the frightened whinnies of the horses within the stable could be heard.

Arnath got to his feet and looked around. Despite their precautions, several buildings within town were on fire. Though the blazes were only small, starting to catch, there was nothing they could do about them. Sending troops to fight the fires would be an outright invitation for the necromancer to move beyond the confines of the lake. Sickened by the notion that Kroman's Town could be razed this night, Arnath looked away, to check on the damage that had been done closer by.

Havanth lay face down on the shore, his back emitting black smoke, his booted feet floating listlessly in the water. Lorta was pinned under the felled tree branch, a long spike of wood protruding from his head. Behind Heflynn, Grentoss had been thrown backwards in the grass. The old mage lay sprawled, his eyes vacantly locked on the stars above, a smoking wound in his chest.

Mego limped by behind Arnath, supporting both Trenth, whose one hand looked as though it had been thoroughly mashed, and Apaulon, whose neck was ringed with black lightning scars.

Arnath turned back the to lake, which now vented undulating wafts of steam from all the power that had been blasted through it. The spectral necromancer floated amongst the rising wisps of vapour; its height visibly reduced. The undulations within its smoky black folds began to swirl again, and Arnath knew it was gathering power to strike once more. How... How could they stop this?

"Enough!"

All heads, including the proximate one atop the dark spire, turned towards the road next to the stables. There, Garthe had emerged and was walking onto grassy field by the remaining lake gate, his infuriated gaze levelled across the lake.

Arnath felt just as Illona did, as she rushed to him and held onto one of his triage bloodied sleeves, begging him not to go. "Please, love, he'll kill you."

Garthe pulled his arm free, held her hand reassuringly for a moment, saying "If I don't, he'll kill us all. Trust in me."

And then Garthe continued on, across the eastern edge of the lake.

"What is it you want? What is it you think I can do for you that makes any of this destruction worth while?!" Garthe yelled across the water.

"Life." The gravelly, echoing voice said, flatly, as though Garthe was supposed to understand its meaning.

"And what makes you believe I can give you life again?"

"Your old master, who has spoken within me since the day I absorbed his essence, firmly believed you would grow into the greatest mage of your time, perhaps of all time. So great was his faith in your healing powers. You will use those powers to restore me to a young body. I will begin my life again, and begin my conquest anew... Chosen one."

The necromancer finished speaking as Garthe neared Arnath. When their eyes met, it took everything they had not to burst out laughing. From within their merged undead essences, impish Morgosh had grifted the necromancer Alathuum from beyond the grave with his lies. The non-corporeal necromancer truly believed Garthe was the all-powerful "Chosen One" Morgosh had created as a means to con unknowing folk out of food and shelter.

Trellith could see Shrakar, his head poking up from behind the damaged boathouse, his thoughts whirling. He looked at Arnath and Garthe, agape. "Morgosh brought him to us. He fooled him into seeking us out so we could destroy him."

Arnath nodded at this, and said, "After he was killed and absorbed by the stone, Morgosh must have become privy to the necromancer's plan. Our old mage saw the scope of the threat and sent the necromancer on a mission to find the only people Morgosh knew he could trust to do away with this thing – Us. I say we oblige him."

Resolute in what needed to be done, Garthe turned and held his hand out to Trellith. Trellith looked, saw the stitched wad of one of Garthe's combat grenades and quickly snatched it from the boy's hand. Trellith crossed behind Arnath to stand with Heflynn, where he pulled a longbow arrow from the quiver on the prince's back – one with leather thong affixed behind the fletching.

Assured Trellith understood the plan, Garthe walked over to Grentoss' body and knelt, closing the dead mage's eyes. He then plucked up the power stone from where it had fallen on the grass and secreted it into his palm.

The form atop the spire appeared agitated and called out, "Why delay the inevitable, boy? I will have my life back!"

Garthe returned to stand on Arnath's left, and whispered, "Ready."

Arnath turned right, saw Heflynn nock the thonged-arrow that now had sack-cloth grenade dangling from it. Trellith stood ready beside the prince's right hand, a long pipe-match ready to strike and light the fibrous wick dangling from the grenade. Arnath then turned toward the boathouse, his eyes meeting Shrakar's across the corner of the lake. He gave the half-Orc a hand signal, letting Shrakar know it was time to give all they had. Shrakar nodded and unsheathed his giant axe.

Both Arnath and Heflynn exhaled deep, steadying breaths, as Garthe once again turned to the lake, saying, "You want life? You call this life? To cut a swath of destruction in your original life, then again in death, and then to have restored again, only to use it for more destruction? That is not life."

Garthe waved his arm at all the people around the lake, and at the town beyond. "This is. Places like this are life. To be surrounded by people, friends and companions. That is life. Not some lust for conquest over others, others would not even share a drink and pipe with you. What kind of life is it to blindly believe you have no equal, and therefore you have permission to crush all that you see?"

Arnath himself believed in the words Garthe spoke, the words that so troubled the specter of the dark mage. He could not have been prouder of the son he had fostered these many years.

Garthe's words had greatly rankled the necromancer. The spire trembled, the body-shape atop it losing cohesion. As Garthe spoke, a guttural snarl began to grow in volume from the center of the lake.

"You wish to cut down, rather than embrace. You wish to dominate, rather than uplift. You wish fear, rather than respect. You would perpetuate hate, rather than love. For that reason alone, you don't deserve life..."

The building snarl coming from the spectral necromancer had grown into a full-on roar of hatred in Garthe's direction.

"... You deserve to remain dead."

Garthe held up his hand, and pointed the power stone at the spire and unleashed all the power he had through it. The thick red beam that came forth screamed across the lake and impacted with the spire. The spire shuddered, its black layers coming apart, revealing the veiled colours beneath...

And the live-stone floating within the necromancer's spectral chest.

Arnath turned over his shoulder, where he could hear Heflynn once again pulling back his bow, and the whick on the grenade already crackling. "My prince..."

"Yes, captain." Heflynn said, awaiting the command.

"Send that thing back to the darkness."

As soon as Arnath heard the spring of the bow from behind him, and felt the rush of wind as the arrow flew past his shoulder, he called out, "Volley!"

Everyone around the lake still able to fight let their weapons fly. Closest by the spire, Shrakar threw his great war axe, and it woop-woop-wooped through the air, bashing through the base under the necromancer's "body", scattering the black, smoky particles in all directions.

As the necromancer's defenses were being burned away by the power stone, it could muster little help against the multitude of weapons flung its way. It tried anyway, and that was the distraction needed. It would only take one weapon to end it.

Heflynn's arrow flew true, flashing across the lake, and when it struck and smashed through the live-stone, the grenade went off. All could hear the momentary impact that shattered the crystalline structure, and the popping blast of the grenade. The anguished howl of the necromancer as its hate-filled, thousand-year plan came to an end was cut abruptly short as the thunderclap of a tremendous explosion ripped outwards from the center of the spire.

So violent was the force of the shockwave, everyone on shore was blown off their feet. A great many windows in Kroman's Town shattered instantly. The surge of energy thrust down into the lake with such incredible force, most of the water was displaced, blasted into the air, soaking the grass, trees and the road in the deluge. The blast wave of water crashed into the buildings in the town, and instantaneously quenched the fires throughout.

For several moments, everyone was blinded by the powerfully propelled monsoon all around them. First, the forceful deluge slammed into them as it roared away from the lake, then, after a mercifully still moment, it reversed direction under gravity's pull and began to crash like a flash flood back into the lake bed.

Arnath clung to the grass as the displaced water roared back into the lake, cascading over him with the force of a raging river. When it felt the near-tidal force had finished washing past his body, he looked up.

Very slowly, Arnath stood up on shaky legs, surveyed the damage all around and began to count the living.

*

It took all of the remaining fall and the winter that followed for Kroman's Town to recover. Not only was there the extensive damage to the buildings, which Kroman's got little help repairing, as Solindar had its own damage to contend with. There were also the bolder-sized chunks of the mound and fin that had to be hauled away. These were taken to the graveyard, and hewn down into tombstones for many of the dead, but for one that remained by the lake as a commemorative stone.

In the days that followed the costly battle, the legion of King's guard already present were able to help with the grisly task of dealing with the dead and injured that were spread across the lakeside and town. All-in-all, twenty-three people were killed in the battle, and a little more than half that number were injured, some quite gravely.

The dead and injured amongst the King's guard were taken to the inner kingdom, to be buried with honours in the guard cemetery, or recover in the barracks at Sa'ensbourg, near the palace. Listrelle's body was eventually recovered from Solindar, and buried in the great cemetery in the fields south of the palace by an honour guard and accompanied by the royal family. Mage Orpha took the body of Grentoss to be interred at the tomb of all mages near the valley where the guard cemetery stood. Guardsmen had been dispatched to find the body of Shinthala for the same purpose, but had little luck finding her amongst the rubble of Solmairyth. Those in the know, Arnath and his fellows, knew they would likely never find her, her body and mage essence were likely completely absorbed to grow the power of the necromancer's corporeal manifestation, just as Morgosh's had, all those years ago.

Amongst those lost from Kroman's Town were Mayor Bumpol, Sheriff Daruun – who was struck down when the cart barricade was lashed with the powerful lightning blasts - and Fernlow, who was crushed when the blasts struck the top of the mound. Grovan, the old tailor, died when his heart failed, so panic stricken was he during the battle.

Lorta, Tellifar and six others from Solindar had perished in the fighting. The King himself attended Lorta's funeral, to honour the great elf who had constructed so many wonderous buildings throughout the kingdom, the last of which was Arnath's Outpost in Kroman's Town.

Once Havanth was buried and Grentoss' body was taken away, Valdara took over leadership of their party, and they set forth, with a hired crew of elves from Solindar, to fully plunder the treasure room under the Kolifarii Falls. Though it was estimated by the bank in Solindar that Valdara was the richest woman in the kingdom, outside of the palace, she expressed interest in returning to Kroman's Town and taking over the sheriff's post. She and the others – Trenth, Mego and Ogron – had kept Havanth's word, and transferred a sizeable sum, a king's ransom in fact, into the outpost's account in Solindar. The proprietors of the outpost were not yet of a mindset to celebrate the fact that they'd be rich until the end of their days. The grim realities of recent events still hung heavy in their minds.

Though the dead of Kroman's Town were buried fairly quickly, it took some time for the town to organize a proper ceremony. Mayor Bumpol, who normally put together such things, was among the dead. Eventually a new mayor, Kewin, was elected by show of hands in the Briny Sea. Prince Heflynn oversaw the election. Many townsfolk kept suggesting he himself be mayor, and could not be made to understand that members of the royal family were not legally allowed to hold elected offices within the kingdom. Kewin's first act as mayor was to hold his wedding to Anya, who was quite visibly pregnant, at the Briny Sea, a celebration all from far and wide were invited to.

After the wedding, which was attended by Shimar, Taishen and a large retinue from Solindar, Shimalena returned home to Solindar with them. An entire swath of her town required rebuilding, and she very much felt she was needed. Though she was long estranged from her traditionalist family, their deaths in the destruction of Solmairyth hit her quite hard, and she felt the need to be around her own kind for a time.

Garthe was more than understanding, encouraging her to go. She had to heal. Besides, Garthe had become so busy healing others since the battle, that he was almost entirely absent company to anyone he felt close to. He could barely react when Illona too left Kroman's Town for her month of training at the post office in Morley. Once the last of the injured were fully healed, and his cases became day-to-day, he began to miss both Shimalena and Illona terribly.

Between the ridiculously busy nature of his practice and the loss of his two closest friends, Garthe did not at first notice the melancholy that had taken over the outpost in the meantime. All three of his surrogate fathers – Arnath, Trellith and Shrakar – seemed quite quiet and dour, and Garthe wondered if they had been since the battle took place. He quickly realized they were plagued by the same question that nagged at the back of his mind. Were they responsible for what happened?

It was a somewhat viciously circular argument to have with one's self. Did their intended treasure raid of the Arkonian ruins set off the chain of events that led to so, so many deaths? They had lost friends and companions as a result – the first of which being Morgosh, who died there in Arkonia, his very body and soul cannibalized by the inert necromancer lurking within the live-stone. Though it might be easy to sway the blame towards Morgosh himself, since mages were entirely responsible for minding any magical dangers a party might face in their quests. That, paired with their supposition that Morgosh had fooled the necromancer from within and sent it on a crash course through the kingdom after Garthe made it a pretty sound argument. But placing the blame at the dead mage's feet felt petty, for they were placing the responsibility on a companion who could no longer defend himself.

Prince Heflynn, who continued to live in the apartment on the first floor until he could find contractors to refurbish the octagonal cottage by the first cut out the eastern road, was able to salve some of the wounds in the outpost - by once again bringing forth the notion that kingdom should be informed when and where attempts to profit from the leavings of the ancient world where made. Instead of no one being any wiser when a threat resulted from something like the Arkonian necromancer being accidentally freed – and it was an accident, he assured them – why not have a system in place to inform the authorities when such potentially dangerous precincts were being breached?

Presented like that, especially after they had seen the worst that could happen up close, Arnath began to see the benefit of such a mandate. If not something as formal as permits, why not some kind of registry to inform the kingdom when a group of fools was going to potentially unleash the wrath of a mountain dragon by trying to steal its treasure? As restrictive as he first felt the notion to be, the battle with the necromancer had changed his mind. Just as they were when they were young, most adventurers were drunken, unthinking fools, and a registry might sober them up to the one, over-arching social responsibility involved in a life without any other responsibilities at all. Arnath was more than fine with that.

*

It wasn't until the following spring that a light seemed to show at the end of the tunnel of the over-arching gloom in their lives.

Not only had the outpost's reputation grown, having obtained the TO for Traveller's Outpost on all new, royally-approved maps, the town itself had grown in reputation, casting off the stigma of having had their old outpost destroyed by dark magics years ago. No – now it was a place where great heroes fought to destroy a necromancer from the ancient world. *That's right, veterans of the battle of Isthmar, the valiant King's Guard, even one of the princes of the realm. That's right, right here by this lake.* Kewin didn't need to be the promoting showman that Bumpol was. People were passing through town in droves, if just to ride their carts by the lake, to look at the battle scars on the fin and the mound.

Kewin posted on the town board that Kroman's was without a gentlemen's tailor, and more. Entire businesses that stood empty since soon after the outpost disaster were in dire need now that the town was fully revitalized. People from towns near and far enquired about where they could open such businesses, and quite quickly. A priest of the light had even come through town, looking for a suitable space for a small temple. His services were utilized that very night, when the entire town came out to say farewell to their dead. The priest did leave early on in the night though, when the large wake held at the Briny Sea began to snowball into licentious revelry. It was a party in Kroman's Town, after all.

As purveyors of food and drink, along with Gaila and Hamly, Durnly and his outpost neighbours couldn't be more pleased. Though the Briny Sea was never fully full, but for larger celebrations, it was never, ever empty either. The balcony, which looked over the now-storied lake, was always full, and with more people always waiting to be seated. Durnly nearly fell to his one knee with joy when Shimalena came back to Kroman's Town. Someone had to watch the floor whilst he took delivery after delivery from their many suppliers.

Garthe and Illona were ecstatic to see Shimalena as well. With Garthe's workload reduced to people passing through town with teething children, or the maladies of the Kroman's elderly towns folk, and the occasional training yard injury, he had time to spend with both of them, and they made the best of it. It felt exactly like it had before, but for moments when Shimalena would become quiet and distant. Or when she would drink too much cider, and bring up something she never had before – Having a family.

Illona didn't worry too greatly about the little changes. She had experienced so many big ones in the past year. Not only did she leave Kroman's for a whole month and train in Morley, making as many new friends as there were people in Kroman's Town, once she was done training, she was immediately appointed, likely with Prince Heflynn's intercession, as Post Master General of Kroman's Town, officially taking over from the retired Miss Minidell. Whilst her heart clung to her two great friends and loves, she also thrilled in a life wherein a post from the palace needed immediate delivery, and she'd be off like a shot on the back of Princess Dragonfly, sometimes with an escort of Guardsmen.

The members of the King's Guard who at first reluctantly came into town to train at the outpost now had to wait for scheduled sessions, so keenly were their ranks wanting to master skills taught to them by the heroes who fought beside the King at Isthmar, and then defeated the necromancer, right here, outside their very door.

Arnath was glad of the occasional days, like today, when he could train with more experienced guardsmen, like Apaulon and those from his cohort. He'd noted Apaulon had become quite a fine, even dangerous, swordsmen under his tutelage. Arnath guessed the experience with the necromancer had filled the young soldier with something his sense of duty needed – The understanding of the urgency of a true threat. His appearance had changed too. Garthe was able to completely heal and fade away the lightning scars around his neck, but the tuft of stark white hair that appeared after that night around his window's peak seemed to be there for good. Apaulon didn't mind that much. He was easy to spot in the field amongst his similarly uniformed fellows, and it served as a daily reminder in the looking glass of what he and the others had endured.

Squaring off as he did now with Arnath, both of them holding weighted wooden swords, he tried to remember all the older captain had taught him. *Watch the body, not the hand holding the sword. The feet will move before the sword thrusts.* Circling each other, Apaulon didn't worry Arnath would hurt him, more that he'd make a fool of himself and disappoint the captain. Even if he ended up on his backside, he'd still learn something.

Apaulon thrust in quickly, and immediately found Arnath's free hand clamped around his wrist, and his body flailing to find the ground. By the time he was on his back, his fellow guardsmen, seated on the ground nearby, even those on the climbing wall, were laughing at him.

"Laugh if you must," Arnath said, offering Apaulon his hand, "But, don't let your laughter wipe the lesson away."

After Apaulon was on his feet and brushing himself off, Arnath turned toward the young guardsmen sitting on the ground, pointing his wooden sword at them. "What did he do wrong?"

The young men and women on the ground all looked dumbstruck when confronted by the big warrior. Among them, a blond girl said, "He went for the shoulder opposite your sword arm."

"Exactly. And?"

"Once his arm was extended, you were free to do anything you wanted with it… Including chopping it off." The girl said, her eyes on Apaulon's like an extra sting of admonishment.

"Too right." Arnath said, dropping his wooden sword in the sand. "Now, all of you, on the wall, down here."

The guardsmen working with Shrakar on the wall slowly climbed down and moved into the yard. Apaulon and his cohort went to the wall. Arnath said to Shrakar, "I'm taking a breather. You work with them in the yard on shield work, have Apaulon work them on the wall, doing side-to-sides."

Shrakar nodded he understood, waved Arnath on his way, stepped from the wall, and picked up one of the last remaining tall shields left in their training arsenal, the rest having been burned or blasted apart fighting the necromancer. Until the artisans of Solindar re-supplied them, this one would have to do. Shrakar turned the shield sideways, presented its width to the nearby soldiers who had just come from the wall, and said, "Shields up!"

Three of the guardsmen grabbed up smaller round shields, placed them against Shrakar's and heaved against his unmovable weight.

Seeing they were in good hands, Arnath gulped down some water from a pitcher by the door, and went inside. He immediately heard Trellith saying, "No! Listen! The only ones who will know where you are going will be us, the proprietors, the prince, who is the royal arcane investigator and Master Orpha, the royal mage. No one is going to beat you to your prize because of that information. It's so the King's guard knows what they are up against if you free a demon hoard from whatever treasure vault you are plundering. You've heard of what happened, right over that very lake down the hill, I assume?"

Arnath had heard, and himself had, the very same conversation repeatedly since the mandate was put in place. Luckily, this time, the sword-belted warrior in road-beaten leathers on the opposite side of the front counter from Trellith grudgingly took the quill without further argument, withdrew a pathetically tattered map fragment from his coat and began to write in the new registrar book on the counter – The one dedicated to logging the destinations of their treasure seeking adventurer guests. Still feeling put upon, the leather clad man smacked the quill down on the counter and stormed away.

As Arnath reached the counter, the front door swung open and Merynda was there in the shaft of warm afternoon sunlight. Across the street behind her, a cartload of spring vegetables she'd brought was being unloaded by Durnly and the Briny Sea kitchen staff.

"Delivery day. Care for a walk?" Merynda said, her outstretched hand ushering him to join her. She looked over the counter and smiled at Trellith, playfully asking, "Can I take the captain away from you for a while?"

Feigning gumption, Trellith said, "I suppose our business could survive a portion of one day without our illustrious captain lurking about."

"Good of you to say, my trusted lieutenant." Arnath jibed, and turned to make for the door, but the piteous look on the Merynda's face froze him in his tracks.

She pointed at his waist and smirked, saying, "Come now, love, you don't need that. I'll protect you; I promise."

Arnath looked down, realizing from a near-lifetime of habit his sword was still belted on. She was right – He wouldn't need it on a romantic walk around the lake. Especially in a town now teeming with King's guard. He unfastened the belt and stepped behind the counter.

Arnath caught a wry wink from Trellith as he coiled the belt around the scabbard. Turning from his friend, he looked up into Merynda's eyes, seeing his future there, the one the adventuring road had never allowed him. Arnath reached up and hung up his sword, hoping, if not today, then some day soon, it would be for good.

ABOUT THE AUTHOR

T hough new to the world of publishing, author Devon Richards is a Hollywood optioned screenwriter with several film projects in various states of development. He is also a prolific song writer, bass player, guitarist and is actively working on an album for independent release.

While not traditional in commercial writing, Devon Richards plans to explore as many genres as possible. This first novel, "Where All Roads Lead", is an epic fantasy that plays with many of the tropes of the genre. He has published fiction in not only fantasy, but also the Horror and Noir genres. Along with an "All Roads" sequel, he is also working on a book close to his formative 80's underground years - an alternative culture-based noir.

An expert chef, he resides in Toronto, Canada